STOLEN LEGACY

STOLEN LEGACY

A NOVEL BY
DIANE & DAVID MUNSON

MicahHouse
media

Grand Rapids, Michigan

Some Scripture quotations are taken from the HOLY BIBLE, NEW INTERNATIONAL VERSION®. NIV®. Copyright ©1973, 1978, 1984 by Biblica ®. Used by permission. All rights reserved.

Some Scripture quotations are taken from the Holy Bible, King James Version, Cambridge, 1769.

This is a work of fiction. Names, characters, places, and incidents either are the product of the authors' imaginations or are used fictitiously. Where real people, events, establishments, locales, or organizations appear, they are used fictitiously.

DEDICATION

Stolen Legacy is dedicated to the countless surviving veterans of our U.S. armed forces and those of our Allies, and to the memory of those who've passed or died in combat. Our freedom to write and pursue our dreams in a democratic society is the result of their sacrifice. We are grateful to the men and women who served in WWII and those who helped the Dutch Resistance, including Diane Reen. You all have our heartfelt thanks!

> *"For I know the plans I have for you," declares the Lord.*
> *"Plans to give you hope and a future."*
> Jeremiah 29:11 (NIV)

ACKNOWLEDGMENTS

It is one thing to write a novel. It's quite another to see that novel become a book to hold and to delve into. We thank Micah House Media and those supporting them for assembling *Stolen Legacy* into the book we delight in promoting and we hope you will enjoy reading. Thank you, Pamela Guerrieri, for your editorial adjustments to our creation. We appreciate the creativity of Jeremy Culp, for his laying out the pages that fit between the stunning cover, which he also designed.

ABOUT THE AUTHORS

ExFeds, Diane and David Munson write High Velocity Suspense novels that stand alone, with some of the characters reappearing. The Munsons call their novels "factional fiction" because they write books based on their exciting and dangerous careers.

Diane Munson has been an attorney for more than thirty years. She has served as a Federal Prosecutor in Washington, D.C., and with the Reagan Administration, appointed by Attorney General Edwin Meese, as Deputy Administrator/Acting Administrator of the Office of Juvenile Justice and Delinquency Prevention. She worked with the Justice Department, U.S. Congress, and White House on policy and legal issues. More recently she has been in a general law practice.

David Munson served as a Special Agent with the Naval Investigative Service (now NCIS), and U.S. Drug Enforcement Administration over a twenty-seven year career. As an undercover agent, he infiltrated international drug smuggling organizations, and traveled with drug dealers. He met their suppliers in foreign countries, helped fly their drugs to the U.S., feigning surprise when shipments were seized by law enforcement. Later his true identity was revealed when he testified against group members in court. While assigned to DEA headquarters in Washington, D.C., David served two years as a Congressional Fellow with the Senate Permanent Subcommittee on Investigations.

As Diane and David research and write, they thank the Lord for the blessings of faith and family. They are busy collaborating on their next novel.

WWW.DIANEANDDAVIDMUNSON.COM

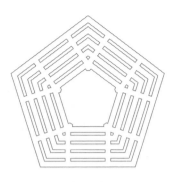

PROLOGUE

SEPTEMBER 11, 2008
ARLINGTON COUNTY, VIRGINIA

Federal Agent Eva Montanna perched on a backless bench southwest of the Pentagon desperate for answers. The one hundred and eighty-three other benches surrounding her represented the souls who had perished here seven years earlier. She clutched a moist hanky in her hand, grabbing at memories of her twin sister, Jillie, who died in the attack. A passenger plane, piloted by deranged terrorists, had plunged into the office where Jillie worked as a military prosecutor.

Eva's heart broke for her vibrant and strong sister. The President's words from an hour earlier provided no comfort: *Seven years ago at this hour, a doomed airliner plunged from the sky, split the rock and steel of this building, and changed our world forever. The years that followed have seen justice delivered to evil men and battles fought in distant lands. But each day on this year—each year on this day, our thoughts return to this place.*

For Eva, the fight had just begun. A tear rolled down her cheek, which she swiped away with her hanky. Though she and Jillie had committed their lives to pursuing justice, now it was up to Eva. Their dad loved to brag when introducing them, *"Meet my daughters, the agent and the prosecutor. Eva nails 'em and Jillie jails 'em."*

Eva choked back a sob. Since losing her twin sister, she drove herself harder to capture the guilty. Her younger twin, by several minutes, had always needed her protection, and on 9/11/2001, Eva wasn't there. Looking down, she saw the engraving honoring her sister. She traced with her finger the grooves spelling out *Jillian Vander Goes,* and recalled battles they'd fought together as young girls. Her mind veered to one summer they spent at Grandpa and Grandma Vander Goes' farm in Zeeland, Michigan. She pictured Jillie laughing under the huge beech tree...

Eva giggled with her ten-year-old sister, Jillie, in the farmyard. Wearing identical purple outfits and heart-shaped sunglasses, both girls counted their newfound treasures from their summer vacation.

"Look!" Eva cried, holding up a small red rock. "It's from Grandpa Marty."

Jillie tickled her sister's cheek with a blue feather. "Grandma Joanne gave me this!"

They both giggled again. That is, until a dark shadow crept across their blanket under the beech tree.

"What are 'ya makin' so much noise about?" the older boy said.

Eva hid her treasures behind her back. "It's our party. You aren't invited."

"Sit by me, Ricky." Jillie made room for him on the blanket.

"Let me see what you're hiding."

Ricky O'Neal reached over and grabbed Jillie's feather.

"Leave her alone."

Eva snatched the feather from his hands. As she handed it to Jillie, Ricky swiped her red rock that had tumbled to the blanket.

"It's a dumb rock."

"Give it back!" Eva leapt to her feet. "Grandpa found it in Lake Michigan."

"If you can catch me."

Ricky took off with her rock and Eva chased him around the tree. He zigged and zagged through the yard before speeding on his longer legs toward his grandfather's farm down the road. Eva tossed off her sunglasses and ran after him. He barged into his grandmother's house, banging the screen door behind him. Eva knocked and knocked, but no one came.

Finally Grandmother O'Neal appeared behind the screen door, wiping her hands on an apron. "Are you one of Martin's twin granddaughters?"

"Yes, and Ricky stole my rock," she answered breathlessly.

"Which twin are you?"

"I'm Eva, the toughest one."

"Well, Eva, my grandson is no thief. You go home. Tell your grandfather Martin to keep you there."

Grandmother O'Neal banged the door shut in Eva's face. She fumed but knew there was nothing to do but go back to the farm. Jillie stood at the end of the long driveway.

"Did he give you our red rock?" she asked.

"Nah. Don't let that creep back in the yard." Eva wiggled her finger at Jillie. "We need Grandpa's help."

They hurried past wire fencing on the side of the garage. Brown chickens pecked around the dirt. Inside the garage, Eva walked up to her grandpa, who stood at his workbench. Next to him, a red coffee can was attached to a small electric motor. It turned slowly. Something banged in the can.

"Do you have anything we can hide our treasures in?" Eva asked.

Jillie wrinkled her nose. "Ricky took the red rock you gave us."

"That's too bad." Grandpa reached up to a shelf. "I have better rocks up here."

As he pulled a yellow tin can from a shelf, it rattled. Eva clapped her hands in delight. Grandpa dumped the contents onto his workbench.

"Take this." He gave her the yellow can and pointed to smooth, shiny stones on the bench. "These Petoskey stones are valuable once they're polished up."

"Cool," Eva said. "They're prettier than the one Ricky stoled."

Grandpa started whistling. He pulled the electric plug from the wall. Eva and Jillie watched as he tipped the machine on its side and removed the cover off the red coffee can. He held it out so the girls could see inside.

"I'm polishing Petoskey stones with this liquid abrasive. When they're done, they'll shine just like these here on the bench. I found these beauties up north, on the beach of Lake Michigan."

He picked up two shiny stones and placed them in the bottom of Eva's yellow can. "Here's one for each of you. Now, don't let Ricky see them."

"We won't!"

Eva sped with the can to the beech tree, with Jillie close behind. Eva popped off the lid. Her "younger" sister put in their collection of feathers, acorns, and a dried turtle shell. They set the can at the base of the tree. Jillie added on top pictures she'd drawn of them at the beach.

"Let's swing."

Eva headed for the tire swing Grandpa had hung on the tree. She climbed on the tire and straddled the rope, coaxing Jillie, "Give me a push, then hop on."

Soon, Jillie was sitting inside the tire below Eva. Their blond hair blew in the breeze as they drifted to and fro. Around the corner of the house came Ricky, holding his hand next to his jeans' pocket. Eva spotted him first.

"Jillie, stop the swing. Here comes the thief."

Her sister dragged her feet until the swing quit moving. In a flash, Ricky was upon them.

"You can't come in our yard," Eva ordered.

"My grandmother says I have to give your stone back."

Eva reached out her hand from her perch above him. "Give it to me."

Ricky reached into his pocket and took out a baby garter snake with three stripes on its back. He thrust it toward Jillie and she screamed.

Eva reached down and yanked the little creature above her head.

"Thank you! Is this a trade for the rock?"

"No way." Ricky dug furiously into his pocket and reached his hand toward Jillie.

"Here's your stupid rock. I found the snake on the way here."

Eva admired the little snake, which coiled around her hand. "I don't think we want the rock. We have nicer ones, and now we have a snake."

Ricky shoved the rock into his pocket. "I only showed you the snake because I need a can to put it in."

He looked over at their yellow can and took one step toward it. Jillie leapt from the swing, followed by Eva. All three collided under the tree. Jillie grabbed the can and fled toward Grandpa in the garage.

Eva looked at her empty hand. "Where did the snake go?"

She searched along the ground with Ricky helping.

"You lost my snake," he grumbled.

Eva shook her head. "Nope, it's ours. You just gave it to us."

Jillie joined the search party. "Grandpa's guarding our can. He says Ricky should go home."

"No way. I want my snake."

Eva stood upright. "Go ahead and look all you want. He's miles away. It's your fault for trying to steal our coffee can."

"I'm keeping the rock then."

Ricky headed for his grandma's house.

"You can have it. We have nicer ones," Eva yelled behind him.

He disappeared around the corner of the house.

Eva whispered in her sister's ear, "Let's bury our can where Ricky can't find it."

The two girls waited for Grandpa to leave the garage. Eva borrowed his shovel. Jillie opened the screen door into the chicken yard and stood guard against Ricky's surprise attacks. Eva quickly buried the can in the sandy soil near the garage, smoothing the dirt over their treasure. Feeling clever, Eva joined Jillie outside the fence.

"When should we dig this up?" Jillie wondered aloud.

"When we're old enough to drive Dad's car, we'll come from Virginia ourselves. That'll teach Ricky to swipe our stuff. Let's wash up."

In the living room, Eva surprised Grandma Joanne. She looked up from her book with red eyes.

"Grandma, are you hurt?" Eva asked.

Her grandma wiped away her tears. "I'm fine, little one. Are you and Jillie ready to open your present?"

She scurried into the kitchen and handed them each a wrapped package. "This is for my favorite granddaughters."

Eva grinned. "We're your only ones."

"Yes, sweetie, and I'm happy you are here. Open your presents."

Eva ripped off the paper. Inside a little box was a gold necklace with a charm.

"It's a shoe."

"Not just any shoe. A wooden Dutch shoe. Your heritage is Dutch, you know. Let me put them on you."

She fastened the gold chain around their necks. "Your grandpa's parents were born in the Netherlands. Maybe someday you will visit there."

Eva headed for the back door with Jillie in hot pursuit. Grandma protested. "Don't wear your necklaces outside. You might lose them."

Jillie stopped. "Eva, if we go out there, Ricky will sneak back."

"Is Ricky O'Neal bothering you girls?" Grandma's hands were on her hips.

"He stole our rock," Eva said. "When I chased him to his house, his grandmother wasn't nice to me."

Grandma Joanne took off her apron. "Don't worry about Mrs. O'Neal. She doesn't like me either. In fact, that's probably why she acted mean to you."

Eva dropped down on the kitchen chair. She loved a good story.

"Why doesn't she like you, Grandma?"

Jillie crept up to the table and sat. So did Grandma. "It's something silly, like Ricky taking your stone. His grandma thinks I took something of hers."

"Oh no!" Jillie objected. "You didn't, did you?"

Grandma Joanne's cheeks blushed. "Ricky's Grandma used to be Helen Barnes who lived on the neighboring farm. Her parents knew Grandpa Marty's parents, but this is not for young girls like you two. You go check on Grandpa."

Eva wrinkled her nose. "It is for us girls. Did Helen like Grandpa and wanna marry him?"

Grandma Joanne turned in surprise. "Yes! When Grandpa was in the war, Helen wrote him letters. She set her cap on him. When he came home with me as his new wife, she got her knickers in a knot."

"What are knickers, Grandma?" Eva asked, frowning.

Grandma blushed again. "When you graduate from high school, I'll let you read my diary. It's all in there."

Eva came over and hugged her grandma. "I'm glad you're my grandmother and not the other one. I'll love you forever."

Jarred back to the present by sounds of soft crying, Eva clenched her fists, thinking of all the pain. Grieving families wandered the grounds for their time alone following the memorial service. A man and teenage boy walked to another bench shaped like a bent springboard attached to the ground at one end.

She stirred on Jillie's bench. Soon the public would be allowed to enter. A thought pierced Eva's mind. Would her life, and her family, ever be free from the influences of evil? Then she recalled what Grandpa Vander Goes wrote in his letter saying he couldn't attend the memorial.

"I lived with Aunt Deane in the Netherlands when Hitler invaded, and did all I could to help the Resistance. I've since regretted not doing more. Perhaps you can visit me soon and read my war journals. Don't let evil around us discourage you. Remember Jesus' promise, 'I am going to prepare a place for you. And if I go and prepare a place for you, I will come back and take you to be with me that you also may be where I am.'"

Grandpa had never told Eva that he resisted the Nazis. What had he done? No wonder she and Jillie were determined to pursue justice. While Eva waited to be in the heaven Jesus spoke of, she must continue Grandpa Marty's and Jillie's quest. Peace replaced her angst and Eva stood, gazing across the memorial where other families gathered to honor those who died.

She gave a final look at Jillie's name on the bench. Duty called. This afternoon, she'd attend a hearing on Capitol Hill to stop the threat of terrorism in Cuba and Latin America. Her orders were clear. First and foremost, Eva must remain strong in her faith. She would do all in her power to uphold justice, and protect her family, no matter the cost. What price had Grandpa Marty paid against the Nazis, she wondered.

Eva left the Pentagon filled with a deep desire to find out and to uncover just what Marty meant in his letter about his fight against evil.

1

JUNE – FIVE YEARS LATER, ZEELAND, MICHIGAN

Federal Agent Eva Montanna tore after the suspect with tremendous speed. Her heart banged against her ribs. She fled across a slippery slope, the reassuring grip of her Glock giving her courage to pursue the woman. No matter how Eva tried, she couldn't breach the distance. Her prey was escaping with astonishing speed.

Fury rose within Eva. She pulled in extra air, urging her legs to ramp it up and catch the woman. A federal agent couldn't simply fire at a fleeing felon without cause. Still, if the woman turned and pointed her gun, Eva could shoot. She would shoot.

But what if the woman never quit running?

Eva yelled again, "Federal agent! I said stop!"

The suspect dressed in black sped down the hill. Eva drew nearer. But her foot collided against a rock. She careened onto the wet grass, her body sliding dangerously close to the mountain's edge. Eva stifled a scream.

The woman turned, raising her gun. Eva's eyes locked onto the woman's vivid turquoise-blue eyes. Fear jolted through her. Where was her Glock?

A noisy bell rang. Eva's eyes flew open. Where was she?

To the erratic beating of her heart, she surveyed old-fashioned furniture spread about the room in a hodgepodge fashion. Eva tried shaking off her grogginess. She felt exhausted from working so many hours just to get away on vacation. A colorful watercolor of a woman hung on the living room wall above her. She was lying on a couch. Okay, she was in Grandpa Marty's house in Zeeland, Michigan. Eva and her family had arrived yesterday for a two-week vacation.

The eerie dream bothered her. She mentally zipped through her past cases, not recognizing anyone with such odd-colored eyes. What about the woman's gun? Eva had seen one like it—in a WWII museum she'd visited near Washington D.C. It looked much like a German P38. Eva roused herself and stood, convinced neither the woman nor the gun had any bearing on her life.

"Grandpa," she called. "Are you here?"

She glimpsed out the front window. A white van drove off. Had she actually heard the doorbell ring? The front door closed, and Marty emerged from the front hallway.

He stared at a box. "I thought maybe it was Ralph returning my journal."

"Your neighbor has your war journals?" Eva blinked.

"Well, he took only one, but for the life of me, I don't remember why."

Marty tossed her a quizzical look. Eva came closer.

"Ralph brought back the journal," she said. "Now we can begin your memoirs."

"It's addressed to me," Marty replied, flexing his brow.

The way the box was taped rather sloppily planted a seed of suspicion in Eva's mind.

"Grandpa, why would Ralph wrap your journal in brown paper?"

"I never said he gave me this." Marty wore a crooked grin.

Impatience erupted in Eva. Had she entered the Twilight Zone? He continued fumbling with the paper. She leaned over to tear it off, but tugged too hard, sending the package crashing to the tile.

With both hands, she snatched up the box and shook it. Suspicion burrowed into her well-trained mind. Why did Ralph want Marty's World War II writings anyway?

"This is too light for a journal," she said. "And there's no postmark."

Marty reached for his package. Eva refused to hand it over until she knew more.

"Not until you tell me who gave you this. If Ralph didn't bring this, who did? Was it your mail carrier?"

"Nope. It was one of those trucks."

"Do you mean a brown truck with a man in uniform?"

"No." Marty raised his chin. "But I see how tough you are questioning me, just like I see on TV."

"You have nothing to fear from me, Grandpa. Let's open your box."

His fingers were too weak to break the tape, so Eva grabbed a pair of scissors. After snipping the tape, she ripped off the brown wrapping. He pulled a pair of plaid slippers from the box. He plopped down on a kitchen chair and tried them on.

"They're a perfect fit." Delight rang in his voice.

Eva peered inside the box, looking for a card. "I wonder who sent them."

Nothing indicated who sent the gift. Stymied, she checked the brown paper for clues. Carriers used bar codes and scanners. This parcel had none.

Marty lifted up his slipper-clad feet. "Eva Marie, since your grandma, my Joanne, passed away, several church widows fuss over me. They make me feel kind of old."

"You don't act your age," Eva replied, crackling the brown paper. "You reached the door before I even left the couch."

She set the wrapping and box on the kitchen table. Marty took off his slippers and shoved them back into the box.

"Maybe it's the dreams keeping me up at night that are aging me," he said.

"What dreams?"

Marty ignored her question, asking, "Where's Scott and my great-grandkids? My time with them will end too soon."

"Good question." Eva checked her watch. "My sweetie and the three kiddos should be back from the beach by now."

She picked up the old-fashioned wall phone and dialed Scott's cell number. It went to his voicemail. Her haunting dream tugged at her mind, and she was curious what dreams Marty had. The mystery slippers arriving suddenly also disturbed her. Her family was late and she couldn't reach Scott. Worry bolted through her. Scott rarely turned off his phone.

2

Eva pressed her lips together and gathered her wits. She pulled out bread and sliced turkey for lunch. "Grandpa, tell me what dreams are keeping you awake."

"Oh, they're nothing." Marty set the box of slippers on a nearby stool.

"That's what you claimed in Israel, but we both know it was something more."

He looked away, prompting her to add, "You and I both dreamed an earthquake hit the small nation *before* it happened."

"Some memories have faded. That's one of them. But the day I met Joanne is firmly etched in my mind."

"Does Grandma appear in your dreams?" Eva could understand he'd dream of his departed wife who he married after World War II ended.

"Most nights she does," he replied, his voice wavering. "She tells me something. Only, in my dreams, I can never hear what she says."

Eva walked over and patted his hand. "I pray God refreshes your spirit."

"I'm glad you came here for vacation. Is the coffee ready?"

"Not quite."

She stepped to the sink and fixed the coffee. Dark clouds swept past the window. Ominous weather should bring her crew racing home from the beach. She mulled over Marty's dreams, vowing to help him make a fresh start by working on his memoirs. After lunch, she'd contact Ralph and demand he return the journal.

Eva toasted raisin bread, spread the butter, and layered in cheese and turkey. She nestled a dill pickle on each plate, and brought one to Marty. Tempting smells of melting cheese did nothing to break his stare.

"Why don't you enjoy lunch and then we'll revisit your delivery person."

"I can get my coffee."

Although Eva protested, he shot from his chair and poured a cup. He picked up her plate with his other hand, managing both deftly. "Here's your lunch, Eva. Let me say grace."

After giving thanks for their food, Marty dove into his sandwich. Eva nibbled hers.

Then she asked evenly, "What did the person look like who delivered the box?"

"Dunno," he quipped, his half-eaten pickle poised in the air.

"Okay. Man or woman? Older or younger than you?"

Marty's shoulders sagged under his striped shirt and he plunked down the pickle.

"He was young. Twenty-something, I guess."

"Good. Did he say your name?"

"Fiddlesticks." Marty coughed out a sigh. "My brain's mud."

Car doors slamming preceded the thunder of the Montanna kids' feet. Relief flooded through Eva until they marched in the back door dropping wet towels on the floor.

"Stop!" She extended her hand like a traffic cop. "Go outside. Remove your shoes and brush sand off your feet."

Scott entered barefooted, carrying his shoes, and wearing a sheepish grin. "The beach was a blast," he said.

"Yeah, Mom!" her teenage daughter Kaley cried. "The waves were huge."

Andy, their oldest son, tossed a football on the floor. "You should've seen Dutch's head bobbing out there. He swims pretty good."

"What?" Eva's eyes rounded. She whirled on Scott. "You agreed to keep the kids out of the water if the waves were rough. Is that why you didn't answer my call?"

"You called?" Scott fumbled getting his cell phone out of the holder. "Oops, my battery is dead."

He plugged in his phone and then lifted a slipper. "I should be lecturing you. You certainly blew our budget on these."

"I did not." Eva bristled. "They're not even ours. They arrived for Grandpa."

Andy slipped out. So did Kaley, who prodded her youngest brother

Dutch out the kitchen door. Their footsteps thumping up the steps made Eva breathe in deeply. She needed to dial it down a notch.

Scott faced Marty with a gleam in his eye. "Who is the rich lady chasing you?"

"Scott, did you surprise me with these?" Marty asked. "Eva and I are clueless."

"Not me." Scott held up a plaid slipper as if admiring a piece of crystal. "But some rich lady must be your secret admirer. Angus Plaid is produced in Canada. It's expensive there and even more so in the U.S. They make this plaid into scarves, hats, and the like. I've not seen slippers made from Angus though."

"Wait." Eva snatched the slipper from Scott's hand. "Working for Immigration and Customs, I come across Scottish plaids. Maybe these are cheap knockoffs."

Scott flashed a knowing smile. "Okay, Marty, which wealthy lady is after you?"

"None." He shoved hands into his pockets. "The slippers arrived by courier."

Not appreciating Scott's humor—especially not after Marty had revealed his troubled dreams of Grandma—Eva tapped her husband's back hoping he'd get the hint.

"How do you know they're so expensive?" she asked Scott.

"When I was White House press secretary, we declared gifts valued over a hundred bucks. The Canadians gave my aide an Angus scarf, which she reported."

"I have no friends in Canada," Marty exclaimed.

The next instant, he hurried to the fridge and opened the door. He removed a package of cookies. "When I told Helen you were coming, she baked cookies. Boy, everything she cooks is delicious."

"Who is Helen?" Eva folded her arms.

"You know, I lease my farmland to her grandsons."

"The kids should enjoy her treats. Scott and I will run upstairs and collect them."

She steered Scott by his elbow out of the kitchen. When they turned the corner into the hall, she smiled up at him.

"Grandpa is worried about the slippers. Perhaps you are right and his friend Helen sent them. I'd like to figure this out and start on his journals."

Scott squared his shoulders. "Can I help solve the riddle?"

"Sure. Get Marty's journal from Ralph next door."

"You got it." Scott folded her into his arms. "I missed you at the beach."

She leaned against his chest. "Hmm. You smell like coconut. I promise I won't work on Grandpa's memoirs for the entire vacation."

Marty hustled from the kitchen, his gray hair sticking up in the back. "My mind is in a tizzy. Have you seen my gold watch? I had it when I answered the door."

Eva pushed back from Scott and he helped her look under every table, chair, and sofa. They checked beneath the bench seat in the hall. But Grandpa's one-hundred-year-old watch had disappeared.

3

For Eva, Marty's missing watch deepened the mystery of the slippers. After she made lunch for the rest of her family, she combed the house for the watch, coming up empty-handed. She urged Marty to rejoin them around the kitchen table. They sipped coffee while Scott and the kids ate ham and cheese sandwiches.

"Gramps," Andy said, gesturing with his arms. "You should've seen the guy kite surfing. The wind pulled his kite down in the waves. Water sprayed over his head. The kite lifted him so high in the air, he did a one-eighty before hittin' the water again."

With his pursed lips and cheerless expression, Marty seemed uninterested in Andy's animated story. Eva offered a remedy.

"Who wants apple pie and ice cream?"

"Me!" Dutch shouted. "Ice cream, ice cream, we all scream for ice cream!"

"You get an extra scoop for your poem," Eva said with a smile.

She cut the pie into six slices, crowning each piece with vanilla ice cream.

"None for me." Marty waved off his dessert.

"But apple pie is your favorite." Eva set the plate in front of him anyway.

Marty shrugged. "My appetite's gone."

Eva looked at Scott, wanting him to do something. Rather than coax Marty, he improvised, eating Marty's piece as well as his own. Eva couldn't figure out what bothered Marty besides the slippers. Before she settled on a reason, Dutch put down his spoon.

"Wanna climb Gramp's big tree?" he asked Andy.

"Sure. Race ya!"

Andy stormed out the door, followed by Dutch. Marty caught their enthusiasm.

"Time to check for the mail." He rose from the table. "Might stir my appetite."

He left the room, and Eva said, "I'm unsure what to do. Grandpa seems lost."

"Yeah," Kaley agreed. "When I came down this morning, I found him staring out the window. I asked what he was doing and he said he was watching for deer."

Scott covered Eva's hand with his. "Last evening, I saw a doe head into the cornfield. Deer probably keep him occupied when we're not here."

"That's just it. Grandpa has lots to do with us here. Why wouldn't he eat his pie?"

"He's not hungry. Just because you aren't chasing bad guys, don't go looking for problems around here." Scott took his plate to the sink. "Or, maybe he's worried about his journal. I'll go see if Ralph is done with it."

He slipped out the back door. Kaley came over, her pretty eyes filled with concern. "Mom, is our being here too much for Gramps? He's used to quiet."

"Your maturity amazes me. I never thought of that."

"My brothers overwhelm me sometimes." Kaley managed a grin.

"Me too." Eva laughed. "You go on a lark with your dad and brothers. Grandpa and I will crack open his journals."

"What's this?" Kaley picked up the box. "Dad sent you flowers?"

"No, pumpkin. Someone sent Grandpa a pair of slippers."

Kaley spun the box around, examining it.

"Yesterday when you and Dad drove to town, I went outside and saw a flower truck parked by the driveway. The driver walked to his truck carrying a box like this."

Eva twisted around and gazed out the front door window. She'd seen a white van earlier. Or had she dreamt it?

"Did Grandpa say he received a delivery yesterday?" Eva quizzed.

"He was asleep in the chair. He probably didn't hear the flower guy ring the bell."

"A guy?" Eva stepped closer. "You saw a guy?"

"Ah … I'm not sure." Kaley lifted her shoulders. "He was slightly built. Might have been a girl wearing pants."

Eva zoomed in on Kaley like a laser.

"Which flower company was it?"

"Did I say flowers, Mom? It was a white van. I assumed it was a flower van. I don't think it said flowers. Maybe flowers were painted on the door."

The back door slamming interrupted Eva's interrogation. Scott tossed his Detroit Tigers cap on the bench.

"That was a bust. Ralph's playing warrior at a re-enactment down at the lakeshore."

Eva frowned. "How do you know where he is then?"

"His son told me. Before you fire off a dozen questions, Junior has no idea where to look for Marty's journal."

"Okay, I buy that." Eva thrust her hands on her hips. "Ralph borrowed Grandpa's journal for war research."

Scott wiped his brow. "He comes home Sunday. Meantime, what's our agenda for this second day of our hard-earned vacation?"

"I'm checking on Gramps." Kaley hurried past. "He should have his mail."

Eva's eyes lingered on Scott's. "I don't like Grandpa's memories being where I can't reach them."

Scott pulled her to him, lightly kissing her forehead.

"That's my wife, the federal agent who is always ready to seize control."

"We have a new problem," she countered, recapping Kaley's flower van story.

Andy waltzed into the kitchen popping gum and blowing a purple bubble.

When his bubble burst, he asked, "Dad, wanna check out the waves again? Kaley said we have to beat it for a while."

Eva's ringing cell phone split the air. She grabbed her phone. The screen told her it was her task force partner, FBI Agent Griff Topping.

"I should take this call," she told Scott. "You decide what comes next."

Eva went into the living room asking Griff, "What's wrong?"

"What do you mean? Can't I call and see if you're having a nice vacation?"

"Nice try, Griff, but you're all work and no play. Why are you really calling?"

He cleared his throat. "Now that I've confirmed you're loafing at the beach, I do recall my other reason."

Crackling noises made Eva press the phone to her ear.

She heard Griff say, "… suspicious caller. I took the woman's number, but said I couldn't reach you right away."

"Could I call when I'm back in the office? My vacation is just starting."

"Right. You deserve a rest."

Eva laughed, picturing Griff's grin. "I'd do the same for you," she kidded back. "If another 'suspicious caller' comes looking for me, pretend you don't know where I am."

"Will do, but she did claim it was urgent."

Eva's heart plummeted. "Well, if it's a true emergency, give me her name."

"You sure? You're still on vacation, right?"

"And my time off is speeding by each second. What's her name?"

"Delores Fontaine."

Eva's mind thumbed through files of her past cases, stopping at a Chinese relic. Then she remembered. Yet Griff sounded as if he hadn't a clue.

"Griff, do you know her?"

"Nope. She refused to tell me anything on the phone."

"Think a moment. Delores is the art curator for a wealthy family foundation. She gave key evidence in my arrest of a Chinese general who smuggled artifacts."

Griff chuckled. "Your memory's sharper than mine. Dawn says I should take fish oil. How could I forget Delores? That exciting caper had you going undercover."

"I never approved of how her case ended." Eva walked over to Marty's desk and pulled out paper and a pen. "Okay, I'm ready for her number."

"No way. I wouldn't dream of interrupting your family time."

"Griff, please!"

"I shouldn't have bothered you. Enjoy the beach!"

The line went dead. Eva pocketed her phone, stymied once again.

4

va tossed and turned that night. She'd made a few calls, trying to track down who sent Marty the slippers. Old, forgotten cases rampaged through her mind like wild horses. Adrenaline shot through her veins. Her eyelids refused to close. She tried to lie still, but regret made her restless.

Grandpa's mind was fixed on his wife, but Eva had never been close to her. Rather, Grandma Joanne mostly kept to herself, sending greeting cards and scarves she'd knitted for Kaley and Andy. She died the year Eva and Griff had risked their lives on the island of Socotra.

Eva clenched her teeth thinking about that terrorism case. Justice had been hard to come by. She blinked back moonlight shining through lacy curtains and remembered. Little Marty, who everyone called Dutch, was born that same year. What a blessing he was. Overwhelmed with love for her young son, Eva relinquished her angst, and finally slept.

That is until a noise startled her awake. She tossed back the sheet and went swiftly to the window. The sun's rays lit the backyard, but the clock proclaimed it wasn't yet eight. Eva changed into shorts and a T-shirt and grabbed her cell phone.

She found Marty at the kitchen table with his Bible and sat beside him. "You're up early." Eva peered at the pages. "What are you studying?"

He smoothed a page. "Jeremiah. The weeping prophet's message is uplifting."

"He's not high on my reading list. I'm happy if I read a Psalm each day."

"With time on my hands after Joanne's death ..." Marty's voice broke.

Compassion surged through Eva. She touched his arm.

"Am I imagining it, or are you missing her more lately?"

He wiped his eyes. "After you and I traveled to Israel a few months ago, I realized I don't like being alone. It's wrong, but I already feel lonely for when you leave."

Ah, one mystery solved, she thought. To Marty, she said, "We'll miss you too. With our jobs, Scott and I are unable to move here."

"I know that." He slid a finger down the page. "Jeremiah says God has plans to give me a hope and a future. Living out this truth is hard."

Eva wrapped her arms around his neck. "Faith is believing when we cannot see around the corner. How about breakfast? Eggs and sausage?"

"Toast and juice is enough."

"You got it."

While bread toasted, Eva checked her phone for e-mails. Sure enough, Griff had sent Delores' number. After serving Marty breakfast, she sauntered out to the backyard and sat on a swing hanging from a mighty beech tree.

With her back to the house and her eyes gazing into green rows of corn, she phoned Delores. What if Delores didn't answer a "blocked" call? Eva would never leave her personal number on a voicemail.

An alto voice answered, "Hello?"

"This is Agent Montanna. I received your message."

"Oh, Eva. I couldn't figure out who was calling with a blocked number."

"What can I do for you?"

Delores whispered, "I have information. Can we meet next Wednesday? I live in D.C. now."

Eva refused to cut short her vacation. "Give me some idea. It's been years."

"Eva, I appreciate what you did for me last time we met. What I have uncovered is along the same lines as before."

Eva seized onto the possibilities. "You mean stolen or smuggled art?"

"Correct. Think Dutch Masters."

"Delores, you have my attention. But I am out of town."

Eva suggested a date to meet when she returned and ended the call. Momentum to dig into Marty's journals surged through her veins. Time was marching on. She went inside, finding the house quiet. Where was everyone? She heard voices in the basement and plunged down the steps.

"What am I missing?"

"Gramps wants the Chinese checkers," Kaley said, snooping in a cabinet.

Andy slumped on a battered couch, plugging his nose. "Phew, it stinks."

"It's dampness," Marty explained. "Sorry I didn't clean up before you came."

Eva spotted the checkerboard on a shelf and pulled it down.

"I love this game," she said. "Grandpa, you should teach the kiddos to play."

"Maybe, but look here, Andy." Marty held a metal device. "I've had my juice harp since I was a youngster like you."

He stuck a harp in his mouth. With his finger, he twitched a wire that looked like a bobby pin extending across his open mouth. The juice harp vibrated and tinny sounds of *Old MacDonald Had a Farm* filled the basement. Eva and Scott sang a duet to his juice harp, giving them all a jolly laugh.

Kaley stood with her arms crossed, breaking the magic. "I'm invited to play volleyball with the youth group. Can I drive the van?"

Eva's eyes shot toward Scott. Let her husband decide.

"Sure," he said. "I'll ride along and say hello to Pastor Dekker. Let me know what time to pick you up."

"Can't I go by myself?" Kaley kicked a beanbag pillow.

Eva faced her. "Grandpa's truck is too small if the rest of us have to leave."

"Let her take my truck." Marty rose from an overstuffed chair.

"No," Eva said. "You don't have insurance for a teenage driver."

"Fiddlesticks. I'll call my agent."

Scott dropped an arm around Marty's shoulder. "Another time. I want to ask Pastor Dekker about Saturday's softball challenge. He wants me to pitch."

Marty took the hint, his eyes downcast.

"Where did you find such a unique instrument?" Eva asked, changing the subject.

"In a box of memories from my youth." He flashed a nostalgic smile and pointed to an old steamer trunk. "That's how we made music. If we couldn't buy a juice harp, we put wax paper around a comb, put that to our lips, and hummed through it."

"No way!" Andy looked perplexed. "You made music through a comb?"

Marty's eyes shone. "I kid you not. That was the forerunner to the rock band."

"Gramps, what else are you hiding in here?"

Andy peered in the trunk, but Marty shut the lid.

"Not so fast. I don't want to reveal all my valuable old trinkets at once."

"Kaley and I are off to church," Scott announced. "Get your stuff, kiddo."

"Can I come along, Dad?" Dutch looked up at Scott who towered over him.

Eva's heart skipped a beat. Her son was growing up fast. She tousled his blond hair.

"Sure. Take Andy too. Then Grandpa and I will pour over his journals."

Andy flew up the steps. Dutch tore after him. Kaley lagged behind Scott as she slowly climbed the steps.

Marty laid a hand on Eva's arm. "My journals are in that old trunk."

"Good. Let's get started. I installed new software on my computer. You talk and the program types what you say."

Marty rubbed his arms. "You read them first. I wouldn't know what to say."

Eva opened the trunk, removing several leather-bound journals before closing the lid. Marty took the journals and hugged them to his chest.

"These are my war journals, except for the one Ralph borrowed."

"Oh, that reminds me. Scott checked and Ralph is due back Sunday. Are you ready to spend some time in World War II?"

Eva's periwinkle eyes searched his blue ones. In the dim light she saw a shadow flicker over his face. Were there things he didn't want to face from his war years?

She snapped off the light and followed him upstairs. In the kitchen, she brewed fresh coffee. After setting out more chocolate cookies, Eva sat next to him at the table.

"Let's start with something easy. Where did you and Grandma meet?"

Marty bit into a cookie, his eyes drifting away.

"Someone's walking in the backyard!" he cried.

Eva leapt from her chair and glared out the sliding glass window, wishing she had binoculars. "I don't see anyone," she finally said.

"He was there all right, walking fast." Marty tossed his head. "Maybe it was Ralph's son. Eva Marie, I have something else on my mind."

She returned to the table deciding that Marty didn't want to talk about Grandma. Things weren't coming together on this vacation as she'd expected.

Though eager to delve into his journals, she said, "Grandpa, I'm all ears."

"Good. I want you to see Holland's windmill. It's just like the one I hid Jews in during World War II. Stepping inside transports me back in time. Will you come?"

"Sure. When do you want to go?"

"Why, right now." Marty rubbed his chin. "Helen is giving tours. Biting into her cookie made me remember."

He sure was talking a lot about Helen. Eva set aside the journals.

"Certainly, I want to meet your friend. I'll leave Scott a note. He and the kids can meet us later for lunch. Also, I found a store that sells Angus plaid. Gather your slippers. We'll see if Valerie's Boutique knows who bought them."

Eva secured her keys and readied herself for a new adventure. These days with Marty seemed like a perpetual whirlwind.

5

Eva spotted De Zwaan, the towering windmill, looming ahead as Marty drove his truck down a flower-studded driveway. The Dutch landmark looked majestic, its four large sails etching the blue sky. All threats of storms had passed. Eva admired the flat land, thinking the Netherlands countryside must be similar. In her travels, she'd never made it out of Schiphol airport.

Marty had insisted on driving the few miles from his farm and Eva let him. He wheeled his "baby" into a parking spot beneath a tree.

"I like parking in the shade. This old truck has no air conditioning."

Eva hopped out to photograph a group of red dahlias.

"Look at these huge blooms. My mother would love it here."

Marty slammed the truck door. "Well, she and my son never come to Michigan. Marcia and Clifford are too busy with their own lives."

"Ever since Jillie died, Mom isn't the same. She and Father roam the earth looking for peace. They're in Nepal, helping at an orphanage."

"Peace is not a state of mind, Eva Marie. Jesus is the giver."

She smiled at him. "You're so right. I am blessed to be here with you. Let's walk this stunning garden and trust Jesus to solve our future dilemmas."

"Okay." Marty pointed to the flags along the path. "I love these Dutch flags."

He handed Eva his keys and she slid them with her camera into her purse. She took his arm. Flags flying from different parts of the Netherlands surrounded them. As she saw the replica of a Dutch village, her earlier talk with Delores Fontaine came roaring back. Perhaps Marty could shed light on one aspect.

"Grandpa, you're a trained artist. What do you know of the Dutch Masters?"

He stopped and whirled his head. "That came out of the blue."

"It's related to a case of mine. I know of Rembrandt, of course."

"It depends on the era, but you should consider Ver Meer. His 'Girl with the Pearl Earring' is famous. Also, Jan van Eyck was a Flemish painter who died in the fifteenth century. I say Flemish, but back then, the whole area was known as the Low Countries and part of the Netherlands."

"Besides Rembrandt, I've never seen any of their actual paintings. Have you?"

Marty lifted his chin. "My dear, have I! Some say van Eyck invented oil painting. These artists' works are priceless. They've been bought by museums and are protected by expensive security systems."

"We Dutch have reason to be proud," Eva said, guiding him down the path. "And for you, even more than you know."

"Do I sense another mystery?" Eva asked, curiosity bubbling within her.

They reached the steps leading to the windmill. He grasped the handrail.

"Family legend has it that our ancestor, Peter Vander Goes, was a well-to-do official in the Netherlands. Aunt Deane says he lent money to Johann Gutenberg for the first printing press. You've heard of that invention?"

She smiled. "It was as revolutionary as the computer. But is he connected to one of these famous Dutch artists?"

"Aunt Deane told me much of the tale. It's a bit hazy, but Peter was a hero. I wrote our ancient family history in some journals I can't find."

Eva followed him up the steps. "Did Ralph borrow them too?"

"No." Marty shook his head. "But I have more somewhere."

"I'll help you find them. Scott's tracing his family line. I want to see how far back we can place the Vander Goes tree."

A tour group was just starting. A young woman in costume detailed the inner workings of the mill, then ushered them to the upper level. Eva strolled onto the balcony, leaving Marty chatting with the guide about the milling process. So Marty had spent time in a mill just like this one. Gusty winds blew her long blond locks into her eyes. She brushed away her hair and was surprised to see black horses galloping in the fields.

"Those are Frisian horses," a husky voice said.

Eva turned and faced a woman dressed in a bright blue and white costume.

"Remember Ricky's grandmother Helen?" Marty's blue eyes danced with delight.

The two women shook hands, with Eva recalling Helen's mischievous grandson. Of course, she had not seen Ricky since she was a girl.

"Do you volunteer at the mill?" Eva asked.

"I do." Helen fiddled with her glasses. "Marty and I knew each other moons ago. My father farmed his fields when Marty sailed to Holland. He and I are reconnecting."

"Our lives often take curious turns," Eva replied. "I look forward to his journals."

Helen's eyebrows arched. "Oh? Am I in those, Marty?"

He grinned. Eva began to suspect this trip to the windmill had everything to do with Helen and little to do with Marty's past memories. She opened her purse.

"Grandpa, are you ready to head to your truck?"

Helen answered for him. "I'm taking him upstairs to see where we grind wheat. Want to join us?"

Eva started to say yes, then decided not to. The galloping Frisian horses and steady winds might clear her mind and she'd find answers to the puzzles stumping her. But hadn't she come here to learn of Marty's life in the Netherlands?

"All right. Lead the way."

"Come, I want to show you something." Marty's face glowed.

He darted inside with gusto. Eva followed Helen. They climbed curving stairs that clung to the mill's inner wall. On the third floor, Eva hovered behind Marty, who inched his way into a waiting group of tourists.

Helen gestured with her arms, telling how the working windmill had been relocated to Michigan more than sixty years ago. It was originally built in the Netherlands in 1761 and sustained heavy damage in the Second World War.

"Outside, around the base, you can see one of the original blades riddled with bullet holes," Helen said. "The gashes resulted from battles with Nazis."

Marty leaned back, whispering to Eva, "Later I will tell you how I tangled with a German soldier. I forgot about the incident until we walked inside the mill."

Eva raised her eyebrows. But she said nothing because the tour was winding its way down another stairway. Helen explained how some mills in the Netherlands pumped water from behind dykes to reclaim farm fields.

"During the war, millers had a dangerous job. They issued warnings to citizens by stopping the sails in various positions. The German occupiers never knew these codes."

Marty nodded heartily and Eva made a mental note to follow up. When they reached the cool brick-lined base of the mill, Marty lingered, speaking to Helen in quiet tones. Eva headed outside where she snapped photos of the stately structure that held many secrets behind its walls, just like Marty.

She waited on a wooden bench until he joined her.

"I invited Helen for lunch. We're just friends, but we're both alone."

"Oh! Speaking of lunch, I had left Scott a note saying that we'd meet him and the boys for lunch at one. We'd better head out."

Eva urged Marty to hurry, but he dawdled, pointing out other attractions in the park. Families gathered around a Dutch street organ belting out a lively tune. Then he showed her the merry-go-round with hand painted horses.

"I miss bringing Joanne here."

Eva tugged his sleeve toward the truck. "Would you like to return to the Netherlands?"

"Seeing the Dutch row houses and the mill brings memories flooding back."

Was he finally going to open up?

"Then our trip here is worthwhile," she said. "After lunch, we'll check on your slippers at the boutique. Then we'll start on your memoirs with no more delays."

She started digging in her purse for his keys.

"Oh no!" Marty cried.

He sounded so upset Eva concluded he wasn't interested. He never spoke of the war dangers he faced or if he fought. Only recently did she learn of Eli Rosenbaum, the Jewish man Marty had saved from the Nazis.

"It's all right." Eva combed through her purse. "Where did I put your keys?"

She'd just caught hold of them when Marty yelled, "Hey, Eva, look!"

Her head snapped upward. Her eyes bulged. Marty's truck had shrunk several inches and sat close to the asphalt like some chopped hot rod.

"Your truck is dangerously low. Do you check the air in your tires?"

"It's crazy … It's crazy," he kept repeating.

She scurried to the truck. The reason for the odd change became painfully obvious. "Your tires are flat."

Eva wiped her forehead in the rising heat. Had vandals flattened his tires? Things didn't add up. She bent over. Deep gashes lined the sidewalls on both front and rear tires on the driver's side. Both tires on the passenger side had been slashed too. Four tires were destroyed.

"I can't believe this," she sputtered.

Amazed that such a crime could occur in broad daylight in a nice town like Holland, Eva did a three-sixty. She saw no one suspicious lurking in the parking lot, just a bus letting out elderly people. Eva looked into the front seat. Although the windows were open, Marty's slipper box was still on the seat.

"Oh boy! We left the windows down and doors unlocked."

He shrugged. "I don't have AC so I keep windows open in summer. Besides, who'd steal it? Young thieves couldn't figure out how to drive the stick."

"Well, we're sidelined." Eva pulled out her phone. "Road service can bring the truck to a tire store. No one carries four spare tires."

"Len does my work."

Eva punched in Scott's number. Turned out he and the boys were already at the restaurant, but he agreed to come right over. Marty didn't know Len's number, so Eva searched in her smart phone for his number. She arranged for Len to bring his tow truck. Marty eased into his Chevy to wait.

"Look here." He held up a bouquet of flowers tied with ribbon. "Someone saw my tires were flat and left these. How nice."

Eva slid behind the wheel to examine the flowers. She recalled Kaley saying she'd seen a white van with flowers painted on the side. This bore looking into. Perhaps Helen left them in Marty's truck.

After all, she hadn't begun their tour, a younger girl did. But would such a friendly woman slash Marty's tires? Eva shuddered. Perhaps Helen had an evil streak like in some horror flick. Even stranger, the box of slippers sat untouched in the unlocked truck.

Then Eva spied it—a note folded beneath the ribbon. She opened it. Shock waves jolted through her.

> *Martin Vander Goes, you despicable traitor, I hate you. Return my stolen property or else your life is worth nothing. You and your family are being watched. If you notify the police, you will have more trouble than you ever imagined possible. You're no different than the thief Kuipers.*

Eva's hands shook. She turned aside to keep Marty from reading the hate-filled words. Anger roared through her veins like a torrential flood. Who threatened her sweet and wonderful grandpa? She wanted to scream, but instead, she inhaled, trying to calm down.

The mysterious slippers had set off a cascade of events like dominoes. She didn't yet know the perpetrator, but Eva knew one thing. Slashed tires pointed to a deliberate act by someone. The note mentioned Kuipers. Who was he and what role did he play in this?

"Grandpa?"

He had gone. Her heart fluttering, Eva jumped out of the antique Chevy and found him setting a jack under the rear of the truck.

"Someone left a note," she said. "It says you took something. Do you have any idea what that means?"

He straightened his back, his face a portrait of confusion.

"I always try to live as an honest man."

Marty inserted the jack handle, but Eva touched his hand.

"Road service is coming to take your truck to a tire store."

"If you say so." He shrugged and returned the jack to the truck bed.

Eva struggled to find a kernel of truth. "Are you in conflict with anyone? Helen is a friend, but is there more to it?"

Marty thrust his hands on his hips, glaring at Eva in an unusual way.

"I am no idiot. As a Christian, I aim to treat others as I wish to be treated."

"Of course, Grandpa. I can't understand why anyone would slash your tires."

He tilted his head as if deep in thought. "I eat dinner at Helen's once a week. Also, I give a widow lady a ride to church, but I'm not courting her either. Ralph objected when I put in a fence post, but I moved it. We're friends. I have no enemies."

A large flatbed truck ground to a noisy stop behind the pickup. Len hustled out and whistled. "Wow. You got someone real ornery. Your tires are all slashed."

"It's incredible," Eva replied. "We have no explanation."

Len was all smiles. "Let me load his baby. You both ride up front with me."

"My husband is coming. We'll follow behind you and buy the new tires."

Len lowered the flatbed with Marty supervising. Eva used her fingertips to carefully snatch the note off the front seat. Troubles were mounting fast. She wished Scott would get here. Maybe he could get Marty to tell him things he didn't want Eva to know.

6

Eva seized a tissue from her purse and wrapped it around the note. Thoughts of how to best check for fingerprints consumed her mind. Scott wheeled into the parking lot, spinning gravel. He sped to help Len. Eva shoved the note, tissue and all, into her pocket. Dutch and Andy ran over to watch the truck being hoisted on the flatbed.

Marty strode up to Eva, wiping his hands on his pant leg. "Seeing your son helped me to remember. I don't know if it's important."

"Tell me."

"The delivery boy asked if my last name was Dutch."

"Good. Did you see flowers painted on the delivery truck?"

"Nope." Marty turned his blue eyes to her. "But I signed my name to a clipboard."

"That's helpful to know. I think I should call Chief Talsma."

As Eva reached for her cell to phone the police chief, the note fell from her pocket. The wind stirred the tissue, blowing it away. Marty chased it and picked up the piece of paper. He scanned the note, his face turning pale.

"This is terrible. Who wrote such a thing? And with my name on it!"

Eva hurried him to their van and nestled him into the middle seat. She called Andy over. "Hop in and start telling stories to Grandpa. He's upset about his tires."

"Sure, Mom."

Fury at the unknown mounted. Eva crammed the note into purse. Her blood pressure rose on the drive to the tire store. Scott offered to bring Marty back for his truck when it was good as new.

"We have a bigger problem," Eva told him behind a tire display. "I won't talk about it here."

Scott stared. "What's happened besides some freak slashing Marty's tires?"

"Sshh. Our slasher left a note. I'll tell you more at home."

He grinned, but Eva saw nothing funny in this mess. Her whole body shook with adrenaline. She was keyed about getting back to the farm but stopped on the way for Chinese takeout. No one had eaten lunch. Eva corralled her sons, instructing them to wash their hands. Then she dished up hot plates for everyone but herself.

She couldn't eat with the world collapsing around her. Instead, she took the tissue and note from her purse. Holding the letter by its edges, she examined the underside, seeing nothing else. Eva retrieved a baggie from the pantry and slid the note inside, asking Marty, "Where's your telephone book?"

He looked up from his chicken chow mien. "You're not calling the police?"

"Mom, are you reporting Gramps' tires?" Andy held a fork near his mouth.

"Not yet," Eva assured. "I'm checking to see if any local company delivered Grandpa's slippers."

"Okay, we can do that much." Marty sounded relieved.

He walked to a desk and pulled out a small yellow book. Eva called Valerie's Boutique, but they hadn't sold the Angus plaid slippers. The clerk tried to entice Eva to stop in for their sweater sale. Defeat dogged her with every courier service she found that hadn't delivered the package. Scott finished his meal and went outside to toss a football in the yard with Andy and Dutch.

Marty paced while Eva finished her last call. She set her phone on the counter.

"With no tracking number, neither UPS nor FedEx could help."

"The note said not to involve the police. What can we do?"

"Listen, Grandpa. Lance Talsma may be the local police chief, but he's also your friend. We should tell him about your flattened tires."

Marty's lips drooped. "What if someone means to hurt you or my great-grandkids? I could never forgive myself."

"I'll be careful how I handle this."

She punched in Talsma's number. His voicemail clicked on. The ringing doorbell made her jump. Marty dropped a cup, which rolled across the linoleum. Eva hung up and answered the door, expecting some new trauma.

There on the front porch stood Scott with the bouquet of flowers from the truck. He flashed a funny smile.

"I found these in the van. You have my house key. All the doors are locked, as they should be."

"Thanks, but I'm throwing those weeds in the trash."

Scott scowled at the idea. "You still sound upset. What can I do?"

Eva ushered him into the kitchen. It was time for light to shine on the darkness.

"Pull up a chair next to Marty. We need God's help sorting this out."

Using tissues like potholders, she gently tugged the letter from the baggie. She carefully unfolded it, saying, "Read but don't touch. My prints are smeared all over the paper."

Scott silently read the typed letter, his face growing beet red.

"What piece of scum threatens to hurt my family?" he roared.

"Sshh. We don't want the boys hearing. That note was tucked in the flowers. I've been trying to find who delivered the slippers, but I've struck out. The package had no tracking numbers. Marty can't remember the kid who delivered it."

Scott's cheeks bulged before he blew out a breath.

"What about your cases? Who's on your enemies list?"

"I have a few," Eva spat. "One escaped terrorist is on my mind, but Grandpa, you have no connection to a Romanian."

Marty shook his head. "I'm going upstairs to my room to pray. Please don't call Chief Talsma until I come down."

He left Scott and Eva to sort things out.

"I'll have the brown paper and box checked for prints," she said. "Where did we put those?"

Scott rushed to the garage and came back. "Grab an oven mitt. The box and paper are on top of the trash can. At least the garbage truck hasn't come yet."

Eva pulled on the mitts and stowed the wrapping and box in a big trash bag.

"Have you called the flower companies? Kaley saw a flower van near the house," Scott said.

Eva sighed. "I should've done that. Look up the numbers for me."

She nodded at the phone book as she wrapped a twisty tie around the plastic bag. Scott flipped open the yellow pages.

Before writing down a single number, he said, "A threat against a federal agent brings in other feds. Call the FBI."

"Brilliant." Eva snapped her fingers. "I'll phone Griff. I can also take the evidence to our ICE office in Grand Rapids."

"If we leave soon, we can make it before five." Scott headed for the garage.

"You don't need to come," Eva called.

Scott held firm. "We don't split up until we catch whoever's behind this. What would have happened if Kaley had driven Marty's truck by herself?"

"Our family could be in danger," Eva agreed. "Drive to the church and pull Kaley out of her volleyball tournament. I'll round up Grandpa and the boys."

Seconds later, Scott backed down the driveway. Eva let the others know of their change in plans. She then made another phone call, not to florists, but to Chief Talsma.

She advised him of the threat, adding, "We're taking the evidence to the ICE office in Grand Rapids. Will you swing by while we're gone and look around?"

"Sure. I've known Marty for years. He taught my daughter how to paint watercolors. I won't let anything happen to him on my watch."

They exchanged cell numbers, with Eva promising to call if she spotted suspicious characters on the road. She was ready to hang up, when Talsma asked her to consider something else.

"Could it be someone wants you folks to leave the house?"

"I don't think so. No one was here when the truck was vandalized."

"But the slashed tires delayed your return, correct?" Talsma shot back.

Eva gripped her phone. "Yes."

"Was anything removed from the house while you were away?"

"Good question. Marty's gold watch is missing. But he may have misplaced it. We'll do an inventory when we come home."

"My officers and I will drive by the house until this is resolved."

Eva thanked him and hung up. Her sons were stomping their feet on the front porch. "Don't go anywhere," she hollered through the front window.

Eva checked the backdoor locks before racing upstairs. Marty fumbled with a shopping bag in his room.

"We need to head downstairs, Grandpa. Scott will be back with Kaley soon."

"Take this. You may think me odd, but it has my will, checkbook, and important papers I don't want to leave lying around."

"You should keep your papers in a safety deposit box, but we'll take them along."

"That note has me seeing things from a new perspective. My life is in God's hands, but I want to be prepared. Where did you put my journals, by the way?"

"I'll grab your journals on the way out."

Like a mother hen, she herded Marty downstairs and out the front door. Eva tossed his journals in the shopping bag and locked the front door. Scott turned in the drive, and the rest of the family loaded into the van. After making sure everyone had put on their seat belts, Eva punched in the number for FBI Agent Griff Topping.

From the third row, Andy complained, "Mom, that Chinese grub is long gone."

"I only ate a candy bar during the volleyball game," Kaley said.

Scott joined in. "Anyone else hungry besides me?"

"Me!" Dutch echoed.

Marty said, "Nothing for me."

Eva turned to ask, "How about a chocolate shake?"

He shook his head, causing Eva to wonder if she should involve him in this trip to the ICE office. But she was uncomfortable leaving him alone. She cast a sideways glance at Scott. "Turn off at Hudsonville."

Scott pushed back. "I hope you know what you're doing, Eva. If we run into traffic, we won't make it by five."

"Then we'll go back tomorrow. What kind of mother lets her children go hungry?"

"You're right."

Scott exited the freeway and found a nearby fast food restaurant. He shouted their order into a metal menu board. Their food was bagged and ready in minutes. He drove off while Eva handed out boxes of chicken strips and apple fries.

All the while, her eyes swept the rearview mirror. Eva's mind pulsed with the unknown. Who could be out there stalking her and her family? And more importantly, why?

7

Eva drained her coffee and munched on apple fries before popping a peppermint in her mouth. A gentle rain started. Scott turned on the wipers. Eva phoned Griff on her cell, and thankfully, he answered on the first ring.

"Hey, it's Eva. I've a story to tell you."

"Make it quick. Dawn has a doctor's appointment and I'm meeting her there."

"Is anything wrong? Your wife comes before a new case."

"Just routine. I promised to take her to dinner afterwards. What's up?"

Out of habit, Eva lowered her voice. "I'm heading to ICE in Grand Rapids with Scott and the kids. Grandpa's truck was vandalized by someone who left a threatening note. If ICE can't help, will you look into the evidence for me?"

"Are we talking about some disgruntled punk you put away?"

"Ah ... I thought of Andrei, but I can't say more at the moment."

Griff cleared his throat. "Right. After you and I testified at Andrei Enescu's international terrorism trial, he escaped from federal prison. I thought I heard Interpol had tracked him to his homeland in Transylvania."

"Maybe you could double-check."

"Will do. Does Marty have enemies?"

"None that I've nailed down," Eva replied softly.

The gentle shower turned to torrents. Rain pummeled the van's roof, the loud sounds competing with Griff's voice. Scott's knuckles were white as he hung on to the wheel. Cars splashed rainwater against the windshield, making it hard to see.

"Griff, I have to call you back. If you're busy with Dawn, I'll leave a message."

Eva ended the call abruptly. She pulled down her visor and looked in the mirror. The kids were quiet, eating their food. Marty held his shake with both hands. Eva refocused her eyes to the road ahead. She saw the danger before she knew what was happening.

"Look out!" she yelled. "A truck!"

Scott swerved left as the cargo truck veered into their lane. The van hydroplaned toward the median. Eva's pulse rocketed.

God, protect us!

Seconds later, their van slowed. Scott eased back into his lane. Eva forced out a sigh, the peril of being pushed off the road seemingly over. But the near miss with the metal barrier made her think. Who was coming after them? She hoped Griff might offer fresh insight; however, she'd have to wait to find out.

"Whew!" Marty said. "I haven't seen rain this hard since I was in gale force winds on Lake Michigan."

"What happened, Gramps?" Andy chimed.

Marty chuckled. "I crossed Lake Michigan in a giant storm on the steamship *Milwaukee Clipper*. It was really scary."

Kaley made a terrific noise drinking the last of her shake, then asked, "Were you alone or was Nana with you?"

"No, I was alone. My stomach didn't like the waves much."

"Dad, can I go on the *Milwaukee Clipper*?"

"Yes, Andy, you can," Marty answered, crumpling up his food bag. "She's a museum ship docked in Muskegon, not far from here. The *Clipper* has been replaced by a faster boat that carries families and their cars to Milwaukee. The new one rides atop the water."

Kaley and Andy were of one mind. "We want to see them both!"

"If we have time," Eva said.

Groans erupted from the back. Slashed tires and a vicious note bore the earmarks of a ruined vacation.

Scott leaned toward her and whispered, "If we stay busy—"

"Right, I won't worry so much."

Her eyes drifted to the side mirror. No cars seemed to be following on their bumper. The rain stopped as unexpectedly as it began. That meant Eva could dart into the ICE office building with no umbrella. After they left the freeway, Scott navigated the one-way streets in downtown Grand Rapids as if he'd grown up in the city.

He slowed in front of a tall brick building. "We'll spin by President Ford's museum. I want to photograph his tomb."

"I'll call your cell when I'm done." Eva opened the door.

"Sounds like a plan."

She hopped out, grasping her large plastic bag of evidence. Eva shot past the Stars and Stripes and approached a wall of glass. The young clerk eyed her cautiously. She held up her badge.

"Sorry, you missed the boss," he said.

"How can that be?" Eva said, lifting her chin. "Agent Little was expecting me."

"He and the other agents dashed to the airport. The airline found a suspicious package on an inbound flight. He said to leave your evidence with me."

The clerk seemed eager to help, but could Eva trust him? She thrust her badge into a jeans pocket and gripped the plastic bag tightly. The ringing phone nudged her toward a decision. After the clerk took the call and hung up, Eva asked for his name.

"Clark Hollis."

"Okay, Clark, you're busy. Find a registered mail package and we'll send this stuff via express mail to Virginia. I'll package it up for you."

He nodded and buzzed open the entry door, allowing Eva to enter. She quickly learned Clark aspired to become an agent after college. He helped her photocopy the note. Using gloves, Eva secured the note into a glassine evidence bag. They flattened the box and folded the brown paper. Eva hand wrote Griff's address at the FBI.

"You're lucky, Agent Montanna."

"No one's told me that lately," she said grinning. "How so?"

"Because I was about to head for my mail run when you burst in."

"So you're sure you can get my package to the post office before it closes?"

"As sure as my dog eats his treat in one gulp."

"I'm counting on you."

Eva folded her photocopy of the note and stowed this in her purse. She tried calling Griff again. His voicemail clicked on, so she left a message.

"Expect a package. Call me when you're back from dinner. I don't care what time. I won't rest until the monster threatening my family is caught."

She phoned Scott, pocketed her cell, and thanked Clark for his help.

"Look me up if you ever get to Washington."

"Thanks, Agent Montanna. I should close up so I can mail this in time."

Eva stepped outside, watching from the overhang for Scott to drive up. Her mind sized up the case of the mystery slippers. Whoever sent them was savvy enough to know Marty's slipper size. They knew where he lived. They'd also tracked his truck. Furthermore, they dropped off the horrid note with an ugly bouquet of flowers.

The entire scenario smacked of a demented mind. Perhaps one of Eva's arrestees was to blame. Andrei Enescu had shouted vile things at her when the marshals led him away in handcuffs after the jury convicted him.

Yet, something nagged at her. The note never mentioned Eva being a federal agent. Maybe the threat had no tie with her or her job. She needed to draw more info from Marty. Some local might be holding a grudge.

Then she remembered Ralph had borrowed the journal. Perhaps he'd loaned something valuable to Marty, who had forgotten to return the "something." It was a flimsy connection, but Eva would make it a point to meet Ralph on Sunday when he returned from the WWII reenactment.

Every passing car caught her eye. She examined every driver and none seemed to notice her. All the same, she couldn't shake the feeling that a pair of eyes watched her. Scott pulled to the curb, and she climbed in.

"Everyone okay?" she asked, buckling her seat belt.

Kaley spoke up first. "Mom, there's some cool murals along the river."

"They're left from the annual Art Prize Grand Rapids holds every September," Marty answered. "I missed last year, but you should see the spectacular art."

"Gramps, why not enter your work?" Kaley asked.

Eva didn't hear his reply. Her thoughts lingered on how the person had known she and Marty were at the windmill. They must have been followed, perhaps by Kaley's flower truck. It was all so maddening. Scott zoomed onto the freeway, heading to Zeeland. Eva leaned back and mentally replayed what she knew.

For one thing, being a target made it hard to be objective. She wanted Griff's opinion. Two skilled federal agents should piece this together. Too bad Marty's tires were slashed in a parking lot with no security cameras. At least the note and wrapping were on their way to the FBI for analysis.

Also, Chief Talsma knew no one bent on harming Marty. Her grandpa was clueless, yet he seemed reluctant to share something. Eva tented her fingers. Was that true? His memory revved in spurts, like a car engine with a faulty fuel pump.

She pulled down the visor and glanced in the mirror. Dutch had fallen asleep and so had Marty. Love for her family coursed through her. Eva touched Scott's forearm.

"God prompted our visit to Marty, but why is this happening?"

"We'll get the answers we need at just the right time. Do you have to stop?"

Eva shook her head. If only God wouldn't delay showing her how to protect her family.

8

Back at the farmhouse, Eva tried to lighten her mood by cooking spaghetti. But as the sauce bubbled, so did her anxiety. Whoever threatened Marty had a twisted mind and the kind of anger that squeezed hope from the heart. She concluded something else. He was dangerous.

She'd certainly experienced her share of wackos in her years on the job. But Marty's situation posed something worse: a direct threat to her family. Eva lowered the heat on the sauce. She sliced radishes and threw them on a lettuce salad, concern embedding deep within her. What else should she be doing?

Dinner came and went with Eva no closer to answers. Scott played dominoes with the children until their bedtime. Marty snoozed in his favorite chair, the day's events zapping his strength. Finally, when the kids were upstairs and out of earshot, Eva felt free to tackle the threatening note with Scott and Marty.

"We need more to go on," she said. "What am I missing?"

Marty got up and plugged in the hot water carafe. When it boiled, he poured them herbal tea. The trio sat around the kitchen table and sipped the spicy tea. Marty's red-rimmed eyes betrayed how the stress wore on him. This mad scheme by some vengeful person was hurting a man Eva dearly loved.

"My FBI partner is checking if it's some hoax by a felon I put behind bars," Eva offered, hoping to calm his nerves.

"Hmmph." He simply looked away.

"Grandpa, I want you to feel safe in your house."

Marty pursed his lips. "I won't be safe here ever again. I should have sold the farm to Mr. Barnes before the war. But Joanne and I did enjoy living here after the war."

Eva's senses went on alert. What was Grandpa about to divulge?

"But you have regrets?" she prodded.

"Eva Marie, you blew out candles on your tenth birthday right at this table. We've had happy times, but I suppose our family has its share of enemies."

"That surprises me," Scott said. "In this community you've helped build schools and gave food for the poor from your crops."

"Who are our enemies?" Eva plunked down her cup.

She hoped Marty would give her something to go on.

He twisted his fingers around his cup. "I recall something I'd rather not. The day after I arrived in the Netherlands, the Germans invaded. Aunt Deane had already helped Eli Rosenbaum and his parents make a new home in Middleburg. They had faced tremendous discrimination in Germany."

"I met Eli in Israel," Eva replied. "You two had an amazing reunion there. Are you saying he means you harm?"

"Dear me, no! There are some things I never told you ..." Marty's voice ebbed away and he drank his tea.

Eva drummed her fingers on the blue tablecloth. "Let me see if I understand. Some crazed Nazi you crossed in the war is behind this?"

To her ears, such a possibility seemed far-fetched. Still, the world had gone so haywire, anything was possible. She gazed at her copy of the note and had no trouble forming a picture of a hateful fiend, a nut who hoarded dozens of guns in the basement, waiting to strike. Ready to snap cold handcuffs on the guy's wrists, chills raced up Eva's spine. She must stop imagining the worst. Was her faith in God a mere nothing in a crisis?

"Grandpa, let me try again," Eva said, struggling to assess the facts. "Maybe someone you and Eli know is behind this."

Eva looked at his tired eyes and stopped. She rose and wiggled the back door handle. It was locked, but the dead bolt wasn't. She threw it closed. Marty got up and stalked down the hall to the bathroom as if he was a man on a mission.

Eva stayed right behind him wondering if she should go in. When he didn't close the door, she followed. So did Scott. Marty went to a narrow wall that enclosed the bathtub and shower. He lifted and removed a wood panel that had been painted to blend with the wall. Eva looked at the exposed water pipes and wondered.

She shot a questioning look at Scott and he shrugged. As if a magician revealing a rabbit in a hat, Marty reached into the hole and pulled out a large green satin cloth. He handed this to Eva. She was surprised by the heavy weight. What was in here?

Marty replaced the panel, telling her, "Hundreds of years ago, Lady Douglas traveled from Scotland to marry Lord Jan Vander Goes in the Netherlands."

Marty straightened his back. He motioned her to his den, where he promptly sat.

"Whew, I almost forgot about hiding these. Unwrap the cloth. See what's inside."

Eva gently placed the bundle on his desk. After untying a cord that held the fabric closed, she stepped back. He unrolled a piece of linen. It reminded Eva of a wall calendar Marty once bought her overseas.

But this piece of linen was no calendar. Expertly sewn into the shape of trees, old family names filled the air with mystery. Eva held her breath as he unrolled twelve linen scrolls.

Scott whistled. Marty touched one with a wobbly finger. "These are all of Eva's ancestors. Each generation of Vander Goes women, including Aunt Deane, sewed one of these linen scrolls. You can imagine how old some of these are."

With great care, Eva picked up a faded one. "I never learned more than a few words in Dutch."

Marty translated, telling her that Peter Vander Goes was appointed judge for Duke Phillip the Good in the year 1452.

"Eva, maybe your love of justice comes from him."

She squinted at the tiny letters. "What do our ancestors have to do with who is stalking you?"

"I have more artifacts."

Marty lifted up three leather-bound journals, each wrapped in waxed paper.

"Here are the family journals I mentioned. At sixteen, I worked for the Zeeland Record, and I wanted to be a journalist. If you start reading, you may find what you're looking for. Events from the past are swirling in my mind. I don't know anymore what's important."

He swayed on his feet and gripped the back of the chair to steady himself. Eva stared at an open journal as if an answer to the riddle would spring from the pages.

"So, these journals are different from the ones we took earlier?"

Marty stroked the leather. "During the long days of surviving the Germans, Aunt Deane and I found relief from fear by talking about family.

I wrote furiously. These three journals contain history that Deane recounted from hundreds of years ago. My other ones are about the war."

"But Ralph still has one of your war journals?"

"I'm not sure what he has." Marty seemed to sink into the chair.

Eva turned to Scott whispering, "Take Grandpa to bed?"

Shoving her grandfather's history under her arm, Eva went to the kitchen where she lifted the lace curtains. Looking down the drive, no movements caught her eye. She heard nothing unusual. She poured a glass of milk and snagged an apple. In the den, she put down her snack. Trusty legal pad at her elbow, Eva cracked open the first journal.

The year was 1455. In high school, she'd studied the War of the Roses, which broke England apart; however, Eva knew little about her ancestors from the Middle Ages. Though she was fascinated about Peter Vander Goes being a judge for a powerful duke, the pressing danger against her family forced her to save this volume for later. Surely the threats weren't linked to folks that lived that long ago.

Marty seemed to hint his war years held the key. She flipped to the first page of his journal from 1940, fingering the worn pages. Would they bring her closer to the truth? There was one way to find out.

Eva began reading. She soon realized Marty had written his journal more like a novel than just jotting down events. It didn't take her long to become immersed in his exciting tale.

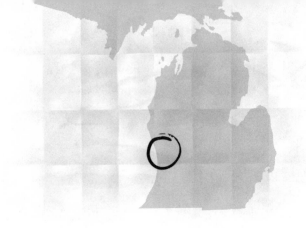

9

MARCH 1940 – ZEELAND, MICHIGAN

Martin Vander Goes plunged down the steps of the Zeeland Post Office. The sun's rays beat on his head, making him wish he'd ridden his bike. A slight breeze stirred as he held up his letter bearing foreign stamps. Was Aunt Deane sending good news from the Netherlands? He was about to open his letter when a hand clapped his back.

"Martin, this heat's unbearable. Can you believe it's March?"

Martin spun around, not knowing how to answer Mr. Barnes. The neighboring farmer tugged at his overalls.

"What have you decided, Martin? It's time for me to begin planting."

Martin hid Deane's letter behind his back. "I know you and other farmers like trading jokes at mail time. So I walked into town to find you. I'm not sure if I should lease you the farm."

"It's like this, see." The stocky farmer outlined his proposal to lease Martin's acreage, and thrust out his fat lower lip. "Give your answer soon, or you'll endanger my crop."

"My father respected you, but Reverend Hartema says I should sell the farm and live with him and his wife. He's become like the father I lost."

Mr. Barnes stiffened. "Your father wouldn't approve of you selling the family home. You lease the land to me, and you stay in your homestead. It also preserves the place for when you and Helen … ah … decide to marry."

Marry Helen? Martin flexed his brow. He was a classmate of Barnes' daughter, but marry Helen? He had better end this inquisition. Too many memories of his recently deceased parents were flooding his heart.

"No," he said. "I won't decide standing here in the scorching sun. I'll stop by tomorrow."

The demanding farmer wasn't finished. "Reading your letter may help grease your way. Who's writin' you from across the pond?"

Mr. Barnes' incessant questions wore Martin out.

"My father's sister sent a letter from Holland," he quipped and turned his back on the nosy farmer. He began the long walk home.

"Tomorrow then!" Mr. Barnes called.

His heart heavy, Martin jammed the letter in his pocket. Misery dogged his strides. Whatever Aunt Deane had to say, he'd read away from prying eyes. The farther he walked, the more he lingered on his father's fatal tractor accident that took his life. Shock had rattled Martin to the core. But even worse, a few days later, his mother's heart gave out. She'd taken to her bed, and never got up again.

That makes me an orphan, Martin thought, kicking up dust with his shoes. He choked back a sob. Reverend Hartema wanted him to move in with him and his wife. After conducting the joint funeral, they invited Martin over for supper most evenings. He owed them a lot. Eating one solid meal a day kept him alive. The Hartemas had no children, so it would be like being with family.

But Mr. Barnes called himself Father's closest friend. Leasing him the farm would allow Martin to stay in his childhood home. He'd reached the rusty gate already. Paint peeled off the side of the house. Weeds grew along the walk. His spirits sank.

"I can't farm," he muttered. "I barely have enough money for food."

Truth was he had no seed corn or dairy cows. He'd sold everything, even his beloved horse, to pay the property taxes. Though he liked running errands and writing short articles for *The Zeeland Record*, his future here looked bleak.

Worry overwhelmed him. He slipped through the squeaky gate and went into the house where his father's overalls hanging on the back peg brought bitter tears. A hard thought pierced his lonely heart. Mr. Barnes cared nothing for him. He wanted to marry Martin off to Helen and get the land.

He yanked open the icebox, chipping away at the ice using the pick like a weapon. When his pain finally eased, he filled his glass with ice and strode to the pump. Though he worked it furiously, no water came out. Was it broken?

The house was falling apart before his eyes. Grief squeezed his lungs until he couldn't breathe. He scurried outside for air, only to stumble on gnarled roots of the giant oak tree. He fell on soft grass. A bluebird landed on a hanging branch above him. The way the tiny bird gazed at him quizzically made Martin think his mother was checking on him.

He picked himself up and brushed at the grass stain on his knee. A storm raged within him. Just then he glimpsed something yellow on the ground. It was Deane's letter. Wind stirred the thin envelope as if saying, "Open me. I won't be forgotten." He lunged for it and slid his thumb under the envelope.

Before he could read it, a shrill voice called, "Martin, are you hiding by the tree? Mama wants to know if you're eating supper with us."

He snapped up his head. Helen Barnes stood by her bicycle, a welcoming smile plastered on her freckled face. Martin's lips parted. Though she was the cutest girl in school, she delighted in showing off her smarts, raising her hand for every question, and besting him every time.

And what of her dad's hints of marriage? Martin was ready to wave her off. Then his stomach growled, changing his mind. The Hartemas were gone for the day and Helen's mother was a wonderful cook.

"Okay, Helen. I'll walk over at six. I have things to do first."

"Do you want to talk about your letter? Is it from your aunt in the Netherlands?"

"Never mind," he shot back.

She hopped on her bike. "Mama's fixing fried chicken. Bring your appetite, but leave your grumpy attitude at home."

Helen rode off, her pigtails flying behind her. To avoid another delay, Martin ripped open the envelope. He walked slowly into the house and read his letter.

Dear Martin,

    In these sad days, remember our Heavenly Father knows your needs before you speak them to Him. I long to see you! Come and sail to Rotterdam. My neighbor Simon Visser will pick you up in his fishing boat and bring you to Middleburg. Stay here as long as you like. I will finish telling you stories of our family heritage. Yesterday a man came to see me and I would like your opinion on dealing with the situation. Your father taught you well and you are the head of your family. Telegram your arrival date.

All my love, Aunt Deane.

Leave his home and sail to the Netherlands?

Impossible!

He had no money to cross the Atlantic. He'd sold one of his paintings of Lake Michigan, which earned a few dollars for bread and milk. Martin strode to the desk by the window. He let out a ragged breath. Here, Mother had taught him how to paint. His finger touched tubes of oil paints and tiny brushes arranged in neat rows.

Somewhere in his stubborn boy's heart, he felt wanted by his family thread overseas. When his tall Dutch aunt visited from the Netherlands three years ago, Martin could barely keep up with her when they'd ridden bikes. Her strong legs pumped up the hill leading to the lakeshore as if it was nothing. Along the shores of Lake Michigan, she'd spun fascinating stories of their Dutch ancestors who had been persecuted for their Christian faith. Deane mentioned rare jewels and an ancient silver chalice. But then one day she'd announced, "I return home. My friend is ill. God will provide another time for me to finish my stories."

His mind back in the present, Martin set down his brush. A longing to know more about his brave ancestors filled him. Maybe he could even paint in the Netherlands, where the famous painter Rembrandt had been born.

The future beckoned. There by his mother's desk, Martin made a life-changing decision. He locked the front door behind him, confidence rising in his chest.

Let Mr. Barnes lease the farm. Martin had other plans.

He'd sail the Atlantic Ocean and visit the land where his parents were born. He'd travel beyond Michigan and discover his family's legacy. The letter tucked safely in his back pocket, Martin ran to his bike, ready to begin life anew.

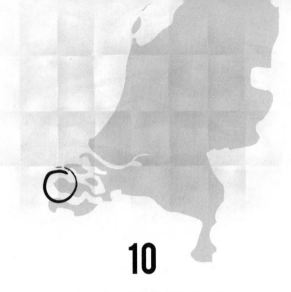

10

MAY 9, 1940 – THE NETHERLANDS

Martin arrived in Middleburg less than two months later. Standing on Simon's small craft that brought him here from Rotterdam, he enjoyed the relief from the ever-moving sea.

"Hot diggity. I'm here!"

Martin swiveled his head, admiring neat brick buildings lining the waterway. Though his legs felt wobbly, he graciously tipped his cap to the muscular fisherman.

"Simon, on the Atlantic the ship ran into gigantic swells. I thought I was a goner."

"Many a good man lost his life on that sea," Simon said in passable English. "Tell your *tante* I come later to her party. First I clean my boat."

A broad smile etched Martin's face. "I know nothing about a party, but I'll tell Aunt Deane. Thanks for getting me here safely."

"*Ja.*"

A man of few words, Simon handed up Martin's bag as he stepped onto the canal wall. Martin stowed his paint box under his arm. The fabric bag he slung over his shoulder. He'd left America's shores a scared seventeen-year-old, and was disembarking in Middleburg a man. Having crossed the wide ocean during a powerful storm, he'd never once become sick. Rather, he ate with sailors and sketched faces of New Yorkers bound for European travels.

What flat land this was, yet so vibrant green and colorful. Tempted to stop and paint every flower and Dutch citizen he saw, he thought of Helen Barnes. She begged him to write and send sketches of his new homeland. Her tears at his bon voyage dinner sizzled through his mind. Had he done right in leaving the farm?

Several women cycled past on their bikes, jolting Martin to reality. Deane was waiting for him. Why dwell on the sorrowful past? New adventures called. He was ready for whatever God brought his way. Martin struck out along the canal watching low-slung boats pass by, their captains hauling in ropes. A voice shouting startled him.

"Stop, young man. You are new to our town."

Martin whirled around. "Yes?"

He faced a stout man in blue uniform. The policeman's high hat and gleaming black boots gave him a foreboding look. Surely Martin hadn't gotten into trouble already. On the voyage from Rotterdam, Simon mentioned a skirmish between Germany and Russia over Poland, but that didn't involve the Netherlands.

"What do you do here?" the officer's tone rang with authority.

Martin formed his reply carefully, wary of his Dutch words. "Sir, I am in Middleburg to visit my *tante*."

"What is her name?"

Martin swallowed, glancing about the square. Wasn't that her address across the street? He was about to point at her door when a man in wooden shoes and local dress stalked up, complaining his bicycle was stolen. This distracted the policeman long enough for Martin to shoot across the street.

He scrambled to Deane's door, where uncertainty assailed him. Did she live along the waterway? Father always said she lived near the magnificent town hall. Martin pulled Deane's telegram from his back pocket. Sure enough, this should be her home. He knocked on the door until a well-dressed woman peered out. But Martin didn't recognize her.

He cleared his throat. "My *Tante* Deane is expecting me."

His German was satisfactory, but her German mutterings in reply puzzled him. She let him in a blue and white tiled foyer. He sat on a cushioned bench, cradling his paints in his arms. Loud voices spilled from another room. He listened, but could make nothing of the ruckus.

Maybe this was the wrong house. If Deane didn't appear soon, he would leave. Meanwhile, he relished a rest with his eyes closed.

In a flash, cold fingers stroked his cheeks. Martin's eyes flew open. A tall woman with snapping blue eyes bent over and gazed at him.

"Aunt Deane!"

She folded her arms around him and kissed his cheek.

"Martin, at last." Her English was laced with a soft Dutch accent.

He got to his feet. "Sorry, but my ship arrived a day late because of a storm."

"Simon sent me word. You and I have much to discuss."

"Oh, he'll come later to your party, whatever that means."

"We expected you yesterday and were prepared to celebrate today without you." Deane smiled. "You made it in time. Come and meet my friends."

In a cozy parlor, Deane introduced him to Mr. Rosenbaum and his wife, who had answered the door. She stared with dark, sullen eyes. Neither she nor her husband spoke much English. Their teenage son sat in the corner, thumbing through a book.

Deane's comment about "having much to discuss" piqued Martin's curiosity. But he held his tongue, shaking everyone's hand, saying in his best Dutch, "*Goedemiddag.*" The adults chatted of Queen Wilhelmina, which didn't interest Martin.

So he walked over to Eli Rosenbaum. The boy held up a book. It appeared to be in German prompting Martin to ask, "Am I right, you are from Germany?"

"Munich," Eli said, keeping his nose in the book.

Martin tried to engage him. "Have you ever been to America?"

"No." Eli snapped the book closed. "But I want to. My Papaw lives there, you know."

Martin did not know, but the boy's command of English pleased him. He told Eli so.

"How long are you staying with your aunt?"

"I'm not sure," Martin answered. "My parents both died recently. I'm making a new start. When did you come here from Germany?"

Eli's lean face clouded. "After Papaw moved to America."

"Where does he live?"

Before Martin found out, another of Deane's friends approached. Deep lines crinkled around the older man's thick moustache. He gazed at Martin with merry eyes.

"I am Willem de Mulder. Deane and I are long-time friends. You have her bright blue eyes and strong jaw." He pulled a gold chain dangling from his vest pocket and removed a round gold watch. "Your grandfather made this. Look at the tiny lettering on the back."

Martin pulled one from his pocket. "This was my father's. It too was made by my grandfather."

Deane hurried over, her brows creased for some reason.

"You have met Willem. He is the miller who operates the windmill not far from here."

Mr. de Mulder's eyes sparkled. "My son serves in our Army or else he would welcome you."

"When can I tour Middleburg?" Martin asked Deane. "I'd like to ride your bike over the bridge and see the ancient town hall. It's from the Middle Ages, right?"

"You will visit many places, even my jewelry store. First, you rest."

"But I'm interested in seeing things and painting pictures. Besides, I'm not tired."

A loud clatter outside the window brought Deane racing to the window. She drew aside a lace curtain. A man with a grotesque face peered in.

"Constable Kuipers is calling a council meeting at town hall," he said.

She dropped the curtain with a cluck of her tongue. She pulled Martin aside. "Beware of Constable Kuipers. He seeks to grab power around town."

"I will do as you say. Can I go with you to the hall?"

She motioned at her friends. "You see we have much food in your honor."

Eli spoke to his parents in German. He walked over to Martin with a shy smile.

"My parents will permit me to show you the town."

Deane smoothed her blouse sleeve. "All right. You boys enjoy the sights. Kuipers has called a meeting and I will go. Meet back here for supper at six."

AFTER EXPLORING MIDDLEBURG, Martin sat cross-legged on the grass near the windmill, sketching its enormous sails. Eli waited patiently for him to finish.

"The paint I add later," Martin explained as he finished the drawing.

Eli pointed west. "My home is that way. I can show you a nest of swans by the canal."

"Okay. I'll have more subjects to paint."

Martin folded his paper. Then he and Eli sprinted across the flat land with Eli showing him their furniture shop.

"We live in the apartment upstairs."

"You should be safe here for life, Eli. I don't want to leave Middleburg either."

The two boys kidded as they strolled to the water's edge. To Martin, laughing hadn't come as easily of late. Many boats bobbed along the canal and they became engrossed in watching men repair fishing nets.

"You and I are the same, Eli," Martin said.

"I think not." Eli tossed his head. "You are much older than thirteen."

"Yes!" Martin laughed. "I'm almost eighteen. I don't mean our ages."

Eli looked at Martin with questioning eyes. "Are you also Jewish?"

"No, I'm a Christian. I was thinking that you left your home and so did I."

"But we can never return to Germany."

"Why not?"

Martin wondered what kept them from their homeland. Eli nodded at a fisherman with a white chin beard and brown cap tilted low over his eyes.

"Do you recognize Simon? He supplies us with fish and comes to our home for Shabbat. So does Deane. They too are Christians."

Martin waved at Simon, telling Eli, "He brought me here from Rotterdam. But what is Shabbat? Some kind of game?"

Eli folded his cap between his hands and looked across the water.

"In my faith tradition, we take a day of rest to remember what God has done. When we lived in Germany, we stopped having Shabbat. My mother was too afraid. We were forbidden from going to synagogue. Here, we can observe our Friday evening service and meal. Will you and Deane join us tomorrow?"

"I'd like to. But I'll ask if she has anything planned."

"My stomach urges me back to your party. I have eaten nothing since breakfast."

Martin clapped him on the back. "Me either. Eli, I wonder if your Shabbat is like our Sunday. We attend church, eat a nice meal, and rest before going to evening service at church."

"I suppose so. I have only ever been in a synagogue."

"Well, I've never been in one of those."

As they walked toward Deane's house, Martin noticed children skipping and carrying schoolbooks. "Eli, why aren't you in school?"

Eli donned his cap. "Why? I stayed home to welcome you. We owe Deane so much. She found our Middleburg apartment after we fled Germany."

"You and I have something else in common. She found me a home too."

"My family and I honor you too, Martin," Eli replied in all seriousness.

"Then make it snappy, my friend. I could eat a horse."

They started to run, and Martin smiled inwardly. His caring aunt had given the Rosenbaums and Martin a new start. He couldn't wait to hear her captivating stories. Maybe tonight after dinner she'd entertain them all.

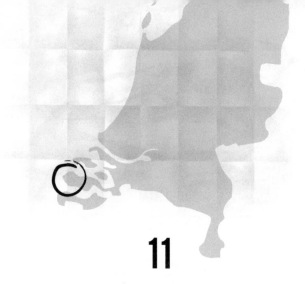

11

MAY 10, 1940 – THE NETHERLANDS

Martin's celebration lasted well beyond eleven o'clock. He fell exhausted into bed. A prayer of thanks to God on his lips, he remembered nothing else until low humming sounds ruined his sleep. Loud banging startled him awake. He sat up to listen.

"*Gevaar! Gevaar!*"

His mind tumbled. Was he still sailing on *The Voyager*? Were they in danger of hitting the rocks? A door creaked open. Shrill voices talking excitedly in Dutch cleared his mind. He was at Deane's home in Middleburg. Seconds later, she burst into his room.

"Martin, get dressed. Simon just came. Something terrible is happening."

Anxiety pulsed through him. "Did someone die?"

"Hurry downstairs. I will tell you."

He threw back the covers. Surprised to see he was already in his clothes, Martin jumped from bed. When he reached the first floor, he expected to see people belonging to the earsplitting voices he'd just heard. But Deane was alone in the parlor.

"Where's Simon?" Martin rubbed sleep from his eyes.

"Warning others."

Deane turned on the radio. Martin leaned closer, trying to sort out the trouble.

"Germany bombs our airfield!" Deane's eyes sparked with fire. "They invade the Netherlands!"

Martin flinched. His pulse thudded in his ears. Would he have to fight? Rapid pounding on the front door magnified his fear. He darted to open it, but pulled back.

Deane glanced out the side window. "All right, Martin. Go ahead."

He threw open the door, letting in Mr. de Mulder and the Rosenbaums. Eli latched onto Martin's arm, shaking it so hard he thought his arm would twist off.

"Eli, slow down." Martin stepped backwards. "The airfield is bombed. What about in Middleburg?"

The boy doubled his fists. "Hitler wants to kill us off!"

Willem de Mulder's knees gave way. He sunk to the floor. Martin hurried to help him into a chair.

"My son fights," de Mulder said, his voice quavering. "Our prime minister was wrong. He said Germany would leave us alone like in the First World War."

All color drained from Mr. Rosenbaum's face. The slight Jewish man flashed a panicky look. He whispered in his wife's ear, and she shrieked. Her husband put an arm around her and she buried her face into his shoulder. Martin struggled to grasp the awful truth.

"If the Dutch go to war, America will help," he offered.

Deane shook her head. "This is not America's war. The British and French fight against Germany."

"*Ja.*" de Mulder rose to his feet. "With any luck, they will send troops."

"Luck has nothing … listen!" Deane commanded. "The announcer says our brave soldiers are resisting."

This quieted their tongues. She and the others huddled around the set. Martin waited breathlessly for news that America would save them. But the announcer leveled a crippling blow.

Martin's hands flew to his face. "Your warplanes are being smashed!"

"I knew it," Eli sobbed. "We will die, just like my family in Germany."

Panic thundered through Martin's veins. He froze in place. War was nearly on his doorstep. He should have stayed in Michigan. Why did God allow dreadful things to happen to him?

Deane whirled on him as if knowing his cowardly thoughts. She gripped his shoulders.

"Martin, we must fight and we will!"

Defiance radiating from her shining eyes drove out his doubt. He broke free from her viselike grip. "I can shoot a gun. Father took me hunting for deer and pheasant."

Willem de Mulder strode over. Towering over Martin, he jabbed a finger at his eyes.

"Killing a man is far worse than shooting food for your table."

"But I will, if I have to." Martin hoped his courage would match his bravado.

"I came to tell you the grave news and met Rosenbaum on the way." de Mulder snatched the doorknob. "We should gather weapons and supplies."

"We will do what is necessary." Deane lifted her shoulders. "First we should pray for God's protection."

After glaring at her for a moment, de Mulder said gruffly, "Leave religion out of it. Our Army is strong and will beat the rascals."

He clomped out in his wooden shoes and slammed the door. Deane turned her attention to Mrs. Rosenbaum who wept softly. Eli flitted about the room. Martin encouraged him to stop and talk.

"The Dutch are fighting," he said.

The teenager could only wring his hands. "It is too late."

Martin steadied himself. Hadn't Father and Mother trained him not to give way to fear? Though he urged Eli to sit on the sofa, his friend remained standing and fidgeting.

"Most Germans hate us Jews. Have you ever read Hitler's book?"

"No. My father refused to allow *Mein Kampf* in the house."

"Each page details his evil mind." Eli's widening eyes revealed his escalating fright. "Papaw escaped to New York three years ago. My papa refused to leave the bank or our home in Munich. He believed we would be safe."

"I am glad you finally left," Martin said with feeling. "Is any family still in Germany?"

"No. They seized our home and money."

Home! Martin's heart banged in his chest like their old radiator did. Qualms over being in a war zone battered his tired brain. Then he remembered what his father once said.

"Eli, my father told me Germany used mustard gas in the Great War. He said, 'Son, I pray every day you will never fight in war. May God protect your life.'"

The younger boy shook his fists. "After Germany lost, they blamed us Jews for stealing their money. They will not stop until they control everyone."

"My father fought in that first war and survived. We will too, Eli."

Martin vowed to have his father's courage in standing up to the Germans.

"Wait!" Deane held up her hand by the radio. "The French are sending paratroopers."

Mr. Rosenbaum clamped a hand on Eli's shoulder. "Son, we go home."

"I hope to see you again." Eli tilted his chin. "We may not have Shabbat this evening."

Martin whispered back, "I will pray for you and your parents."

Eli's eyes misted. He hustled out the rear door behind his mother, his papa's hand resting on his shoulder. Deane wasted no time wagging a finger at Martin.

"Follow me."

He stood his ground. "Where are your guns?"

"This is no time for questions. You are needed."

He moistened his dry lips, but asked nothing more. She propelled him with a heavy hand to her jewelry shop next door. They entered the store, the boards groaning beneath their feet. Martin looked around at beautiful displays.

A sterling silver tray sat atop a glass sales counter. On the tray sat a coffee server, creamer bowl, and sugar container, also made of silver. Behind glass doors on glass shelves, gold and silver pocket watches were laid in neat rows. Gold watch chains of various lengths hung on a velvet board. Some were adorned with gold knives, their blades folded closed.

Deane hurried to a large, dark green safe, which was taller than Martin and had double doors. She turned the combination dial on the front, but stopped.

"Look here."

She carefully removed a high, rectangular painting that hung on the wall next to the safe. Then Deane turned the frame around and pointed to the upper section.

"Martin, look closely. This number seventeen is the first number of my safe combination. You need to know if something happens to me."

"Please don't say such things. I need you alive …" His voice broke.

Her eyes searched his with a burning intensity. She patted his hand. "I must tell you. You are my only remaining family member. No one else knows the numbers to open the safe."

"Okay, I'll listen. But I refuse to believe anything will happen to you."

"Watch carefully."

She whirled the dial several times around to the left. After stopping at seventeen, she pointed to the picture frame's right side. "See this number six?"

He nodded and she continued her instructions.

"It is the second number. Turn the dial right, one time around. Pass the six, stopping at it the second time around." Deane's finger rested near a third number penciled on the frame's bottom section. "Then turn back to the left and stop at this number."

Martin watched what she did when she stopped at the third number. Deane pulled hard on the handle and opened the safe. Quickly she replaced the windmill painting on the wall.

"Martin, I know these numbers by heart. You should too."

She swung open the double doors. Inside the safe on its many shelves were more watches and engraved silver items. Her voice fell to a mere whisper.

"Never tell anyone what I am about to show you. This is part of our family's legacy from four hundred years ago."

Her hands trembled as she opened a drawer and took out a metal case with a separate lock. She inserted a small key and removed a velvet bag. Deane drew open the top.

"Look inside," she ordered.

Martin squinted. He could hardly believe his eyes.

"Those are diamonds and rubies, right?"

"*Ja.* This valuable necklace we must protect at all costs."

"Where did such beautiful jewelry come from?"

Deane closed the bag. "I will tell you later of its heritage. Now, we finish our work."

She locked the metal case, pinned the key under her sweater, and rushed to the counter. After sliding open the interior door, she snatched up watches and chains, asking Martin to help hide them. He picked up the silver coffee tray and service. Deane secured more watches and silver pieces in the safe before locking the door and spinning the dial.

"I imagine German soldiers will steal anything small and valuable as souvenirs of their conquests," she explained, speeding back to the empty counter.

Here, she arranged costume jewelry. She stepped behind a railing and turned on a globe lantern dangling over the jeweler's bench above her high stool. Martin imagined her working in this tight corner. The dozens of wooden boxes filled with watch and clock parts amazed him.

Deane slid these boxes into drawer openings below the bench. "No need to display valuable items to tempt the wicked."

She scattered a few cheap watches and pens in the display case, then she faced Martin, her eyes determined.

"In the back storage room are several cuckoo clocks that need mending. Bring them here and set them on this case."

Martin completed his task. With every breath, he grew more concerned for their safety. After displaying the broken clocks, Deane locked the glass case with another key, which she also pinned inside her sweater. Their silent journey back to her home next door was interrupted by angry shouts from the street.

Once he reached the house and locked the doors, Martin's anxiety spilled over.

"What will the Germans do to us? Will I have to fight in the Dutch Army? Eli is terrified. His family left Germany and doesn't feel safe here."

"Martin, God sees us in our hour of need. We must be strong and courageous."

"If the Germans fight …" He lost his train of thought. Fear immobilized him.

Deane took his shaking hands into her strong ones.

"Your papa fought for America in 'the war to end all wars.' He survived the muddy trenches of France. I stayed here, at home with my mother. Then my brother, your papa, married your mother. Now you are with me. I will watch over you, but we must make a plan."

Bang! Bang!

Harsh knocks rattled the back door. Deane became still as a statue. Dark thunderclouds passed through her blue eyes, and Martin vowed in his boy heart to take care of her. He pushed out his chest ready to defend their home.

"Should I see who's there?" he hissed.

"We need to develop a code with our friends. Let me check behind the curtain."

She pulled aside the lace and then dropped it, her face twisted.

"It is Kuipers, the constable I warned you about. His wife is German. I do not trust either of them."

Deane opened the door a mere inch, but Kuipers thrust in his foot. His bulky body wasn't far behind. Martin shrank to the far wall. This was the same policeman who stopped him yesterday when he first arrived in town.

Kuipers lunged at Deane. "Is your boat out front on the canal?"

"The last I saw, yes." Deane folded her arms. "Why do you ask?"

"I am taking it for the men."

Deane clucked her tongue. "My tiny rowboat is not of much use. What men need it?"

"The Dutch Army," Kuipers snapped. "The Germans are fast approaching."

The gruff policeman cast a dark eye at Martin. "I have seen you before."

"Never mind him," Deane replied with authority.

"Hmmph. My wife is organizing food. You must see her at once."

"I will do all I can to help our fighting men."

Kuipers spun on his thick heels and left. Deane pressed a finger to her lips.

Martin waited some moments before confiding, "He accosted me yesterday in the square. I never admitted I am your nephew."

Deane turned the lock with a swift click. "You will learn who to trust. It is best if Kuipers forgets you are here. For now anyway."

"Why? Am I trouble for you? I could sail home, but I have already rented out the farm."

"No, no. You stay with me. Every port is being watched. Danger is everywhere. I do not want anyone thinking you will fight."

Martin swallowed. His throat felt raw. He was hungry and thirsty, but such things didn't matter. Middleburg wasn't safe from the Germans. He and Deane might have to flee any second. Sounds of airplanes flying over their heads made him jump.

"The Germans are going to drop bombs on our heads!" he cried, covering his head.

Deane tapped his back. He dropped his arms and she motioned him to the window. She pointed up at the sky. "Those are our airplanes."

Martin didn't know what to think or do. He'd just arrived yesterday and his mind was jumbled. Finally an idea took shape.

"Aunt Deane, I will defend and protect you. I am not afraid to take up arms."

She nodded briskly and turned on the radio. In an agitated tone, the announcer said, "The Germans are strafing Dutch positions in Zeeland. Our men face danger on all sides."

Martin shuddered. It was one thing to shoot pheasant and deer for the dinner table. Could he kill a man?

Deane punctured his thoughts with a request. "Martin, go invite the Rosenbaums for Friday night supper. We will eat their Shabbat meal here. All together we will pray to God for help in this crisis."

Martin hesitated for a second. At the daring look in Deane's eyes, he tossed on his cap and slipped from the house. He stopped and listened. Guns firing in the distance pummeled his ears. Were the Germans that close? If he kept to the buildings he should be okay. He retraced his steps from yesterday to Eli's, being careful to avoid Kuipers at all costs.

THOUGH AFRAID, THE ROSENBAUMS CAME to Deane's for Shabbat. Awestruck, Martin watched Mrs. Rosenbaum light two candles. She spoke in melodic Hebrew over the flames. Yellow shadows glimmered against the drawn drapes. This was nothing like church back home. Deane, who sat erect next to Mrs. Rosenbaum, was a portrait of strength. On Marty's right, Eli acted less antsy than he had earlier. And being united in Deane's dining room seemed to cast out Martin's terrors of the night.

Germany was invading, but here they sat, ready to enjoy a meal. Mr. Rosenbaum rose, walked around the table, and stood behind his son. He placed both hands on Eli's head. He said something in Hebrew before reclaiming his seat around the dining room table.

Martin whispered to his friend, "What did your papa say to you?"

"He gave the traditional blessing, 'May I be like the sons of Joseph, Ephraim, and Manasseh.'"

Before Martin could ask him to explain, Deane folded her hands in front of her.

"Thank you for blessing your family. Now, I would like to ask Jehovah, who sees us here in this situation, for His mighty help."

She closed her eyes. So did Martin. He joined her in his heart as she prayed aloud, "The God of Abraham and Jacob is here in our midst. We are thankful for His provisions and safekeeping. He provided for His people through the sufferings of Joseph in Egypt, and has sustained Jesus and the descendants of His disciples ever since. May God protect and guide us. Amen."

Deane opened her eyes, lifting a cover off a soup tureen and a napkin from the bread. "This may not be your traditional Shabbat dinner, but Martin and I did our best. He cut stew vegetables and bought challah bread from Wisenheimer's bakery. And we have pickled herring with onion."

"Eli, soldiers are fighting miles from here." Martin leaned on his elbow. "Soon, the Dutch will beat those Germans to smithereens."

The boy's eyes bulged. "I was so scared, I ran all the way here, Martin."

"Deane's faith is strong, like Joseph's." Martin passed Eli the breadbasket. "I want to be brave like he was when his brothers sold him into slavery."

"The rabbi teaches of Joseph. Jacob favored him, which made his brothers jealous. After Joseph was imprisoned, he became a great leader. Years later, he saved his father and brothers during a famine."

While Eli dipped his bread into a dish of salt, Martin mulled over Eli's description.

"I think the Jews are like Joseph," Martin said. "You were favored by God and then enslaved and persecuted."

"If only Jehovah would save us from the powerful Nazis."

Martin gazed at his friend, strength building in his heart. "I pray God will rescue our families from their evil grip, just as He did for Joseph. The Israelites even took Joseph's bones to the Promised Land when they left Egypt."

"Maybe one day we will go there."

"I want to, after the war." Martin picked up his bread. "Why do you dip bread in salt?"

"Salt never spoils. It is a symbol of our eternal covenant with God."

"So bread has an important role in your Jewish faith too."

Eli nodded. "Jehovah sent manna, morning and night, when my ancestors fled into the wilderness."

Martin thrust his slice into the coarse salt and enjoyed the intense saltiness. As the adults talked among themselves, he savored this meal around the table. Such a time may not come again with Germans a breath away. Was this the right time to share what else was on his heart?

He set down his spoon. "God used Moses to spare your people from Pharaoh. Then He sent Jesus to save us all. Jesus Messiah said He is the bread of life."

Eli looked at his mother who served more soup to Deane. He said in a hush, "I am not sure Jesus is the Messiah. Perhaps you and I can talk about it later."

"I can show you the Bible verses where Jesus said He was the Son of God."

"Sometime I would like you to show me." Eli hunched his shoulders. "This is Germany all over again. There, we celebrated Shabbat with the drapes shut. Now our tormenters pursue us to the Netherlands."

Martin touched Eli's forearm. "You're safe in our home."

"We are not safe anywhere. My parents listen to British reports on our crystal radio."

"All I know is what I heard on the ship. Men were upset by Germany invading Poland. Deane says Hitler wants to control Dutch seaports."

Eli toyed with his spoon. "In Munich, they killed everyone in my family, except for us and Papaw in New York."

Sorrow pierced Martin. He no longer felt like eating. Most of Eli's family was gone. Martin's parents were too, but they hadn't been murdered. Could he ever understand such hatred? He glanced at Eli whose cheeks blazed red. He looked afraid.

Martin wanted to help. What could he do? He chewed his bread in silence, the coarse salt burning his tongue. With Germany battling for the Netherlands, what would tomorrow bring?

12

Early the next morning, Martin turned down the lamp, extinguishing the flame. He and Deane had stayed up all night praying, talking, and singing hymns. A raucous noise in the alley brought them both to the curtain.

"I don't see anything," Martin said, straining his eyes.

Deane peered out. "It is nothing. Some cats are living near the shed. Let us hope our soldiers fighting on our eastern border have swift victory."

Her voice sounded strong despite her lack of sleep.

"Should we eat before I leave to check on our Jewish friends?" he asked.

"I will slice bread and cheese. I have a clock to repair by noon."

They ate quickly. Deane slipped on her wooden shoes. He stayed by the door, unsure what surprises lurked outside.

"Shall I go with you to the shop?" he asked.

A knock on the back door startled them both. Martin lifted the curtain. Eli stood there, twisting his cap. Martin opened the door, and Eli burst in, his arms waving.

"French soldiers are falling from the sky! Come see!"

Martin swiped his cap off the back peg, but Deane grabbed his arm. "Stay clear of the fighting and report back to me."

He banged the door closed. Hastening along the canal with Eli, he stared at the sky, disappointed to see nothing but white puffy clouds.

"Where are the parachutes?"

"Over this way," Eli said. "I have been scouting since the sun came up."

Even on his shorter legs, Eli surpassed Martin going around the corner heading for the northern edge of town. Several soldiers blazed past with their big guns. They must have already dropped from planes.

Martin gazed skyward. "Look! Soldiers are falling like manna from heaven."

He watched them land and gathered their collapsing chutes into a ball. The soldiers stuffed them beneath fallen tree limbs or rocks before scurrying away to join their units.

"Those soldiers look ready to beat the Germans." Martin approved of their rapid movements.

"They head for Bergen Op Zoom."

"Where?" Martin still didn't know his Dutch geography.

Eli pointed east. "To our border with Germany. de Mulder's son fights there."

Martin's mind convulsed at the thought of having to shoot a man. But he should prepare himself. The war was creeping closer every day. Airplanes roared low overhead. Martin looked up again.

"They're not Dutch!"

He dove to the ground, pulling Eli down with him. The planes flew past without shooting.

Martin nudged Eli. "They must've been French planes."

"I banged my knee," the younger boy complained.

Martin reached out to lift him up. "What are your parents doing this morning?"

"I forgot. Papa wants me to help him find cans of fuel for his truck."

Martin offered to go along, and they headed for Eli's apartment, sticking to the back alleyways.

On the way, Martin said, "I can hardly imagine what it's like to live under Hitler."

"They ruined our lives, Martin." Eli slowed his steps. "I could not attend school. One night, police smashed windows in every Jewish shop. Soldiers hauled my older brothers to a concentration camp, where they died. My uncle and cousin were shot in the street. We broke free of the Germans, forever, I thought."

Martin kicked a stone. When he'd been Eli's age, he had no concerns of being killed. Even when he helped his father plant corn in ninety-degree heat, he cooled off by swimming in Lake Michigan. Shame enveloped him.

"How terrible for you, Eli."

"My mother still has nightmares of Kristallnacht." Eli raised his fist. "Our synagogue was burned to the ground. Police rounded up our men. Because Papa knew Deane, she found us the apartment to live in. Papa opened his furniture store."

"How does my aunt know your papa? She never told me."

Eli cracked a slight smile. "Your grandfather and my grandfather were friends."

"I never knew my grandfather Vander Goes."

The teen shrugged and Martin nudged him forward. They rounded a corner. Out of nowhere, a strong hand grabbed Martin's shoulder. He beat the hand with his fists, thinking it was Kuipers. The man's fingers sunk into his flesh.

"Where do you boys live? Will you take me there?"

Martin strained against the stranger's hand, struggling to get away. He trusted no one.

"Why should I tell you?" he hissed.

"Your life and mine may depend on it," came the man's swift reply.

"You don't sound Dutch or French. Who are you?"

"I might ask you the same. Your Dutch accent sounds American."

Martin caught a glimpse of Eli walking backward, *away* from his apartment.

The tall stranger pulled out a roll of Dutch guilders. "I need your help to find Deane Vander Goes."

"Why?" Martin eyed a heavily armed French paratrooper storming by without giving aid.

"I heard you talking. The Germans will invade this island in days, if not hours. You are not safe here and neither am I."

Martin considered the slender man dressed in tweed trousers and olive green trench coat. "You're no Dutchman. Who are you and where are you from?"

"Am I right, you are from across the pond?"

Shots rang in the distance. The man seized Martin's forearm.

"Take me to Deane's home. I will pay you handsomely for it."

Eli slipped away, perhaps to warn Deane. Martin debated what to do. This was no sleepy Michigan town where he had no enemies. In war, peculiar things happened. He'd better learn fast or his life would be over.

"It's not far," he said, motioning with his hand.

They set out, going along the tree line, which should give Eli time to tell Deane. Waves of doubt battered Martin's mind. He asked God to help, just as Joseph did in the Old Testament. He trod on, praying silently. *Heavenly*

Father, if this man means trouble, please prevent him from hurting me. This is war and I am in the thick of it. Protect Eli and Deane. Show me what I should do.

When they reached Deane's row house, Martin took the man around to the rear door.

"Wait here," he ordered.

He hurried to the kitchen, nearly colliding with Deane as she rushed in.

"A man offered me money!" he said. "He wants you. I think he's British."

She put a finger to her lips. "Eli cautioned me about the man in the square. Where is he?"

"By the rear door."

Deane pursed her lips as if deep in thought. Then she went to the back entryway.

The man held out his hand. "Friends told me to see Deane Vander Goes."

Martin's eyes shifted from Deane to the man. What would she do?

She lifted her chin ever so slightly. "To whom am I speaking?"

"Blake Attwood. Is there someplace we can talk alone? Henri Winkelman sent me."

Martin peered closely at Deane, anxious to know if he'd done right in bringing Mr. Attwood here. Her eyes gleamed and relief coursed through him.

"Martin, take Eli out by the front," she said. "Mr. Attwood and I will talk here."

He led Eli out on the canal side, and asked him to return after helping his father.

"We must plan how to survive the siege."

Eli looked nervous, folding his cap. "I told Papa we should flee to England. He is looking into it."

Without another word, Eli stole down the street. Martin locked the front door and crept to the kitchen. The hallway door stood open, so he stepped inside, letting Deane know he was listening. She didn't object to his presence.

"French reconnaissance troops are here," Mr. Attwood was saying. "His Majesty needs me home in England. Henri insists Deane Vander Goes can make a connection for me. You have an old family name?"

"Our Vander Goes family roots run deep here, sir. We have lived in Holland since the fourteenth century. What type of connection do you need?"

Mr. Attwood peeled Dutch guilders from a thick wad. "Will this secure a boat? Germany will rule your country within the week, or even days."

"But we fight." Deane's blue eyes held no fear. "Our soldiers are brave men."

"You will never crush Hitler's forces. He has been building air superiority for years. Your government has not fortified the coastal regions or your eastern border with Germany. I can rendezvous with a British vessel off the coast, but I need help. It is imperative I report to my government what I have seen if we are to give aid."

Deane took his money. "My fisherman friend may help you for nothing. Still, your guilders may prove useful in another way."

She wagged her finger at Martin. Flexing his brows, he followed her into the front hall.

"Who is Henri Winkelman?" he asked. "What if he sent a Nazi in disguise?"

"Do not fear. I have known General Winkelman since he was a colonel. He bought his wife's wedding ring from me. He is high in our government."

"So Mr. Attwood must be trustworthy and we should assist him. What should I do?"

"Take these guilders to Simon. See if he is able to take our British friend in his boat."

"It will be good to see Simon again." Martin put the money in his pocket. As an afterthought, he told his aunt, "Eli is finding fuel for his papa, but he's coming back."

Deane clucked her tongue. "After what this British gentleman told us, I want you to bring the Rosenbaums here after you meet with Simon."

Martin donned his cap, and hustled out. Kuipers came stalking from the corner, his black boots glittering in the sunlight. Martin darted back into the house. He nodded at Deane and Mr. Attwood, who sat around the kitchen table talking.

"I won't be long." Martin promptly left by the back door.

With Kuipers nosing around the neighborhood, Martin avoided going directly to Simon. Instead, he sauntered to the corner and gazed back over his shoulder. Good. Kuipers was nowhere in sight. As Martin poked his head around the corner, he looked straight into a policeman's chest. It was Kuipers.

"Where are you sneaking off to?"

"On an errand, sir. And I must be quick about it."

Martin scurried down an alley, making sure Kuipers wasn't on his trail. Moments later, he opened the heavy door to the stairway next door to Rosenbaum's furniture shop. He dashed up the steps, clearing two at a time.

Eli answered the door, his hair sticking up. "Papa and Mama are gone!" His voice climbed to a fevered pitch. "The Germans took them!"

Martin shut the door behind him. He lowered his voice, hoping to calm his friend.

"The Germans aren't here yet. French soldiers fight with the Dutch. Your parents are getting fuel. Leave them a note to meet you at our house. Then come with me, on my mission."

Eli reluctantly wrote his note. Then they shot down the brick-lined street. Martin peeked around the corner toward the canal. Kuipers was talking to an elderly man on a bicycle. The man raised his arms in protest and Kuipers pulled him off the bike, punching him in the face. The man cowered on the ground, holding up his hands. Kuipers kicked him in the stomach.

"It is Councilman Roosevelt!" Eli hissed.

Martin lurched forward to intervene when Kuipers pulled out his gun and fired. The man crumpled to the ground.

"Aghh!" Eli cried, pushing his hands on his ears.

"Sshh!" Martin hissed.

He pulled Eli's arm and dragged him to a doorway. "Stay out of sight. Kuipers just killed him. If he saw us, we're dead too."

Eli's eyes widened with fright. His lower lip trembled.

"By killing a Dutch official, Kuipers just picked sides," Martin said. "Scram!"

Eli took off, but Martin glanced once more at Kuipers. He stood staring into the canal. Councilman Roosevelt's body was gone; only his bicycle remained. Martin needed to reach Simon, but he couldn't go there with Kuipers on the rampage. With one swift movement, the constable lifted the bicycle and tossed it into the canal.

Martin's pulse raced as he joined Eli in the alley. They reached Deane's house scared out of their wits. They rushed inside to tell her, but she wasn't there.

"I'll check upstairs. Stay here."

Martin looked in every room on the second floor with no success. He trudged downstairs, uncertain where Deane and Mr. Attwood had gone. Had they too run afoul of the mad Kuipers? Martin should never have left her alone.

He breathed in deeply. "Eli, I will never forget seeing that man, dead on the ground."

"This is life under the Nazis. Fear never goes away."

"Deane and Mr. Attwood aren't here," Martin said, growing concerned.

"She's probably showing off her shop."

"You're right!" Martin pushed Eli out the door. "I still have to find Simon for him."

"Why does he need Simon?"

"To sail to England."

Eli stopped. "Maybe he can take—"

"Get going," Martin interrupted. "Before Kuipers shows up in the alley."

Eli nodded and they ran into Deane's jewelry shop where Mr. Attwood turned up the volume of the radio.

The announcer said, "The news is grim. Prime Minister Chamberlain has resigned."

Deane scowled, looking concerned. "Is that a serious blow?"

"Not in my book." Mr. Attwood clasped his hands behind his back. "It was time for Neville Chamberlain to go. Adolf Hitler runs rings around him."

Martin stepped forward. "Mr. Attwood, I haven't gone to Simon. I just witnessed something terribly wicked."

Deane shut off the radio and Martin spoke fast, telling how Kuipers shot an innocent man. Mr. Attwood's eyes darkened. He strode to the front window, ostensibly gazing at a motorcycle racing by. Then he turned.

"What Martin saw is disturbing. We must avoid your constable at all costs."

Martin tried grasping the situation. "Mr. Attwood, can you still go to England if you don't have a prime minister?"

"I say, my name is Blake. It is even more imperative that I get home. Within the hour His Majesty King George will ensure a strong leader wages this war."

Deane interrupted with a question of her own. "Did Kuipers see you, Martin?"

"I don't think so. Eli and I veered course." Martin gripped his cap. "I don't want Kuipers knowing of Blake or my mission to help."

Deane squared her shoulders. "You did right. Go tell Simon everything."

Martin thrust on his cap. Before he left, Deane asked Eli, "Where are your parents? I told Martin to bring them here."

"Sorry to disappoint you again." Martin felt rattled to the core. "We left them a note to come here. Come on, Eli."

"You never disappoint me, Martin." Deane touched his shoulder. "Be careful."

He nodded and rushed from the shop. Eli stayed close behind him. They both stole to the walkway along the canal. Martin saw a few fishermen, none that he recognized.

"I don't see Kuipers at least."

They scampered to the place where Simon kept his boat. Only, his boat was gone. Martin walked up to a fisherman who stood by Simon's shed.

"Excuse me, do you know where Simon is?"

The man glared with his bloodshot eyes. "Transporting soldiers. Come back tomorrow."

"Okay, what time?"

"How should I know? We are at war. Do not bother me again with your nonsense."

The rugged fisherman fixed an eye on Martin as if daring him to contradict him.

Should he do as the gruff fisherman commanded or wait for Simon?

Armed soldiers, rifles at the ready, marched toward them. Martin yanked Eli behind a fishing shanty. He watched until the soldiers swiftly passed, heading for town. Then he leaned against the shanty.

"Whew. They were Dutch."

Hands trembling, Eli pulled his cap low over his forehead. "I do not feel safe here."

"Let's go back to Deane's house. If your parents aren't there, we'll look for them."

A few minutes later, Martin pushed open Deane's front door. All of her doors should stay locked, so he decided to talk with her about getting a key. Deane beckoned them into the parlor. Blake kept his post by the window. He looked more casual, having removed his trench coat and loosened his tie.

"Will Simon help?" she asked hopefully.

Martin cast a furtive glance toward Blake. "Simon's ferrying soldiers on his boat. A fisherman, who acted very rude, said he'd return tomorrow."

Blake seemed to take news in stride. He picked up his coat and straightened his tie.

"I will seek another way. Thanks for your efforts."

Deane rested a hand on Eli's shoulder. "Your parents are in the kitchen. We will join you after we decide what is to be done."

Eli somberly removed his cap and stepped into the kitchen.

Deane lifted her hands. "The Rosenbaums have a family staying with them from Amsterdam. They are homeless."

"Proceed carefully," Blake cautioned. "In these perilous times, your neighbor may become your enemy."

"I have known my neighbors for more than thirty years," Deane replied with fervor.

"My dear Deane, war pushes many to the brink and begs the question what are we capable of. You will soon find out. I should push off."

"No!" Martin declared. "The moment I wake up, I'll run over and see Simon. Won't you stay and tell us how to fight back?"

Deane stepped forward. "Blake, you are welcome here. We have room to make you comfortable. And Martin is correct. You have certain skills to benefit us."

After glancing over his shoulder toward the kitchen, Blake dropped his coat back to the sofa. "The first rule in war is to ascertain who your friends are. Then stick together like a hand in a glove. Unfortunately, some fellow Brits are spying for Germany, which makes my job to defeat tyranny all the harder."

His speech finished, he sauntered to the window. Deane headed for the kitchen to confer with the Rosenbaums about their friends.

"Be careful," Martin warned her. "Kuipers is on the prowl."

Curious about the mysterious man who traveled through the Netherlands, he joined him at the window. Blake lifted up the lace curtain.

"Hitler considers the Dutch part of his Aryan race. His henchmen may go easy at first. Eventually, they will control everything."

"Will the Dutch go down in flames?"

Blake let the curtain fall. "Hitler will subsume Holland into the Third Reich. The more you resist, the more he will clamp down on your freedoms."

Martin could hardly believe he'd been thrust into war—his father's worst fear. But he would not give in to terror.

"If the Dutch are defeated, can I help you British in the fight?"

"That is worth some thought." Blake ran a hand through his curly hair. "Say nothing to your aunt just yet."

"Agreed. Eli and his family want refuge in England. Can they go with you?"

"That is not possible," Blake replied. "There may be another way. When Germany seizes control, any Jew living in Holland is at risk."

"My pastor in America taught the Jews are God's people. We must care for them."

"I cannot understand Hitler's maniacal hatred of Jews."

The Brit dropped his eyes to fuss with something in his pocket. Martin couldn't tell what he was doing until he handed Martin more guilders.

"What's this for? You already gave me enough for Simon's boat."

"My dear chap," Blake said, dismissing Martin's objection with a wave. "Holland has more than a thousand printing presses. If you stay in this country, you will be useful to the British cause by developing an underground newspaper."

"How did you know I wrote for a newspaper in the States?"

"A lucky guess. You are a smart lad." A sly smile etched across Blake's face. "Trustworthy contacts are vital. Let me advise you how to build a network."

Martin listened to Blake's ideas, feeling foolish thinking of past articles he'd penned about crops and the local fair. As they talked, admiration grew for the stranger he'd met hours ago. He saw a glimmer of hope for the first time since Germany's attack. He might be useful in this dreadful conflict after all.

13

Martin worked hard and slept little the next few nights. He lay on the bed fully dressed in case he had to flee on a second's notice. Adrenaline pulsed through him. He folded his arms under his head and stared at the ceiling. The evil conquerors marched nearer each day. Radio reports blared the Dutch army was being overrun by German *blitzkriegs*.

Martin was riddled with doubt. Shouldn't he fight with the Dutch soldiers? Deane forbade him from taking up arms. Didn't he also belong to the Netherlands? Blake, the British intelligence officer, suggested Martin start organizing the neighborhood. It was all so confusing.

He rolled up on his elbow and listened. A scuffing sound outside his room launched him to his feet. Martin treaded lightly down to the kitchen, stopping in the doorway.

"Aunt Deane, you're up already."

"I made hot tea," she said as if the hot brew would solve their problems.

She hovered over the teapot, silently pouring a cup. He gratefully took his and eased into a chair. He blew on the steaming liquid.

"I guess you couldn't sleep either."

"A little. I have been in much prayer." She topped off her tea and perched on a chair across the table from him. "Our soldiers are being killed. Defeat is imminent."

Martin offered no comforting words. Rather, he ate the dry bread and avoided the scalding tea. He assumed Deane shared his bleak thoughts. Life would be difficult for them, but more so for the Rosenbaums and Jewish families with the Germans in power.

"Should I go to Simon or is Blake remaining in Middleburg to gather intelligence?"

Deane rose and nestled bread and cheese in a basket, which she covered with a towel.

"Take these to the Helmholdts from church. Their son is in the Army and his wife is ill. I had a vivid dream last night, Martin."

He stood and gazed down into her tired eyes. "What has God shown you this time?"

"This dream was like no other I have ever had." She laid a hand on his arm. "German airplanes smashed Middleburg to pieces. In the rubble, I found a precious ruby, like the ones set in our family necklace. The red color sparkled among broken bricks. I saved it from the ruins, knowing I had found the heart of God."

"Do you mean we should hide our necklace in a safer place?"

"I believe my dream has a deeper meaning. Jesus shed His blood so all will be saved, even the Germans. Jesus is more precious to us than any ruby. No matter what we face, we must *never* relinquish our faith. Promise me that you will not."

Her eyes shone brightly through her tears. Martin snatched her hand.

"God is with me, I know," he said, feeling power in the words as he said them. "I will try to tell others how He protected me since Mother and Father died."

Deane patted his hand. "That is what I ask."

"How do we live in war? Kuipers already killed a man. Will I have to kill?"

"The most dangerous place is outside the will of God. If you ask, He will show you each day what to do."

She handed Martin the basket and gave him the address. "Deliver this, and then see if Simon is back. Tell him it is urgent that he take our guest to sea. Bring back any fish he has. Bring these extra guilders."

Martin stuffed the money into his pocket. He set his mind to evade Kuipers and eased out the back door, checking over his shoulder for the lethal policeman as he walked about a quarter-mile. He was about to cross the street, when a motorcycle zoomed around the curve heading straight for him. The driver, whose rifle was slung across his back, screeched to a halt in front of Martin. The French soldier held up his hand and turned off his engine.

"*Wachten!*" he ordered in fractured Dutch.

A column of French military trucks loaded with troops, and some towing artillery, lumbered into view. Excitement sizzled through Martin.

He stepped closer asking in English, "How far are you going?"

Trucks continued rolling past. The soldier slid his helmet back on his head. Pointing at Martin, he posed a question of his own.

"American?"

"Yes."

The French private smiled broadly. "My uncle, he marry American woman. They live in Jersey. I spend one year there."

"I'm from Michigan." Martin gestured at the lead truck disappearing toward the east. "Where are you headed?"

"The Germans won most of the Netherlands and approach Zeeland. We assist your troops at Moerdijk. We do not let them capture your Vlissingen port."

The last convoy truck approached. The private yanked his helmet forward.

"I hurry to front."

He kick-started the motorcycle and blasted off. Martin sped two streets over and delivered the food. Then he rushed to the canal, spying Simon's boat tied at its mooring. He found him standing by the canal talking to Mr. Grossman. The younger man owned the kosher butcher shop and attended synagogue with the Rosenbaums. Martin saw Mr. Grossman hand something to Simon before walking away. He figured the butcher wanted Simon's help in fleeing the Netherlands.

Martin strode forward and greeted Deane's friend. The fisherman looked worn out.

"Deane and I are concerned for you," Martin said. "Is everything okay?"

Simon wiped his brow. "I may take a sudden journey for a sick and elderly gentleman. Is Deane well?"

"She and I have a new fishing assistant who must be taken to his fleet. He gave Deane this to hire you."

Martin tried to give Simon the guilders, but he refused the money.

"We insist." Martin tightened his jaw. "It may prove useful for your fishing business later. And my aunt says it is urgent."

"Just who is your assistant?"

Martin kept a watchful eye while explaining how he and Blake met, vaguely mentioning his overseas connections. "He is on a mission to return to his prime minister," was all he dared say.

Simon stroked his white beard. "I understand. He is welcome to come aboard. When?"

"Within the next few days. Meanwhile, we need fresh fish for lunch."

"*Ja.* I have something special for you."

Simon hopped down to his boat. Seconds later, he held up a giant specimen.

Martin swallowed hard. "No herring?"

"The Lord says we should be grateful for our daily bread." Simon flashed a crooked grin.

"Oh, I give thanks for my bread. It is your slimy eel I despise."

Simon grunted. "No time to fish. I am busy ferrying soldiers."

"Okay. Deane will be happy if I buy your slippery fellow."

Martin counted out more guilders and plopped the eel into his empty basket.

"I'll be in touch. Will you be going out again before I bring your new assistant?"

Simon shrugged his ample shoulders. "If I do, I will send word."

Martin touched the bill of his cap and headed for home.

As he neared Deane's row house, Eli stopped him. "Come with me to the mill. I heard explosions beyond the ridge."

Martin stopped long enough to put the dreaded eel in the kitchen, calling out, "I'm leaving with Eli."

Then they scurried along the canal before turning north. A French soldier barreled past, hollering about the Germans. Martin heard what he said, but kept going on to the mill. Willem de Mulder was tending to his boisterous chickens.

"We heard explosions." Martin rushed by. "We wanna see how close the Germans are."

"Martin, stop. We take a look from the mill."

Mr. de Mulder hustled them up the steep stairs to the high floor where he ground the flour. Martin bolted to a small square window. With his heart pounding, he surveyed Middleburg, once so beautiful and alive with color. Thick billows of dark smoke rose in the east. He gulped at the awful sight, and whirled to face the miller, anxiety rising in his chest.

"A French soldier said the Germans are at Moerdijk and steamrolling this way. They're smashing everything."

"My son is at the front," de Mulder said, his eyes watering. "German planes and artillery weaken Zeeland's defenses. Soon they will be here."

Eli hung back. "If Germany conquers the Dutch, where can we go?"

At the boy's terrified voice, Martin struggled for an answer.

"I asked Mr. Attwood to take you along," he blurted, "but he has a secret mission."

Mr. de Mulder straightened his back. "Who is Mr. Attwood? How can he help Eli's family?"

"He's a friend." Realizing his mistake, Martin turned back to watch the fighting.

From his vantage point the battle looked far away, but reality seeped in. The Germans would conquer the Dutch as they had the Polish. He faced Eli, wanting to alleviate his fears.

"Deane and I invite you and your parents to live in our home. We have two extra bedrooms."

A black cloud lifted from Eli's face. "Mama will be happy."

"I must set the mill's sails to warn of the Germans," de Mulder interrupted. "You had better caution your families."

Martin snapped to attention. He galloped down the steps with Eli close behind. They burst out the mill's lower door. Rapid explosions erupted from anti-aircraft artillery near the canal. Tracers streaked toward a German Messerschmitt speeding toward Vlissingen. The Messerschmitt dove, both its engines roaring. The German pilot aimed his plane straight for Dutch soldiers manning the big gun.

Martin ducked behind a tree. Machine gunfire blazed from the Messerschmitt. Dutch soldiers spun around in their platform. Tracers from their guns flew skyward toward the fighter.

Boom!

A thick cloud of smoke engulfed the German fighter. The plane tumbled in the air, spiraling toward the marsh. A trail of smoke belched behind it.

Martin grabbed his friend's shirtsleeve.

"Eli, let's beat it!"

Martin pumped his legs hard, reaching the village outskirts. His chest heaved beneath his ribs. Eli managed to stay on his heels. When they veered down the street behind Deane's, he found no signs of war. He suspected that would soon end.

He pushed Eli into the open back door and caught his breath. The wall clock struck twice, and then Martin heard the unmistakable rumble of trucks. He strode to the large parlor window and yanked back the sheers.

"More French troops are on their way to Moerdijk."

Eli backed out of the room. "I should tell my parents about living here. Mama cried all last night. I heard her through the thin wall."

Martin followed him out the back door.

"I'm going to see if Deane's in her shop."

They parted, and Martin found Deane by her large safe. Blake was at the window, turning over the windmill painting in the sunlight. Deane motioned Martin to come in.

"Blake appreciates art as we do." Her eyes grew stormy. "Hitler has other plans for us."

Martin fought to catch his breath. "Germans haven't captured Zeeland, but they're fighting at Moerdijk. From the mill, Eli and I saw smoke billowing just east of here."

Blake calmly centered the windmill painting back on the wall. "I will remain in your home until I leave. Is everything set with Simon?"

"He needs to know when you must leave, but he is ready." Martin felt his pulse recede.

Deane sighed and leaned against the safe. "Kuipers was in here earlier, strutting around, touching everything."

"I say, Deane." Blake stroked his chin. "Folks in England are all busy digging and hiding their valuables. You should follow suit."

She picked up a large metal box from below the counter, which she handed to Martin.

"I was going to put this in the safe. It is rather full with jewelry. Take it to the house."

Deane led him to the rear door and whispered, "Find the shovel and bury this outside."

"What's in here?" he asked, cradling the box under his arm.

"Vander Goes family scrolls and other heirlooms I showed Blake. There are also some extra guilders, which we may need to survive in the future."

"Where's the key for this box?"

She pointed to the bottom of her sweater. Martin nodded. Outside, he grabbed the shovel. An idea came to him. To keep Kuipers from finding the spot where he would actually bury the box, Martin disturbed the soil near the foundation. Then he parked his bicycle over the mound.

Next, he dug furiously and then secreted the family treasures beneath the shed. Martin set flowerpots over the fresh soil. He stepped around the storage shed to view what was going on down the street. There at his feet lay a rifle.

He snatched up the weapon and carried it into the house along with the shovel. Both could be handy against attacking soldiers. Voices in the parlor drew him to investigate. Deane and Blake sat listening to a British broadcast on the radio. Deane must have brought him via the front entrance so he wouldn't see Martin digging. Martin entered the room quietly, setting the rifle and shovel at his feet by his chair. Blake wrote in a small notebook.

The announcer crisply intoned, "Our new prime minister, Winston Churchill, is about to speak to the House of Commons."

Churchill's voice boomed, his authority to fight the Nazis filling the room. Martin grabbed his journal, and in pencil recorded the historic speech. When the prime minister finished, Martin wiped his eyes. The man's great courage inspired Martin deeply.

The announcer had other news, blurting in a high-pitched tone, "Stay tuned for further updates about France and the English Channel. Meanwhile, Mr. and Mrs. Herring of Triton will celebrate their sixtieth wedding anniversary at the town library on the evening of the fifteenth."

Blake wrote feverishly before looking over at Martin. "Simon needs to take me out Wednesday evening."

"I will make sure his boat is moored," Martin said, closing his journal.

"It is imperative. The elderly couple named Herring refers to my code name within British Intelligence. Triton is no English town, but is the *HMS Triton*, one of our submarines. In two days, they will look for me at a rendezvous point."

Martin nodded, finally understanding why Blake couldn't take Eli to England. The Brit's eyes locked onto the rifle. "Where did you get that gun?"

"It appeared by the shed and I grabbed it."

"Brilliant. You may need it soon. Please find a lamp for me to burn this paper."

Deane turned off the radio. "I am going upstairs to pray," she said, leaving quietly.

Martin picked up an oil-burning lamp on a side table, his fingers shaking. His father's words on his deathbed dove at Martin like an attacking hawk. *You are a smart boy, Martin. Care for your mother and believe in the Lord, my son. His plans are best and they are good.*

Smoke tickling Martin's nose brought his mind careening to the present. As he watched the paper burn, he knew he must be more assured like Blake. He set his jaw and asked him for advice going forward. Blake washed the ashes down the kitchen sink.

"Be wary of newcomers," Blake said smirking. "Except for me, of course. Seriously, go see Oostenburg, the undertaker. Tell him I sent you. He needs help with his printing press."

Martin lifted his chin, curiosity building. Who was Blake Attwood really?

14

Wednesday morning dawned with the faint stink of smoke. If only it would rain. Martin ignored the odor and did everything Deane asked. He checked on the Rosenbaums, bicycled food to their church, and burned papers. He met Simon in the shadows behind his shed by the canal. His chores complete, he left Deane and Blake listening to the kitchen radio. He needed time alone.

In the parlor, he jotted a few lines in his journal. Chaos was everywhere. Shops were shuttered. A few Dutch flags still waved, but the future looked bleak. Martin set down his pencil. He wanted to help Oostenburg with the underground newspaper. With the world about to plummet to an end, would it make any difference?

Still, Winston Churchill wasn't about to give up. Martin shouldn't either. Blake's idea took shape in his mind, and Martin started writing his first article about the war. Words spilled onto the paper. Then he wondered if something was missing. Blake's opinion mattered, so Martin crossed into the kitchen, his article in hand.

"Has your Vander Goes family always lived in Middleburg?" Blake asked Deane. He stood when Martin walked in.

Martin lifted his paper. "I need an honest opinion on the article I just finished."

"I am interested, chap." Blake resumed his seat.

At Deane's encouraging smile, Martin cleared his throat and began reading evenly, as if he was a radio announcer.

"Britain's new leader rose to power after Chamberlain resigned. Winston Churchill boasts a long record of military service, most recently as the First Lord of the Admiralty. He challenged the Nazi war machine in his recent speech by imploring the world to stand up against the National Socialists of Germany. Mr. Churchill infused his listeners with strength and resolve. Dutch citizens, hear his words; they will stir you to action."

Martin's eyes shifted to Blake, whose eyes beamed approval. Deane sat riveted, her hands around her teacup. Their rapt attention gave Martin the pluck he needed to continue.

"Churchill's voice was thick with emotion as he said, 'We have before us many, many long months of struggle and of suffering. You ask, what is our policy? It is to wage war, by sea, land, and air, with all our might and with all the strength that God can give us; to wage war against a monstrous tyranny, never surpassed in the dark and lamentable catalogue of human crime.'"

Blake rapped his palm on the table. "Martin, you captured his speech word for word."

"There's more. Should I keep reading?"

Deane wiped her nose with a white hankie. "Please. I could hardly listen to his speech, my heart fluttered so."

Martin found her sudden outburst perplexing. She'd always acted in control. He smoothed his paper, confidence building in his chest.

"The British leader desires God's help against the Germans. Mr. Churchill rallied us to fight tyranny when he said, 'You ask, what is our aim? I can answer in one word: victory; victory at all costs, victory in spite of all terror, victory, however long and hard the road may be; for without victory, there is no survival.'"

Martin glanced at Deane. Tears rolled down her cheeks. She was as stirred as he'd been by Churchill's call to arms.

Motorcycles blasting past the house ended Martin's recital. He ran to open the front door to get a glimpse of what was happening. Two Dutch soldiers sprinted behind several speeding motorbikes. In a surprise move, Kuipers rushed toward Martin in his black polished boots.

Desperate to warn Blake, Martin called, "Aunt Deane, put on tea. We have company!"

He spun around and managed to reach the kitchen ahead of Kuipers. Relief flooded him. Blake was not to be seen.

"I need sugar," Kuipers demanded.

Deane's hands flew to her hips. "Our soldiers shoot Germans with sugar instead of bullets?"

"Do not be smart. Sugar is essential to the war effort. Give me yours along with bread."

Deane clucked her tongue, but went into the closet where she kept food supplies. Martin blocked the door, preventing Kuipers from seeing inside the storehouse. She nudged by Martin with several items in her hands. She gave Kuipers a tin of sugar and half a loaf of bread.

"There is no time for baking. If you have not noticed, we are embroiled in a war."

"Holding back needed supplies will mean trouble for you."

"Yes, I kept bread slices for our lunch," Deane replied, her voice hard as nails. "Or do you want us to starve?"

Kuipers snatched the food. He cast an ominous look at Martin and left out the back door.

"He is trouble, that one." Deane shook her head. "We should eat before he takes our butter. It is good he did not count three slices. Run Blake's lunch upstairs. "

Martin checked, but Blake wasn't in the guest bedroom. Where did he go? Martin returned to the kitchen where he joined Deane at the table.

"I talked earlier with Simon. He is ready for our guest to arrive at eight o'clock."

"You grow braver by the day." Deane stirred a speck of sugar in her tea.

Martin held up a finger. "And more wary of Kuipers. He'll steal everything we have."

"One day we will push the Germans from our country."

"That is wishful thinking." Martin gulped his tea and wiped his mouth on his sleeve.

Blake sauntered through the back door. "My word, that was close. From a hole in your outhouse, I watched the policeman leave the yard."

"Sshh," Deane whispered. "London is broadcasting."

Martin turned up the radio in time to hear heart-stopping news.

"The army has capitulated!" he cried. "Queen Wilhelmina escaped to England!"

"Our queen does not give up." Deane leveled a stern gaze at Martin. "Nor do we."

Blake coolly poured himself tea from the pot. "Your queen goes to England for help."

Deane rose and looked out the window. When she turned, her face was a mixture of fury and strength. "Martin, go tell the Rosenbaums. There is no time to lose."

Alarm pulsed through him. Would he run into Kuipers again? He forced himself out of the chair. Moments later, wearing his grandfather's ragged fisherman's cap, he hopped on his bike. He pedaled the roundabout way to the furniture store, managing to avoid Kuipers' ever-roving eye. A "closed" sign hung in Mr. Rosenbaum's store window.

Martin cleared the rickety steps and knocked on the apartment door, using their pre-arranged code. Eli let him in. Martin fought for composure, but his limbs trembled.

"The Dutch government has collapsed," he said. "The queen has fled to England."

Mrs. Rosenbaum sunk to the sofa in tears. Her husband steadied himself on a chair. Eli looked panic-stricken, wiping his eyes. Martin looped an arm around his friend.

"You and your parents will live with us."

"Papa will not leave," Eli whispered. "He refuses to let Germans push him around."

Martin feared for Eli. His papa's stubbornness might bring him trouble.

"Well, come for dinner. We can talk things over."

After Eli discussed this idea with his parents, Mr. Rosenbaum folded his thin hands. "We come."

Eli sighed deeply, his roving eyes betraying his terror at what lay ahead. Martin gripped his bony shoulder. "We won't let them take you."

Martin blasted out the door and down the steps. Tears for Eli burned his eyes and he dashed them away. This was the right time to act on Blake's tip to contact the undertaker. He bicycled to the mortuary, where he stopped pedaling just inside the fence and rested his feet on the ground. Oostenburg hammered nails in a casket. Stacks of coffins were piled all around him.

Horror sizzled through Martin. So many soldiers must be dying.

A lovely young woman wearing a pretty dress walked up to him.

"My father is busy, you see," she said, a lilt in her voice. "Do you need his service?"

Martin hadn't expected to meet anyone except Mr. Oostenburg. Besides, her good looks distracted his mind.

"I am Lucy Oostenberg," she said.

Martin figured Lucy was a year or two younger than he was. "My *tante* is Deane Vander Goes. I am—"

"Oh, you are her nephew Martin," she interrupted. "We missed your party as my mother fell ill. We thought it best to stay home."

"How is your mother?"

"She remains in bed, so I help my father."

"It must be hard to see so much death."

She shrugged. "I am more used to it each day."

Martin set the standard on his bicycle and stepped closer. "I wanted to speak to your father about something in particular."

"What about?" Lucy asked, eyeing him closely.

"I wrote articles for my newspaper in Zeeland, Michigan. If he is interested, I can return."

Lucy twisted her hands and glanced toward her father who pounded the nails.

"He will want to speak with you, Martin. Can you return after dinner?"

"Perhaps tomorrow."

A large black car rolled up, its window lowered. It was Kuipers. Martin did not react. He didn't want the policeman guessing he had something to hide.

"Vander Goes, what are you doing?"

"Visiting friends." Martin smiled at Lucy.

Kuipers leaned his sizable head out the window. "Who died?"

In that moment of hesitation, Martin willed his eyes not to flinch.

"No one I know," he replied. "But many brave soldiers have lost their lives."

Kuipers swept an arm toward the coffins. "A German governor will soon lead our country. Vander Goes, let me see your passport."

"I left it at my Aunt Deane's. Do you want me to get it?"

"You no longer live in America. I enforce the laws and you will do as I say."

Martin bit down on his lip. His loathing for Kuipers increased each day. But rather than tell the arrogant policeman what he thought, Martin turned to Lucy.

"I will tell my *tante* you said hello."

Martin got on his bike and wheeled away, his legs pumping with great strength until he reached the alley behind Deane's home. He dropped his bike by the shed, and stormed in the house. His search for his aunt proved fruitless. Next he tried the jewelry store. A tiny bell rang on the door when he entered. She must have just connected a warning bell.

He saw Deane by the safe, her back to him. She locked it shut.

"Are they coming?"

"Yes, for dinner. Eli's papa is stubborn, thinking the Nazis are bullying him."

Her eyes misted over. "Kuipers came while you were gone. He questioned me about Eli and his family. I led him to believe they are leaving for England."

"Is Blake taking them after all?"

"No. Consider carefully what I have just told you."

Martin shoved his hands in his pockets, digesting her words.

"Okay, I get it. They must leave their home at once. Our dinner is their going away celebration. Kuipers stopped me, boasting of his rise to power."

Deane pinned the lockbox key to her sweater. She grabbed his arms.

"We must stay strong. Did not the Lord Himself tell Joshua to have courage before he led the Israelites to the Promised Land?"

A wave of fear passed through Martin. He grabbed her hand.

"We will face it together, Aunt."

The bell rang. Martin spun on his heels, steeling himself to confront Kuipers. But it was Blake, bringing news.

"Churchill is addressing Parliament. You may want to hear another historic event."

Deane thrust a "closed" sign in the window and locked her shop. The trio returned to the house. Once settled in the parlor, Deane turned on the radio. Martin searched for his pencil and his journal. As Churchill's forceful words hung in the air, Martin wrote everything he could. When the broadcast was over, Blake turned off the radio.

"We Brits are in full scale war against Germany. I need to leave Holland."

Deane snapped to life. "Martin, make sure Simon is ready for our guest."

Martin folded his arms in protest, not wanting to tangle again with Kuipers. "Simon already promised me this morning to be ready after supper."

"Never mind," Deane replied. "Our government collapsed. His plans could have changed."

"You would make a good sergeant in the Army," Martin said thoughtfully. Then he left the house, riding to Simon, who was fixing one of his nets.

"Did you bring in any herring?" Martin asked.

"This is no time to fish. I make it look like I am."

"Deane sent me. You are having supper with us at eight, right?"

Simon winked and bent over his net.

Martin wanted to ensure the Dutchman knew he wasn't really taking supper with them.

"At that time, I'll bring my fishing assistant. He's interested in catching slippery eel out on the open waters."

"It is my honor to partake of such a delicious meal with your aunt." Simon reached into his blue coat and handed Martin a note. "Give her this."

Martin grabbed the note, curious what Simon had written. Later, when he gave Deane the note, she slipped it into her apron pocket. Martin shrugged. He was getting used to her taciturn ways. Blake wasn't around, but Martin wanted to ask him about Churchill's strong beliefs. Victory at all costs, he'd said. Martin went to the parlor and opened his journal. Chewing the end of his pencil, he wondered. What would be the cost of being conquered by the Germans? What would it take to beat them?

MARTIN SET OUT FIVE BLUE AND WHITE bowls on the dining room table when he heard one knock and then another. He opened the back door and Eli stumbled in, his brow glistening with sweat.

"Mama is afraid to leave the house."

Martin partially shut the door. "Then you should stay and eat."

"Papa wants me right back."

Eli looked longingly toward the stove, where a big pot of soup simmered. Deane scooped boiled potatoes into a bowl, and ladled the onion soup into another pan. Martin settled these into a basket, which he gave to Eli.

"Tell your parents we are here for you," Deane said. "There is no need to hide in fear."

Eli thanked her profusely for the food and slipped out. Deane dished hot soup in a large tureen, telling Martin to run upstairs.

"Tell Blake the Rosenbaums are not coming. He may as well join us at the table."

Blake gratefully accepted and brought down his trench coat and a small leather bag. Neither he nor Deane said much at the table. Martin speared a potato with his fork, plunging the entire morsel into his mouth. Who knew when he might eat again?

When one of Deane's many clocks chimed fifteen minutes until eight o'clock, Blake pushed away from the table. Martin gobbled the rest of his soup and brought the empty bowl to the kitchen sink. Blake did likewise.

The risk of sneaking the British agent from the country weighed heavily on Martin.

"Simon is waiting," he told Blake. "Are you ready?"

"I will never forget your kindness to me. I just need my coat."

Deane gave Blake a wrapped parcel. "Eat this egg sandwich later."

By his wide smile, Blake seemed pleased by her thoughtful gesture. He wiggled into his trench coat, and cinched the belt. Martin put on his grand-father's old cap.

"It's almost dark. We'll keep to the alley at first."

"I pray for your safe passage," Deane whispered as she closed the door behind them.

Martin slipped into the twilight, aware of the present danger.

Walking alongside Martin, Blake said in hushed tones, "Thanks, old chap."

"Me old? I'm seventeen. You can't be much older."

"Sorry to offend. It's something we Brits say."

"Yeah. I know what you mean. Back home we say 'you guys,' even to girls."

They reached the alley. Martin scanned up one side and down the other before stepping out of the yard. Thankfully, he saw no one to interfere with their journey.

"We should be in the clear. Kuipers prowls around during the day. By now, he's at home with his wife, wolfing down his apple strudel."

Martin stepped with purpose down the alley, his respect growing for Blake. "You have lots of responsibility for England. More than I can do."

Blake lifted the collar of his trench coat around his neck. "I have trained to serve my country since a wee lad. Special military schools and the like. Here I am at twenty-one, fleeing Germany's advance. I await my next assignment."

At the alley's end, Martin pressed a finger to his lips. "Keep quiet until we get you to Simon's boat. I'm sure you know how voices carry by water."

"You learn quickly, my friend."

The pair remained in the shadows as they darted along the canal.

"Someone is coming." Blake grabbed Martin's arm and they hid in a doorway.

Martin pressed his body sideways. So did Blake until a man in dark clothing passed. Was he a Dutchman or German? Martin couldn't tell. He trusted no one without proof of their loyalty.

"Simon's boat is just ahead," Martin whispered. "Let's go before we meet one of Kuipers' cronies."

Blake kept his voice low. "You are wise to be on guard. Allegiances fluc-tuate. Yet, I am relieved by Deane's confidence in Simon."

"She's known him all her life. He brought me here in his boat from Rotterdam."

"My life is in his hands."

"And in God's. Don't forget Deane and I pray for you."

Water lapped against the canal wall. Simon's boat stood ready. Martin listened for suspicious sounds. All seemed quiet and no one walked on the dock. Had Simon made sure the other fishermen would be gone at this hour? Martin rapped softly on Simon's shed door and waited. Seconds later, he knocked again. The door opened a crack.

"It's me, Martin."

The door opened a few more inches. Martin squeezed through, followed by Blake. Arms folded, Simon stepped back, prompting Martin to quickly introduce his "fishing assistant."

"You have Blake's guilders to pay for fuel."

Simon eyed the Brit. "Brave Dutch soldiers tried to protect our northern border, but were crushed. They had to surrender. Here in Middleburg, we fight on."

Blake tightened the collar of his trench coat. "My government sent soldiers. Without support, they were forced into retreat."

"In time, we will win." Martin balled his fists, wanting Germany's defeat in days and not weeks.

"Well said, but be prepared for privations and treachery." Blake handed a folded paper to Martin. "Take that to the man I mentioned earlier."

Martin opened a crude drawing. "It's a map."

"German locations are marked from Middleburg to Vlissengin. Your undertaker knows what to do with it. After Simon takes me fishing, I will share the information with my superiors."

Martin stuffed the map into his shoe and gripped Blake's hand.

"God's speed," he said. "I must hurry back to Deane."

"I hope the God you speak of listens to you. He and I are not on speaking terms."

Simon ended their talk by picking up his lantern and swinging open the door. He headed for his boat. Blake gave Martin a good-bye nod, and hurried behind Simon. Martin stayed in the shadows long enough to see Blake crouch onto coiled ropes. Simon draped a net over him, turned on his motor, and launched into the canal toward the sea.

Martin lifted up a prayer for patrolling German soldiers to be blind to Simon and Blake's voyage. His senses keen, he strode over to Mr. Oostenburg's with the map safely in his shoe. Grim determination propelled his steps. He was now part of a network of men and women who risked their lives to bring the Nazi regime down in flames.

15

On Thursday night, with Blake Attwood gone to Britain, Martin fidgeted with the radio. He and Deane listened to the news, which grew more horrific by the second. He snapped off the radio.

"I can't listen to any more!"

Deane clutched her family Bible. "The Germans run roughshod over my beloved Holland. Fires burn from the Rotterdam blitz. They killed so many people."

"It's terrible. Eight hundred men, women, and children murdered by the Nazis!"

"Martin, we must stay calm. The Dutch Army still fights here in Zeeland."

"Do you think we can control the southern coast?"

His question hung in the air. It seemed as if the Dutch could do nothing to repel the marauding enemy. Deane wiped her eyes and opened the Bible. After reading aloud two verses in the book of Psalms, her gaze at Martin held great sadness.

He reached out a hand. "Aunt Deane, what else is wrong?"

She simply rested her chin in her hands, and he wondered if he should ask. He had an idea of what bothered her.

"Is everything all right with Simon?"

"He is concerned for me."

"Did he tell you so in his note?"

"That personal matter is between the two of us. I suggest you and I find sleep. Only God knows what tomorrow brings."

"Whatever troubles you, I'm here. If not for you, I would be alone."

She rose, closing the thick Bible. "And without you, I would face this war alone. I had another dream last night, but I will tell you in the morning. *Goede nacht,* Martin."

With Deane picking up the oil lamp, he checked the back door lock. Satisfied all was secure, he climbed the stairs to his room, which he found too stuffy. He opened the window and sat on the bed, removing his slippers. Below his window, a cat screamed.

Ferocious, guttural cries drove Martin back to the window. He heard two cats fighting in the dark night. Eventually, one beast must have won because the brawl ended. The intense fight stirred something harsh in Martin's spirit, a ruthlessness he'd never felt before.

The night air trembling with peculiar sounds, he dropped to his bed. Hours passed, but he found no rest from his tortured thoughts. Exhaustion seeped into his bones. He gave up trying to sleep and shoved on his slippers.

Downstairs, a light burned in the kitchen. Deane sat at the table, her hands gripping an empty cup. She looked so forlorn Martin felt moved to share his distress. Though he swallowed, his throat felt dry as dust.

"Germans are killing people all over Holland and in Europe. I struggled all night, but hate is lodged in my belly. I burn to kill every one of them."

His confession left a bitter aftertaste on his lips. Deane gaped at him intently. Was she ashamed? Then her features softened, and she laid a hand on the family Bible.

"Martin, Jesus died on the cross to pay the penalty for our sins. He cried aloud, 'Father, forgive them, for they know not what they do.' The Lord showed me last night in my dream that we must also forgive these Nazis."

He pounded the table. "And let such evil go unchecked? No!"

"Martin, I love you like my own son. Please listen. Hatred is the seed of all evil. Do not become like them. When I die, I do not want to face my Lord with malice in my heart. Let Him heal your wrath. Our faith teaches vengeance belongs to God and God alone."

"I refuse to be weak in the face of the enemy."

Deane's piercing look penetrated his soul. "You are right," she finally said. "We will stay strong and seek to do His will, which is perfect. But be yoked with light and not darkness."

Martin's mind retreated to a time when he and his father had plowed the big garden behind the garage with old Betsy the mule. As they had walked the row together, Father explained, "Martin, being yoked with Jesus means you don't pull the load by yourself."

Martin battled fierce anger. A desire to wipe out their enemy banished all thoughts of his loving father.

"This must be wrong." He clenched his fists and stalked to the parlor. Bright morning light shone through the lace curtains, nearly blinding him. Martin choked back tears.

"Oh God, help me! I don't want to ever take a man's life because of hatred. If I must take the life of an enemy, let it only be in defense of another."

A few deep breaths later, he felt his heart calming. He wiped his eyes on his sleeve. Martin returned to the kitchen a different man. The burden of saving the country rolled off his shoulders. Deane sat very still with her eyes tightly closed. At sounds of his steps, she opened them.

"Did you pour out your heart to Him, Martin?"

The words stuck in his throat, and he nodded. She seemed to understand because she smiled at him, a smile he would never forget, because in that instant, a tremendous explosion rocked the entire house. A glass lamp crashed to the floor, spilling oil. Martin leapt to mop it up with a towel.

He heard a whistling sound.

BOOM!

Deane grabbed his shoulder. "The Germans are bombing. Get under the heavy table."

They plunged beneath the sturdy oak table. Martin threw his arms over his head. More explosions rattled the windows and his racing heart.

"Aren't we safer outside?" Martin asked.

"*Ja!* Run!"

Martin shot out the door and past the garden shed. He and Deane crouched outside, but bombs continued falling, one right after another. Screams surrounded them. Martin clapped his hands over his ears, loathing that shrill whistling sound of falling bombs.

He scrambled up from his knees and with Deane, hobbled past the corner. They dodged frightened, howling dogs. Hundreds of people ran in every direction. Panic seized him, but somehow he kept running. A row house on the adjoining street burst into flames. Bricks tumbled from the sky. One glanced against Martin's bare arm.

The sight of his own blood spurred him on. He made an instant decision.

"Aunt Deane, we need to flee the city. German bombs will flatten every building."

Her fingers dug into his arm. "I have a pain in my chest. Wait a moment."

Martin breathed a silent prayer for God's help to survive this onslaught. Then he whispered, "Can you run now?"

"*Ja.*"

Her voice a bare whisper, he helped her flee through the park, past the windmill, and up the slight ridge. A few other neighbors shared his idea. One lady tottered in her clogged shoes until she threw them off, running in her bare feet.

When Deane stopped to catch her breath, Martin asked, "Should we keep going?"

"*Ja*, to the edge of the field."

They scurried into a farmer's barren field. Deane lifted her skirt to climb over a low-lying wooden fence. He helped her down. A panicked cow headed straight for them. Martin acted quickly. He pushed Deane back up over the fence and climbed right behind her. The cow rumbled past, mooing mournfully as she went.

Martin wiped his forehead. "That was close."

"Maybe her calf is dead." Deane leaned her hands on her knees, breathing heavily. "But you see how God protected us. I am grateful."

"Look at the dark smoke and flames pouring from town."

They waited a few moments to make sure there were no more rampaging cows. Martin scanned the sky for planes. He saw several in the distance, but they seemed to be flying away. Deane pointed to town folks gathered beneath a far tree.

"Come. Let us see what our neighbors need."

MARTIN AND DEANE DIDN'T RETURN HOME for hours after the bombing ended. They helped so many people find shelter whose homes and lives were shattered. At last, he secured Deane's arm as they picked their way through piles of smoldering timbers. They reached her shop and Deane unlocked the door, using the key she'd pinned to her sweater.

Every clock lay smashed on the floor. Martin bent over and began gathering the pieces. Deane put a hand on his shoulder.

"First, we check the house. Then we go find Eli and his parents."

Martin dropped the clockworks with a thud. Passing by the counter, he was surprised to see the windmill painting hanging by the giant safe as if there hadn't been one bomb. He walked out into the backyard, covering his nose against the awful stench. Deane's shed was ruined.

He started moving aside chunks of split wood.

"This is where I buried your boxes."

Deane clucked her tongue. "The earth looks undisturbed. I want to see inside our home."

The rear door stood open. They went in and Martin quickly secured the door. Broken plates and cups littered the kitchen floor.

"Look at your Bible, Aunt. It's not been touched," Martin said on his way to the stairs.

On the second level, he darted into every room. He returned to the kitchen with good news. "One smashed window is all. I need a board to cover the opening."

"Praises to God," Deane said, straightening her back by the stove.

A single knock rapping against the door jarred Martin's nerves. Seconds passed before he heard another single knock.

"A friend is calling," Deane said. "Open the door."

Martin let in Eli's parents. Mr. Rosenbaum's lips parted, but he made no sound. He looked stricken. Martin helped him to sit.

"Tell us what has happened," he urged.

Mrs. Rosenbaum's voice sounded shrill as she sobbed, "D'ey has our son."

"Someone took Eli?" Martin stumbled backward. "Have the Germans arrived then?"

Mr. Rosenbaum wailed, "My son, my son! Eli go check on Grossman. I watch from window. Two men take him at gunpoint."

Martin fired off questions.

"Which way did they go? Was it Kuipers? Or were they soldiers?"

"No uniform." Mr. Rosenbaum sought Deane's eyes. "Eli fight. D'ey hit his face."

Deane enfolded Mrs. Rosenbaum in her arms and led her to a chair. Then she turned to Martin. "See if you can learn anything."

Martin edged out the back door, pulling on his cap as he ran through the alley to the street. Danger rose to meet him. Putrid smells mingled with smoke. He choked back rising bile and fought sheer panic. Where to even begin looking? What if Eli had already been killed?

An idea lit his muddled brain. He could run to the mill and see if Mr. de Mulder knew anything. Pressing his back against the row houses, he reached the corner without trouble. He sped to the bridge, but before crossing, he looked down. That's when he saw them.

Two women lay on the ground behind low bushes, their hands clapped over their ears. Had they been shot? Martin scooted down the hill, trying not to fall.

"What happened? Are you hurt?"

They both sat up, tears streaming down their faces. One girl's black eyes and hair shone like coal. The other girl's chestnut brown hair hung in her eyes.

The brown-haired girl said between sobs, "Two men knocked us off our bicycles and stole them."

Her friend interrupted, "They were German soldiers dressed in Dutch clothes."

"They probably parachuted in behind our lines," Martin said.

"*Ja,*" the first girl agreed. "Without our bicycles, we cannot ride home to my farm. It is too far."

"Who are you?" Martin inquired.

"I am Yaffa Levi. This is my friend Rebekah Abrams, who came here after Rotterdam was bombed. All our parents are dead."

Martin felt pity for them. "Yaffa, who can help you with your farm?"

Giving no answer, she rubbed her eyes. Rebekah tried standing, but slipped on the slope. Martin helped both girls to their feet.

"I am sorry. My parents died too," he said with tenderness. "Yaffa and Rebekah, follow me to the mill. It is close by. Mr. De Mulder will know what to do."

The two young women exchanged glances, but didn't stir.

Martin held up a hand. "I sense you don't recognize my accent. I'm American, and live here with my *Tante* Deane. She owns the jewelry shop. If you delay, I bear no responsibility if you're injured."

Rebekah dusted off her knees and stared at Martin.

"You did not tell us your name," she scolded.

"Martin Vander Goes," he replied. "You know I'm no German soldier, but make up your own minds."

He turned on his heels and climbed up the bank. Rebekah caught up to him.

"My brother died on the *Simon Bolivar* last year trying to reach England. It hit German mines and sunk."

Martin turned an eye toward her face, streaked with dirt. "I never heard of the ship, but I'm sorry. What happened to your parents?"

"They were killed recently in Rotterdam when Germany bombed!" She clamped her hand over her mouth. "I found them covered with blood. Yaffa and I are out of our senses. Please help!"

Martin slowed his steps. Sorrow filled his heart for this young woman. She was alone in the world just like he'd been before sailing to Aunt Deane's.

"You're in shock. My parents died last February in the States. You and Yaffa must hurry. The mill is down this road."

"Yaffa," Rebekah called. "Come quickly."

Echoes of gunfire ricocheting off the brick buildings caused Martin to duck behind a tree. During a lull in the shooting, he hurried both girls over to de Mulder's home. Other than one boarded up window, the small house next to the mill didn't appear damaged from the bombs. Their chickens were pecking in the front yard. The miller's wife reluctantly let them in.

"These girls are orphans," Martin explained. "Yaffa lived on a farm, but I don't see how she can manage that by herself."

Mrs. de Mulder spoke in such comforting tones to Yaffa that the girl burst into sobs. Rebekah's eyes were wet, but she seemed able to control her emotions.

Martin introduced Rebekah. "German bombs destroyed her parents in Rotterdam. If you can help these two girls, I must find Eli Rosenbaum. Men seized him this afternoon. Did you see or hear anything?"

"Ask my husband. He is in the mill."

Martin dashed next door, where sadly the miller knew nothing. Martin stepped outside the safety of the windmill, unsure what to do next. Sounds of yelling and battle cries split the air.

Then he recalled Deane's recent words, "The most dangerous place is outside the will of God."

Searching for one small boy in the town of Middelburg, under heavy siege, would be harder than catching a slippery eel with his bare hands. Odds were Martin would never find Eli. But he didn't believe in chances. God had a plan and Martin needed His guidance.

"Father," he called, the wind tearing away his words. "Help me find Eli."

The fighting seemed to have shifted south of town, so he went north. He forged a path up the ridge, away from the canal. Martin walked on, plugging his nose as he stumbled past a dead cow. The barn door was closed. He stopped in his tracks. That door usually stood open.

And why was the neighborhood dog digging by the door? The furry animal, its tail lopped off, dug furiously at the dirt. The mutt's food could be locked in the barn. Still, it might be worth a closer look. He climbed the wooden fence, then crept to the barn. A wounded German soldier with a loaded gun might be lurking inside. Perhaps he was being foolish, but Martin walked up to the dog. He listened, hearing nothing but the dog scratching.

Wondering who was in the barn, Martin asked in German, "*Wer ist da?*"

No answer. He called again, "*Wer ist da?*"

The dog smelled Martin's pant leg and barked. Then the mutt continued digging.

Martin lifted the wooden latch that held the two doors closed. Holding his breath, he opened the barn door. The dog shot right inside. Daylight shining through the cracks provided little light. Martin hoped he wouldn't run into any German soldiers. After all, the door had been locked from the outside. As the dog scampered into a dark corner, Martin heard a muffled plea.

He peered and saw the mutt sniffing around something large on the earthen floor. Martin's eyes adjusted to the dim light. A person leaned against the barn wall. He rushed over and found Eli tied at the wrists and feet, his trousers torn at the knee.

"Eli, it's me, Martin!" he cried, jerking the rag out of Eli's mouth.

Eli choked and coughed. Martin pulled the rope off his wrists.

"Who did this to you?"

"Not sure," Eli said with a moan. "Two men pointed a gun, demanding to know where Grossman went. I did not know. They hit my head, and I woke up here, alone."

"Your papa saw it all and sent me after you."

"How did you find me here in this barn?"

"I wish I could take credit for being smarter than Sherlock Holmes, but God brought me here. He used that ugly dog."

Martin helped Eli to his feet. "Can you walk?"

"I guess so, but my head hurts."

Eli took a wobbly step, so Martin snatched his arm. "Let's beat it before the men return."

"Good idea."

They shooed their new four-legged friend from the barn, and Martin latched the door. They made it safely to the cross street by Deane's, where they spotted three wagons being pulled by large horses. Marching German soldiers sang with gusto about their Fatherland.

Fury pulsed through Martin. "Get going, Eli. The Germans are here!"

They rounded the corner and Martin glanced behind him. The German convey passed through the intersection. He made a mad dash for Deane's with Eli keeping stride. By tonight, the Rosenbaums might be living in Deane's home.

16

Martin had again miscalculated. Mr. Rosenbaum still refused to leave his apartment. Late the following evening, as the sun touched the western horizon, Martin hiked over to see how Rebekah and Yaffa were doing at de Mulder's. It took a long while for Mrs. de Mulder to finally answer his coded knock.

"I brought bread and herring for you and your guests," he said.

She let him in and took the food without smiling. "Rebekah and Yaffa spent the afternoon hiding on the mill's top floor. It has been a stressful day."

Martin looked around the cramped, but tidy house. Yaffa huddled on a small chair. Her pair of knitting needles clacked away. Rebekah stood in a corner wearing a sweater too big for her. She gazed at Martin with large, luminous, black eyes. He stared back in wonder. She hadn't been so beautiful when he found her crying in the grass.

His heart skipped a beat and he managed a smile. "I must return home, but my aunt wanted to make sure everyone was all right."

He didn't tell Rebekah it had been his idea to bring food.

"Off with you, lad, before darkness falls." Mrs. de Mulder set the food on the table. "You want to be able to spot any Germans coming at you."

She hustled him out, but not before he stole a final glance at Rebekah. Did a smile grace her lips as she blinked at him? He would never know. Mrs. de Mulder closed the door.

He blew out his breath on the outside step. Fires raged all over the city.

The historic town hall was rubble, smashed to smithereens. Martin wiped sweat from his brow. He walked to the top of the ridge to survey what might be happening. He figured now that the Germans had crushed the Dutch, they'd send in someone to run the country.

The setting sun gave sufficient light for him to scale a tree as he'd done growing up. Hand over hand he climbed several feet up the tree before looking out between the branches. To the east Dutch soldiers skirmished with German troops. Soldiers wearing blue, green, and khaki uniforms zigzagged across fields of tulips, smashing flowers beneath their boots.

In the distance, he saw a German shoot a Dutch soldier at point-blank range. The soldier slumped to the ground. Could Martin help? A bullet whistled through the leaves above his head. He climbed down the tree, shock and horror battering his mind.

German soldiers barged into an adjoining field. Martin crawled on his stomach toward the fallen Dutch soldier. His fingers felt a faint pulse on the man's neck. Lying in the cover of red and yellow tulips, he applied pressure on the man's shoulder wound. Then he crept away to find Dr. Smit.

Back in town, he spied the doctor riding his bicycle, careening around the corner and away from the action. Martin waved him down.

"A Dutch soldier is shot and bleeding."

Without saying a word, the doctor turned his bicycle and pedaled behind Martin, who raced to where the soldier had fallen. But the soldier had vanished.

"What do you mean by flagging me down? No one is here." Smit's eyes bulged.

"Psst." The faint sound came from behind a tree. A young boy with a dirty face motioned for Martin and the doctor to come near. They did and he pointed to rows of tulips.

"The soldier's eyes flew open," the boy said. "He jumped up, shouted in Dutch, and ran off holding his gun."

Dr. Smit nodded. "*Ja.* He had a minor wound. Excuse me, I hurry to my clinic."

The harried doctor hopped on his bicycle and rode off. Sick at heart, Martin trudged home. Deane looked up when he burst in the door. She was reading her Bible. His heart beat erratically. Tears stung his eyes.

"Broken bodies are floating on the water. Death and destruction are everywhere!"

He swiped at his eyes, choking back a sob. Deane hurried over and kissed his forehead.

"My dear one, sit and tell me everything."

Martin dropped into a chair. "Middleburg is done for. Dutch soldiers are still fighting, but the end is near. What can we do?"

"Trust our Lord, Martin. I was reading the Twenty-third Psalm. Put these words into your mind: 'Yea, though I walk through the valley of the shadow of death, I will fear no evil, for Thou art with me.'"

He laid his head on his arms. In his heart, he knew Deane was right. Who but God knew what each day would bring? Still, he had to figure some way to live under the Germans.

Martin lifted his eyes. Deane was pouring out tea. She slid a cup to him. "Drink this right away. The hot liquid will nourish you."

He sipped some and said with feeling, "Yaffa and Rebekah are frightened. I worry for those Jewish girls whose parents are gone."

"They are all right at the de Mulders. You delivered the food?"

"Yes. Do you think the miller and his wife will agree to let them live there?"

"They might."

"But what will happen when de Mulder's son comes home from fighting?"

Deane fell silent. At length, she replied, "They are good people. We shall see what can be done for all our Jewish friends."

Martin drank his tea with a question on his lips. How long would Middleburg be safe for Rebekah and Yaffa?

THE NEXT FEW WEEKS PASSED IN A BLUR. Martin and Deane gave aid to the homeless and wounded, their home becoming a beacon. One morning after he'd served everyone in their house breakfast, Martin walked down the street to assess the situation. In one hand, he clutched his journal. With the other, he plugged his nose against the stench of fires smoldering in the wreckage.

He wanted to weep. Everywhere he turned, he saw buildings leveled and bricks tossed into heaping piles. His Dutch neighbors clawed through the ruin. Sometimes they snatched out a candle or other item they could reuse. One devastating image after another pierced his mind.

On a stone wall, he sat and jotted notes. Mr. Oostenberg had hired him to write a regular column. The undertaker used his morgue to print an underground Dutch newspaper in secret during the night. During the day he built caskets and buried the dead.

Martin's lead sentence: Holland is no more.

He wrote of Germany usurping control, installing a new government under the leadership of an Austrian Nazi named Seyss-Inquart. Queen

Wilhelmina remained in England, but she'd also fired Prime Minister Dirk Jan de Geer who promoted reaching a peace agreement with Germany. Disgusted by German arrogance, Martin jumped from the wall. Eli scooted past, his head drooping. Martin hurried after him and tapped his shoulder.

"Why are you rushing off without saying a word to me?"

Eli twirled around, his eyes wide. He gripped a bundle to his chest.

"These clothes belong to the Goldman's son who died," he said in a hoarse whisper. "His parents escape tonight to England. They gave me their son's clothes."

"They are leaving? How?"

"They slammed the door before I could ask."

"You'd better go home. I am off to observe and write my article."

Before Eli slipped away, the Third Reich's latest collaborator drove up. The sun reflected off Kuipers' black German car. The newly-installed head constable leaned out the open window and pointed a stubby finger at Eli.

"You, come over here."

Eli shot a furtive glance at Martin as if asking for help. Martin followed Eli to the car.

"Rosenbaum, tell your father that I want him to come see me this afternoon. I stopped at his furniture store, and he has a closed sign in the window. All Jews must register."

"Register for what?" Martin gazed down at Kuipers.

"A new order is being handed down from the Third Reich. Vander Goes, you and your *tante* should make sure your neighbors comply."

Martin clamped his mouth shut. He understood nothing of this new order. It was probably something Kuipers made up to bully Jewish merchants.

Kuipers jabbed his finger at Eli. "I never believed you were going to England. Tell your father to stop by police headquarters at four. I am busy rounding up criminals."

"We want to go to England." Eli's thin arms shook. "I will tell Papa what you said."

Contempt burned in Martin's belly. The powerful policeman used his intimidating tactics against some Jewish family every day. At least he drove off without making any more threats. Martin laid a hand on Eli's shoulder and felt his bones.

"Eli, run home and ask your parents to hurry to our home. A family we had staying in the attic left yesterday for Amsterdam to live with their relatives. You can wait no longer to leave your home. I am forming a new plan."

"What plan?"

Martin looked over his shoulder. "We do not discuss such things on the street. Hurry home while I finish my assignment."

He took out his pencil and a clean sheet of paper from his journal. He leaned against an aging tree. After sketching the scene with bold strokes, he walked up over the ridge, where he finished his black and white drawing. The stark landscape mirrored the bleakness he felt inside.

Mrs. de Mulder rushed up. "They captured our son!"

"Better captured than dead," Martin replied, folding his drawing.

Her hands flew to her face. "Being in the hands of Germans might be worse than death."

"I am sorry he's been taken. They may keep him alive, as Dutch soldiers are made to work in German factories. I will ask Kuipers where your son might go."

"But why would Kuipers tell you anything?" Mrs. de Mulder countered.

Martin rubbed his chin. "Perhaps you are right. My aunt … ah … mends his clocks. I will tell her at once."

With that, he strode home carrying his journal under his arm. Burdens for his friends seared his heart. Within the hour, Mr. Rosenbaum signed a handwritten bill of sale transferring ownership of his furniture truck to Deane. Then he took jewelry and silver candlesticks from his wife's satchel.

"Here are d' pieces, Miss Deane. I think you agree d'ey are worth d' price we agreed. I accept less for d' truck, since you promise to help my customers."

Deane slipped off her apron, gathering the items in its folds. Mrs. Rosenbaum slid a handkerchief from her sleeve and dabbed her eyes.

Her husband placed his arm around her. "Now, now. If we leave in d' middle of d' night, we need 'dis money from Miss Deane."

"Here is the amount we agreed upon." Deane handed Mr. Rosenbaum a stack of guilders. "If things improve, you buy them back. I will try not to sell your candlesticks or truck. We should get you settled into your new home upstairs."

Eli watched the exchange with tight lips.

Martin handed his friend an oil lamp. "Follow me."

Soon the Rosenbaums relocated to the attic, where they would live in hiding from Kuipers and the Third Reich.

After dinner and as night fell, Deane instructed Martin, "Drive their truck to the boat landing. Abandon it where local fishing boats depart to sea. That should convince Kuipers they have left the area."

He fulfilled her request, and then stopped at Simon's. But his boat was gone so Martin went on home. Deane and the Rosenbaums were practicing their hasty ascent to the attic if unwanted visitors should arrive.

Martin slept better that night, knowing Eli was under his roof and he could look after his friend. On the days that followed, after Deane fed her new "family" members, they washed all plates immediately to hide the evidence. When the lights were on, Martin closed the drapes as they all listened to the crystal radio, one of the few possessions the Rosenbaums brought along.

One evening, the announcer said: "Jews are disappearing from Amsterdam and Rotterdam. Those who have not fled are being taken to work in German factories."

A sudden banging on the rear door sent Mr. and Mrs. Rosenbaum scurrying from the room toward the attic. Eli grabbed the radio and headed upstairs. Martin surveyed the room for any evidence the Rosenbaums lived there. He saw nothing to give away their presence.

"Open up!" came a shout from behind the door.

Loud banging continued until Deane opened the door. Constable Kuipers forced his way in with a German officer. The officer's uniform had the dreaded SS insignia. A Ruger pistol clung to his shiny belt. Martin didn't like his vulture-like eyes.

Kuipers pushed past Deane and entered the parlor.

"What do you want?" she demanded.

Kuipers raised his fist at her. "Have you seen the Rosenbaums?"

His eyes were concealed below the visor of his uniform hat. His ample chin protruded nearly as far as the visor.

"Well?"

Deane wiped her hands on her apron. "Yes, I saw Mr. Rosenbaum several days ago." She glanced from the officer to Kuipers. "Has he done something wrong?"

Kuipers stepped closer. "Where did you see him?"

"He came to me and offered to sell his truck. I purchased it."

"A truck," he snapped. "You have no need for a truck."

"And you have no need for Rosenbaum," Deane replied.

Kuipers raised his chin and stared down at her so fiercely that Martin worried for his aunt. Would Kuipers and the SS officer haul her away?

"Why do you need a truck?" Kuipers insisted. "To aid our enemy?"

"For my clock and jewelry business. I do not carry a grandfather clock on a bicycle."

"Why should he sell you a truck he uses in his furniture business?"

"Mr. Rosenbaum mentioned he had relatives in Rotterdam," Deane explained.

"A lie! We found his truck abandoned by the docks. His shop is empty. He fled the country."

The German officer's hand flew to his pistol and he glared at Deane. "You said you gave him money," he said in fluent Dutch. "To aid his flight?"

Deane shook her head. "No, I merely bought his truck."

"What proof do you have? How did the truck get to the docks?" Kuipers insisted.

Deane walked into the parlor. The German officer followed her, craning his neck as he went. Martin's pulse raced. He feared Kuipers would climb the stairs and search for the Rosenbaums any second. Deane picked up the bill of sale and thrust it at the constable.

"I paid for the truck, but Mr. Rosenbaum wanted to use it for one more day. I agreed. You have found my truck. Please return it to me."

"You are so stupid," Kuipers scolded. "Did you not see he was preparing to escape?"

"What do you mean, escape? Is he under some kind of arrest? I have never known Mr. Rosenbaum to commit an offense."

Kuipers wagged his finger. "I am not free to tell you all I know. If you learn where the Rosenbaums are, inform me immediately."

He headed toward the door, but then stopped, pointing at Martin. "Do you have a pistol?"

"No," Martin answered sharply.

Kuipers pushed out his chin and nodded toward the SS officer. "Someone shot and wounded one of our officers when he questioned a woman about ration cards. A witness says the shots came from the direction of this flat."

The German officer walked toward the stairway to the attic, but Deane stepped in front of him. "We keep no guns in this house. We abhor war and violence."

The officer put one boot on the first step as if debating what to do. Martin said a silent prayer for God to protect the Rosenbaums.

Kuipers lifted his hat slightly before dropping it back in place. "Send your nephew to my station. He can retrieve the truck."

He gestured to the officer and in a flurry they left Deane's house.

Martin sagged against the wall. "Good thing he didn't ask about guns in the shop."

"Jesus is unwilling that any should perish. You and I should bring Him our needs."

There in the kitchen, Martin and Deane held hands and prayed.

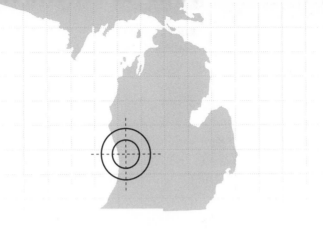

17

JUNE IN ZEELAND, MICHIGAN

va put down Grandpa Marty's journal, forcing her mind back to the present. She was not in World War II or the Netherlands, but in Zeeland, Michigan, at Marty's farm. Her husband Scott had ushered their three kids to bed hours ago. She leaned back in the leather chair. Because Marty rarely talked about his wartime experiences, fresh and intriguing questions leapt from every page.

She rubbed her tired eyes and read his entry for October 1940. He'd started using fake names for his contacts in the Dutch Resistance. What were the true identities of "Homer" and "Reverend Brave"? How could she ever track down these people?

Her heart began pounding at what she read next. She put herself on guard to the secret life he'd once lived. Eli Rosenbaum's name kept appearing.

"Is Eli behind the threats?" she muttered. "He lives in Israel, but what about his family?"

Scott's cold lips against her neck startled her. She smiled up at him and he snatched a seat next to her.

"Uh, oh," he quipped. "I knew it would happen. Talking to one's self is a bad sign."

"I've good reason. Look what I found."

She slid the journal over for Scott to read. He scanned the page before lifting his eyes to hers.

"Marty says he used the gun he found and kept in the shop. He shot a German collaborator who abused a woman."

Eva sighed. "I find it hard to think my gentle grandpa shot a man. Still, he was in war. He was trying to save a life."

"Eva, maybe this 'collaborator' sent the plaid slippers and left the note."

"It seems far-fetched."

Scott flipped back a page. "What about Eli Rosenbaum and his family in hiding? From what you told me before, Marty and his aunt kept them alive."

"I met Eli when Marty and I visited Israel a few months back. He is charming. There's no way he is involved in this."

"You're instincts are usually right." Scott's finger skimmed the page. "Marty says here he worked for Reverend Brave, and a man named Homer."

"Those aren't their real names. Marty wrote that entry five months after the German invasion. The Nazis seized control and didn't allow Jews to be promoted or keep government jobs. Jewish companies were forced to register with the authorities. Reverend Brave, as Marty called him, organized a protest meeting."

Scott handed Eva the journal. "Who's this Kuipers fellow who rounds up Jews? Marty wrote Kuipers forced them to register with authorities."

"He was a police constable who constantly checked on Marty and Aunt Deane." Eva scowled. "I guess they installed a special alarm to alert Eli and his family when Kuipers showed up. He is definitely Marty's enemy."

"Maybe Kuipers is still alive and after Marty for revenge."

"Grandpa saw him kill more than once. I should see if he was tried for war crimes." Eva began pacing the room. "But it all happened so long ago. My training says there's no connection."

Scott rose and shut the journal. "Enough. You seem stressed."

"I am, and my neck hurts."

"Trouble always ends up in your neck and shoulders. Want a nice rubdown?"

"Sounds like a perfect way to relax."

Eva shut her eyes, letting Scott massage the tight knot in her neck.

Ring.

Scott dropped his hands.

Ring.

Eva dove to answer the house phone.

"This is Eva," she said, thinking Lance Talsma was calling her back.

Heavy breathing echoed against her ear.

"Who is this?" she demanded.

"Put Martin on the phone."

Eva glanced at Scott. "Who is this calling for Martin?"

The man erupted in a cynical laugh. "Your grandfather is a dead duck if he does not return what he has taken."

Fear clawed at Eva's throat.

"What are you talking about?" she hissed into the phone.

"Martin knows."

The connection went dead. Eva grabbed at Scott's arm, digging her fingernails in his flesh and telling him everything the caller said.

"Eva, why didn't you put the phone on speaker?"

"I didn't think fast enough. My mind is spinning. Let's take Marty and the kids and leave."

Scott enveloped Eva into his strong arms. "I have an idea."

Eva pulled away, her heart thudding in her chest.

"I'm exploding with anger and want to rip apart whoever is doing this. But that won't stop the fiend, whoever he is."

"Eva, I said I have an idea."

"I'm listening." She stalked to the window and looked out.

"Really?"

She whirled to face Scott. "Yes, now I am."

When Scott told her, she thought his suggestion made sense. She plucked up the phone and hit *67 to trace the call. But she ended up slamming down the receiver.

"No voicemail clicked on."

"We're not defeated. We regroup."

Eva whirled on him. "Easy to say. A madman's lurking out there, and I'm no closer to finding him."

"Call Chief Talsma. Ask him to come over."

Eva bit her bottom lip in frustration. Did she taste blood? She had to get a grip on her surging emotions.

"Once again, Scott, as my partner in this search, you are brilliant."

She phoned Talsma, hoping he'd answer. He did and agreed to have a patrol car drive by and check the neighborhood. Eva promised to call if she found anything strange.

After securing every door, Eva and Scott went to bed. She slept little. Winds and rain pelted against the windows and roof. She kept her gun loaded in the side drawer by the bed. Scott fell right to sleep, waking up thirty minutes later. He punched the pillow beneath his head a few times.

"I can't sleep."

Eva sat up. "Me neither."

"What else did you find in Marty's journals?"

"He and Deane were looking for ways to survive the Nazi takeover when I quit. His experiences make me wonder what is coming for our family and our country."

Scott found her hand in the dark. "Jesus said in the final times, there would be wars and rumors of wars all around."

"Each day is a fight. We don't know how long we have on this earth before Christ comes to call us home."

Eva stayed quiet for some time. The next thing she heard was a rustling sound. She leaned on her elbow and listened. Scott's heavy breathing told her that he'd gone to sleep. Had rain falling on the roof made the funny sound?

Then Eva heard footsteps going down the hall. She scurried to follow the apparition down the stairs, steeling herself to tackle the retreating shadow. The subdued light made it difficult to see who was in the house. But when the man opened the fridge, she saw Marty dressed in blue jeans and a shirt. Relieved, she approached him.

"Grandpa, you gave me a start. What are you doing up at this hour?"

He lifted up his foot, showing off his new slippers.

"Aren't these special? I decided to make your grandmother's special Dutch pancakes. Kaley loves 'em. So do I."

"It's five thirty in the morning. Go back to bed. I'll help you fix pancakes later."

"Old ghosts are haunting me, Eva Marie."

Her mind alerted to the "collaborator" he'd shot in Middleburg years ago. Perhaps if he talked about what happened, she would learn the truth faster than by combing his journals. She led him to a chair.

"Can you think of anyone who wants to hurt you?"

He tilted his head as if deep in thought.

Eva tried again. "You wrote about shooting a German who was abusing a woman. Can you tell me about it?"

"I'll try." He wet his lips and looked her in the eye. "At first, the Germans eased us into their control. Then it became the worst terror of my life. With enemies all around, I trusted no one. But I don't remember the soldier you're asking about."

"In your journal, I read how the Dutch government collapsed. Despite the war, you and Deane did save Eli and his family."

Marty's face fell. "Yes. That is one good thing. After my parents died in the spring of forty, I felt turned inside out, sort of hollow. To be thrown into a brutal conflict took every ounce of my faith to survive. It's a miracle I even lived."

"After you and I visited Eli in Israel, I felt strongly I should visit you. It's no accident I'm here when this troubling conflict is thrust upon you."

He searched her face with his watery blue eyes and shrugged.

She patted his rough hands. "We're both awake to stay. Want coffee?"

When he smiled, she set the pot to brew. Eva pulled out two cups and sliced Dutch date nut bread. After they sipped coffee and ate the bread, Marty surprised her.

"Eva Marie, there are things you don't know. I never wanted my son, your father, to find out."

Adrenaline shot through her.

"Do you want to tell me?"

"Eva …I …" His voice fell away.

Maybe she should have plowed ahead and finished his journals. But that disturbing call had ended her quest. She decided to tell Marty about it.

"Last night, someone called for you," she said. "I asked for his name, but all he did was laugh wildly. He claimed something would happen if you don't give him what he wants. Do you have anything belonging to someone else?"

Marty visibly flinched. "No."

"I didn't think so, but what does he want?"

Eva had to find a way to pry open his memory. She poured him more coffee. He simply stared down at his slippers.

"Something is rubbing on my plantar wart."

"Let me see."

Marty took off the offending slipper and Eva wasted no time shoving her hand inside.

"No wonder it's bothering you. There's a hard lump under the insole."

She snatched a paring knife from a drawer and sliced the insole. What she saw made her spin around. Eva pressed her finger to her lips, and then opened the fridge and shoved the slipper inside.

"What's wrong with you?" Marty called.

She stepped closer and whispered in his ear, "There's a listening device in your slipper. I want to examine it, but you must stay quiet."

"I don't understand. How can someone listen to us through my slipper?"

Eva again put a finger to her lips. Marty nodded and she removed the slipper from the refrigerator. Silence filled the tiny room as she ripped out the insole. Then she opened a drawer and took out a pair of tongs meant for ice. But she had something else in mind.

She inserted the tongs in the slipper and extracted a small implement made of plastic and metal. Holding it in the air, like a dentist examining an extracted molar, Eva turned it around beneath the kitchen light.

Finally, she winked at Marty.

"It's okay to talk. This isn't a listening device. It's a GPS device."

Marty squinted at her prize. "You got me there. What is it?"

Eva lowered the tongs and put the device on the table.

"During World War II, pilots used a compass and watched stars to figure out their location. If this little gizmo had been installed in those airplanes, they would've known exactly where they were. A GPS is a Global Positioning System that sends a signal to satellites and tells whoever put it there exactly where your slippers are."

Marty's eyes flickered to the other slipper on his foot. He looked totally confused. Eva wondered how to make him understand. Before she could explain further, he toggled his head and stared out the kitchen window at the cornfield.

"What are you looking at, Grandpa?"

"It's this time of morning," he paused, his smile fleeting. "I am reminded of deer hunting. Things look different at dawn and at dusk."

"How so?"

He pointed toward the field. "Last night before darkness fell, I saw something in the corn plants beyond the garage. Just something moving among the stalks, but I couldn't tell if it was a deer. It was too big to be a raccoon."

"Maybe I should go check."

Eva stalked to the window. Marty came over and shrugged.

"It could be tricks of light," he said. "One early morning, I was hunting and focused my sights on what I was sure was a deer. I held my fire because the animal never stirred. When daylight lit the field, guess what? I'd almost shot a milkweed plant."

Eva rubbed her hands together. "I'm not so sure."

"I learned tricks of light and use them in my paintings."

"You mentioned in your journals you liked to paint and draw. Why have I never seen your work?"

A shadow crossed his eyes. "Do you want to see them, Eva?"

"Yes, if you'll show me."

"I'd like nothing better. Your grandmother wanted me to keep my paintings in the garage. Follow me."

Eva gazed at her grandfather and debated. She should investigate the GPS. Still, there was little to be done at such an early hour.

"Let me at least call Chief Talsma."

After leaving a message for him, Eva said, "Okay, take me to the garage. You have me curious."

Whatever he kept out there might unravel the mystery deepening around her family. Scott rushed into the kitchen carrying Dutch, who was crying.

"He had a bad dream," Scott explained.

Dutch lifted up his arms to her. "Mommy."

"Maybe you're hungry." Eva tousled his hair. "How about Grandpa's special pancakes?"

At his enthusiastic, "Yes!" Eva decided exploring the garage could wait. Her mind pulsed with unanswered questions. Was the "abuser" Marty wrote of connected to the threatening note? Last night's caller had the voice of a younger man.

She got out flour for pancakes, anxiety rolling in her stomach. She had to show Scott the GPS she'd found in Marty's slipper. His reaction would confirm her next move.

18

Eva changed into her jeans, and returned to the kitchen where she cooked sausage and pancakes. She was pouring syrup when her cell phone rang. She left the table to talk to Chief Talsma, who said he'd come right over. Eva returned to the table and finished her breakfast.

"Well, pardner, what would you like to do today?" Scott asked Andy.

Their oldest son stabbed his fork into the sausage, holding it in midair. "I wanna fly one of those remote controlled planes, only we don't have one."

"Why not go the beach?" Eva asked.

"Whoop, whoop!" Andy hollered. "I heard rain last night. That means some pretty cool stuff probably washed up on the beach."

Kaley set down her glass of juice. "Yeah, I'd like to find driftwood to paint."

"My one and only great-granddaughter takes after me," Marty said proudly. "She loves to paint."

Kaley's cheeks turned a rosy hue and she giggled.

"Okay." Scott formed a circle in the air with his finger. "Get your swimsuits. I'll hunt up beach towels."

Marty set his dishes in the sink, which prompted the teens to leave the table. Kaley ushered Dutch upstairs. Eva immediately showed Scott the GPS.

"You found this where?" He stared, arching his eyebrows.

Fresh anger stirred within Eva. "In Marty's plaid slipper. Chief Talsma will be here any minute. That's why you have to leave with the kids."

"Okay, but what's this high-tech thing doing in his slipper?"

"It might be a weird prank, or it could be a real tracking device."

"Eva," he said her name so intently that she shuddered. Scott rarely used such a firm tone with her.

He grabbed her hands. "You're a trained federal agent with lots of skills, but we need help."

"That's why I called Chief Talsma."

"The kids and I will spend an hour jumping the waves, then I'm coming back to decide what should be done."

With the boys laughing and thumping down the stairs, Eva pressed a finger to her lips. Scott nodded and kissed her cheek.

"Keep your cell phone handy, and I mean it."

"You too, sweetie," Eva replied.

She strode outside while Scott went to find the towels. Some minutes later, Eva waved as her family drove off in the van. With Chief Talsma not here yet, and Marty still inside, Eva went to check out the cornfield. Had her grandpa really seen someone back there?

She ducked into a long ribbon of green. The farmer who rented Marty's land had planted his corn early. The maturing plants flourished in neat rows and grew as tall as Eva. Wait, were those footprints in the damp ground?

Someone had been standing in her row. Fresh footprints covered older prints and headed in all directions. Eva placed her foot into one of the prints. It fit her size. Could this have been a woman? She started tracking the prints to the east, but then heard gravel crunching. Must be the chief.

Eva plunged out of the green corn and reached the driveway just as Talsma rolled to a stop in his police car. He eased long legs from the car. Rising to his full six-foot-four inches, he clipped his car keys to his gun belt.

"You come here on vacation and get right to work," he said. "Don't you ever relax?"

Eva clenched her teeth. He meant to be lighthearted, but she couldn't rest until she caught whoever was stalking her family. Before she could take him into the house, Marty shuffled up.

He somberly shook hands with the chief and then pushed the opener for the detached garage. One of the enormous doors rattled open.

"I'm going to show Eva something important. Do you want to see?"

"Chief," Eva said, pocketing her hands. "This should take a minute. Then I'll show you that item in the house."

Talsma pursed his lips. "You go ahead. I'll phone my deputy and let him know where I am."

"I store my paintings up here in the attic." Marty headed for the stairway at the rear of the garage. "My friend says they're valuable."

With one eye on the steep steps, Eva warned, "Take your time."

"I made it up here last week. Everything about that painting still haunts me."

Eva climbed the steps, making sure she stayed behind Marty. He went straight to a corner. With amazing strength, he shoved aside a battered trunk and wooden chair.

He removed a blanket from unframed drawings. "These are my war sketches. You see the awful destruction from German bombs. Your grandmother refused to let me display them in the house."

"You have real talent," Eva said, admiring his work. "Your drawings make it seem like I'm standing among the ruins."

He held up a small watercolor of a woman wearing a vibrant Dutch costume. "Meet Aunt Deane. You have her periwinkle eyes."

"I had only seen her black and white photo. Your painting brings her to life."

A haunting smile graced Marty's face. He yanked open the lid of a beat-up trunk. With gnarled hands, he lifted out a large blue and white cloth dotted with windmills. He tugged the cloth tenderly, as if valuable treasure lay inside.

The cloth fell away. Eva saw a framed painting of a beautiful woman. Her dark hair fell to her shoulders and she held a bunch of yellow tulips. A hint of sorrow in her black eyes made Eva wonder. She stepped closer to examine the face.

"Who is she?"

Marty stayed quiet for so long that Eva twisted her head to look at him. He stood unmoving as if in a trance.

"Grandpa, is she real? Do you know her?"

Marty set down the painting. He bowed his head and wiped his eyes.

"I won't push you into remembering something you'd rather forget," Eva said gently. "It's just that I have to find out if your war years are linked to the slippers or threatening note."

She hugged his bony shoulders. He kissed her forehead and pulled back.

"I'm not so frail yet. Did you read in my journal about Rebekah?"

"Yes. You hid her and another young woman with the de Mulders."

Marty pointed to the painting. "She is Rebekah. I met her and Yaffa often, always in the mill. I brought them food coupons. My contact in the Dutch Resistance falsified those so we could buy extra food. Over time I memorized her face. She never knew I painted her."

"You should bring your work in the house. I see why you say they're valuable."

"I agree, Eva. It's time they leave this musty old garage."

"You pick out some and I will carry them."

Marty handed her Aunt Deane's painting and a few of his sketches. Then he lifted Rebekah's painting and headed toward the stairs. Eva had other ideas.

"I'll carry everything. Use the railing, please."

She secured the paintings and sketches beneath one arm and followed him down the stairs. His steps seemed to have renewed purpose. Eva wanted to learn more of his years in the war, but first she had to deal with the GPS in the slippers.

Once outside, Eva told Chief Talsma about the footprints she'd spied in the cornrows. She clutched the paintings, feeling a cramp in her arm.

His hand flew to his holster. "Okay, I'll investigate, but let me eyeball that device you found. Where is it?"

"In the refrigerator. Come on, and I'll show you."

Talsma stalked beside her, reaching the house before she did. A dozen "whys" burned in her mind as she set Marty's works on a hall table. Her grandpa must have gone upstairs, perhaps to mull over his time in the Netherlands.

Talsma settled his lanky frame into a chair around the dining room table. Eva retrieved a small towel from the fridge. At the table, she unfolded the towel to reveal one plaid slipper.

"I normally don't put footwear on the table, but this is evidence."

"What kind of package did the slippers arrive in?"

"A box wrapped in brown paper, with no return address. As I said, it's something much more. Look."

She used ice tongs to remove the device from the slipper. Expertly using the implement as if she were a surgeon, she held the tiny device aloft.

"I thought it was a listening device, but I now believe it's a GPS, complete with its own battery. This is evidence of a sinister plot."

"I've never seen anything like it." Talsma reached for the tongs.

Marty walked up to the table asking, "Is the evidence in my slipper from one of your cases, Eva?"

Before she could answer, Talsma faced Marty, waving the tongs. "Someone is more interested in where you go than in what you say."

"That's exactly what I decided," Eva said, with grit in her voice.

A puzzled look on his face, Marty dropped into the chair. "I don't understand."

"We need coffee."

Eva turned to the sink, ran cold water in the decanter, and filled the coffee maker.

"Chief, while the coffee brews, you write down what I say. Then we'll see if you have any other ideas for narrowing our search."

Eva measured dark roast into the coffee basket, and mentioned last night's strange phone call. "I view it as another threat. The male caller's voice was deep and gruff."

Marty fidgeted with the tongs. "I might have recognized his voice, if I heard it."

"You were in bed," Eva said, raising her voice above the sputtering coffee maker.

"Let's eat something with our coffee." Marty wandered over to the cupboard. "Where are those fritters? Oh, here they are."

He unwrapped the fritters and Eva arranged the sweets on a tray. She set the goodies on the table and poured hot brew into three mugs.

Talsma took an apple fritter. "Thanks. I skipped breakfast."

"Enjoy," Eva said. "They're from a Dutch bakery in Holland."

As they ate their pastries, Marty's eyes flew to a windmill painting that hung on the dining room wall. Eva sensed she should ask him about it. But Talsma pressed her for more information about the phone call and the slippers.

Eva gripped her mug. "I contacted several local boutiques, but I'm stumped. You've been chief for years. Does some local have it in for my grandpa?"

"Every small city has its share of lightweights," Talsma said, helping himself to more coffee. "As far as I know, our citizens cherish you, Marty."

Marty couldn't take his eyes off the painting.

"Which puts us back to square one." Eva sighed. "Chief, did you find any connection to a flower company?"

Talsma handed her the tongs with a grimace on his chiseled face. "You need more sophistication than what my department offers."

"I understand you're a small, local department," Eva said. "The FBI is examining the note and packaging for prints. They'll need another week at least."

"Send this GPS to the FBI lab." Talsma drummed his fingers on the table.

Eva held up both palms. "I plan to."

"Right."

Did Eva only imagine the defeat resounding in the chief's voice? She cleared her throat, thinking how best to probe the depths of Marty's mind without stressing him out. She laced her fingers together and leaned toward him.

"Grandpa, someone's tracking you. Any old school chums holding a grudge?"

Talsma grinned. "What have you been up to, old-timer, that somebody wants to keep tabs on you?"

"I sure wish I knew, Chief," Marty replied, tearing off a piece of his fritter.

His eyes darted from Eva to Talsma. Worry pummeled her heart. Scott would be home soon with the kids and she was miles from solving anything.

Talsma untangled his long legs from under the table and stood. "Eva, you didn't answer when Marty asked you earlier. Could this be related to one of your cases?"

His penetrating question forced her mental gears to turn.

"I've wracked my brain. I keep my family separate from work, especially from Grandpa in Michigan. I've never worked a case here."

Bright lights reflected across the ceiling. Eva strained her neck to see out the front window. Their van was pulling into the driveway. She grabbed the tongs.

"Here comes Scott. I don't want the kids knowing about these threats."

Talsma rubbed his chin. "My deputies can drive by, but that's a short-term fix."

Eva wrapped the towel around the slipper, hiding it behind a pickle jar in the fridge.

"I've made up my mind," she said. "We keep the GPS in the slipper. Grandpa, you're coming with us to Virginia. Once there, our tech can analyze it."

"Uh, oh." Talsma shook his head. "If you drive to Virginia with the GPS, whoever is following you will obtain your address."

"You're right!" Eva slammed the fridge door. "My mind is mush. I need to think more clearly about what to do with the GPS."

Marty rose from the table. "I just remembered something about the note."

He shot from the house and over to the garage as if on an urgent mission. Eva bolted after him, with Talsma following. Eva stopped at the van window.

"Go in the house with the kids," she told Scott and then headed up to the garage attic.

Marty flipped open the old trunk. He peered in and cried, "It's gone!"

She crouched beside him.

"What's gone?"

"The painting I thought of. It was here last week."

"Are you sure this is where you last saw it?"

"Eva, I'm getting older, but not totally forgetful. I kept looking at the windmill painting and my mind finally snapped. Last week, the other one was in this trunk."

Talsma elbowed his way closer to the trunk. "Okay, you got me. What did you paint?"

"The note insinuated I'm a thief, like Kuipers. He was the Dutch policeman who stole Deane's jewelry and turned traitor. I've never stolen anything, and I'm not a traitor. But I did paint him and his Gestapo thug who had us living in terror in our own home."

Thoughts of footprints in the cornfield sailed through Eva's mind. So did a lot of other ideas. Did Marty know what he was talking about? Who would gain by taking his WWII paintings? She scanned the attic, hoping to spot stray artwork.

"So one of your pictures from the Netherlands is missing?"

"Yes, yes. Please listen. It was here and now it's gone."

Talsma's right hand flew to the holstered gun. "You mean it's stolen?"

"Yes! I'll show you what they took."

Eva did a double take. "How can you show us if it's been taken?"

Marty waved them off and hurried to another trunk. "I used pencil to sketch on a small canvas what I wanted to paint. Then I'd try to find a larger canvas to paint on."

He fumbled at the bottom of the trunk and turned with a pained look. "They're not here either. This is your grandma's fault!"

"How can that be?" Eva asked, comprehending none of this.

"She never approved of my war paintings or anything else I did."

Chief Talsma shot Eva a pointed look. She shook her head, concerned that she had finally entered the twilight zone here in Zeeland, Michigan. She heard the van doors slamming outside.

"We need to head downstairs. Grandpa, what do you mean about Grandma Joanne? She's no longer alive. How can she have anything to do with this?"

His hands trembling, Marty blinked rapidly. Eva imagined his heart was pounding.

"After I returned from the war, I married Joanne. Because of my nightmares, she insisted we make a new future without painful memories haunting me. I don't mean to blame her, but she urged me to keep my paintings and things up here. A few years ago, I did bring my journals into the house."

Eva tossed him a warm smile, but he wasn't looking at her. He stared into the trunk, filled with scraps of canvas.

"Do you want to file a report for theft, Eva?" Talsma's hand rested on his gun.

She shook her head. "No, I need to talk with Scott. Do me a favor?"

"Name it."

"Will you drive by the cornfield on the back side? Those footprints are making me nervous."

19

Later in the farmhouse, Eva kept evading Scott's questions about Chief Talsma's conclusions. Andy, Kaley, and Dutch played a board game with Marty around the dining room table.

She whispered to Scott, "Not in front of you-know-who. Want to help me cook?"

He went over to the sink and washed his hands.

"Okay, Eva. What can I do?"

"Fire up the grill and cook the chicken thighs."

Eva got out salad fixings, making sure to keep the towel-wrapped slipper behind the pickles. She sliced tomatoes and fried potatoes. Marty even hauled out a lacy tablecloth and candles. The family gathered to eat a home-cooked meal.

"Aunt Deane always set a proper table. During those desperate war years, she made soup from vegetable peelings and tulip bulbs."

"Yuck," Dutch said, holding out his tongue.

Scott reached for his hand. "Son, we have better things to eat. Grandpa Marty's memories remind us to be thankful."

He bowed his head and everyone closed their eyes.

"Almighty God, You are our protector. Keep watch over us here in this cozy house. We are grateful for our family, our food, and our health. Thank You, Jesus."

When Scott finished, he gazed intently at Eva. She recognized his probing look, which meant he was itching to find out what she and Talsma had decided.

She simply passed the salad. "Well, kids, enjoy tonight. Our vacation is drawing to a close."

"But Mom," Andy wailed, "the church is having a softball match. I'm pitching."

She smiled. "We're all having a fun time. But Grandpa and I talked it over while you were at the beach. He's coming to Virginia with us."

Marty grinned. "Andy, I hope you don't mind missing your game."

"Nope." Andy selected a red radish and doused it with salt. "You're the best, Gramps. Wait till you see my baseball signed by Hank Greenberg."

"He was a mighty fine slugger." Marty nibbled his salad.

Eva felt momentary relief until Scott pushed back his half-eaten plate. Leaning forward, he asked, "When do we leave?"

She couldn't hold him at bay much longer. Tension over events sizzled in the air.

"First thing in the morning. After dessert, I have to go for a drive. Maybe I'll pop over to the market and buy treats for our ride home."

"Can I come along?" Dutch asked, shoving a piece of chicken in his mouth.

Eva had something more troubling on her mind than Dutch's cookie choice. "Not this time."

"But you don't get the right chips. I don't like the plain ole' kind."

Scott intervened. "Buddy, let Mom go. You and I will challenge each other at checkers. Kaley and Andy can pack and by that time, Mom will return with taco chips."

Eva quietly mouthed, "Thank you."

She served ice cream, and then Eva washed the dishes. Marty drifted to his comfortable chair in the family room and promptly fell asleep. Scott hauled out checkers, letting Dutch win the first game. Andy and Kaley packed and came down to watch a family video from an earlier vacation at Holland Beach. Eva glanced out the window. The sky was no longer streaked with any pink. Night had fallen.

She grabbed her purse. On the way to the back door, Scott snagged her elbow. "What gives?"

"I'm taking a short buzz around the neighborhood. Chief Talsma called to say he, too, found suspicious footprints behind the house."

Scott's eyes brimmed with questions, so she added in a bare whisper, "Someone took one of Marty's pictures from the garage. I'm checking for anything out of the routine."

She slipped out the back door, patting her semi-automatic Glock in a fanny pack around her waist. In the van, she fastened the seat belt and started the engine. Windows down, she rolled down the driveway and turned north on 88th Avenue.

Quiet engulfed her on the country road. In this farming community, there were no city blocks. Instead, all roads were set about a mile apart. At the next intersection, she turned east for a mile, and then drove right. Lights from an occasional farmhouse showed how few farms dotted the huge fields. Eva paralleled Marty's road before cranking another right turn.

As she approached 88th Avenue, her lights revealed a few spots where the tall grass looked trampled. Were those footsteps leading from the road to the cornfield? There were no homes on this right side of the road. So Eva figured those footprints hadn't come from Marty's neighbors.

A quarter-mile from the stop sign, her lights bounced off taillight reflectors. She slowed and saw a van parked on the shoulder. Her mind calculated. It wouldn't be uncommon for cars to park alongside the road during hunting season. Hunters left the fields after the last scrap of light disappeared. But this was summer and not hunting season. Besides, most hunters didn't drive Nissan vans. Perhaps this driver had engine trouble.

Eva eased her vehicle to the shoulder, stopping a few inches behind the white Nissan van. No one appeared to be inside. The tires were inflated, and the van seemed too new to have broken down. She killed her lights and cut the engine. Eva sat in the darkness, listening to crickets chirping in the distance and thinking. Marty's neighbors drove trucks or SUVs with four-wheel drive. This van was more like a family vehicle.

She figured out something else, equally troubling. This area was within walking distance from Marty's garage and near where she'd seen the footprints. To find out for sure, she raised the windows and removed her keys before sliding out. After quietly closing the door, Eva roamed past the Nissan. It was too dark to see inside. She tested the hood with her hand; the metal felt as cool as the night air.

Pulling her fanny pack to her right side, where her gun would be in easy reach, Eva stepped across the drainage ditch. She entered a row of corn. All her senses were on maximum alert. She walked a block toward Marty's farmhouse and stopped.

Her breathing echoed in her ears. Ahead and to her left, a mercury vapor light, common in many farmers' yards, gave enough light to see in front of her. This farmer probably did as Marty did. He set the light with a sensor so it came on at dark and clicked off at dawn.

Why hadn't she grabbed a flashlight? She knew better. But she had her smart phone. Eva snapped the cell from its holder, pressing the "on" button before walking again. Corn leaves brushed against her clothes, making a swishing sound. She occasionally stepped into a new row to get closer to Marty's garage. Each time she heard the rustling noise.

She'd walked several hundred yards, when a different sound startled her. Eva stopped and held her breath.

Whoosh –Whoosh – Whoosh.

Something or someone else was hitting the cornstalks. Eva widened her eyes, but to no avail. Darkness surrounded her. A running deer might create such a noise. Thumps of heavy footsteps pounded in her ears.

Eva crouched, ready to pounce. Shadows blocked the distant yard light. She couldn't see who was coming. Suddenly, something crashed right in front of her.

A blow to her body knocked Eva to the ground, forcing air from her lungs. "Agghh!" she cried.

She struggled to her feet, becoming twisted in the stalks. Someone ran away toward her van. Eva reached for her gun. But she couldn't use it, not yet.

Instead she shouted, "Stop! Federal agent!"

The person did not stop. Eva raced after the retreating footsteps. Her earlier confusion had cost her vital time. She huffed and puffed, crashing through the tall corn. Her lungs ached each time she breathed.

A door slammed. Gravel spun. Eva's arms whacked at the tall stalks, pushing herself from the corn. The license number, she had to get the license number.

She finally broke free, in time to see the white van roaring down the country road. Eva strained, but couldn't read the license plate. The car's lights weren't on.

"Why didn't I memorize the stupid number when I first pulled up?"

She was disgusted with herself. Then something worse happened. She patted her jeans pockets and couldn't find her keys. As the Nissan turned left at the stop sign ahead, its lights came on. And here was Eva fumbling around in her fanny pack. Finally, her strong fingers grasped her keys along with her gun.

She hopped in her van and spun off. But she saw no one after driving into town or even around the area. Eva gave up and went back to Marty's in defeat. She noticed the side door to his garage standing open. Someone had come back for a second time. What were they looking for?

Whoever slammed Eva minutes ago might have sent the slippers and threatening note. He might have taken Marty's sketches too. Or could it all be a coincidence? The truth proved as elusive as her search in the cornfield.

20

Eva stepped into the light of Marty's kitchen and saw her slacks were covered in debris. She dashed to the mudroom where she dusted herself off. If only she could as easily rid herself of the doubts assailing her mind.

Taking a deep breath, she strode into the living room. "Scott, I just had a run-in outside. Someone clobbered me in the cornfield."

"Yes, I see."

He came over to pluck a green leaf from her hair. "Are you okay?"

"My ego isn't. I failed to get the license number. Thankfully, we're leaving in the morning. It's too dangerous here."

"I'm no trained investigator, but won't whoever is behind these threats simply follow us?"

Concern rang in his voice and Eva had to admit he was right. She laid her hands on his shoulders and looked into his eyes.

"We need to close up here. I'll call Chief Talsma and devise a plan. Meanwhile, Grandpa should pack a single bag."

"I helped him gather his shaver and a few clothes earlier. Let me see what else he needs. You lock up."

Scott rested a hand upon her cheek before heading from the room. Eva pulled out her cell phone and a few minutes later, she and the chief forged a getaway plan.

After that, she spent a restless night trading places with Scott staying awake. Her eyes were wide open when the sun poked its rays above the cornstalks. Her plan came together smoothly and by eight o'clock every door on the Montanna van stood open.

Chief Talsma came to lend a hand. He stepped into the large door opening and fastened a carrier between the rails of the roof rack. Scott stood ready to hoist up two suitcases and a duffel bag.

"Marty's things go on top," he said. "He has too much stuff for a single bag."

Eva nodded toward the house. "Are you finished in the basement?"

"Yup. I shut off the water pump and drained the pipes. I set his furnace to come on if temperatures dip below forty-five. The house should be all right if Marty doesn't return before winter."

"See if you can get him and the kids settled inside. I'm taking one last look."

Eva returned to their bedroom, carrying the shoebox and slippers under her arm. They'd left nothing behind. After checking the bathroom, she went into Marty's room. Socks were crumpled on the bed. These she stuffed in her pocket. She paused in the dining room to admire the windmill painting. She'd forgotten to ask Marty if he had painted it. Perhaps this was the mill where he'd hidden Rebekah and Yaffa.

To have this familiar painting with him in Virginia might ease his transition. Eva took it off the wall, tucking the heavy painting under her arm along with the shoebox. She'd finished sweeping through the house when she recalled Marty's journals.

She stowed them in a leather bag, hoisted the strap over her shoulder, and locked the rear door. A strange foreboding dogged her steps back to the van.

When he saw the windmill painting, Scott grimaced. But without a complaint, he found room in the back of the van for it. Eva crammed in the leather bag and shoebox. Though tightly packed in the van, Marty and the kids sang "Old McDonald Had a Farm."

She got into the passenger seat and turned to smile at Andy in the far back seat.

"Did you pack everything?"

"Yeah, Mom."

"And you, Kaley?"

"I did, but Dad made me leave my driftwood behind."

"Right, but it's stored in the garage attic. We'll return and then you can bring the wood home. How are you doing, Grandpa?"

Marty sat behind Scott with a wide smile. "Happy to spend more time with you all."

"Me too." Eva looked out the windshield at Scott, who was walking around their van inspecting tires and the luggage rack. He finished his inspection and

shook Chief Talsma's hand. Then Scott slid behind the wheel and they were
ready to go.

The chief leaned on the open windowsill. "My officers patrolled in town
and out here in the neighborhood. They didn't spot the white van you saw
last night, Eva, or anything else suspicious."

She dipped her head and handed Talsma her business card.

"You and the folks from church are fantastic to help us escape."

"No problem. You're like family." Talsma tapped the sill. "Marty was my
Sunday school teacher. We won't say how many years ago that was."

Marty's chuckle gave Eva peace of mind that he'd be okay on the long trip.

Talsma gestured at the farmhouse. "We'll keep an eye on things here. I'll
pick up Marty's mail every few weeks from the postmaster, discard the junk,
and send the rest to your office address."

He slapped his hand on the roof of the van. "I'll follow you out of town
to clean your tail."

Scott rolled down the driveway. On the drive through Zeeland, Kaley
and Andy kept up a constant banter about the cool waves at the beach.
Eva scanned the driver of each passing car. They approached the last traffic
light before the expressway when Eva saw Talsma flash his bright lights. He
cranked a U-turn into the gas station. Scott eased up to cruising speed and
raised his window.

Eva took out her cell phone and punched in some numbers.

When FBI Agent Griff Topping answered she said, "Hey, it's Eva. We're
heading home. There are things I need to tell you."

"Want to do that now or later?"

"Ah ... later. Marty is coming home with us. I will bring his slippers to you."

"Eva, here's what I want you to do."

Griff fired off some instructions. Meanwhile, she dug in the slipper box
and her purse.

"Okay, Griff. I can do that. I'll call when I'm done."

Eva ended their call and directed Scott to head for the airport. He
checked his right mirror before changing lanes.

"Why? What's going on?" he asked.

"Griff has a great idea to keep whoever is monitoring the GPS from
knowing where we're going."

"What does he have in mind?"

"You drive to the airport. I go in and disconnect the battery. Whoever
is tracking us will think Marty boarded a flight and the device was found by
TSA or inadvertently disabled."

"Our buddy Griff comes through again."

While Scott put both hands on the wheel and zoomed toward the airport, Eva pulled the device from the slipper. When they reached the airport, Scott and family waited in the drop-off lane. Eva completed her mission with no complications. The battery disconnected, she returned to the van, not looking forward to the tedious twelve-hour drive to Virginia.

EVA AND HER FAMILY LEFT BREEZEWOOD, Pennsylvania, when she phoned Griff. It was almost seven o'clock and they still had more than an hour of the twelve-hour trip to go. When Griff answered, she asked him for a favor, telling him it was "urgent." He agreed to meet them after eight.

"Make it the Golden Arches just off the Washington beltway in Virginia," he said. "You can buy me one of those cheap ice cream cones."

"You got it."

Eva pocketed her phone and kept her eyes on the rearview mirror. No white vans hugged their bumper. Andy and Kaley started a heated exchange about which one of them had a better idea of how to spend their summer before school started.

"If we have a yard sale," Kaley said, "we can use the money we earn to help the church fund for the poor."

"Or buy my radio-controlled airplane," Andy countered.

Eva turned her head. "Dad will be stopping for ice cream pretty soon."

That stirred Dutch from his nap. "Ice cream! I want some!"

"Sure, buddy. It's coming up." Scott exited the highway and wheeled into an empty spot beside Griff's Impala in the back of the lot.

He took Marty and the kids in for a much-needed treat while Eva hopped into Griff's front seat, slipper box in hand.

"Sorry, I couldn't say more on the road," she said. "I don't want to alarm my kids."

Griff took a swig of his coffee. "You've had one lousy vacation."

"It's hard when our loved ones are targeted."

"If it helps, I am praying for you, Eva."

"It sure does." She popped open the box. "The power of living in God's plan means everything to me. Here are the mystery slippers."

Griff picked up the plastic envelope containing the tracking device. "And these appeared at your grandfather's home with the GPS inserted in one slipper?"

"That's about it." Eva nodded briskly. "Your suggestion was a good one. We drove to the Grand Rapids airport, where I took out the tiny battery.

When you reactivate it, hopefully whoever's tracking the GPS will assume Marty's flight disrupted the signal."

"The FBI lab will analyze and then reactivate the device in Virginia. We'll see who shows up. Have you any idea who is behind this?"

"I figure some felon is trying to discover where I live." Eva patted her fanny pack containing her Glock.

"There should be an easier way to find you."

She folded her arms. "Andrei Enescu is clever. What's the status of our Romanian escapee?"

"Interpol is on his case, but I've heard nothing for a few days. He left Transylvania. The last we knew, he was seen on a video in Paris. He's not shown up on any phone intercepts."

"Hmm." Eva's mind churned. "Griff, let me ask you. What does Andrei gain by targeting me?"

"That remains to be seen. Revenge might be high on his list."

"I think Marty's activities in World War II are key. His journals contain interesting clues, but each time I get close to pulling from him some possible link, I get sidetracked."

Griff put the slipper and baggie of evidence into a larger zip bag. "Just remember, I'm a phone call away."

Car doors slammed, prompting Eva to glance over her shoulder.

"Looks like Scott and the kids are ready to leave. Do you want a cone?"

Griff held up his coffee cup. "This will keep me awake until I reach home. Say hello to Grandpa Marty for me."

"Did I tell you why we left so suddenly?" Eva reached for the door handle.

"You found the GPS, right?"

"Yes, but something more disturbing happened. I was talking with Scott about Marty's journals when the phone rang. Not my cell, but the landline."

"Who called?"

Eva pressed her lips together. Her pulse jumped even remembering the threat.

"A man said he'd hurt Marty if he didn't give the man what he wanted."

"Did you recognize his voice? Did he speak with an accent?"

"No. So I say that rules out Andrei."

Griff palmed his moustache. "What if Andrei hired someone to make the call?"

"I thought of that too. But the caller seemed to focus in on Marty."

"Did he say anything else noteworthy?"

Eva's mind replayed the man's words. Then she slugged Griff on the arm.

"You've done it again. He called Marty my grandfather. How did he know I'm his granddaughter?"

"We need to find out. First thing in the morning, I'll check on Andrei with Interpol and take the GPS to the lab. You and I need to create a plan using the device as bait."

"I'll be up all night trying to figure that out."

Eva got out and even though Griff drove off with the GPS, the weight of not getting that van's license number ate at her insides. She returned to their van where Scott handed her a yogurt parfait.

"You need nourishment."

Eva gazed at her husband and wanted to weep. He was such a jewel. Her family meant the world to her. How could she protect them with an unknown enemy getting nearer all the time?

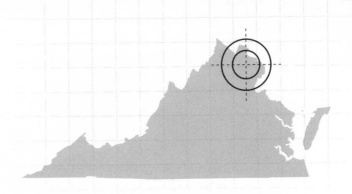

21

BULL RUN, VIRGINIA

It was a few days later when FBI Special Agent Griff Topping drove from the task force building in Manassas. Lydia Neff, the FBI intelligence analyst on the task force, buckled her seat belt while balancing a shoebox and a notepad on her lap.

"Thanks for helping to arrange this caper," Griff said, pulling through the open gate. "I began to think I wouldn't find a place to hide the slippers."

"You know, when my husband and I moved here from Dallas, Eva was the first person to say hello at our new church. She pulled some strings to get me here."

"Looks like Dallas' loss is our gain."

They passed a welcome sign to the historic city of Bull Run, Virginia. He glanced at the address on Lydia's pad and turned the Chevy Impala onto Bethlehem Road.

"What did you find out about the GPS?"

Lydia sighed. "I've never seen one like it. Homeland Security should evaluate the device, but now we're bringing it to the decoy house."

"The slippers are the bait to catch whoever is after Eva. Hey, we beat the Marshals and the ICE tech crew."

Griff eased his Bucar into a driveway. Things looked quiet around the modest home with no cars in the yard … almost too quiet. A crumpled ad hung from the doorknob, telegraphing no one was home.

"We'd better pull that off the door."

"Sure." Lydia looked at her watch. "This is my first assignment for JTTF. I'm learning how the agencies work together. Our FBI lab examined the slipper device, but from here, ICE techs are taking over."

"You've nailed it." Griff shut off the ignition and lowered the window. "Since Eva is with ICE, they want to protect her. The FBI would do the same for me and you."

"I guess she's made enemies in her career."

Griff adjusted his mirror to see approaching cars. "She works high-profile cases, some with me. We've traveled to island hideouts of Middle Eastern terrorists and arrested them. She's cornered Chinese military big-shots."

"Precisely why I'm an analyst." Lydia pushed up her wire-framed glasses. "The Bureau tried convincing me to be a special agent, but this way I support my husband in ministry and am available to raise our kids."

"And hearing of threats against Eva, you're convinced you chose correctly."

"Exactly. Why did someone rig slippers with a GPS and send them to Eva's grandfather?"

Griff tapped the shoebox resting on the seat between them.

"That's why you and I are at this house, to learn more. Eva is careful not to disclose personal info. Yet someone discovered her grandpa is Martin Vander Goes and where he lives. They're betting finding him will lead to Eva."

"Who knew Eva and her family were vacationing with Marty in Michigan?"

"Good question, Lydia. My wife and I did. I should ask Eva who else."

"Griff, it's more than coincidence that I track assets for forfeiture. When I heard you needed a decoy house to appear as Eva's, I thought of this one." Lydia nodded at the ranch-style house in front of them.

"How did you get the Marshal's Service to agree?"

She smiled shyly. "The drug task force arrested a gang using this house to make methamphetamine. I processed the legal claim."

"A meth lab?" Griff pulled out a stick of gum, offering one to Lydia. "This looks more like an older person's home. Plus, it's in a nice neighborhood."

"Weird, huh? A twenty-something woman inherited her grandma's house. Her meth freak friends convinced her to let them cook their illegal stuff in the basement. It's been thoroughly cleaned. We're not in danger going inside."

Griff snorted. "Good!"

"I asked the U.S. Marshal if we could install video surveillance in here until the public auction. He liked the idea so," she snapped her fingers, "voila."

"Lydia, you missed your calling as a special agent." He tapped his watch face. "The tech guys are late."

She swiveled her head around. "Nope. They're here."

Griff and Lydia hopped out and were met by Deputy U.S. Marshal Rod Grainger. Four ICE techs spilled from two black trucks, complete with ladders on top. Cable and high speed Internet logos adorned the side panels. The neighbors shouldn't suspect these were the feds coming to wire the house.

Deputy Grainger grunted, "Hello," inserted a key, and stalked into the house. Griff went back for a bag of assorted items and snatched the ad off the door handle. He lagged behind the techs, while Lydia brought up the rear with her manila folder and the plaid slippers. Boone Dalton assigned tasks to his three techies. Soon all four returned to their trucks. One hauled down ladders and climbed a telephone pole on the property line. Boone went to the basement. Two others sauntered off to the garage.

Griff gazed through pale sheers covering the front window. "Lydia, I hope the folks across the street think they're about to get a new neighbor."

"Well they are, aren't they? Only no one will be here to welcome with cookies."

The two of them got busy arranging the decoy to make it look like Eva's house. After an hour or so, Griff assembled the team in "Eva's" living room, complete with pillows and magazines. Boone held up a computer tablet with four small pictures.

"This is the feed from our surveillance cameras." He pointed to the screen. "See the driveway in this frame. Here you see the open garage door from a camera atop the telephone pole. And we're all in the living room in this one."

Griff surveyed the pictures and nodded his approval.

Meanwhile, Lydia spun around. "I wonder if I can locate the camera."

Even though the screen on the tablet showed her pointing directly at the hidden camera, Griff couldn't spot the actual camera lens.

Boone pulled on latex gloves. "Y'all can give me the slippers now."

"Are you from Georgia, by any chance?" Griff asked, handing over the box.

"Yes, sir. I hail from St. Simons Island, a stone's throw from Brunswick. I miss my sweet tea and fishin' for supper."

"Once we wrap up this caper, I'll be giving your home state my regards when I head down to FLETC."

Boone picked up the mini-device, his eyes widening.

"Sir, this is no cheap commercial transmitter. It's high quality. The battery is disconnected, so it's not transmitting our location. With a battery saver, if it's not moving, the GPS turns on once in a while to transmit the location, then goes dormant."

"It last transmitted at the airport in Grand Rapids, Michigan," Griff said. He hadn't heard of any new problems for Eva since she arrived home. "I'm curious to see how long it takes before someone pokes around here in response to the transmitter."

Boone returned the GPS to the slipper. "Y'all should put these where Gramps would keep 'em."

"Everything looks in order." Deputy Marshal Grainger jangled his keys. "If you don't mind, I want to lock up."

Griff took the hint and motioned Boone to bring his tablet. They hurried to the bedroom. The tablet showed them walking from the living room, with the fourth frame revealing they had entered the bedroom. Griff set the GPS-laden slipper by the bed, making sure the slippers were visible to the camera.

"Okay, we're done."

Boone stopped in the hall. "This data is fed to the JTTF office and monitored twenty-four seven. We have the list of who to notify if anything happens. We start with you, sir, and then Special Agent Montanna, right?"

"Correct."

They packed up, leaving not one iota of evidence to suggest the FBI had ever been there. Deputy Marshal Grainger locked the door while Lydia scooted to Griff's Impala. Griff started the car, but Boone rushed up, holding his computer screen. The image showed them clearly as if a bird watched from its perch above.

"The office will be monitorin' all activity here, sir."

"A stellar job, Boone. Let's quickly trap whoever's after Agent Montanna."

Griff raised the window and roared off, dropping Lydia at the office. He headed for home with doubts nagging at him. He didn't want to let Eva down, but he wondered. Were he and Eva on the right track?

EVA WAS GLAD TO BE BACK IN VIRGINIA. She leaned forward in her chair, talking to Griff on the phone in her makeshift home office.

"The slippers are transmitting as we speak," he said.

Eva fiddled with her keyboard. "I can't wait to snap cuffs on our stalker."

"And I won't rest until he's caught."

"Griff, you're the best. I mean that."

"ICE techs are monitoring round the clock. Just watch your back."

"I always do. Anything new on Andrei?"

"Nope."

"That would be too easy. Say hello to Dawn," Eva said, hanging up.

She casually thumbed through Marty's journal looking for where she'd last left off. Her fingers snagged a folded piece of paper she'd not seen before. The contents of the tattered note surprised Eva.

> *Martin, I've kept quiet too long. I hoped you would work things out between the two of you. As a Christian, you know your duty. You owe my grandson Ricky the money and you should pay him. He is angry. I can no longer defend you. Please make things right.*

Helen Barnes O'Neal

Eva's eyes tore through the note again. It had no date. Helen was Marty's friend and volunteer guide at the windmill in Holland, Michigan. Ricky O'Neal was her grandson, who gave Eva trouble on her childhood visits to Marty's farm. This note revealed something she would never have dreamed. Marty's enemy was from Eva's past: Ricky O'Neal.

This clue drove her with renewed fervor to Marty's journal. His next entry occurred more than one year after Germany invaded Holland. Eva focused her eyes, eager to stop whoever was behind this terrible hoax against her family.

22

JULY 4, 1941 – MIDDLEBURG, NETHERLANDS

It might be Independence Day back in the States, but Martin Vander Goes had nothing to celebrate. Living conditions in occupied Holland were harsh. The German regime was clamping down, just as the British agent, Blake Attwood, had predicted to Martin last year. The sun hadn't risen yet, but Martin had a job to do.

He slipped out of bed fully dressed and went downstairs where he rested a hand on the doorknob. His heart thudded. Aunt Deane was up in the attic with the Rosenbaums and another Jewish family. He decided to boil tea and wait for Deane to come down. Upstairs, she couldn't hear someone knocking on the doors. The special alarm worked only if someone in the house pressed it. Kuipers or his henchmen might burst in and find the Jews living upstairs.

Martin had taken great pains to build a walled-off area where they could hide. He'd also installed the panic button. Despite his precautions, worry for Deane and his friends consumed his mind and kept him awake on most nights. Every Jew had been ordered to move to Amsterdam. Of course, Kuipers erroneously believed the Rosenbaums had already gone to England.

Eli and his parents were careful never to go outside except at night when they could use the facilities in the backyard. Martin had also convinced Rebekah and Yaffa not to register with the authorities. Since they'd come to

Middleburg after the Rotterdam bombing, only Martin and Deane knew they lived with the de Mulders. Well, Simon the fisherman also knew.

Martin heated water on the stove, then poured it into a teapot. With the tea steeping, he took what he needed for his next mission. The back steps started creaking, so Deane must be on her way down from the attic. He could leave now. Stepping outside, he collided against a wall-like chest, crushing his nose.

"Ouch!" Martin fell back. "Why are you lurking by our door?"

Kuipers touched the brim of his high hat. "Where are you going so early?"

"I should be free to leave my own house."

"What are you up to in there? I saw lights moving from the attic to the kitchen."

"Why are you here?" Martin asked, hoping to buy time for Deane and whatever she was doing.

Suddenly he recalled what was under his jacket. Martin fought panic. He hugged his arms to his sides, but his heart raced at being discovered. Bread and pieces of cheese rested inside his flimsy jacket. If they fell out and Kuipers saw the food, all would be over. He and Deane would be hauled off to a prison camp.

"I must talk with Deane." Kuipers' voice echoed in the still morning.

Martin failed to react, which caused the constable to square his shoulders and puff up like a porcupine. Light shining from the kitchen lamp through the open door magnified his forbidding form.

"Are you going to inform her that I am here?"

Kuipers leaned so close that Martin smelled his fishy breath. The foul odor tickled his nose, and he fought the urge to sneeze. Even a twitch of his arms would spell disaster.

"I would like to help, but she's praying as she does every morning at this hour."

"Your aunt's religious dogma is not my concern. I demand to see her."

Martin felt rooted to the doorway. What if Deane had returned to the attic? Kuipers had already spied her lamp. Martin heard a step behind him and cautiously turned.

"What is going on, Martin?" Deane asked.

Kuipers' nostrils flared. "Your nephew refused to find you."

She serenely folded her sweater against her neck. "I am here, as you see."

"Take me to your shop. It is my twentieth wedding anniversary."

Martin clenched his jaw. Kuipers was always sneaking around Deane's jewelry store, asking for special deals. But what could Martin do? If his arms lifted even a fraction, the secreted food would fall out. The risk was great.

In her soft Dutch accent, she told Martin, "Run over as planned and tell Mrs. de Mulder our knitting group meets tomorrow and not this afternoon. I will take Constable Kuipers to select a necklace for his wife."

"This time I want you to give me something extra special," Kuipers spat, his voice hard as nails.

Give me? Martin glared at Deane, trying to read what she was telling him with her eyes. No doubt Kuipers would take a valuable necklace for free. Martin felt a chunk of cheese start to slip. Sweat beaded on his forehead. Deane must have sensed his dilemma because she nestled a hand on his arm and squeezed.

"Go along, Martin."

"Okay, Aunt. But I'll be right back."

He gave Kuipers a warning look and angled past the policeman. He somehow managed to get on his bicycle without spilling the food, but only after Kuipers was safely in the store. Minutes later, Martin knocked at de Mulder's side door, his heart hammering in his chest.

Besides taking bread, he worried about his secret assignment to deliver false identity cards for the Dutch Resistance. Everyone in Holland had to carry an identity card. Several fake ones rested in the bottom of his hollowed-out wooden shoe. Yet it wasn't the danger in delivering the papers that made him fidgety.

Concern over leaving Deane alone with Kuipers battered his mind. The constable was in league with Hitler's men, and wielded absolute power over his Dutch countrymen. Kuipers enforced every harsh rule against Jews. He'd evicted several Jewish families that once lived along the coast and sent them to Germany.

Jews were forbidden to interact with the Dutch, ride the tram, or be seen in public. Martin knocked on de Mulder's door more forcefully. He doubled his fists, wanting to pound sense into Kuipers. Mrs. de Mulder opened the door a fraction.

"Are Yaffa and Rebekah well?" Martin whispered.

She nodded, snatching the bread and cheese. Her eyes were filled with sorrow. Mrs. de Mulder was such a jovial woman who always wore a friendly smile. Not so this morning. Though Martin felt the papers beneath his heavy sock and sweat dripped into his eyes, he had to find out what had happened.

"Deane and I want to know your troubles."

The good lady ushered him inside and shut the door. She wiped her eyes. "Our son has been sent to a concentration camp!"

"We will do what we can to find him."

"Sshh." She shook her head. "Last night, Rebekah and Yaffa went to obtain visas for England. A German soldier questioned them. Reverend Brave, you know who I mean, happened to walk by and convinced the soldier Rebekah and Yaffa are his cousins. They are sobbing upstairs in the mill. My husband says they must leave."

Fear and suspicion swirled in Martin's mind. "Can I see them?"

"I tried reassuring them, but they are young girls, just seventeen, like you."

"We must do something, but Kuipers is at Deane's going through her jewelry."

A look of fear crossed her face. "He comes here looking for bread and ordering my husband to hand over all the flour he can carry away. Martin, go quickly. I put the girls on the third level, near the storage bin."

He left the house, checking for the German sentry guard. Every second's delay meant his false papers might be found. He risked prison or worse. At that moment, the guard's back was turned. Was he lighting a cigarette?

Martin sped to the mill and up the wooden steps. At the third level, he stopped and listened. Hearing nothing but blood pounding in his ears, he whistled a few bars from Beethoven. Rebekah used to play the "Ninth Symphony" on her violin. He heard a sob. Rebekah darted from behind the wooden staircase, holding out her arms.

He took her hands into his. "Mrs. de Mulder told me of your being questioned. You are safe here."

"Not for long." Rebekah dropped her hands. Her dark tresses shivered against her shoulders. "Yaffa and I are frightened out of our wits. We are caged animals. Where can we go?"

"We'll make a plan. I want to see you both safe."

"The de Mulders have been good to us these past months. Isn't that so, Yaffa?"

Yaffa huddled on the stairs, pulling her sweater around her arms. Tears cascaded down her cheeks. "I had a terrifying thought after we were stopped. What if the de Mulders were shot because of us? Rebekah and I believe we should leave."

Rebekah wiped her eyes. Martin's mind buzzed with a question. How could he get them out with the Gestapo watching everyone?

"I promise to talk with my aunt," he said. "First I must tell you something."

He motioned Rebekah closer and gazed into her eyes. His heart ached for the pain he saw in them. He reached out for her hands again.

"Almighty God sees you in this place. You and Yaffa worship Him in different ways than I do, but you must rely on Him to protect you. I had a dream."

Yaffa, ever the mystical one, came over and stood at Martin's right side.

"Tell me of your dream," she urged, drying her tears on her sweater sleeve.

"I harvested wheat, but a fire burned it all. Strong rain saved me and my horse. Then a beautiful rainbow filled the sky. You know the rainbow is God's promise to us on earth."

Yaffa shivered and buttoned her sweater. "Do not speak of God's promises. Why let the Germans invade in the first place?"

"Jehovah's ways are not our ways." Rebekah leaned against the wooden wall. "My mother, rest her soul, always told me so when she lit the candles on the Sabbath. My faith is wavering, yet I thank you for reminding me. I am not alone."

Martin's eyes shifted from Yaffa's scowl to Rebekah's trembling smile. In that moment, something pure flooded his heart. These many months he had a strong desire to protect Rebekah, but this was more—something solid to build a life upon. If this insane war ever ended, he would tell her of his deep feelings for her.

Her dark eyes searched his face, and in that look, he wondered. Did she feel the same heart connection?

Yaffa's whimper burst the magic moment.

He turned his head. "Yaffa, I brought Mrs. de Mulder bread for your breakfast. Let me get Deane's advice on what is to be done."

"Do not leave us here!" Yaffa coughed out a sob. "Kuipers will send us to the camps!"

Martin walked to the steps. He needed to drop off the identity cards.

"Deane is alone with Kuipers," he explained. "I must go for now."

Rebekah clutched at his arm. "Be careful. He is a man to be feared."

"Rebekah, I saw him kill a man for no reason. What do you know?"

"Have you seen his large black automobile?"

"*Ja.*" Martin paused, enjoying her touch. "His Citroen Avant is very expensive."

"The Germans have taken everyone's autos, yet Kuipers keeps his."

Martin knew enough not to trust the chief constable, but he hadn't considered his car.

"You're right, Rebekah. I am always careful around him."

She dropped her hands. "Yesterday, I saw him from the window talking with the Gestapo."

"I must seet to my aunt. Stay here until I return."

Martin trod down the steps, anxiety pumping through his veins. Rebekah would be excellent working alongside him in the Dutch Resistance. But the moment he stepped from the mill, he knew that would never be. Her life was in constant danger of being discovered and sent to a concentration camp.

ON HIS LAST STOP, Martin delivered his false identity cards and hurried home. Kuipers' shiny Citroen sat parked in front of Deane's shop. Feeling every bit her protector, Martin strode into her jewelry store where she was showing Kuipers several necklaces on the counter. He'd taken off his police cap. Sweat glistened on his brow.

"None of these will do." The burly policeman shook his round head.

Deane swiveled on her shoes and returned to the double door safe. Kuipers snuck up behind her. As she reached inside, Martin tried warning her, but his tongue stayed glued to the roof of his mouth.

Kuipers peered in, jabbing a chubby finger. "There! Show me that beauty."

Deane drew out a stunning ruby and diamond necklace. Martin could scarcely believe Kuipers wrapped his grubby hands around their family heirloom.

"My wife must have this necklace."

"I am sorry," Deane said. "It is not for sale."

Kuipers forced his cap on his head. "You will give me this. I offer you no guilders."

"Take it at your own risk." Deane lifted her shoulders.

"Risk? Is it cursed?"

"I do not know. Nor do I know its history. A German SS officer covered with medals brought it here and insisted I store it for him."

Martin stood still. Would Kuipers believe Deane's fib?

"Which SS officer? How did he get such a necklace?"

"He said I didn't need to know his name." Deane glared back. "I assume he plundered the jewels as you intend to do. Perhaps he even killed for it."

Kuipers' pudgy face blanched. Deane remained cool under fire. She gently took the necklace from his fingers and returned it to the safe. Then she set a blue case on the counter.

"I plead with you. Choose this one. It will prove safer for us both."

She popped open the case and stole a glance at Martin. He couldn't read her look. Was she frightened? He finally thought of a way to come to her aid.

"*Tante,* I gave Mrs. de Mulder your message." Martin crossed his arms. "She is baking bread. The constable is to come and retrieve his loaves within the quarter hour."

Kuipers stroked his chin. "Most kind, I am sure. This delicate gold neck-lace will look pretty on my wife. How old is it, did you say?"

"I did not say, but it is valuable. Notice the diamond pendant."

Deane's hand seemed to tremble as she lifted the necklace. Martin thought hard. What did Kuipers have over Deane? He longed to smash his fists into the constable's weak spot, his fat midsection. But Martin realized violence wouldn't keep Kuipers from collaborating with the Nazis.

"My wife will wear this fine piece at the Commissar's dinner party next week," Kuipers boasted. "Wrap it for me."

Deane lifted the gorgeous gold necklace from the blue velvet case and held it up as if saying good-bye. Tears pooled in her eyes. Just as she nestled the piece in its case, a German soldier marched into the shop. His hands rested on a rifle slung over his shoulder.

"Chief Kuipers, you are needed. An unruly group of Christians from the *kerk* are protesting in front of our headquarters. Their signs claim Jews are being shipped to Germany."

Kuipers' hand went to his pistol. "If you leave this shop before I return for my necklace, I will come to your home."

He shot a warning look at Deane before bustling out with the soldier. As they left, Deane seemed to crumple before Martin's eyes.

"Why has Kuipers made you cry?" Martin insisted on knowing.

She steadied herself on the glass counter. "He found out Yaffa and Rebekah are hiding at de Mulders'. He blackmails me for the gold necklace and anything else his hands select."

"He is a terrible fiend. We must help them find a new home."

"I thank God. The church protest may save their lives."

"You should preserve these." Martin handed her the necklaces lying on the counter. "If Kuipers has his way, you will have nothing left to sell. The caretaker from the train station said his parents had many fine art pieces and money in the bank. The Nazis took everything."

Deane locked the necklaces in the safe. So many questions penetrated Martin's mind that he had trouble voicing them. Finally he said, "Kuipers acts like a German who hates his Dutch countrymen. What if he returns for the necklace and you aren't here?"

"Do not worry about me."

Concern for his aunt electrified Martin's mind. "Kuipers is our mortal enemy and controls a large police force. Everything you and I do from now on will be scrutinized by him."

Deane nodded. "We should discuss this turn of events with the Rosenbaums. But I do not know if we can find places for them as well as the girls."

"Where will Rebekah and Yaffa go?"

"You ask too many questions. Ride your bicycle to the drop-off place for your underground newspaper. Tell your contact to reach our Amsterdam clockmakers. We need instructions for where to hide the girls tonight."

Martin doubted her plan would work. "Why trust those Amsterdam people?"

"Beatrice has been my friend since school days. Her father made the clock in the pantry. They are part of what you and I are doing. For your protection, I say nothing more."

"All right. Did Kuipers hint the Rosenbaums aren't in England, but in our attic?"

"No. We must be careful in finding hiding places for Rebekah and Yaffa. Be quick."

Martin strode to the door, but then turned to tell her of his idea.

"Aunt, if nothing else is arranged, Simon could hide them in his boat."

Deane drew in a deep breath. "*Ja*, he is our safety net."

Martin left the shop. He made sure Kuipers wasn't prowling nearby before jumping on his bike. He pedaled to the market where he bought a pound of potatoes. These he stowed in his wire basket. If stopped, he would say he was taking the produce to someone.

Then he pumped his bicycle to the far edge of town. He passed along their need: immediate and safe houses for two Jewish girls. He rode around aimlessly for thirty minutes, his heart in his throat. Then he returned to the older man, his contact in the Dutch Resistance.

"Your friends must go tonight," he told Martin, handing him a piece of paper.

Martin memorized the details and gave the paper back. The man lit a match. The scrap of paper burned in seconds. Then his contact handed Martin a bundle.

"You are smart to have potatoes. Put them on top of this, your dress for tonight."

Martin did as instructed. With the destinations firmly in his mind, he wheeled home with the potatoes hiding a secret. What other deception would he have to engage in to get Rebekah and Yaffa to safety?

23

Darkness fell quickly. Martin left the mill wearing a police uniform. The Dutch Resistance had gotten his costume from an officer who detested Kuipers and the Nazis. Martin slung the cloth bag concealing a fisherman's jacket and cap over his shoulder. He would change clothes when he reached Simon's rowboat.

Rebekah folded her sweater and placed it in his sack. They walked side-by-side to sounds of crickets. Anxiety rubbed against Martin's every thought. Despite his worry, he noticed Rebekah's pretty print dress and hat. Deane had given her a new outfit, so she'd look like a young lady spending time with her beau. But this outing was no date with his sweetheart. They faced terrible danger if stopped by the Dutch police and questioned.

"Curfew begins at ten o'clock," he cautioned. "We have less than thirty minutes to reach Simon's boat."

She laid a hand on his arm. "You look so official in your police uniform. No soldier will stop us."

"Keep walking, even if someone passes, okay?"

"Whatever you tell me to do, I will do it. I trust you, Martin."

His heart swelled. He placed his hand over hers. The air felt thick with moisture, as if buckets of rain would fall on their heads at any moment. They walked on, with Martin preparing for the worst. The slight pressure of Rebekah's hand reinforced his charge to protect her, to see her safely to Simon's boat and then up the canal.

She let out a tortured groan. "Clouds hide the stars, but I know they are there. Papa taught me about constellations. He and I gazed at the Big Dipper, trying to find the northern star."

"I miss my father too, but I need to tell you something."

As if she hadn't heard, Rebekah talked on about her father and about the stars. She had no clue of the strain pushing against Martin's ribs.

"Papa was a wonderful doctor. He loved science and knew Yaffa's father." She pulled her hand away from his arm. "Until the Germans killed them both!"

"Keep your voice down," he ordered. "I'm sorry for everything, but please listen. We may not see each other for a long time."

A vivid light swept across them, casting their long shadows on the ground. "*Aufhalten!*" a man commanded.

The thunder of running footsteps preceded another command, "*Stoppen!*"

Martin froze in his tracks. So did Rebekah. Bright light formed their silhouettes on the muddy ground next to the path. Martin's eyes followed the beam, which came from across the canal. The spotlight drifted off, leaving them in the dark. Then the beam swept across the water, closing in on a man running along the opposite bank of the canal.

"*Halt!*"

Heavy footsteps sounded from beyond the light. A barrage of gunfire flashed, followed by a single bang. To Martin's horror, the fleeing man fell into a heap. German soldiers ran and circled around his body.

Martin pulled Rebekah's arm and drew her close to his side. They walked briskly in the darkness.

"At first I thought they'd seen us," he said, feeling relieved.

"They are across the canal and cannot reach us. Why did they chase him?"

He glanced over his shoulder into the darkness, his hearing acute for the slightest sound. "Perhaps because they are monsters. Hurry before a patrol reaches this shore."

"So we must outwit them," Rebekah replied, quickening her pace.

"With God's help, we shall."

The next few minutes seemed like an eternity. Martin scanned the path ahead and the water below. His heart beat wildly.

"Where is Simon's boat? It should be tied along the canal."

Then he heard, *blub, blub, blub.*

Martin grabbed her arm and strained to hear. Rebekah stood completely still. The low rumble of a motor left no doubt.

"A German patrol boat!" he hissed.

Light swept along the bank far ahead. The boat was motoring their way. Remembering the running man who had just been shot, Martin resisted the urge to flee. His eyes searched the canal wall ahead. Low, tied in the shadows along the canal, he saw a small vessel.

"I see it!" He tugged on her arm and hurried toward the boat.

The German boat came nearer.

"Sit on the wall," Martin ordered. "I will hold your hand and help you down."

Rebekah complied and Martin eased her into Simon's boat. As arranged, the Dutch fisherman was nowhere around.

"Scurry to the front and lie flat on the bottom," Martin said. Then he scrambled down the canal wall and stepped into the boat. The roar of the patrol boat grew louder.

"Keep very quiet," he whispered.

Simon's boat rose suddenly, being pushed upward by a giant wave from the patrol boat. Intense light streamed across the wall, blinding Martin. He slammed his eyes shut. Then he opened them to check if they could be seen.

Waves battered their small craft, ramming it against the wall. Martin peered up from his crouched position on the boat's floor. At least he didn't detect their shadows. Engine sounds bounced off the canal wall. German voices mixed with the acrid smell of cigarette smoke. The patrol was coming too close.

He held his breath. Would the Germans storm their boat and take them prisoner?

Then an amazing thing happened. The engine noise began to subside. Just when Martin thought it was safe to speak, another dazzling light swept across the top of their hiding place. He ducked, bending his body into a ball. He sensed Rebekah also wasn't moving.

Minutes passed. Noise from the patrol eventually disappeared down the canal.

In total darkness, he whispered to Rebekah, "It's okay to sit, but stay on the floor."

"Is the threat over?"

"We need to get out of here." He stripped off the police hat and jacket.

After shoving his old outfit in the bag, he donned a fisherman's coat and cap. Then he fastened the oars in place. It took great effort to lower them into the water without making a sound. Martin strained to untie the lines. Then his strong arms pulled on the oars and propelled the boat forward.

He aimed for a spot where he'd cross an intersecting canal. Wilderness lay beyond. Another patrol boat could descend on them at any moment. The rhythm of dunking in the oars and pulling against them fueled his desire to save Rebekah from harm. He pulled with great strength and the boat burst through the water.

Martin tipped forward, seeking Rebekah's dark and quiet face. Again, he leaned back and rowed with all his heart. Thoughts of Kuipers' hateful quest to drive all Jews from the Netherlands lit his mind with a fury. The constable meant trouble and Martin did the only thing he could do: He rowed with gusto.

With each stroke, Rebekah's presence gave him incentive to keep going. Rebekah's gasp broke the silence.

"Listen!" she urged.

Martin stopped the oars a fraction above the water. At familiar sounds of a German patrol boat, his heart collided against his ribs. He checked over his shoulder. There, ahead of their little boat, lay the intersection of another canal. Was the patrol boat in that canal? He dropped the oars into the water and pulled again and again. The boat skimmed into the middle of the crossing canals.

Then Martin saw it.

The German boat bore down on them, its searchlights flashing along the canal walls. Had Kuipers alerted the patrol to track them down? Martin strained against the oars, determined to beat his enemy. They glided through the intersection into the darkness.

Rebekah rubbed her arms. "They came so close. Do you think they saw us?"

"No."

He didn't tell her that soon the patrol would reach the same intersection, its searchlight piercing the night, shining directly upon them. He rowed feverishly, the oars making noise as they splashed into the water. Sweat trickling down his forehead burned his eyes. He wiped his sleeve across them to clear the blurring.

"I see a ramp." Rebekah pointed toward the wall.

Martin glanced over his left shoulder and spotted the dock where a Dutch Resistance contact would meet them. He pulled hard on the right oar, and steered the bow toward an opening in a stone wall. That same moment, the patrol boat reached the intersection. Martin's heart flipped.

But then the German boat turned into the canal, motoring away from Martin and Rebekah. The searchlight beamed across the water and swept behind Martin's boat just as they slid into the ramp's opening.

"We made it."

"Oh, Martin, what will happen to me?" Rebekah's voice quivered.

"I will help you out of the boat."

He was sure she meant something else, but Martin didn't want to talk while on the water. Sweat kept dripping in his eyes, but he had no time to wipe them. He silently lowered the oars. Using all his strength, he rowed up to the ramp. He hopped from the boat, and yanking it forcefully, he mustered enough strength to inch it up the ramp.

Rebekah leaned on his hand and stepped out. The boat rocked with her shifting weight, and she stumbled, falling into Martin's arms. He relished the fleeting touch of her hair brushing against his face. Danger swirled around them, forcing his senses to high alert. He helped her stand and guided her toward a path paralleling the canal wall.

"We have a problem." He spoke in a hushed voice. "We must walk the same way the patrol boat just came from."

"I will be very quiet."

Her soft voice stirred his protective instincts. What a dear woman she was and Martin was forced to leave her in the care of another. His mind tumbled.

"Wait," he said, spinning around.

Martin ran to the boat and took her sweater from the bag with his crumpled police uniform. Back on the path, he draped the garment over her shoulders.

Rebekah clung to his arm. "Where am I going?"

"Our contacts assure me that you will be safe."

"I was in Amsterdam once, and do not want to live there. That is where all Dutch Jews must go."

She shivered and sounded so frightened. He wanted to comfort her, but the future wasn't in his hands. If only he could whisk her to his farm in Michigan. Of course, that was impossible unless he smuggled her aboard a freighter. America wasn't letting in Jewish refugees.

Rebekah clutched the sweater. He tried seeing her eyes, but it was too dark. Martin had to lighten her burden.

"Rebekah, you might work at Veenstra's Tulip Farm as their niece. They all have brown eyes and hair. That is why we chose them."

"Thank you for telling me, Martin. It sounds like I will be with a family. I am thankful not to be sent to Westerbork Refugee Camp."

"You won't be taken there. That camp is for German Jews. You are Dutch."

"*Ja.* Hitler declared all German Jews to be stateless. What about Yaffa?"

Rebekah's hand trembled on Martin's arm as he led her along the path.

"At this moment, Deane takes her to a farm in the countryside."

A noise from the weeds startled Martin. He spun around, forcing Rebekah's hand from his arm.

"Come with me," he urged, rushing her toward a low shrub.

A booming voice rang out in the darkness, *"Aufhalten!"*

Martin stopped and Rebakah bumped into him. Sounds of leather boots crushing gravel drew near. The silhouette of a German soldier came into view.

He strode up to them, demanding in excellent Dutch, "Who are you? Where do you go?"

Rebekah seized Martin's arm. He tensed.

"Sir, I am Martin Vander Goes. We are courting."

The soldier stepped very close. "Are you American?"

"Yes, sir," Martin answered, trying to sound deferential, hoping the soldier would leave.

"You are late. I waited a long time. I take her from here."

Relief flooded Martin, but Rebekah's grip tightened. Her sweater slipped to the ground. He held her up and again put the sweater around her shoulders.

"You scared me," Martin said. "I thought you were a German soldier."

"It is safer this way. Come with me; we must hurry."

Rebekah faced Martin. "Thank you so much. I hope to see you again. Be very careful."

She kissed his cheek lightly and turned away. The sight of his innocent friend walking into the gloom with a German soldier pained Martin. But what could he do? He knew the contact was a Dutchman and part of the Resistance, so he had to trust all would be well.

Martin returned to the boat, giving a final look where she had disappeared. He pushed the boat down the ramp and hopped in. Gripping the oars, apprehension over being stopped by the German patrol boat replaced his worry for Rebekah, for the moment.

He started rowing, keeping a constant watch for the German patrol, her bravery piercing his soul. The trip back to Simon's dock was exhausting and Martin couldn't help wondering if he'd ever see Rebekah again.

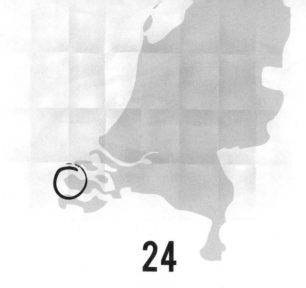

24

A MONTH LATER, MIDDLEBURG, THE NETHERLANDS

The first day of August dawned hot and sultry. Martin stared out the open window from his upstairs bedroom in Deane's house. A German barge streamed by, forcing his mind back to the terror of that night he'd evaded the patrol. Sweat beaded on his forehead in spite of cool air from the open window. He recalled rowing Rebekah in Simon's small boat and delivering her to that faux soldier up the canal.

A month since his secret journey had dragged by. Martin received no comfort from assurances by his Resistance contact. He didn't doubt the man who received Rebekah was a good Dutchman helping Jews find sanctuary in safe homes. The problem was Martin had learned nothing of her whereabouts. Why were his prayers going unanswered?

Desperate for news, he shut the window and went to find Deane. She stood at the stove, dressed neatly as usual, stirring a pot. She wore her hair pulled in a bun behind her head.

"Are you making soup?" he asked to the rumble of his stomach.

Deane tapped the spoon on the pot's edge. "I wanted to make something for you to look forward to."

"That is hard to find these days." He gave his shoulders a fierce shrug.

"Why do you look so unhappy?"

"I have lost my way. What of Rebekah? Or Yaffa? There's been no word if she made it to the dairy farm."

Deane handed him the spoon. "Stir this. My mother always said, 'Deane, a watched pot never boils.'"

"So the soup must boil before we can eat?"

"Yes, but Martin, listen to me." Deane gazed at him tenderly. "What I mean is you will find out in God's time. You have done all you can."

"It is hard waiting on the Lord sometimes."

"*Ja.* Tell that to Simon."

What did she mean? Martin stirred the hot liquid made of vegetables, wanting to ask her, but she went to the bread cupboard for a loaf of rye bread.

When she returned, he asked, "What does Simon have to do with Rebekah? Has something happened to him since I used his boat?"

Deane smiled at him as if he was a two-year-old whose mother had left him alone.

"Simon is fine. He and I have been friends since we were ten years old. When I turned seventeen, he asked me to marry him."

Martin's eyes widened. "I never knew that you and he ... ah ... were in love. He always asks if you are well. Why didn't you marry him?"

"Papa, your grandfather, wanted us to wait until Simon found a steadier occupation. He fished, you see, and still does. Papa wanted him in the jewelry business, but that was too confining for Simon. Anyway, that is over and done with. We stay good friends."

"Why not marry him now? Your papa is in heaven."

Deane snatched back the spoon. "My, this aroma is making me hungry."

"Why not marry Simon, Aunt Deane?"

"Because, my dear boy, he never asked me again. His pride was hurt."

"So you lost happiness because he is too proud to ask again?"

"Even though it is daytime, please close the curtains, Martin." Her cheeks blushing, Deane reached for the bowls. "I do not want our guests being seen. I will set the table. You go and bring everyone down."

Martin hastened up the stairs with a new question. Did Deane mention Simon's marriage proposal because she wanted Martin to speak to him about it? The way she'd opened up over the soup pot seemed so unusual for her. Perhaps she simply wanted Martin to understand the twists and turns of being in love.

Well, in the middle of the German occupation, he couldn't ask Rebekah to come out of hiding and marry him. He reached the top of the stairs and decided: As soon as the British beat the Germans, he would ask her to become his wife.

His mind made up, Martin climbed the narrow stairs winding past the chimney with renewed vigor. He found Eli sitting under the rafters by a tiny window, reading a book. His parents were chatting as they folded clothes. Mrs. Wexler knitted socks. Mr. Wexler tuned his violin. He had been let go from the bank in a nearby town because he was Jewish. The elderly couple had joined the house a week ago.

"Deane has made delicious vegetable soup," Martin said, smiling. "Please join us."

"I am starved." Eli closed his book. "Thanks be to God for food."

Everyone else rose saying, "Thanks be to God."

They followed Martin down the twisting stairs to the kitchen. He sliced bread and asked the blessing. Deane served hot, steaming soup into bowls. As she placed Martin's by his elbow, their telephone rang once. The ringing stopped, and rang twice more. Martin jumped up to answer.

His heart pounded as he listened to the female voice on the other end. "This is Veenstra's Tulip Farm. Tell Deane the rudbeckia plant she left here is thriving."

Before Martin fired off a single question, the phone line died in his ear. The caller had hung up. He returned to the table where Deane held her spoon in midair.

"Well?" Her eyebrows lifted a fraction.

Martin grinned nervously and repeated the message word for word. She ladled soup into the seventh bowl. Then Deane started humming a hymn that sounded like "Amazing Grace."

He stored in his heart the good news. Rebekah was alive and well at Veenstra's Tulip Farm. Martin ate his soup, and the evening flew by. He wrote an article for the underground paper criticizing Dr. Seyss-Inquart and the Dutch National Socialist Party. The regime, which ruled from the Hague, was nothing but an evil puppet for Hitler.

Martin pulled on his cap and bicycled with his completed article to the undertaker's home. Lucy Oostenberg let him in. She shut the door and picked up a paper bag.

"Are you going out?" Martin removed his cap. "Is your father home?"

"He is out back, but I will call him."

Lucy left Martin to wait by the door, her large Dutch skirt swaying as she walked away. He took something from beneath his shirt, and when Mr. Oostenberg hustled in, Martin smoothed a sheet of paper.

"I wrote this, encouraging our citizens to stand up for what is right."

The undertaker wiped his brow. "We must stay vigilant. I overheard

Kuipers tell a policeman his officers should spare no effort in stopping any-one who frustrates the Nazis."

"You're not thinking of closing down the paper?" Martin asked with concern.

"Not at present. Our press works night and day."

With a curt nod, Mr. Oostenberg snatched Martin's article and left the room.

Lucy opened the front door. "Father is afraid to have you and others coming to our home. In the future, drop your articles in a hiding spot. I will show you where."

She led him a block away, to a bombed-out dwelling. In a shattered ves-tibule, she opened a small rusted door.

"Leave them here, where the milkman used to deliver bottles. I will check each night."

"The Nazis are cracking down. We can't be too careful," he replied, turn-ing to leave.

She stopped him. "Martin, make sure no one sees you drop them."

"You and your father have nothing to fear from me."

He watched her walk away, her skirt swinging in the breeze. Martin jumped on his bike, grateful that even though there were many Dutch col-laborators, there were those like Lucy, brave Dutch citizens. Minutes later, he kept watch by Deane's front window, gazing out toward the canal. Locals rode past on rickety bikes. An occasional Dutch constable shot by on a mo-torcycle. Life went on, yet nothing was normal.

Food was scarce. Dutch men were rounded up to work in factories in Germany. Each sunrise brought some new deprivation, especially for Jews. They couldn't own businesses or mingle with non-Jews. Jewish mothers aban-doned their babies on doorsteps of Christians, who gladly cared for the in-fants. But the Germans foiled the Christians too, by threatening to imprison any Netherlanders who took in Jewish babies.

So to protect their Jewish "family" upstairs, each night Martin stayed at the window, to watch, listen, and learn. He could observe anyone approach-ing the house from the canal. He kept his vigil for another thirty minutes and then his eyes felt strained. Night was setting in.

A knock brought him to the kitchen. At the second knock, he peered out the back window. Mr. Grossman, the Jewish butcher, stood on the stoop with his wife.

Deane came in, wringing her hands. "Did I hear the coded knock?"

"It's the butcher and his wife."

With alacrity, she opened the door slightly, but Mr. Grossman squeezed through. His wife carried a satchel.

"Pardon our intrusion. Is it safe for us to enter?"

Deane stepped aside and quickly closed the door behind them. "What has happened?"

"My wife and I have been packed for weeks in such a case. You see, we received a summons to take the train to Amsterdam. We never went. Tonight, the police burst into our meat shop. You know we live in back. We fled into the alley and ran here."

Mrs. Grossman wept in her handkerchief. Deane took her by the arm to a chair.

Mr. Grossman seemed to sag before Martin's eyes.

"Where can we go? The SS is on our heels."

"Our daughter!" Mrs. Grossman shrieked. "She practices her flute at the Center."

It took Deane some minutes to cajole the couple to admit the whole story. And then his aunt flashed Martin a penetrating look. "Do you know Adele Grossman?"

"Yes, she helped her father in his meat shop."

"Take the delivery truck to the Center and bring her here. Be sure to park the truck in the alley."

Martin's hand flew to the doorknob, but he hesitated. "Curfew falls in a few minutes."

"Oh, yes," Deane said softly. "Take this pretty scarf for her head."

He grabbed the scarf Deane used on cold mornings and went out into the nearly dark alley. The printing on the black delivery truck had been changed from *Rosenbaum's Goods* to *Vander Goes' Jewelry and Clocks*. Martin was about to roll down the alley when Mr. Grossman opened the passenger door.

"I go along to get my daughter."

Martin was torn. If they were stopped …

"All right, but ride in the back."

While still in the alley, Mr. Grossman changed places. Martin shifted into first gear and released the clutch. He drove slowly to the street. His headlights swept across a German Army detachment. A soldier with his cigarette hanging from his lips lurched in front of Martin. He flashed the palm of his open hand facing the truck.

Martin jammed on the brakes.

Mr. Grossman whispered, "Are we caught?"

"Sshh!"

Martin lowered the window.

The soldier peered in. "Your headlamps are on. Do you know the directive?"

"I'm sorry, I forgot," Martin stammered.

"Your papers!" the soldier ordered. "I must see your papers."

Martin handed a form that Deane had prepared.

"You are American. Why are you here?"

"I visit my aunt, the jeweler. The war prevents me from returning to the States."

A second soldier rushed from the dark shadows and walked alongside the truck with a scowl. This taller soldier approached the driver's door.

"What are you doing at nighttime in this truck?"

Martin heard a choking sound from the rear. Sweat pooled under his arms. He flung his hand out the open window and tapped the lettering. "This belongs to my aunt for her shop. I'm supposed to take measurements for an old grandfather clock."

The soldier handed Martin his paper and waved him forward. "Remember. No lights. Curfew begins in five minutes. Get off the street."

Martin released the clutch and proceeded forward, this time with no lights. To his dismay, Mr. Grossman kept up a running banter in the back.

"Turn at the intersection and drive by my house. What if they already have Adele?"

"I will chance it, but only for a moment. Then we drive straight to the Center."

In another half-mile, Martin cranked a turn toward Grossman's butcher shop. He stopped and the butcher crawled up behind the driver's seat. He snorted loudly.

"Be quiet. Do you want us arrested? You heard the soldier. Curfew will begin."

A terrible scene unfolded before Martin's eyes. Next to the Grossman's shop and home, German soldiers held torches. Men in black coats herded people into the back of a military truck.

Mr. Grossman moaned. "Oh! They are from our synagogue. I gave them refuge in my home. Our synagogue is covered with Nazi swastikas. They are taking my chair."

Martin thrust the van into reverse. Soldiers hauled furniture from the Grossman's home behind his shop, and shoved their goods into a second truck. Martin backed down the street and crept along without his lights. Though sobbing, Grossman directed him to the Center, where the town's orchestra rehearsed.

"Stay in the truck," Martin whispered.

He shut the door and barreled into the Center. Adele snapped her flute case shut.

"Come quickly," Martin told her. "Your father is in my truck."

"Why should I believe you?"

"You know me. I am Martin, Deane's nephew. The police raided your house, and your parents escaped to ours. Put on Deane's scarf, and let's go."

Adele squeezed her arms into a coat too small for her, but she wouldn't wear the scarf.

"Listen, I want the police to think you are my aunt. It's curfew, so leave quickly."

The teenager rolled her eyes. She set the scarf on her head, the ends fluttering as they walked outside. Martin helped her into the rear of the delivery truck where Adele started scolding her father. Martin closed the door quietly, hoping her voice hadn't already carried down the street.

He drove to Deane's using the alley from the opposite end to avoid a repeat encounter with the soldiers. After nudging the truck alongside her house, he hurried out. His coded knocks prompted Deane to open the rear door. Martin pointed at the truck and rushed to get the Grossmans. In seconds, they slipped into the kitchen behind him.

"You found my daughter!" Mrs. Grossman cried.

Martin held a finger to his lips. "German soldiers are sacking your butcher shop. They're loading Jewish families into a truck. At least Adele is safe."

But Adele didn't seem grateful to be rescued.

"I will never be taken," she boldly proclaimed, holding her flute case.

Deane flinched. "My dear, speak softly while you are in this house. I will not have you putting us in danger."

"My daughter, listen to your elders and start obeying." Mrs. Grossman dabbed her eyes at the kitchen table.

Adele had no idea of cooperating.

"No," she said pouting. "We must stop the Nazis before they slaughter every Jew on earth."

"How do you propose doing that if you are shot?" Deane asked.

She glared so intently at the teen that Martin did a double take. He'd never heard Deane speak harshly to any of their guests. Adele pushed out her bottom lip.

Martin nudged Deane to the parlor, where he whispered in her ear, "I don't trust her. Letting them stay is putting the Rosenbaums and Wexlers at risk."

"Tonight they remain." Deane clasped her hands. "We cannot throw them out after curfew. They can stay in my room."

"Where will you sleep?"

She motioned behind her. "In the chair. Say nothing to the Grossmans about others living here."

"Aunt Deane, I'll keep watch down here tonight. You take my room."

She agreed and they returned to the kitchen with doubt ringing in Martin's ears.

Mr. Grossman announced, "Adele has something to say."

The girl's cheeks reddened as she murmured, "Sorry to sound difficult. I am afraid of strangers. It is my way."

"Be more careful in future." Deane lifted her chin. "You may all sleep in my room. It may be crowded, but come morning, we will sort out what is to be done."

Martin pointed to the end of the alley. "Keep the lights dim. Soldiers are patrolling the side street. They demanded my papers but let me go."

"Be quiet going upstairs," Deane cautioned.

She led the way while Martin checked the curtains for any unwanted cracks. A few minutes later, Deane emerged from the stairwell. Her wide eyes betrayed her concern.

"At dawn, ride and tell de Mulder the Gestapo raided Mr. Grossman's shop." She spoke with authority. "Our miller must set the sails on the windmill to warn others of the danger."

"Yes, I agree. We are in peril, from Adele."

Martin picked up the lamp, desiring nothing more than to throw the flute-playing troublemaker out onto the street.

25

The next two weeks ground along, with Martin in a state of worry over the Grossmans living in the house. The Rosenbaums and Wexlers had insisted they were welcome, so three families, eight in total, all squeezed into the attic. Thursday morning, Martin hiked the stairs with bread and cheese for their breakfast. Eli rushed to meet him.

"She has done it, Martin. Her parents will never tell you. They like it here."

"What has Adele done now?" Anger surged through Martin. "Yesterday, she and Mr. Wexler argued over her playing Bach on her flute while he practiced Beethoven on his violin. I have a mind to hide both instruments."

"It is worse. She left, taking her flute."

"Adele is gone? She's wanted by the Germans. If caught, she'll lead the occupiers here. Where did she go?"

Eli shook his head violently. "Ten minutes ago, she snuck out. I think she is going to play with the youth orchestra. She is the first chair for flutes. I saw her putting on her hat, and I tried stopping her. She will not be denied her chance to be a great musician."

Martin struggled to control his surging emotions. He handed Eli the food. "Eat your breakfast, but say nothing to the others just yet. I will bring her back."

Once back downstairs, Martin told Deane of his quest to find the errant daughter.

"Take the truck," she said, narrowing her eyes. "This is a serious breach."

"Her parents have spoiled her for too long. She is beyond amending."

Martin grabbed his cap and shot into the delivery truck. He drove the streets deliberately, fury pummeling his chest. He cast a sideways glance down a side street. There strode a young woman, wearing a purple flowered dress and black hat.

He turned the corner and parked alongside the curb. A couple of elderly Dutch women walked by and smiled. He knew them and waved. Adele walked toward the Center, swinging her flute case. Martin crossed the street just as the deputy constable roared by on his motorcycle.

As if Adele was his wild and petulant younger sister, Martin looped his arm around her free one, telling her in a firm voice, "Come with me."

"Leave me alone," she flung back at him, tossing her head.

Martin tightened his grip on her arm.

"Make a scene, and you'll be sorry. Kuipers' deputy just went by. He might've seen you."

"I do not care if he did. We must fight back. Do you know the Germans have forbidden all Jewish children to attend school? I refuse to be shut away in that hot attic."

"Don't you care for your parents? I refuse to debate with you on the sidewalk."

The deputy's motorcycle careened around the corner, heading straight for them. Adele pulled away her arm. The motorcycle passed by, but Martin couldn't see if the constable turned his head. Maybe they'd get away this time.

"Get in the truck," he ordered.

She angled away from him, so he walked to the truck, glancing over his shoulder. He saw her following, muttering all the way. Her brazen nature drove him mad. He opened the passenger door, whispering for her to scramble to the back. She did, but reluctantly. Martin shut her in and drove straight home.

As they entered the alley, he said, "You have fortitude, I give you that much. Being strong-willed is laudable, but war is no place for stupidity."

She edged closer toward the front.

"You dare call me stupid. My parents scrimped and saved so I could be taught by the greatest masters. I will take my rightful place in the National Orchestra of the Netherlands!"

What Deane had told him recently about Simon's youthful pride pricked Martin's conscience. Adele was veering down the same rocky path. The Bible said something about haughty pride going before a fall, but Martin was too upset to recall the exact verse. Adele wouldn't care anyway.

There was only one way to deal with this unruly teenager, and he would do it. He used coded knocks on Deane's back door, and then scurried to open the truck's delivery door. He grabbed the puffed-up Adele and pulled her by the hand inside to the parlor.

To her mother who sat weeping on the sofa, Martin said, "So you discovered your daughter defied orders to stay in the house and not be seen."

Mrs. Grossman flew to her daughter and hugged her.

"Mama, do not treat me like a child." Adele pushed her mother away.

Martin yanked Adele's arm and put her in a chair. He spun around, facing Mrs. Grossman and Deane.

"She was sauntering down the avenue with her flute. She wants to play music with her friends."

Deane's hands flew to her face. "No! Everyone thinks the Grossmans left the country."

"Exactly," Martin replied. "If they're found here, the Wexlers and Rosenbaums will be exposed. That is unacceptable."

His eyes flashed heat at Adele. "You could've gotten your parents and all of us arrested. You have no regard for others. You are selfish."

Mrs. Grossman lifted her hands to her daughter's round face. "She is young and—"

"Sit down and quit defending her," Martin barked.

He shook a finger at Adele, his voice icy cold. "Leave this house again, and I will shoot you. I will also shoot your parents. You will not get us all killed or imprisoned."

Deane breathed in sharply, but didn't correct him. This was war.

Adele's father hurried in.

"What is happening?" He blinked his eyes rapidly.

Martin told him everything, adding, "I informed Adele that if she does something so dangerous again I will shoot her and you. Of course, I don't want to, but you must control her. Others' lives are at stake. If she leaves and is questioned, everyone in this house is as good as dead."

Mr. Grossman collapsed in a chair. "Will you give us another chance?"

"What do you think, Aunt?" Martin asked.

Deane gazed at Martin and then the Grossmans. Because she hesitated, Martin decided for her.

"Adele, you and your family have one more chance. It is a matter of life and death."

He glared at her, willing the obstinate girl to contradict him. The hard glint in her eyes made him doubt. Perhaps he would regret showing her mercy after all.

26

DECEMBER 7, 1941 – MIDDELBURG, THE NETHERLANDS

With God's refugees hidden in the upper attic, Martin listened to music on the BBC with the volume low. He didn't want the neighbors to know they still had a radio. Deane perched on a side chair knitting a scarf. She looked tired. Light snow fell outside the window.

"Word is Germany abandons its fight for Moscow," he told his aunt.

She stopped her needles. "This could be a turning point. What else have you heard?"

"The Soviet Union is launching a major offensive to repel German troops. Oh, and Mr. Wexler asked to speak to me today."

"Oh?" Her fingers smoothed the knitted scarf on her lap.

"Yes. He confided Adele is hiding bread behind some books."

Deane's eyes clouded.

"What are we to do with that ungrateful child? She is not carrying it away from the table, so she must steal it from the kitchen. She will cause bugs or mice."

Martin picked up the earphones for the crystal radio. "I told Mr. Wexler the next time there's a problem, he should organize a meeting of the attic community and hold a tribunal with Adele at the center."

"What would come of that?"

"I don't know." Martin dropped the earphones over the top of his head. "They live together and share the same faith. Let them work it out."

Ads from the radio filled Martin's ears, when the announcer interrupted, "Many feel the United States will now enter the war against Germany, as well as Japan."

Martin looked at Deane, whose fingers were once again flying with her knitting.

"We repeat: Japan launched a massive air assault on the U.S. Naval base at Pearl Harbor in Hawaii. Initial reports claim heavy loss of ships and lives. Millions of people and the nations around the world await President Roosevelt's reaction."

Martin snatched the earphones from his head. He jumped to his feet.

"Aunt Deane! Japan bombed our Navy base in Hawaii. Lots of people died."

She dropped her knitting to the floor and came over to him, thrusting her hands on his shoulders. "God cannot be pleased. What is happening to this world?"

"I'll stay with you," he insisted. "You need my protection."

A loud rap on the back door startled them both. There was a pause, then a second knock. Martin sped to the kitchen and opened the door. Deane followed behind. Simon beckoned from the alley for Martin to come out.

"I'll see what he wants," Martin said.

"Be careful. It is past curfew."

Martin pulled the door closed behind him, his heart pounding.

Simon pulled him close, hissing in his ear, "America is at war with Japan."

"I just heard over the crystal radio."

"You must leave, before it is too late."

"Do you mean because Japan is Germany's ally?"

"It is more complex," Simon said. "Once America fights Germany, you will be arrested as a spy and sent to a German prison. I will smuggle you out on my boat. We need to make immediate arrangements."

Martin jammed his hands into his pockets, his mind a jumble. He'd wanted to fight the Germans for the British, but Deane had convinced him it would be too dangerous. Now he had his important work for the Resistance.

"I appreciate your concern, but Deane can't do without me."

Simon waved in the darkness. "Nah. Deane has survived for years since her father passed. She is a strong woman. She'll be all right."

"No." Martin shook his head. "She has more responsibility every day."

"Oh, you mean the Jews she hides."

Martin was surprised to hear Simon say aloud what could get them killed. "Yes, my aunt and I have other work."

Simon paused. "That is true, but listen. With America at war against Japan, the German soldiers in town will come for you. In days, Hitler will declare war against Roosevelt."

Martin's mind veered in a dozen directions. Simon made sense, but to leave his aunt alone in time of war seemed unthinkable.

"Simon, you move in here and help Deane."

"You suggest such a thing? That would not be proper. Deane is a respected single woman. I am a single man."

"Deane often tells me how much she respects you. Once you wanted to marry her."

"That was long ago. She said no."

Martin tugged on Simon's sleeve. "Now you listen. She was young and immature. Her father influenced her. She never married. Why? If you ask me, she pines for you."

"You speak nonsense, boy." Simon wrenched his arm away.

"Have you ever asked her again?"

"Nah." Simon pulled down the bill of his cap. "She is not the marrying kind."

Martin stepped closer. "I'd consider leaving if Deane has someone to look after her."

"She is a strong woman, I tell you."

"Thanks for offering to help me escape." Martin shook Simon's hand. "I will think and pray about it."

He went back in the house, unsure what to do. He would tell Deane about Simon's warning, leaving out their discussion of her future.

EARLY THE NEXT MORNING, MARTIN invited Simon into the kitchen where the fisherman stood tall, twisting his cap in his hands.

"Has something happened?" Martin asked. "You look upset."

"I did not sleep all night, worrying about you being taken."

Martin faced his friend. "I have not decided, Simon. Am I to leave or stay?"

"It is urgent I speak with Deane. Is she home?"

She came in carrying her Bible, which she set gently on the counter.

"Here I am, Simon," she said softly. "Martin explained you want to help him leave because of Pearl Harbor. He and I talked into the wee hours. Have you decided, Martin?"

Before he opened his lips, Simon rushed toward Deane.

"Can we talk alone?"

"There is nothing my nephew cannot hear. This involves his life."

"Woman, what I want to say is for your ears only."

Martin scampered from the room. He walked to the big window, praying Deane would make the decision God meant for her. A few minutes later, she and Simon came in holding hands. Her cheeks flamed a pretty color, matching her rosy sweater.

"Martin, the most amazing thing has happened. Simon and I are to be married."

"Yippee!"

He kissed her cheek and clapped Simon on the back. The three of them spent the next hour making plans. Deane made an important phone call before going to town with Simon to receive their marriage license. Martin prepared tea. He sliced bread and cheese into thin pieces and arranged them on a platter.

At the double knock, he ushered in Reverend "Brave" and took him to the parlor.

"My aunt should return at any moment," Martin said.

"You and I will witness their nuptials. Then I am needed at the hospital to call on an elderly man who is dying."

Martin heard the front door unlock. Deane waltzed in, wearing the navy blue dress she wore on Sundays. Simon looked stylish in a suit and tie. In a flurry, she brought out the family Bible. This they placed beneath their hands, and exchanged vows to honor and cherish each other before God Almighty. Their pastor lifted up a moving prayer and signed the documents.

Martin urged him to stay for a sandwich, adding, "I want to sketch the wedding scene with you in it."

He drew with great speed the newlyweds standing before the pastor. Everyone drank a cup of tea and then the reverend slipped out. Simon thumped Martin's back.

"Your being my nephew makes me proud."

"Uncle Simon, you are my family too."

Simon's lips curved into a smile. "Let me know when you want to escape. I will contact a merchant marine vessel. My boat is ready."

Martin wiped his forehead, where sweat beaded. "We must avoid German U-boats. They sink many ships."

Deane brought Martin a fresh cup of tea. Her face glowed with true joy. For that Martin was thankful. She deserved one day of happiness.

"Your living here changed my life, Martin. I am not anxious for you to leave."

"I never dreamed when I left Zeeland, Michigan, that you and I would become so close. Like a mother and son."

Deane's eyes glistened with tears. He set down his cup on a table and enfolded her into his arms. She kissed his cheek.

"From here on, you keep to the house. I fear Kuipers may come looking for you."

Martin grasped her cold hands. "He'll be busy for days routing out the last of the local Jews. Hitler has yet to declare war on the United States. But I will do as you suggest."

"Let me carry your messages," Simon offered in a gruff voice.

Just as Martin agreed to everything they suggested, Mrs. Grossman sailed in, her cheeks ablaze. "Adele is gone! I found this note on her blanket."

Martin snapped open the folded piece of paper. His eyes scanned the scribbled words.

"Your trouble is over." He handed Deane the note. "Adele has run off to Berlin with a German violinist who promises her fame. I am sorry for you, Mrs. Grossman, but your headstrong daughter is probably gone forever."

Without reading it, Deane gave the note to her husband Simon. He talked in low tones to the butcher's wife. At length, Mrs. Grossman looked at Deane with tears in her eyes.

"My husband is packing his bags. We are ready to leave if you can find us a place."

She left as quickly as she had entered.

"I will handle this," Simon told Martin.

"We can hope Adele is too busy playing her flute to give evidence about the Rosenbaums and Wexlers," Martin replied.

"The other families may have to move as well, but we will see."

Simon slipped out the back door. Deane sat at the kitchen table and bowed her head as if in prayer. Martin hurried to the front window to watch for Kuipers. He was grateful for how God had intervened for Deane in her marriage.

Then he prayed under his breath, "Dear God, please keep Adele's lips sealed."

27

MAY 15, 1942 – FT. BELVOIR, VIRGINIA

Five months later, Martin sat on his cot writing to Helen back in Michigan. He could hardly believe two years had passed since the Dutch government fell. He looked up from his letter, his mind retracing how he got to Fort Belvoir, Virginia.

Simon had shown great courage in smuggling Martin to a U.S. flag merchant ship for his trip home. That was last December. Of course, Martin mentioned nothing of his hair-raising trip to Helen. He could still feel the anguish of being adrift in the cold and wave-tossed Atlantic for hours. Darkness had engulfed him on all sides.

When the merchant ship finally bobbed alongside Simon's tiny craft, Martin had stumbled up a flimsy rope ladder, with Simon holding it rigid from below. On his voyage to America, Martin battled constant fear of being blown up by a German U-boat. But here he was this morning, dressed in Army green and ready to serve. Even getting aboard that decrepit ship and sailing home had prepared him for boot camp.

He dashed a final sentence to Helen, telling of his graduation yesterday and assignment to an engineering group. Martin addressed his letter and licked it shut. Questions battered his mind, which he hadn't admitted to her. Would he now pick up arms and fight the Germans?

Tomorrow he'd sail the Atlantic for a third time, going to an Army Air

Corps base in England, a place he'd never been before. He dragged his duffel bag from beneath his bunk and opened it. Already, he'd helped build a new apparatus developed here at Ft. Belvoir by Major Lewis Prentiss. Others in Martin's group were mass-producing the elements for a new obstacle course, to be replicated at all Army boot camps.

He opened his Bible, struggling to read Psalm 108 in the dim light. Comfort flooded his soul, and he repeated the words written by King David thousands of years ago. "Be thou exalted, O God, above the heavens: and thy glory above all the earth; That thy beloved may be delivered."

Martin had been delivered from death in the Netherlands. Hadn't God also carried him through the tough days as one of the first "guinea pigs" on the obstacle course? He'd trained on the device as if in a real battle, running at and charging over and around barriers. Martin had crawled under barbed wire with live fire whizzing above him. Scars from cuts and scrapes lined his hands and arms. Still, he'd survived.

His body tensed, his sore muscles aching. The future was mapped out by his superiors and Martin would have to obey. Army engineers had completed facilities for B-17 bombers to assault Germany. He was going to England to support their mission.

Mail call sounded. He rushed from the tent. Helen's letters came faithfully while Deane had written a few times. Martin eagerly awaited her letters, which rarely got through the German censoring system. Waiting in line with other soldiers, he reflected how Deane and Simon carried on the Resistance work. Of course, Deane never said so in her letters.

He read between the lines. She often referred to the Rosenbaums as plants, saying something like, "The yellow rose bush is blooming near the house where you planted it."

"Vander Goes, you have a letter," a private called.

Martin handed over his letter and took one in a pale yellow envelope. He tore into Deane's letter with a wide grin. Simon was down with the flu, but feeling better. She knitted orange caps for the neighbors. Martin smiled. The House of Orange represented Queen Wilhelmina's Dutch government before the German oppressors. Good for her. Wearing orange would aggravate the Nazi oppressors and lift the spirits of Deane's neighbors.

Martin returned to her letter. She was concerned the tulip bulbs might not survive the cold weather. Perhaps she would close the shop as fewer people had money to buy things. Wait!

His heart leapt. What did she mean the rudbekia plant had been torn up? Had something happened to Rebekah? He reread the troubling sentences:

I wish I had better news about the rudbekiah plant. Someone tore it up by the roots and took it away. I do not know where. Keep us in your prayers, dear boy. The day Simon and I married, you called me "mother." Since then, I see you as my son. You are in my prayers for the Lord to bless you and keep you safe.

Love,
Deane and Simon

Tears blurred Martin's eyes. He blinked, spotting Simon's scrawl at the bottom:

The authorities allow me to visit Westerbork. It is now a transit camp. I look there for our friends and pray with them. The next time I write, I may have news of our friends.

Grief tore through Martin. He ran behind the mess hall and dropped beneath a tree. He read Deane's letter over again. Her words broke his heart. The lovely and beautiful Rebekah must have been seized from Veenstra's Tulip Farm.

An icy finger of fear ran down his spine. He shuddered. Did Simon mean Rebekah was being held at Westerbork? She could be sent to a concentration camp. Suddenly those verses in the Psalm took on new meaning.

He pressed Deane's letter into his journal, unsure what to do. In the morning, he'd be shipping out. Hope stirred anew. Perhaps once he reached Britain, he could seek help in contacting the Dutch Resistance. He would do everything he could to find Rebekah.

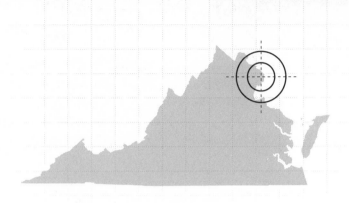

28

AUGUST, EVA'S HOME IN VIRGINIA

Eva sat stunned. She reread Marty's entry for May 15, 1942. It was the last one in this volume. Had Rebekah indeed gone to a concentration camp? Did she survive the war?

On this quiet Saturday morning, Eva gathered her thoughts at the dining room table. Smells of cinnamon from the raisin bread she'd just toasted filled the air. Her family wasn't up yet, giving her time to reflect on where to go next. Who from Marty's past meant to harm him? She longed to ask him about Rebekah, but that might not provide any clues. Besides, she didn't want to cause her grandpa more pain.

Eva poured coffee and let her mind wander, forming a mental picture of the street separating the canal from Deane's home and shop next door. Without getting up to view the painting, Eva imagined the Dutch windmill gracing her living room wall as it once had in Deane's shop.

The seemingly evil Kuipers, the police constable, loomed large. She pictured his greedy hands combing through Deane's jewelry, hoping to extort a nice piece. And what of the ruby necklace Marty wrote about? Perhaps Kuipers had stolen it. Or was he trying to steal it back from Marty?

Eva fired up her laptop and queried his name on multiple search engines. After thirty minutes of searching sites in the Netherlands and Germany, she stumbled upon an obituary written in a Dresden newspaper. Apparently after the war, Kuipers became a noted security chief for East Germany's Stasi.

The lengthy article noted Kuipers left a granddaughter named Trudi Kuipers Russo. She lived in New Jersey. Eva found a social site for Trudi indicating she was a professor at the state university. She tried locating her phone number, but came up empty. She'd try the college on Monday.

At least she knew the constable could no longer come after Grandpa Marty. But Kuipers' daughter might carry a grudge. With renewed interest, Eva thumbed through his journal to remind herself how Marty had described the jewelry. The magnificent ruby necklace was made of silver, diamonds, and fiery red gems. Once again, Eva perused the note from Helen Barnes O'Neal that said Marty owed money to her grandson.

Helen had written in her note: *He is angry about it, and I can no longer defend you.*

Why had Marty tucked it in his journal? What did it all mean?

Shuffling steps behind Eva made her leap from the chair. It was Marty. Her muscles relaxed. My, she was getting jumpy over the slightest sound.

"Good morning, sunshine," she said, borrowing his greeting to her as a child.

Marty stared down at his journal on the kitchen table. Eva motioned for him to sit.

"I've been reading how you graduated from boot camp. Want some coffee?"

"Please. I woke from a dream and couldn't go back to sleep."

She rose and poured him a large cup, adding his sugar and creamer. After setting the mug in front at the table, Eva walked over to the toaster and popped in two slices of raisin bread.

"You like toast with cinnamon, right?"

Marty nodded almost absentmindedly. "Sounds good."

Eva slipped back into her seat and opened Helen's note.

"Can you decipher this for me? You had it in your journal."

"Let me see." Marty took the note and drummed his fingers on the table.

"Why is Ricky O'Neal seeking retribution for an unpaid debt?"

"Oh, that was years ago. Ricky contracted to plow Ralph's driveway. At the same time, Ricky gave me a quote to plow mine for the entire winter. Instead, I hired Tommy Mann from church. On the first snowfall, Tommy cleaned my drive before I ever got out of bed."

"If Tommy plowed your driveway, why does Ricky claim you owe him money?" Eva pushed a stray hair from her eyes.

Martin shrugged. "He and I resolved things after I told him about Tommy. I never knew Ricky ever came with his plow."

"Well, that's as clear as mud." Eva folded the note and asked her next question.

"Grandpa, whatever happened to Deane's ruby necklace, the family heirloom? Did she sell it? She told Kuipers it belonged to an SS officer."

Marty stirred his coffee with a tiny Dutch spoon. He blinked, saying nothing.

"Are you awake yet?" Eva kidded.

"Yes, and I'm quite sure I received the necklace after she died. In fact, I removed it from her safe."

"Did you sell it?"

Marty rubbed the graying stubble on his chin. "No. Did I bring it to Michigan?"

"You never told me. Is it at the farm? What did you do with it?"

"I wrote about it in there, didn't I?" Marty tapped his journal. "Have you finished reading them?"

"Yes. Well, two down. One to go. That's the one Ralph has."

Marty nodded. "What about the necklace?"

"After Pearl Harbor, you joined the Army and are about to leave Fort Belvoir for England. You don't mention the necklace."

The way he sat quietly holding his cup had Eva worried. She ambled over and spread his toast with butter.

Bringing him the treat, she asked, "Want to talk another time?"

"No, I'm reminiscing. Pictures blaze through my mind and I try reaching for them. Before I grasp the moment, it slips from view. Does that make sense?"

His tender look was so precious, tears pricked her eyes. She wanted to help him remember what he needed to remember.

"All right, let's start with this. Did Grandma Joanne wear the necklace?"

"Never."

"Okay. Do you have an idea of its worth?"

Marty nibbled his toast before replying, "Deane said it's worth a fortune, because it's hundreds of years old."

"Eva!" He dropped his toast. "I can see myself burying the necklace in Zeeland."

She reached for his arm. "I read about you hiding family heirlooms in Deane's yard after the Nazis invaded. So the necklace is still beneath Dutch soil?"

"No! I buried it in Zeeland, Michigan. It's under my garage."

Eva blinked. "The garage with the attic, where you stored your paintings? How could you bury it under the thick cement floor?"

Marty gazed at her with his bright, blue eyes and smiled.

"When I first built the garage, it had no cement floor."

"So it's there, beneath the cement?"

He nodded vigorously. "I never dug it up. My mind forgot until you reminded me."

"Who knew you hid the necklace there?"

Eva drank some coffee, waiting for Marty to respond.

His eyes shifted. "Not even your grandma. I never told Joanne because I wanted to preserve the heirloom if we lost our shirts like in the Depression. But, God blessed us so much, I never needed it."

"Grandpa, somebody's been stealing art from your garage. That same person may know you secreted a valuable necklace in there."

"My mind used to be really sharp, but I have lots of memory gaps. That's why I'm happy for my journals. But Eva," he gripped her arm, "that necklace is worth a fortune. Aunt Deane said so. We must rescue it."

She suddenly recalled something important.

"Grandpa, my memory isn't in top shape either. Because Ralph still has your third journal, he may know about the necklace from your writings."

Marty leaned forward. "Ralph likes history. He's tracing his ancestors and is interested in World War II. Oh dear. I gave him my journal to see how people survived back then."

"Did he ever tell you how he's using it?"

In answer, Martin pushed out his lips. Eva's mind reeled.

"Grandpa, we have to find your necklace before it disappears, if it hasn't already."

Her phone rang. She debated answering when she saw Chief Talsma was calling. She hit the button to answer.

"Eva, sorry to bother you on Saturday," he said. "Are you home with your family?"

"Yes. Grandpa and I are chatting about his journal. I was thinking of calling you."

"I'm in his war journals? That surprises me, as I was born the year President Kennedy was shot."

"No, that's not what I meant. I wanted to talk to you about retrieving one of his journals and something else. Chief, what's on your mind?"

"Wait a second, Eva."

She heard squeaking sounds and then a bang. The chief returned to the call.

"I shut my office door," he said. "I apologize because I've a report on my desk and meant to call you. I'm in the office on Saturday to clean up loose ends."

Eva grabbed a sheet of paper to take notes. Marty motioned that he was heading back upstairs.

"No problem, Chief. What's up?"

"After you took Marty to Virginia, my deputy learned of a Nissan dealership in Grand Rapids that rents cars. Someone borrowed a white Nissan van from them the very weekend you saw one on the roadside."

Eva winced. Being tackled in that cornfield by the Nissan driver had wounded her pride. "You say it was 'borrowed.' Who did they loan it to?"

"They don't know. Here's how it was discovered. Recently, they went to rent it out and found someone else's license plate on it. They contacted me because the plate was issued to an elderly couple here in Zeeland."

"Go on," Eva said, jotting notes.

"I interviewed the couple in their home. They own a white Nissan minivan. Get this. The plate currently on their van is the one that belonged on the rental."

"Somebody switched plates."

"Right, Eva. The couple serviced their van the week prior to your arrival. The Zeeland mechanic wrote the license number on the invoice, showing the correct plate."

"Which means the plates were switched just before I saw the Nissan van parked by Marty's field." She'd known that van was fishy.

Talsma coughed into the phone and apologized. "My allergies are kicking up. This thief's a pro, Eva. If I had spotted that van in the area and run the plate, it would have come back to the local couple. We would have thought nothing of it. And the dealership never even knew their white van was gone."

"Did they check the odometer for the distance driven?"

"Yes. The van has two hundred and thirty-eight miles since it was last rented. That's enough to drive here and back to Grand Rapids several times."

"Unbelievable." Eva mused. "Chief, does the dealership run video security? They might have pictures."

"Nope. Already checked."

"Hmm," she murmured, her investigative juices boiling over. There must be some way to track down the renter of that Nissan van. An idea flashed into her mind.

"Can you contact local cab firms? See if any cab went to the dealership during those few days. If someone is working alone, they might have taken a cab."

"Sure, I'll do some checking."

"You've given me fresh evidence to consider. The plot thickens at this end too."

"Is that what you wanted to call me about?"

Eva plunked down her pen. "Chief, I'm thinking about driving up with Marty on Friday. He was reminded how he buried a family heirloom under his garage floor."

"His garage?" Talsma burst out laughing. "That's a new one for me."

"He's sure he buried it before he poured the cement floor. We need to bust up some concrete."

"You can't tackle that alone. Tommy Mann is a contractor and member of our church. He has the proper equipment. Want me to see if he's available for Saturday?"

"Super. Keep me posted on cab companies."

"Consider it done."

"Uh, oh," Eva mumbled, her heart thumping in her chest.

"Is that a no, you don't want me to call Tommy Mann?"

"No, Chief. I mean, yes, call Tommy, but I have to wrap my mind around this. If the Nissan driver knocked me down in the cornfield, that means he saw my van and Virginia license plate."

"You're right, Eva. That's too bad."

"If he's sophisticated enough to borrow a rental car, and use a GPS, then he surely can track my plate and find me in Virginia."

The chief whistled sharply. "But why put a tracking device in those slippers?"

"The tracking device had been delivered before he might have seen my van."

"True enough. Eva, be careful."

"I will," she replied. "Oh, say, I parked behind the Nissan when he was in the cornfield. Maybe he never saw my plate."

"This is gettin' stickier than a pot of glue."

"If you arrange for Tommy, we can be in Zeeland by Friday night."

Talsma said good-bye, and Eva gripped her phone, not at all sure if going to Michigan to hunt for her family's ancient necklace was a smart move to make. She pushed her chair back and went to find Scott. His wonderful logic always helped her sort out the truth.

29

GRANDPA MARTY'S FARM IN ZEELAND, MICHIGAN

va took Friday off and hit the road with Marty. They stopped only for fuel and fast food on the way. She reached Toledo when Griff called her cell.

"How's my partner?" he asked.

Eva glanced at Marty. His head leaned against the window. Good, the phone hadn't wakened him.

"I'm guzzling coffee to stay awake. We're nearing Michigan. What's up?"

"Driving twelve straight hours is a stretch. Glad you're pounding down the java."

"I'm spending the time piecing things together. Anything else I should do?"

"How about meeting me for lunch on Monday?" Griff asked. "Don't ask why."

Eva forced out a sigh. He was being tight-lipped as usual.

"Okay, Monday it is. At our favorite place?"

"Right."

"How about one teeny hint?"

"Drive safely, Eva."

She groaned. "I'll be wondering all the way to Michigan and back what you're being so cagey about."

Griff hung up. Eva turned off the hands free and realized the tank was reaching empty. At the next exit, she bought more coffee and snacks. Marty stayed awake long enough to eat a banana. Eva wheeled back onto the highway, wondering what Griff knew. A few ideas rattled around in her tired brain, but she wouldn't find out until Monday. That irked her for the rest of the trip.

They reached Zeeland as the sun painted the sky a beautiful orange, but Eva didn't stop to admire the sunset. She drove straight to the hotel, about fifteen minutes from Marty's farmhouse. The two queen beds in their shared room looked inviting. The past week had been a whirlwind with Eva working a heavy caseload and arranging with Chief Talsma for Tommy Mann to bring his jackhammer to the farm in the morning.

After settling into their room, Marty slipped into the bathroom to put on his pajamas. Eva phoned Chief Talsma.

"I can meet you at Marty's in the morning," he huffed, sounding out of breath. "Tommy's bringing his heavy equipment."

"Let's make it ten o'clock. That gives us time for breakfast."

"Tommy's all business. It shouldn't take long."

Eva couldn't help yawning. "Let's hope this isn't a wild goose chase."

She ended the call, quickly making another.

"Are you still on the road?" Scott asked.

"We're safe in the hotel, but won't be up much longer. How are you?"

"Missing you. Kaley took our van to choir practice and just got back. Until you're home, I've grounded her driving alone."

"So you made me the bad guy."

"No. It's just safer until we wrap up Marty's situation. I was worried."

Eva's thoughts jumped to the driver of the Nissan possibly knowing their van's license number. Her heart flipped.

"Scott, maybe we should sell the van and buy a new one, with new plates."

"We can discuss it when you're home. Meanwhile, the kids stay with me."

"Now you have me wondering. You gave me the okay to drive out here. Grandpa is so insistent we find the necklace, which could solve this puzzle."

"We prayed about your going and it still seems right to help him. I took vacation. Tomorrow we're heading to Fort Belvoir to scout out where Marty went to boot camp."

Eva yawned. "Take loads of pictures. I want to publish a little book for him."

"That's a super idea. Sleep well, my darling Eva."

His tender words soothed her rattled mind. "I love you, Scott. Always remember that."

He laughed and said, with a lilt in his voice, "I love you too."

Eva turned on the TV to catch the weather report. With the sound muted, she gathered rain was forecast. That shouldn't hinder their search inside the garage. Marty dropped his folded clothes into his suitcase and crawled into the bed near the bathroom.

"Good night, Eva Marie." He pulled the blanket up to his chin. "We both need our sleep. Tomorrow's a busy day."

She picked up her travel case and turned out the lights. Marty's snoring told her he was already in dreamland. After brushing her teeth, Eva tiptoed out of the bathroom, ready for bed. A crack of light streamed in the window. She tugged the drapes, scanning the parking lot for her Explorer.

Her brows flexed. Two cars parked near hers also bore Virginia plates. Strangely, she saw none from West Virginia or Pennsylvania. Three Virginia plates at the same hotel in Holland, Michigan? What were the odds? It might be coincidence or she could've been followed.

Eva concluded anyone following her wouldn't park in the same lot. She adjusted the air on the window air conditioner and set the dial to high. White noise always helped her to sleep.

Not this time. She stayed awake in the lumpy bed, missing her beloved family. Their faces floated through her mind. Griff had promised to touch base if he found out anything at the decoy house. So far, nothing had transpired there. The slippers and the GPS had found a new home, but no one seemed to care. That had Eva stumped.

Finally, she drifted off, waking early to find Marty hunched in a chair near a wall sconce reading his Bible. Eva brought her clothes to the bathroom and dressed. Then she looked up Ralph's phone number.

"Grandpa, call Ralph and tell him we'll be at the farmhouse with a contractor. That way he won't be concerned. Ask him to return your journal."

Eva punched the speaker button on her smart phone. She hit send and handed Marty the phone. It rang a few times before Ralph answered.

"Hello."

Marty looked confused by the cell phone speaker, but did raise it to his ear. He said hesitantly, "Ah … Ralph, it's Marty from next door."

"Hey, Martin. My caller ID said it was a blocked call. I never answer solicitors begging for this, that, and the other thing. My money goes to worthy causes anyways."

"Sorry," Marty replied. "I'm calling from my granddaughter's phone."

Ralph grunted. "That granddaughter of yours has stolen you away from us. But there's nothin' like family. I see Ricky O'Neal movin' his combine down the road. It won't be long and he'll be harvestin' at your place. When ya comin' home?"

Marty pulled the phone away from his ear and held it like a walkie-talkie. "That's what I called to say. We're back to meet with a builder. Don't be concerned if you see a strange truck at my house."

"You're buildin' on at your age?"

"Nope, just a few repairs. Don't worry."

Eva whispered in Marty's ear, "The journal."

"Say, Ralph, my granddaughter is helping me write my memoir. I need my journal back, the one I loaned you."

"Okey dokey, Martin. Stop by when yer at the house. Bye."

Eva took the phone and swiped the red "end" button. Marty stretched his back.

"I could eat a horse. Do we get any breakfast?"

"Sure. Downstairs they even have a homemade waffle machine. I'm glad Ralph will turn over your journal. I keep forgetting to follow up on that, so remind me."

"Yes." Marty laughed heartily. "I like having to remind you not to be forgetful."

On the way to breakfast, Eva replayed Ralph's comments on the phone. She'd suspected him of making the threatening call, but decided he wasn't the caller. The breakfast area was packed. Turned out there was a military reunion in the area. Marty spied a friend from his Army days, an aging WWII survivor. Eva piled eggs and bacon on his plate while he reminisced with his Army buddy. Eva ate her fruit and listened to their stories.

How interesting his buddy should arrive in Holland the very day she brought Marty here. With God, there were no coincidences.

30

Eva loaded her SUV with their suitcases while Marty traded phone numbers with his old friend. Then she drove Marty to the farm on wet roads. The rain had come and gone, leaving occasional puddles. Tommy Mann's mammoth truck and attached air compressor loomed large by the garage. Eva hopped out.

Marty did too, heading straight to Tommy and introducing him to Eva. "He and his wife attend my church. And Tommy runs the family business."

Eva shook the builder's mighty hand. With his day's growth of beard and mud-caked jeans and heavy shoes, he looked like an honest, hardworking guy.

"Tommy, this here's my granddaughter. She's a big-shot in Washington."

"Not really," Eva said. "It's nice to meet Grandpa's friend. Did the chief tell you what we need done?"

Tommy displayed a toothy grin. "You need to break concrete?"

"Right. You look ready for some heavy-duty busting. Hopefully it won't be too hard."

Eva asked Marty to fetch the key from the house so she could unlock the garage. He strolled to the farmhouse, looking at overgrown bushes by the garage. She made a mental note to call the lawn guy and have him prune them.

When Tommy finished hooking up his air compressor, Eva explained, "Grandpa's nearing ninety and just recalled burying a family heirloom in the garage when it had a dirt floor. We need to dig it up."

"No problem."

Tommy went to fetch his tools. Marty returned with the key, entering the garage through the service door. Soon the lights blazed and the three overhead doors were up.

"Wanna show me where to begin?" Tommy asked, dragging in a hose.

"Right there." Marty pointed and spun around.

Then he walked to the right corner of the garage, near where the overhead door track rose and crossed the ceiling.

"Break up about four by four feet," he said.

Tommy lifted his ample shoulders. "You're sure this is the spot?"

"Yup."

Marty wore a boyish grin, as if energized to be digging beneath concrete and coming up with the prize. Tommy marched to his truck and grabbed some ear protectors. He handed a set to Marty, then to Eva.

"This will be loud. Put these on. It may get dusty too. In fact, you might want to move that antique truck."

Eva looked inside of Marty's truck, asking Tommy, "Can we push it out? My husband disconnected the battery."

Marty slid behind the wheel. Good thing Eva kept up her workouts, because she helped the brawny builder push the truck out of the garage. With Marty's baby safely out of harm's way, Tommy started his noisy compressor. He carried a heavy jackhammer to the garage.

Eva clapped on her ear protectors just before *tat-a-tat-tat* echoed in the garage. Her ears pulsed from the loud hammering. She insisted Marty wait in his truck with his protectors on. Tommy blasted away for a good twenty-five minutes, his shoulders heaving up and down. When the compressor finally quit, he pulled a pickaxe and shovel from his truck. Soon the hammering began again. Eva moved to the swing dangling from a large beech tree.

She took a seat, and waited for the pounding to cease. At sounds of a shovel scraping against the cement, Eva sauntered over to watch. Tommy used monstrous motions, digging and piling loose dirt onto the unbroken concrete. After he'd hefted out a foot of dirt from the four-by-four foot square, he looked up. Sweat rolled down his cheeks.

"I don't find a thing. How deep is it buried?"

Eva held up her finger and brought Marty in from the truck. He stared at the gaping hole in the concrete.

"Are you sure you gave Tommy the correct spot?" Eva asked him.

Marty pocketed his hands. "Try digging a foot deeper."

Eva pulled him back from the hole. With each shovel full of dirt Tommy hurled, she expected to see treasure. But time passed, the hole became a foot deeper, and nothing appeared.

Tommy stayed in the hole, kicking dirt. "Should I break up a larger area?"

"Yeah, maybe over this way." Marty pointed toward the center of the garage.

Tommy put on his ear protection, while Eva led Marty from the garage. The jackhammering resumed and Eva returned to the swing. Confusion bubbled within her. She'd driven twelve hours with zilch to show for it. Had Marty's memory totally collapsed?

The hammering was replaced with the sound of Tommy's shovel, when Eva heard him announce, "I've found something. You may want to look at this."

Eva and Marty hurried back into the garage. Tommy held aloft a rusty can, about the size of a one-pound coffee can. He set this on the garage floor.

"That can't be," Marty said, shaking his head. "It's too small."

Eva was baffled. Maybe Grandpa had left the jewels in the Netherlands. Or perhaps he sold them and didn't remember. Tommy leaned on the broken concrete.

"What should I do next?"

It was warm and humid in the garage. Eva wiped her forehead.

"Grandpa?"

Marty rocked on his heels, pulling his arms behind his back as if dazed. Eva glanced at the wall above where Tommy was digging. Her thoughts roamed to her childhood, when she had visited the farm. Back then, Marty raised pigs, chickens, and cows. She'd even chased chickens in this garage.

"Wait a minute."

Eva looked down at the small can, then inspected the wall. A vague recollection filled her mind and she pointed.

"Where's the door for your chickens to come in and out?"

Marty eyed the location. "Back then, this was a garage and chicken coop."

"But you changed the garage," Eva said. "When Jillie and I buried this can in the chicken yard, it was outside the garage. We must have been about ten years old."

Marty walked over and stood beneath the middle overhead door. He studied the floor. "The chicken door was here, before I added the third stall and put in three overhead doors."

"So the chickens ran around right where Tommy is?"

"Yes!" Marty slammed his palm against his forehead. "My mistake. The garage used to be smaller."

He dashed to another spot. "I buried the necklace right here."

"Mrs. Montanna, should I start over?"

"Please, and we'll make it worth your while. Try where Grandpa is standing."

Tommy groaned while climbing out of the hole. He dragged his tools to the next overhead door.

Marty clapped him on the back. "I feel older today than I have in years."

"No problem, sir. I want to find what you're looking for."

Tat-a-tat-tat.

To escape the continual racket, Eva picked up the rusty coffee can and rushed to the swing. Marty followed and dropped beside her, scratching his head.

"It's crazy. Until you mentioned chickens, I'd forgotten about expanding the garage. Most days my memory is solid, but on others it's foggy."

She patted his arm with love. "Don't worry. We'll find it."

If Tommy doesn't collapse, she thought, steadying the swing.

Eva's attention drifted to the can she held. Memories of her twin sister flooded her mind. She and Jillie buried the can to keep Ricky O'Neal from finding it. They had agreed to return when old enough to drive and retrieve their childhood treasures of stones and feather. They never did. Jillie was killed in the Pentagon on September 11, 2001. Eva started swinging, feeling sad. Her sisterly hopes had been cut short by terrorists from the Middle East.

She turned to Marty. "How does it feel being home?"

He surprised her. "I was lonely here. You and the kids are more fun."

"We'd love you to stay with us for as long as you want."

The digging suddenly stopped. Tommy shouted, "Get in here! I found it."

Marty took off. Eva set down the can and scurried into the garage. She heard tires crunching on the drive. Her heart raced. She jerked her head, afraid to see a white Nissan van. Relief flooded her. Chief Talsma climbed from his patrol car.

She waved him inside. "Tommy's found something."

The three of them hovered by the gaping hole while Tommy pushed a shovel around a hard object. "It feels like some old jug."

He wiped dirt away with his gloved hands, and lifted from the earth what looked like an old pickle jug. The gray and brown crock had a lid smeared with tar. Tommy set it on the concrete floor.

"Whoopee!" Marty hollered.

Eva gave him a bear hug. "There, you see? Your memory hasn't failed you."

"Is that it?" Tommy wrinkled his brow. "Do I look for anything else?"

"You can claim victory," Eva said, a wide smile plastered on her face.

"Sweet." Tommy climbed out and shoveled the dirt back in.

Marty snagged a knife from a Peg-Board. He tried cutting away the tar, but his hand shook. Chief Talsma stepped forward.

"Let me help."

"Gladly." Marty gave him the knife. "The tar wasn't this hard when I put it on."

Footsteps on the gravel made Eva turn. She spied a bald-headed man in overalls walking toward them.

"Grandpa, we have company."

Marty set down the jug. "Oh, good, it's Ralph."

He ambled to the door, but Eva shot past him, stopping Ralph before he snagged a ringside seat in the garage. She headed him off under the beech tree.

Ralph narrowed his eyes at her. "So yer the nosy granddaughter."

"I am Marty's granddaughter." She forced a smile. "Thanks for keeping an eye on the place while he's visiting us."

"No problem, little lady." Ralph lifted his ample chin and craned his neck toward the garage. "Hey, Martin, what's goin' on in there?"

Eva stepped into Ralph's field of vision. "We're making repairs before winter closes in."

"So he told me. Here's yer journal, Martin. It was a great help."

Marty clutched his war memories while Ralph stared at the garage.

Eva squared her shoulders. "What did you find interesting in Grandpa's journal?"

"I'm a history buff." Ralph's booted toe launched a pebble down the drive. "What Martin did during the war is remarkable. I didn't make it to the end though."

Marty's lips sagged. "I'd let you keep it, but Eva and I are writing my memoirs."

Ralph gazed at the chief and Tommy in the garage. "I've kept my eyes on yer place, but nothing happened. Farm equipment goin' in and out. When I saw the police car, I thought I missed somethin'."

"Chief Talsma is a family friend and arranged for the contractor." Eva gestured toward the house. "Ralph, can I show you something?"

"Sure, little lady." He dutifully followed with his thumbs on his overall suspenders.

Eva headed for the back door, calling to Marty, "You better check on Tommy."

Just then, the garage door rattled shut. Eva was glad someone heard her. She stopped by muddy footprints, asking Ralph if he'd heard anyone banging on the door.

"Nah. I only seen farm workers 'round here."

Eva pushed her hair behind her ears. Tommy may have knocked on the door and muddied the steps, but they provided a good distraction from events in the garage.

"You're sure?"

Ralph stared at the mud. "Maybe a farm worker wanted the toilet. He'd been surprised Martin's shut the water off."

"Yes, it's better that way."

Eva wanted Ralph to be gone. So she held up her cell phone and pivoted toward her Explorer.

"Ralph, you must excuse me. I've calls to make. Stay in touch."

She lifted the cell to her ear and walked away. Ralph gave a last look at the closed-up garage, and trudged home in his work boots caked with mud. A sneaking suspicion entered Eva's mind that he had caused the muddy prints. Once Ralph left the yard, the garage door shot up. Tommy dragged out a hose and jackhammer. Marty followed, still clutching his journal.

Eva scrambled from her SUV to join the contractor by his truck. "Your strength and patience are amazing. We need to open that jug."

"Chief Talsma already did." Tommy threw the hose in his truck bed. "Should I get my other truck and haul away the busted concrete?"

Eva didn't want Ralph seeing Tommy taking anything out of the garage. "Let's wait until you return in a few months and pour new concrete."

"Sure, whenever you're ready."

"That settles it."

Tommy handed Eva an invoice and she wrote a check for Marty to sign.

He put his journal in Eva's SUV, and then paid Tommy, wearing a grin. "Son, you're a marvel. Greet your folks for me."

"See you next time."

Tommy flung the check in his glove box. With great ease, he loaded the equipment in his monster truck. He maneuvered his rig around Eva's SUV and drove off. She and Marty hurried into the garage and closed the overhead door. Talsma bent his head beneath a florescent light.

"This is amazing, Eva." Talsma arched his eyebrows. "See what Marty buried."

A flame of curiosity shot through her. Eva hurried over. Next to piles of nails lay an oil cloth, spread open on the flat surface to reveal a stunning necklace. Its delicate silver chain was laced with silver medallions. Each medallion was studded with diamonds, and a sparkling red ruby in the center. The gems were so large they looked like costume jewelry.

"Grandpa, is this the necklace Deane saved from Kuipers?"

Marty's face crinkled with a smile. "Yes! She told me it's centuries old."

"This looks like the real deal." The chief gingerly held the necklace between his knobby fingers.

"I've only seen rubies this huge on toy jewelry," Eva said. "But no one saves something like this for centuries unless it's genuine."

Talsma wrapped the necklace back in the cloth. "You had better take this to a safe deposit box, pronto."

"I will in D.C., where I hope to learn more about this fabulous piece."

"Eva, look." Talsma picked up a frayed leather pouch. "There's powder in here."

She untied the leather strings, and peered at gray powder. Her instincts took over, and she pinched some between her fingers. It was gritty, not fine. She started to raise a finger to her lips, but stopped, thinking better of it.

Marty titled his head. "Deane kept that pouch in her safe. It's centuries old too."

"Chief, have you ever seen powdered silver?" Eva asked, completely mystified.

He shook his head and turned to leave.

"Me either." She shut off the bench light.

Talsma raised the overhead door. "I closed this when your neighbor showed up."

"Quick thinking." Eva stepped around chunks of concrete. "I didn't want him seeing what we're doing in here. He has an odd curiosity about Grandpa's life."

Then she recalled something. "Grandpa, did you tell Ralph you turned the water off?"

He blinked. "Is there any reason I shouldn't?"

"No. Everything is fine. Let's push your truck in the garage."

Marty sat behind the wheel while Eva and Talsma nestled the antique truck in its stall. After the garage doors were closed, Marty asked to go into the house. After checking each room, which all looked in order, Eva announced they were ready to go.

But Marty needed another pair of socks.He headed upstairs while Eva secured the necklace into a zip baggie. She noticed that the dining room wall looked bare without the windmill painting. Marty cruised in with a happy face.

"I found this in my drawer." He held up his missing gold watch.

"Oh, I'm so glad. Ready?"

Eva pulled out her keys, and after locking up the house, she hurried outside. Marty wore a grand smile carrying his pocket watch to the SUV. Eva retrieved her can of treasures. Then she assured the chief she'd keep him updated. He trailed them in his cruiser until they reached town.

She put her sunglasses on, musing how the watch just appeared. A deeper mystery was why no one had yet shown up at the decoy house. But until Eva met with Griff, that question would go unanswered. So she hit the gas, traveling through Michigan and Ohio, and stopping for sandwiches. She and Marty chatted about their success until he took a nap.

Her eyelids were growing heavy too and nearing the outskirts of Pittsburgh, Eva pulled into a hotel. She saw several cars with Virginia plates. But she wouldn't be shaken; Virginia was closer to Pennsylvania than Michigan. Marty lifted his head.

"Are we home?" His voice sounded groggy.

"Not quite. We'll stay at this hotel. You're tired and so am I."

"I was having an eerie dream, the same one I had before we left for Michigan. She called to me."

"Grandma did?" Eva shut off the motor, dropping her keys into her purse.

"Rebekah wouldn't leave Simon's boat. She cried to me, 'I am afraid to leave. I will never see you again.'"

Eva reached out and rubbed his arm. "After you brought her to your Dutch Resistance contact, you had word she'd arrived at the tulip farm."

"I know." He choked back tears.

"This trip has been too much for you. You wanted the necklace, but that doesn't bring Rebekah back. I pray the Lord lessens your grief."

"He has, or I couldn't have married your grandmother. It's the dream. Did you read about the sad letter I received?"

Eva wasn't sure. "Deane wrote a plant had been uprooted. Simon added something about Westerbork."

"No, it's a much later letter from 1944." He wiped his eyes.

"Ralph just gave us your last journal, so I need to read it. I see a restaurant inside. Let's order sandwiches and take them up to the room."

"Okay. And bring the necklace. I want to see it before I go to bed."

"It's in my purse, along with my gun. No one will take it from me."

They ate grilled chicken sandwiches in their room. Eva took out Marty's journal and the ruby necklace, which Marty inspected with great interest. He soon fell asleep. To sounds of his snoring, Eva located an entry for 1944 in the third journal. Sadness filled her heart and she understood his pain. Rebekah had been sent to Auschwitz. No one ever heard from her again.

31

On Monday, back at her Virginia home, Eva dragged her tired body to the car. Driving twenty-four hours over the past three days had her teetering on burnout. There was one thing to do—go heavy on caffeine, and she did. She stopped at the bank, and despite the pouring rain, she savored last night's memory of Marty showing Andy his gold watch. He'd promised one day it would be his.

Eva went inside, satisfied Marty wouldn't tell her kids how the two of them had dug up the valuable necklace. Eva secured the jewels and pouch in her safe deposit box. Adding a rider on her homeowner's insurance policy would have to wait until after she'd had her lunch with Griff.

Also, Delores Fontaine had phoned this morning, wanting to discuss stolen art. With everything happening in her life, Eva had forgotten all about Delores, and promised to squeeze her in tomorrow. Eva checked her watch; she was running late.

To make up for lost time, she sped through traffic at the risk of hydroplaning on the slick asphalt. Last Friday when Griff had called, he wouldn't reveal what he knew. Eva hadn't pressed him. Neither of them divulged urgent matters on a cell phone.

But had he discovered something at the decoy house? Eva cranked the final turn, anticipation coursing through her. Her tires spun on the wet gravel in the parking lot.

Past gatherings of hers at Rob's set new records, or changed the direction of international cases. She spotted Griff's Bucar beneath a shady tree, and parked next to it. Her mouth began salivating. The savory sandwiches drew them to Rob's, but so did the privacy. It was here at Rob's that she'd met CIA Agent Bo Rider, interrogated Russian spies, and commenced secret capers known only to her and Griff.

"This should prove enlightening," she said under her breath.

Stepping with purpose into the deli, Eva raised her sunglasses atop her golden locks. Griff waved from his "desk" at the corner table. She pulled out a chair by a full glass of ice water. A server with bright pink hair handed her a menu, but Eva stopped her with an outstretched hand.

"No menu. I'll have your crab cake sandwich, the Birdie, right?"

The server dropped her arm. "How clever, you know our menu by heart. I'm impressed. What to drink?"

"Coffee, black," Eva shot back.

"Sorry. I need to make a fresh pot."

The server pushed out her diamond-studded lip and sauntered away. Eva nodded in her direction.

"If Rob doesn't hire better help, he may go under. When Wally waited tables here, he appeared with hot coffee and his fantastic smile. How's he doing?"

Griff stirred his glass of iced tea. "Wally's in seminary. He's also married; I rarely see him. But we're all praying we'll be at his ordination service one day."

"Certainly." Not content to engage in small talk, Eva changed the subject.

"What's so hot you couldn't tell me on the phone? All the way here, I thought about how we usually christen some exciting, new adventure."

Griff slid his chair closer to her. "Have you been researching your family online?"

She glared. What was Griff driving at? Her brain needed her coffee to even work. Eva saw no server heading her way. She sighed, facing her partner with a frown.

"Griff, be serious. You don't really think that I, as a federal agent, fool with those social media sites or 'find your distant relatives' websites."

"Why not? I've located all kinds of helpful information on them."

"Yes, as an agent tracking down suspects. It's easy to discover everything about a person online. They post profiles advertising their religion, date of birth, and high school. It's like some genius investigator in the sky has hypnotized everyone in the world. Their personal lives are on parade for every cop to see on the web."

"True." Griff leaned on his folded arms. "And for every con man and shyster."

Eva tapped her fingers on the table to emphasize her point. "But criminals can't do what we can. If their privacy settings keep us from seeing what we want, we subpoena the host and get their private information that way."

"But hackers can get what we can get." Griff sipped his cool drink. "With so much personal stuff on the web, we can only hope our government remains trustworthy."

"Yeah," Eva said. "When you and I went to agent's school, we used old-fashioned techniques to catch the guilty."

Griff shrugged. "What a mixed-up system. It's scary thinking how sub-poenas in the wrong hands can obtain copies of subscribers' profile info and copies of every single e-mail."

"Where on earth is my coffee?"

"I don't see our server. Maybe she quit. I had that happen once."

Eva couldn't muster a grin. She tried suppressing her desperation for caffeine.

"Griff, you and I don't have such accounts and we don't 'like' everyone we know. What's up with your lecture?"

"Not everyone is as skeptical as we are. That's why I called a meeting."

Eva flexed her brow. "Are you saying Kaley or Andy has a page on those sites?"

Just then the server rattled a cup of coffee in front of Eva and re-filled Griff's Arnie Palmer. She mumbled something that sounded like, "Sandwiches … right out."

Eva inched her chair closer to the table and tried the coffee. The scalding hot brew burned her lip, which she plunged into the tall glass of ice water.

As her lip cooled, she asked Griff, "What are you telling me?"

"Your grandpa Marty is conducting research all over the Family Finder website."

"No way!" Eva burst out laughing. "He can barely operate the cell phone on our family plan."

"Wrong. I went on that site and typed in his last name of Vander Goes. A thread of searchers is gabbing about descendants of Peter Vander Goes from the Netherlands. He lived there in the fourteen hundreds."

Eva could hardly believe it. "Peter Vander Goes is my ancestor, and something like my great, great, great, great-grandfather. How is the research linked to Marty?"

"Okay. Someone using the name 'Dutch Dingo' claims to be Martin Vander Goes of Zeeland, Michigan. I wondered if it was you or your parents, so I used our connections. Know what I found out?"

"Tell me, please!"

"You don't like being kept in suspense any more than I do. Dutch Dingo is really Clarence O' Leary of Zeeland, MI."

Eva pushed back her coffee cup. "We have no relatives in Zeeland. Grandpa Marty doesn't use an alias. Besides, O'Leary isn't even a Dutch name."

She thought a moment and pulled out her cell. "I have an idea who might know."

Eva dialed the phone and Griff leaned back with a lopsided grin. He appeared to enjoy his little charade, but Eva didn't.

She talked softly into the phone, "Hey, Chief, it's Eva. Sorry to bother you on your cell, but can you talk?"

"Sure," Chief Talsma replied. "How was your drive to Virginia? Did you get your package there safely?"

Eva sipped some water. The ice felt soothing to her throbbing lip.

"All is well," she said. "I'm meeting with an FBI agent friend. He says Clarence O'Leary from Zeeland is researching on the web and claiming to be Grandpa Marty."

"Really! That's his next-door neighbor. You know, he showed up right after Marty pulled the necklace from that old crock. Clarence goes by his middle name, Ralph."

Disgust surged through Eva. "I never heard his neighbor's last name. Marty always refers to him as Ralph."

"Should I go see him?" the chief asked.

"No, not yet. Let me ask Marty if he knows what Ralph's doing. But keep an eye on his house. Marty left a key with Ralph and I'm thinking that isn't a smart idea. Fortunately, Ralph returned Marty's last journal."

"Let me know if you want me to rescue that key."

"I will." Eva plunked her phone back in her purse.

"Griff, you probably figured it out. Dutch Dingo is Marty's neighbor. I don't know if he's researching a novel or what. Even so, he shouldn't be impersonating Marty."

Griff started to speak, but Eva interrupted with her hand in the air.

"I bet Ralph put the GPS device in the slippers!"

He shook his head. "Eva, Ralph knows where you grandfather lives. He doesn't need the GPS."

"But Grandpa left there and is in Virginia."

"Ralph didn't know Marty would go home with you. No need for the GPS."

Her shoulders slumped. "You're right. I need to grasp the facts and put my raw feelings aside. That's difficult when someone you love is under attack."

"Okay." Griff rubbed his hands together. "What if whoever is chatting online with Ralph, thinking he's Marty, has some other reason to find out where Marty goes."

Horror surged through Eva's mind.

"Me, Griff!" she cried. "That person is trying to find me. Even Ralph doesn't know where I live. He could be telling anyone."

"That's a terrible thought. You need protection."

Ms. Pink Hair arrived, so Griff quit talking. She dumped plates of sandwiches in front of them, knocked off a few chips, and hustled to the kitchen without a word.

Griff lowered his voice. "The person posting back and forth with Marty ... I mean Ralph pretending to be Marty, goes by 'Pilgrim Peerage' and lives in England."

"We have no family in England." Eva picked up her sandwich. "Do we?"

"I do, but you've never mentioned being a fellow Brit."

He was about to bite into his Duffer, when he lifted his eyebrows.

"I'd like to ask a blessing. Then I'm gonna enjoy this sandwich."

They bowed their heads, with Griff thanking the Lord for their meal and asking for help in solving the dilemma. Eva lifted her head and glanced at her watch.

"It's too late to call our MI-5 friend. London is five hours ahead of us."

"We'll phone Brewster Miles back at the office."

"Isn't this your office?" Eva joked, but didn't laugh. "If Pilgrim Peerage is Andrei Enescu, I may move my family like Bo Rider did. Whoever collided with me in the cornfield probably saw my van. I'm going to sell it."

"I'll help in whatever way I can, Eva."

"What about Andrei? Where is he?"

"He's disappeared since Interpol last spotted him in Paris."

"Great."

Eva's appetite shriveled. She called Scott on her cell to warn him, but left a message. "Honey, we need to bring the kids to my folks. Call me."

Hanging up, she glanced at Griff, who was well into the rest of his sandwich.

"Am I right to have the kids visit their grandparents?" she asked.

"You can never take enough precautions to protect your family. The wife of a federal prosecutor was shot last week."

A bolt of fear sizzled through Eva. "God help us."

"He does and He will."

Griff was right, but Eva began to feel like she did when her sister Jillie had been killed on September 11th, 2001—alone and afraid. She needed to spend more time praying for her family. With God's direction, she could end this stalking for good.

32

That evening, Eva hugged Scott before he headed to the garage. The kids were already in the Ford Explorer.

"Kiss my folks for me," she said. "Dad will be happy to see Marty. They've not seen each other since last year. Mom and Dad are always on the go."

Scott jangled his keys. "Sure you won't join us?"

"My reports are overdue. Our vacation put me on the wrong side of my boss."

"You never take time off. I'll call when Marty and I leave Richmond."

He kissed her lips lightly before ducking into the garage. Marty rushed up from behind, hooking his watch fob on a belt loop. Eva seized his arm.

"Grandpa, is Ralph researching for you on the Family Finder website?"

Marty stared blankly. "I never heard of it."

"That's all right. Does he call himself Dutch Dingo?"

"Hahahaha," Marty laughed, rearing his head back. "Eva, he's not Dutch."

She pressed. "Ever hear anyone else called by the name of Pilgrim Peerage?"

"No, but I'm so happy I found my watch. I'm showing it to Clifford. It's been too long since I've seen my son."

"Dad is anxious to see you. I'll invite them here soon. See if they can give you some dates when he and Mom aren't traveling."

"Will do, Eva Marie."

Marty slid into the front seat. Eva locked the back door, and then strode to the front window to wave. As they disappeared around the corner, she returned to the kitchen, where she opened the fridge. Greek yogurt looked okay for dinner.

She brought the container back to her desk and thumbed through Marty's last journal. Her finger stopped at the entry where he'd removed the ruby necklace from Deane's safe. Just then, her cell phone rang. Eva snatched it up.

Thinking it was Scott, she asked, "Is everything okay?"

"No, but thanks for asking," Griff said.

"Oh, I thought you were Scott. You sound irritated. What's up?"

"Brewster is out of the country. Not sure when he'll return to Whitehall."

Eva frowned. "We can try phoning him from the SCIF after our meeting."

"What meeting?"

"Tomorrow at noon. You know, the federal prosecutor wants an update about our counterfeit passport case."

"Oh, yeah. Those Yemeni students with phony Danish passports over-stayed their visas." He chuckled. "Good thing I called."

"The prosecutor is ready to issue arrest warrants, but we'd learn more by watching the students longer." Eva leaned back in her chair. "With every-thing going on with Marty, I feel out of the JTTF loop."

"I'm off to the gym. I ate nothing but pizza and burgers all week."

Eva felt her own snug waistband. "Don't forget the Duffer from earlier. You shouldn't have eaten all the chips. See you in the morning."

She looked at her empty yogurt container. Griff mentioning pizza made her stomach growl. But she could lose a few pounds too. Eva was content to peel an orange and head back to her desk.

But as the evening wore on, the layers of the puzzle weren't so easy for Eva to peel back. She made a list of the evidence. Then her mind focused on why Ralph was masquerading as Grandpa Marty on a genealogy website us-ing the name 'Dutch Dingo.' It was an odd name for an Irish neighbor who grew stranger by the day. And until Eva could ask Brewster, she was clueless as to what 'Pilgrim Peerage' had to gain by investigating Marty.

Maybe there was no connection at all to him. Maybe Ralph's subterfuge was harmless and simply a desire to sound credible with his WWII sources. She put aside her many questions and finished her reports. Worry began to flit through her mind. Scott was late. She phoned him on his cell.

"Hi, honey," Scott answered.

"I'm checking to see where you guys are."

Before Scott could answer, she heard the garage door creaking open.

"You're home!" Eva dropped her phone and ran to greet her husband. He helped Marty from the Explorer and they all tramped back into the house. Eva grinned sheepishly at being anxious for nothing.

"How is everyone in Richmond?"

Marty looked tired, but handed Eva a package.

"Your dad sent you these. We had a nice time together."

Eva tore off the flowery paper. She smiled. He'd sent her Dutch peppermints. "This is great. My stash is pretty low."

"To all a good night," Marty said with a wave.

Scott enveloped Eva into his arms. She patted his back.

"I just finished my reports when you drove in. I'd call that perfect timing."

"I'd call you the perfect friend."

Scott kissed the top of her head, making her heart flutter. All of Eva's problems vanished in his tender embrace.

THE PROSECUTOR POSTPONED THEIR MEETING. So Eva arranged to meet Delores Fontaine one hour earlier. Eva forwarded the finished reports to her boss, and left the JTTF office, her Glock safely in her purse. She hopped in her G-car, concerned meeting with the art curator would be a waste of time. Delores had asked Eva to come to her home, so she wouldn't be seen talking to a federal agent.

Traffic was light, so Eva made it to the Arlington apartment complex posthaste. Eva punched in the code Delores had given her and the parking gate rose. Eva rode the elevator to the fifth floor. She knocked once and Delores let her in.

"Sorry to be so secretive, but I'm worried," Delores said, closing the door.

She wore a beige pantsuit, looking as elegant as she had several years ago. At that time, she'd given Eva evidence about artifact smuggling from China. Eva risked posing as an art curator herself and nabbed a famous archaeologist in the bargain.

Eva gripped the woman's hand, noticing that it trembled.

"Delores, I understand you have information for me. I will try to keep your name out of it, if possible."

The woman's shoulders heaved as if she was close to tears. She ushered Eva to one of several upholstered chairs around a rectangular glass table. Artwork donned every wall in the dining and living rooms. Marty would enjoy nosing around in here, Eva thought. She sat and took out a small notepad.

Delores picked up a carafe. "I recall you like strong coffee. This is a dark roast from Costa Rica."

Eva smiled and Delores poured two steaming cups. Then she perched on the edge of a chair across from Eva much like a bird ready to fly away. She blinked her long lashes.

"Ah … based on what happened last time, you are the last person I ever wanted to see again. But I do not know who else to tell."

Eva sampled the coffee and approved the rich taste. She put down her cup.

"You can trust me to do the right thing. When you first called, I was on vacation with my family. You have evidence related to lost or stolen art, correct?"

"Yes." Delores' voice quavered. "I left the Case Foundation after helping with your Nashville sting. I couldn't face them again. My new position is with the Washington Gallery of Art. I took a hush-hush call about a sale of a Dutch Master. It was secretive."

Eva leaned forward, pen in hand. "It's not unusual for an art museum to buy Dutch paintings. Or am I missing something?"

"Well, the way the conversation unfolded, I took it to mean someone wanted to privately sell an extremely old painting."

"Who phoned you, Delores?"

"He refused to give his name."

"That's a problem. Did you recognize his voice from any previous dealings?"

"I may have." Delores looked puzzled. "He sounded like someone I met at a London exhibit, but I never learned his name."

Eva alerted to the British connection. Yesterday afternoon, Griff had phoned Brewster Miles with MI-5, but he was traveling out of the country.

Not wanting Delores to sense she'd just given an important clue, Eva asked in a casual tone, "Did he refer to any previous meeting in London?"

"No, and I kept things vague, saying I was in the middle of a showing and would ring him back. Of course, he insisted on calling me, which he did this morning."

"What did you tell him?" Eva asked, making notes.

"My secretary told him to call me tomorrow. I wanted to talk with you first."

"Why do you need me?"

Delores rose from her seat and walked to the window. She lifted the blind before facing Eva. "He claims to have a twenty-million-dollar Dutch painting. Such an enormous price tells me it's stolen. There are several missing works. Eva, I do not want to be in trouble ever again."

"Would you like me to be present when he calls?"

"Oh, please do," Delores gushed. "That is exactly what I hoped you would say."

"Is there more you're not telling me?" Eva squinted accusingly.

"No!" Delores raised both hands. "Honest, Eva. That's everything I know." Eva stowed the pad in her purse.

"I'll return tomorrow and assume you will permit me to record the conversation."

"Yes." Delores followed Eva to the door. "Whatever you want. I just want to be sure I do nothing illegal."

Eva stepped into the hall and flashed a wink. "Delores, you did right."

Delores gave a wan smile and seemed to melt in her doorway.

On the way to the car, Eva wondered if her informant was being tested by some FBI sting. Maybe Delores thought so too, prompting her to bring in Eva.

33

The following noon, Eva and Griff met with the federal prosecutor and ironed out a strategy. The prosecutor agreed to let them increase surveillance on the Yemeni students using bogus passports. That taken care of, the two agents sped in Griff's Bucar back to ICE headquarters.

Eva sighed. "I saw Delores Fontaine this morning. Her supposed art dealer never called. Another red herring."

"She sounds flighty. Hopefully Brewster will come through."

"You're sure he's back in London?" she asked, popping a Dutch peppermint in her mouth.

"Can I have another one of those? My stomach wants lunch and we've no time."

Eva handed him a mint. Seconds later, Griff steered into a vacant parking spot by a meter.

"Brewster's expecting our call any second," he said. "Come on!"

Eva leapt out. So did Griff, locking the Bucar with his remote. They ran to the front door, but were stopped by security. After flashing their badges, they took the elevator to the Sensitive Compartmented Information Facility. A security officer sat outside the door reading a book. He inspected their credentials and nodded. Eva and Griff both signed in. Only then did the technician admit them into the specially built communications vault, known in the spy industry as the SCIF.

"I can't wait to find out what MI-5 knows about Pilgrim Peerage," Eva said, returning the creds to her purse.

She led Griff to the secure and encrypted telephone. He joined her inside the vault for their secret conversation. Eva punched in the number, then she and Griff donned earphones with microphones. This would allow them both to talk with Brewster Miles.

The ringing phone stopped abruptly with Brewster saying, "You are late. I must leave in fifteen minutes to see the prime minister."

"Blame me," Griff quipped. "D.C. traffic's a nightmare. Eva and I are secure."

Brewster's familiar British accent popped in Eva's ear. "It's splendid talking with two such brilliant friends. I have fine memories of working together."

Eva grinned. A vivid picture popped in her mind as she'd repelled from a helicopter onto the deck of a terrorist ship with Griff and Brewster. This matter wasn't nearly as dangerous. Or was it?

"Brewster, your voice brings to mind our many joint operations."

"Well, mates, based on intel from Griff, it seems we'll be joining forces again."

Griff adjusted his earphone. "Have you discovered the identities of the Family Finder people?"

"I believe so." Brewster paused. "Eva, are you aware that like Griff, you have relatives here in Great Britain?"

Eva arched her eyebrows. "No. My ancestors are from the Netherlands. Someone going by Dutch Dingo is posing on Family Finder as my Grandpa Marty. This Dutch Dingo is really Clarence O'Leary, aka Ralph O'Leary, Marty's neighbor."

"Perhaps Ralph is helping Marty find your family members," Brewster opined. "I do know the Pilgrim Peerage communicating with Ralph is a British woman. I can tell you that she is no ordinary woman."

"How is she linked to Ralph?" Eva scribbled notes on her pad.

"It is interesting how she uses the moniker Pilgrim Peerage. You may know, British aristocracy famously keep detailed records concerning their breeding. Pilgrim Peerage is no exception. Her real name is Brittney Condover. She is the daughter of the Earl of Condover and grew up on a large estate here in England. Eva, have you heard of the earl?"

Eva stopped taking notes in mid-sentence.

"No. Should I have, Brewster?"

"Let me tell you a story and you decide."

Eva glanced at Griff. He shrugged. She quit writing and listened to Brewster's tale of the Condover family.

"The current earl traces his peerage back to Margaret of York. She was sister to our Kings Edward the Fourth and Richard the Third. According to my research, in the fifteenth century there was a Dutch magistrate named Peter Vander Goes."

"He's my ancestor!" Eva cried, her voice bouncing about the SCIF.

Griff covered his ears and Brewster cautioned, "Stay with me. Peter's daughter Grace married Fredrick of Condover, who was an ally of Edward the Fourth. Grace moved to England and her husband was given the title Earl of Condover by King Edward the Fourth for heroic services. Fredrick built a large castle amidst a vast farmland. That castle, Bentley Park, and the title have passed down through the centuries. Brittney Condover is the current earl's granddaughter. By all accounts, Eva, she is your distant cousin."

Eva flinched. Words stuck in her throat. This was all so strange and new. Neither her father nor Marty ever mentioned a family connection to any British earls.

Griff laughed out loud and spoke for her. "So Eva is part of a wealthy and aristocratic family. Is that what you're saying, Brewster?"

"Aristocratic maybe, but perhaps not so wealthy. British gossip rags report the Earl of Condover is about to lose his castle to creditors. That's not uncommon here in England. These vast homes are expensive to maintain and repair. Some owners rent them out for fundraising events and television shows, or contrive other schemes to help pay the enormous costs. The present earl has entered into several financial enterprises, which have largely failed."

Eva scratched a few notes. "I appreciate all you've learned, Brewster. Still, media reports don't warrant our talking to you from the SCIF."

"On the contrary. My country has benefited from my research. Here's why I told Griff that we needed to speak on secure lines. Brittney Condover is more than the daughter of an earl. She is a missing member of our SRR—"

"Your what?" Eva interrupted.

"Sorry, lass," Brewster retorted. "The SRR is our Special Reconnaissance Regiment, a special ops group designed for counter-intelligence operations. They are like your Rangers or SEALS. Miss Condover came to our attention while she was on leave. MI-5 spotted her meeting with a colonel of the Bulgarian Army."

Griff palmed his moustache. "Eva's cousin is in league with former Soviet military types?"

"Hold on." Eva wagged a finger at Griff. "Let's hear what else Brewster knows."

"Thank you, Eva. The colonel is assigned to the Republic of Bulgaria's embassy here in London. We had Brittney under surveillance for some time. She was questioned about meeting the colonel, and claimed he was selling art pieces she wanted to buy for her family's estate."

"That would be Bentley Park," Eva offered, checking her notes. "Is that feasible?"

"Perhaps, except the Condover family has no extra funds to spend on art. Soon after Brittney was interrogated, she disappeared. We are afraid she is in Sofia, or even Moscow. Bulgaria and Russia remain staunch allies."

Griff pointed to his notes, telling Brewster, "Eight weeks ago, Brittney used the name Pilgrim Peerage to communicate online with Marty's neighbor about the Vander Goes family."

Silence on the other end. Finally, Brewster grunted, "Hmmph. That matches the time frame when we questioned her, right before she went AWOL."

Eva didn't believe in coincidence. She shook her head.

"Brewster, what do you make of this?"

"First, we were forced to make massive security changes within the SRR. MI-5 is convinced Brittney Condover went to the dark side. Secondly, I am sorry to burst your bubble. You learn you have an aristocratic British cousin, and then find she's a traitor."

"I can't believe I'm related to a traitor," Eva insisted. "But I'll comb through our family's records and find out."

Griff closed his file. "Eva and I will keep digging over here. If you learn anything important, please advise."

"You can count on me. Cheerio."

With that, the international connection went dead. Eva glared at Griff. He wore a comical grin. Eva didn't see the humor. In fact, her stomach churned.

"Griff, I know what you're thinking. Somewhere down the line, you and I are related. Fine, but my head is reeling. How are we going to find Brittney Condover? What does she want with my family? She sounds dangerous."

Griff's smirk vanished. "You're right. A Special Ops type is trained in fighting, weaponry, and stealth. Watch your back, Eva. I'll be right there watching with you."

"I have an idea. See what you think."

"Let's have it."

"Lydia, the analyst assigned to this case, is pretty good with social media and the Internet. She hacks into Brittney's Family Finder account and changes her password."

"What then?"

"Lydia hijacks the account, and contacts Dutch Dingo, pretending to be Pilgrim Peerage. She says someone hacked her account and lost their correspondence. Now that she has the account under control, he needs to resend his last messages."

Griff snapped his fingers. "I'll talk to Lydia and see if she'll do it."

It was Eva's turn to smile. She left the SCIF with hope blooming in her heart. With Brewster's help, she had just pulled one of the threads unraveling this torturous maze.

34

A few days passed with Eva checking each day how the kids were doing at her folks. She arrived at the task force office late Monday morning, after another meeting with the prosecutor about the passport counterfeiting ring. Coffee was made, so she assumed Griff had been in and left to pursue a lead. She dropped her keys on her desk and poured coffee before phoning her parents.

Andy answered, "Mom, we saw Jamestown where the pilgrims landed."

Eva's mind alerted to Brittney Condover and Pilgrim Peerage, but Andy brought her back to their daily activities.

"It was cool, but mosquitoes ate me alive. Tomorrow we're going to Monticello, where Thomas Jefferson lived. Here's Dutch."

Her youngest son giggled. "Mom, Gramps showed me a new airplane at the store. Can he buy me one?"

"Have fun, buddy, and don't forget your prayers. Put Gramps on the phone."

"I won't forget. Here's Gramps."

Eva sipped her coffee until her dad came on.

He said briskly, "Now Eva, before you get riled, it's a radio-controlled plane. Dutch loves mine and wants one too."

"I hope you're all having a nice time. But Scott and I are teaching our kids to be content with less. Can't he play with yours?"

"Okay, a helicopter isn't as pricey. Our birthday present for him?"

"I suppose you'll have to buy something extravagant for all your grandkids."

"Oh, I already bought Andy a boogie board. And your mother took Kaley shopping. She's decked out for school. New shoes, watch, the whole gambit."

"Thanks, Dad. Enjoy your grandkids. Say hi to Mom and keep in touch."

Eva set her phone on her desk, realizing she was partly to blame for her dad going overboard with gifts. She should take the kids to visit their grandparents more often. A bulging envelope sent from Chief Talsma drew her attention. It contained Grandpa Marty's mail.

She thumbed through a library newsletter and a church envelope with last Sunday's bulletin. Then she logged onto Marty's checking account and paid his electric bill online. At nearly eleven o'clock, Eva still had lots to do before she could leave.

She was spending the afternoon with Marty at the Manassas Battlefield. They hadn't done anything fun together since he came to stay with them. Besides, seeing the Civil War sights might clear her mind, which was stuck on why Ralph studied her family genealogy. Brewster had not called with any new information about Brittney Condover.

To wrap things up, Eva phoned the Tech Group.

"Dale Anderson here."

"Hi, it's Eva. Anything new at the Bethlehem Road decoy house?"

"Let me see." He hummed off-key. "Our log says the equipment is functioning properly."

"So the GPS in the slippers is still working?"

"Right, Eva. It periodically trips our recorders as it emits its location. Oh, wait. Here's a note about a girl riding up the driveway on a bicycle and ringing the doorbell. She cupped her hands around her eyes and peered in the front window."

"I never heard about her." Eva bolted upright in her chair. "How come?"

"Maybe we dropped the ball. Another tech noted she looked like a solicitor."

"If so, she's nosier than most."

"You're welcome to come down here and watch the recording."

Eva stowed her keys in her purse. "I may do that. Thanks for the update."

She was about to hang up when Dale added, "Oh, Eva. Funny story, if you have a minute."

"I have about that much time."

"The marshals hired lawn guys to make it look like the house is lived in. Guess what we found?"

Eva bit down on her lip. "They're not doing drugs again in there?"

"Nothing so sinister. But Rod Grainger, the U.S. Marshal, checked our recordings and discovered the landscapers are cheating the government, charging for more mowing than they are doing."

"At least they're getting something for our work," Eva replied, eager to hang up.

"But here's the hilarious part. Rod told the lawn guys that a curious neighbor is keeping track of them. The guy reduced his bill."

"Hooray for us taxpayers. Something good has come from this fiasco. Gotta run."

Eva jotted a noted for Griff to call if anything happened at the decoy house. More than anything, she needed a clue, any clue, to stop whoever was stalking her family.

LATER THAT EVENING, Eva rested her head on her folded arms next to Marty's journal, sensing the tension inside Aunt Deane's home. Eva had just reread where Marty and Deane feared being discovered by Kuipers with an attic full of Jews. She lifted her head and picked up the last journal, looking for a mention of Kuipers, who seemed to have disappeared from Marty's writing.

Of course, with him joining the Army, Deane hadn't been able to write much. Not with the Germans reading her mail. Eva pulled out an e-mail address and phone number she'd found on the college website for Kuipers' granddaughter, Trudi Kuipers Russo. At eight o'clock, it wasn't too late to call. A voicemail came on so she hung up, not about to leave her home phone number.

Her cell phone vibrated on the desktop, echoing through the slide-out drawer like a snare drum. It was ICE tech-ops center calling. Eva was slow to realize why. She punched the "on" button and said hello.

A young sounding female responded, "This is tech-ops calling. There is activity at one of your sites. My instructions are to call you."

"This is Agent Montanna. I didn't catch your name, agent—"

"Oh, this is Lydia. I'm here alone."

Eva's mental fog lifted. She grabbed her notepad.

"Lydia, what's happening?"

"The alarms activated. I can see a person sneaking around in the house on Bethlehem Road in Bull Run. Should I notify the police?"

"Yes. Have them use secure communications and set up a perimeter. They are not to approach the subject or the house. Explain that you see a person on the video feed."

"Will do."

"Lydia, the map above your desk should show each agent's residence. Call the three nearest ones. Advise them to scoot over to Bethlehem Road. Tell them to make contact with responding local police and arrest anyone coming out. But our agents should wait until either Agent Topping or I arrive before entering the house."

Lydia paused. "Okay, Agent Montanna, you want me to contact police, they don't enter or arrest anyone, and I dispatch nearest agents. Ten four."

"Good job, Lydia. I'll be in my car in two minutes. My radio call sign is TF Two. I'll be on the tech-ops radio channel. Tell the others to go on that channel."

Eva hung up and sprinted into the family room. She interrupted Scott's reading a suspense novel about Israel.

"Honey, something is up at the decoy house where we hid Grandpa's slippers."

She spun on her heels and ran to her bedroom. Eva changed from shorts into jeans and pulled on a sweatshirt. She strapped on her belt, extra clips, and her Glock, stuffing her feet into thick, leather shoes. As she bent to tie them, Scott hurried in.

"You're not going there alone, are you?"

"Nope. Other agents will meet me. I'll phone Griff on the way."

Scott caught her arm as she brushed past. She backed up and gave him a kiss. Then she hugged him real tight.

"Gotta go. I'll call later."

He followed her to the kitchen. Eva grabbed the keys to her unmarked Ford.

"Call when you can," Scott said. "I'll be praying for you!"

"Thanks, sweetheart. I'm glad the kids aren't here. Be careful too."

She hurried to her G-car, where she opened the glove box and turned the channel selector. Eva pulled out the coiled microphone wire until the mic sat in her lap. Slamming the glove box closed, she tapped in Griff's number as she backed down the driveway.

Eva was already heading for the interstate when he said, "Griff here."

"Lydia just called. Someone's at the Manassas safe house. I'm on my way."

"Do you want my help?"

"Bingo. Turn the JTTF radio to channel fourteen. That's the tech-ops group. Other agents are responding. Sign on as TF Nine. Lydia is notifying the local police. We're asking them to sit tight on a perimeter."

"Okay, I'll be on the radio. TF Nine, right?" Griff confirmed.

"Right."

Eva roared onto westbound I-66, keying her microphone and announcing, "TF Two is 10-8 en route to Bull Run."

Eva's radio crackled with: "TF Six is en route, ten minutes out."

She keyed her mic, "Ten four. Base, do you have an update?"

"Local LEOs are responding," Lydia said. "They'll wait in the area."

Eva swung into the passing lane, heartened the local police were on the way. Her speedometer indicated she was speeding at ninety-five miles per hour. She picked up her microphone, only to be interrupted by Griff calling base.

"TF Nine is en route to join TF Two."

Lydia replied, "Ten Four, TF Nine. TF Two and Six are also on air."

In order to bring TF Six and Griff up to date, Eva asked Lydia to explain events at the decoy house.

"Can't see much of the suspect," Lydia said over the radio. "He's moving around. He must have picked up the sensor, because the GPS indicated movement."

"Ten four." Eva pressed her microphone again. "TF Six? Did you copy that?"

"Copy, TF Two. I'm near the target. I'll connect with the LEOs."

Lydia's voice boomed through the speaker, "Suspect running in the house. He's tearing a picture off the wall."

"Any word from the police?" Eva shot back.

"I still have their dispatch on the line. One unit's a block south of the house and another is approaching." Lydia added quickly, "We have a problem. I saw the suspect by the wall. Now there's a big ball of fire."

Eva picked up her mic. "Notify dispatch of the fire. Alert them to arrest anyone seen running in the neighborhood."

"This is TF Six. I'm on scene and following the locals up to the house." A pause, and TF Six added, "Smoke is everywhere. No one's outside."

Eva dropped her speed and exited off Sudley Road. To her south, she spied flashing lights of fire trucks zooming west on a side street. She maneuvered down the ramp onto southbound Sudley.

Another ICE agent announced, "TF Four. I'm on the interstate, ten minutes out."

"This is TF Six at the scene. Back door is wide open. House is fully engulfed. Looks like the suspect got out."

Eva jammed on her brakes and jerked to the side of the road. Should she try to apprehend the suspect?

Lydia blurted, "GPS signal going east through the neighborhood very fast. Suspect must be running."

"Suspect grabbed the GPS slippers," Eva said into her radio. "Base, keep us advised of their direction."

Eva reached into her glove box and turned on a switch. Fire trucks with red lights and sirens passed by, so she raised the volume on the radio. She flipped another switch, activating her microphone.

"Base, my transponder is on. My location should show on your console map."

"Affirmative. I show you on Sudley Road. The GPS signal was heading in your direction, but is dormant now."

"Yes, it would be. To conserve its battery, the GPS only broadcasts periodically."

Eva's eyes flickered through the windshield to the intersection ahead, then to the rearview mirror where she saw the intersections behind her. She watched for anyone on foot. Her radio crackled.

"TF Two, this is TF Nine," Griff said. "I'm going to set up here on Sudley."

Eva keyed her mic. "Good idea. That's where I am now. You set up southbound. I'll flip and cover northbound traffic."

"Ten four," Griff answered.

Eva pulled from her spot, and cranked a U-turn at the next intersection. She wheeled into a fast food restaurant lot. Once again, she surveyed the area, being alert to anyone walking or running.

Her radio crackled with Lydia's voice. "GPS signal is on again. Northbound on Sudley, just north of TF Two."

Eva turned on her headlights, shoved her selector in gear, and raced northbound on Sudley. She jumped back on the air.

"Base, do you see our three units on your console?"

"Negative. I see yours, but not TF Nine. The suspect is ahead of you. Do you want me to notify local police?"

Eva realized Lydia couldn't see Griff on her map. He was on a portable radio and not emitting a GPS signal. Approaching a red light, Eva slowed and looked both ways before proceeding through it. As she stomped on her accelerator, she saw in her rearview mirror Griff blasting through the same red light.

She blinked and focused her eyes ahead of her, desperate to see anyone running. But she saw no one. She keyed her mic. "Suspect must be in a car."

"TF Two," Lydia said. "Suspect is a mile ahead of you."

Eva's radio buzzed. "This is TF Four. I'm entering northbound Sudley. Base, do you see my signal?"

"Four, you are one-half mile behind TF Two. The suspect is ahead of her."

The road narrowed to two lanes. Now in open farmland, Eva became trapped behind a blue van going well below the speed limit. Adrenaline pulsed through her, but she couldn't pass on a curve. The moment the road straightened, she kicked her G-car into passing gear and swerved into the other lane.

She whizzed by the van, glimpsing a video player in the headrest behind the driver playing a child's cartoon. The driver looked like a harried mother going out to the store or heading home, and not a suspect.

Eva keyed her mic. "Base, I just passed a blue family van. Is the GPS signal still ahead of me?"

"You're very close," Lydia said. "The signal's emitting just beyond you."

Eva sped up behind a small tan SUV. Her pulse skyrocketed. This could be the suspect. In her rearview mirror, she saw both TF Nine and Four passing the blue family van at high speeds. Her eyes flew forward. Eva zeroed in on the SUV's Virginia plate. She gripped the wheel, desperate for a safe zone to pass.

She yanked up her microphone, blurting, "Nine and Four, the plate on the tan SUV ahead of me looks like a rental. I'm going to get around it. You both hang back."

Static from other microphones clicked, meaning the agents behind her were using shorthand to confirm they'd heard her. The road straightened. Eva swung into the opposing lane and shot past the van. It was dark inside; she couldn't even see the driver. She darted back into the driving lane and checked her rearview mirror.

Lydia's excited voice broke the silence, "TF Two. You're right in front of the suspect's signal."

Eva grabbed her mic. "Okay, guys, our suspect's in the tan SUV. Get ready!"

But then her mind whirled with what to do. Her training warned of the dangers in attempting traffic stops with police cars. Worse, Eva was driving an unmarked car. Citizens were told not to pull over for unmarked police cars with small flashing red lights, but to find lighted areas such as a gas station. This road was completely dark.

Eva decided if they waited to arrest the suspect until reaching a lighted area, he could use side streets for a car chase or neighborhood houses to hide in.

Back on her radio, Eva announced, "Nine and Four, I'm going to find a straight spot in the road and block the van. We have him boxed in. Get your red lights ready. When you see me stop, use them. Base, notify the police we've located the arson suspect and are attempting a traffic stop. Give them our ten twenty."

Her foot eased off the accelerator until an oncoming sedan went by. When she was a quarter-mile ahead of the suspect, Eva lowered the sun visor over the passenger side of her windshield exposing front and back strobe lights. The road rose slightly, giving her less shoulder room. She threw a toggle switch on the bottom of her dash. In an instant, her car erupted in alternating flashes of LED lights.

Eva pulled into the approaching lane and hit her brakes. The car shimmied. She cranked the wheel to the right, sliding sideways on the pavement. Through her passenger window, she now faced the SUV coming straight at her. Its bright headlights blinded her. The SUV wove all over the road. Two flashing red lights behind the suspect swerved to a stop.

Eva leaped out her door. She drew her Glock and prepared to jump aside if the suspect hit her car or tried passing on the narrow shoulder. But the SUV swerved left and tried to go down the sloping shoulder behind Eva's car. The suspect accelerated.

Gravel flew in the air, zinging by Eva's ears. The drop was too great. Eva cringed. The SUV flipped and rolled down the embankment. It bounced, stopping on its wheels. With the screeching of tires, her partners' cars skidded up to Eva.

Griff hopped out, calling, "Eva, you all right?"

"I'm fine." She pointed dramatically. "Our guy's trapped down in that SUV."

Lights from Griff's Impala shone onto the farm field, revealing one crumpled tan SUV. To Eva's astonishment, the suspect was climbing out the passenger window. He started running into the murky field. Eva saw him carrying a short rifle or shotgun.

"Gun! Gun!" She raised her Glock and tore down the slight embankment.

Adrenaline flooded her veins. She charged after the man running into the darkness. There was barely enough moonlight to see his outline ahead of her.

"Stop! Federal agents!" Eva shouted, plunging through the black night.

She was gaining on him, and her eyes focused like a laser on his gun. She couldn't fire unless he turned and pointed the gun at her.

Griff yelled from behind her, "Stop! Federal agents!"

Knowing he had her back, Eva ran faster. Suddenly the suspect turned to the right. Eva extended her Glock at eye level. With a quick thrust, her quarry threw the rifle and kept running toward the woods in front of him. Once Eva saw him toss the gun, her legs managed even more speed.

She heard Griff panting behind her. Eva drove herself forward, determined to grab the suspect first. Her lungs felt close to exploding.

There was no need to yell anymore. By now he knew federal agents were chasing him. At last, Eva closed the difference. She stretched out her left hand and latched onto his hooded sweatshirt. Their momentum sent both of them sprawling down a hill and into a damp field.

The guy threw a wild punch, landing hard on Eva's shoulder. Pain rocked her. She socked him in the stomach. Somehow, he scrambled to his feet. Griff hit him with a flying tackle. The guy squirmed beneath him. But Ryan Hall, TF Four, ran up with handcuffs.

Eva dragged herself to her feet and joined Ryan, who slammed a knee on the guy's chest. Their captured prey still struggled to get away. Eva finally heard Ryan ratcheting handcuffs on his wrists. Griff was back on his feet and joined Eva, who rubbed her aching shoulder.

"You okay?" Ryan asked, yanking the suspect to his feet.

The hood fell away, revealing long hair. Eva gasped. She'd been chasing a woman, just like in her dream.

Griff chuckled. "Our arsonist is a woman. Go figure."

Back on the road, traffic was blocked and backing up. Police cars with flashing lights crept along the shoulder.

Eva holstered her weapon. "Griff, you two guys take her to Ryan's car. Find out who she is. Once she's secure, grab a light and come back. I'll look for the gun she threw."

Eva groped in the darkness trying to retrace the route she and the female suspect had taken into the field. Moonlight revealed shadows of bent grass, but when the woman had tossed her gun, it must have gone farther off their path.

Her shoulder throbbed as Eva searched everywhere for the discarded weapon. She couldn't find it. Concern for the burning decoy house assailed her mind. She sure hoped no one had been hurt. The marshals wouldn't get much for it at auction now. What would be the repercussions for using a seized house as a decoy?

Eva didn't need this trouble. Some moments in her career had been pretty wild, but she had always stayed clear of disciplinary action. Total destruction of some grandma's seized house might pose a bump in her career path. She also wondered about the gun. Did the suspect always travel with one in her car?

A wavering flashlight came toward Eva. She stopped and drew in a deep breath, waiting for Griff's better light.

"How's your shoulder?" he called.

"It hurts, but I haven't found her gun. I think we ran down this way."

Griff and his flashlight bobbed closer. "The county police asked us to move our cars. Traffic's finally moving again."

"Give me the light. I know where we've been."

She snatched his flashlight and swept the beam across their path.

He followed behind. "Ryan has her in his car."

"Who is she?" Eva asked, aiming the light on the weeds.

"She's carrying a New York driver's license, but isn't saying a word."

"Could be a fake," Eva snapped, sweeping the light across their path.

"This began with a GPS delivered to your grandfather's house in Michigan?"

Eva trained the light ahead of her. "Marty is so low profile, it's probably meant to locate me."

"So she's an assassin sent from New York, thinking the seized house is your home."

"When you put it like that, it makes no sense. If I'm not in it, why burn the house? But then again, why take the GPS slippers before setting the house ablaze?"

"Hey, Eva, shine the light to your left," Griff ordered. "I see something on a patch of stones over there."

They hurried to a rocky indentation in the weeds and stopped. Eva aimed the light on the suspected gun.

"That's no gun," Griff said. "What is it?"

He bent over while Eva trained the light. He picked up pieces of wood with mitered ends. Griff unrolled a painted canvas.

Eva groaned. "It's the cheap garage sale oil painting from the dining room."

"What? We caught ourselves a stupid art thief?" Griff glared at Eva.

She defended herself. "It looked like a long gun. I expected her to turn it toward me."

"Well, your gun is a stupid piece of canvas." Griff stuffed it back around the disassembled frame. "Why this painting?"

"I have no idea. Let's get out of here."

Eva plunged toward the red and blue lights flashing up on the road. Disgust seeped from every pore. Who was the woman? And why steal a worthless painting?

Griff grabbed the flashlight and handed Eva the rolled-up painting. "We can hold her for arson," he said. "But we'll have to turn her over to the locals."

"Oh no!" Eva spat. "She tried burning down what she thought was my house. That's an attempt on the life of a federal agent."

"I don't think so, Eva."

Eva stopped in her tracks. "Why not?"

"I heard the radio traffic." Griff turned toward her in the darkness. "She stayed in the house long enough to know it was uninhabited. That's a lesser felony."

"Maybe you're right, but I'll think of something."

Eva reached the street, ready to unload on one crazy suspect. Then she saw Ryan's car had gone, hopefully with the woman still handcuffed in it.

35

Eva hustled back down the hill to retrieve the slippers from the demolished SUV. Then she watched the crushed vehicle being hoisted onto a wrecker. The tow driver pulled away, heading for the ICE impound lot. Eva gently eased into her unmarked car, babying her shoulder. She desperately needed an ice pack.

In her back seat lay the rolled-up canvas and collapsed picture frame. Griff checked on her a final time on the way to his car.

"I'll be fine once I figure this out," she said.

Griff nodded. "Nothing about this makes sense."

"You're so right. Why steal a corny picture and burn down a house she knows isn't occupied by either Marty or me?"

Eva's cell phone buzzed. She glanced at the screen. It was a blocked call.

"It's probably an agent calling."

Griff started to walk away. "You answer. See you back at headquarters."

Eva answered and found it was Ryan.

"We just arrived at HQ with the female," he said. "We need you for a complete strip search."

Eva gulped. She detested doing strip searches.

"Ryan, what do we know about her?"

"She ain't saying a thing. She has an international driver's license in the name of Amanda Casper. It has a London address and she has a British accent. She carried a throwaway cell phone and magnetic hotel room passkey.

It looks like a Hilton. Agent Wooley just went to the local Hilton to find out at which hotel she's been staying."

"Good work, Ryan. I'll be there in thirty minutes. We'll sort things out, but it's going to be a long night."

The miles to the office were a blur. Eva considered Amanda Casper and replayed her last conversation with Brewster. Was it too bizarre to think Amanda might be Brittney Condover, aka Pilgrim Peerage? Condover was AWOL from British SRR and thought to be hiding in Bulgaria or Russia. Could she really be in the U.S.?

Eva swallowed. This woman might be Eva's distant cousin. That didn't sit well. She rolled to a stop in the parking lot next to Ryan's government ride. After removing the slippers and rolled-up painting, she peered into his back seat, where the prisoner had been sitting minutes before, with her hands cuffed behind her back. Eva couldn't fathom a Montanna or Vander Goes family member being confined as a criminal.

She stalked to the door and swiped her ID badge. Griff pulled in beside her car, so she waited for him to catch up.

"Ryan called," she said. "The woman has no passport, but has an international driver's license in the name of Amanda Casper. She's British."

"Sounds mighty suspicious. Think she's the missing SRR agent?"

"Great minds think alike." Eva held open the door, pain shooting down her arm.

Griff followed her to the task force squad room, where Eva plunked the rolled-up painting on her desk. Ryan came in with a coffee decanter filled with fresh water.

"I'm brewing fresh coffee. Amanda is in the holding cell and cuffed. We're waiting for you to search her." He stared at Eva.

She locked her gun in her desk drawer. "What's she saying?"

"Nada," Ryan said, pouring the water. "She refuses to talk."

"We'll see about that," Eva fired back, heading for the holding cell.

"Oh, wait," Ryan added. "She wondered who the woman was who arrested her."

Eva glanced over her shoulder. "What did you tell her?"

"That she's in no position to ask questions."

"Good. I don't want her knowing my name, not yet."

Eva picked up the international driver's license from Ryan's desk. An unimpressive Amanda Casper stared from the license with shoulder-length brown hair and cold eyes. She might be ten years younger than Eva, but she sure wasn't as fast.

After pulling on a latex glove, Eva steeled her shoulder and headed for the lock-up. She replayed the lung-splitting foot race Amanda had just lost. A nasty thought stopped Eva in her tracks. Amanda might know more about Eva than she did about her.

Eva rested her eye against the peephole in the holding cell's steel door. Amanda sat on a metal bench, her wrists behind her back. She seemed to glare at the stainless steel toilet to her right. Griff stepped up and inserted the large metal key into the lock.

He turned the key. "I'll wait out here. I don't envy your job."

"And I don't trust this arsonist. Stay within earshot."

Griff yanked open the door. Eva went right up to Amanda and snapped the latex on the second glove to emphasize she was in command. What was about to follow was a humiliating experience for prisoners.

Amanda swung her head. She flashed a defiant look.

A jolt of recognition sizzled through Eva. Those eyes! Amanda had the same piercing turquoise eyes as the woman from Eva's dream.

Eva stared back, looking for a Vander Goes family resemblance. She saw none. But to think she'd dreamed about Amanda the day the slippers had arrived was beyond perplexing. It was disturbing.

She prepared her mind for what came next. Again, Eva snapped the latex on her left wrist. "Your driver's license says you are Amanda Casper. Is that your name?"

Icy blue eyes stared back, but Amanda gave no response.

"I assume you're not Amanda. Stand up and turn around so I can remove your cuffs."

The prisoner was slow getting to her feet. When she stood, she turned her back as if used to having her hands cuffed behind her. Eva inserted a key and removed the cuffs. She spun the prisoner around. Amanda stood two inches shorter than Eva.

"Get out of your clothes. Drop them here." Eva pointed to the floor.

The Brit glared, not moving an inch.

"I will not repeat myself. If you don't strip down posthaste, I'll bring four guys in here and we'll all do it for you."

Amanda shot Eva an evil glance, but lifted the hooded sweatshirt over her head. Eva again pointed at the floor. The sweatshirt fell. Next, the woman stepped out of her jeans, calf muscles bulging. Eva figured she had to be the AWOL British SRR agent.

"Are you going to tell me what prompted you to steal items from a house and burn it down? Are you going to tell me why you targeted Martin Vander Goes?"

The Brit kicked off her shoes, answering in a husky voice, "I choose not to answer. You must advise me of my rights."

So the Brit had a voice and one surly attitude. Still, Eva never enjoyed these searches, though they were often part of her job. Undies hit the floor and she ordered Amanda, "Spread your feet."

Using her gloves, Eva finished the indignity of searching for hidden weapons and contraband.

"Okay, put your clothes back on."

Amanda snapped up her jeans and Eva stepped to the door where she clanged the cuffs against the metal. Griff unlocked and opened the door.

"I'll bring you a sandwich later," Eva told the suspect. "You'll remain here through the night."

She pushed the door slightly open and gave Amanda a parting shot. "It is proper to give warnings to persons arrested for violating our criminal laws. But you are a foreigner without a passport, arrested for an act of terror on U.S. soil. You will be sent from here to Gitmo, Cuba."

Griff banged the door shut behind Eva and locked it again. She headed for the squad room.

"Come on, Griff. Let's send Brewster the mug shot Ryan took. Also, send a copy of her driver's license. I'm convinced she's the missing SRR agent, Brittney Condover."

"It's the middle of the night at MI-5, Eva."

"Yes, but I want him seeing her photo first thing in the morning."

Ten minutes later, Eva contacted back channels to forward Amanda's photo and other data to Brewster Miles at MI-5. This method allowed her and Griff to avoid Brewster's counterpart at the British embassy in D.C. She'd just hung up, when Agent Wooley came in.

He tossed his backpack on the floor and dropped in a chair, his legs stretched out. "Based on Amanda's room key, Hilton traced her to the Dulles Airport Hilton."

Eva tapped her keyboard with her fingernails. "So she planned to make a fast exit from the country. We caught her first."

"Good thing too, before she torched any more houses," Griff replied, looking up from his reports. "Want me to head over, search her room?"

Eva pondered his request and then shook her head. "No. Agents Hall and Wooley can finish that job."

Wooley groaned. "I need something besides coffee. Got any food?"

"Hey, Ryan," Eva called to the other agent. "While Griff and I tackle mounds of paperwork, you and John Wooley search her hotel room. John knows the one. On the way back, buy sandwiches and coffee for the crew. Bring something dry and lifeless for our prisoner."

Ryan sauntered in from the evidence room and grabbed his backpack. "You mean like a plain 'ole burger with nothing on it?"

"Exactly. No cheese, no pickle, zip." Eva flashed a smile. "But bring everyone a chocolate shake, including Amanda. I don't want her thinking I'm inhospitable. Only, don't give her a straw."

After Ryan and John left on their assignment, Griff nodded toward the holding cell and tossed Eva a jab.

"I see you treat family just like you treat all your prisoners."

Eva rolled her eyes, refusing to take his bait. Griff had a point though. She didn't care for Amanda Casper or Brittney Condover or whoever and never would accept that she and Eva shared some long lost ancestor. After flexing her fingers, she began typing her report. Time flew.

Hall and Wooley's arrival in the squad room was preceded by the pleasing aroma of burgers and fries. Eva jumped to her feet. She stopped short when she saw what Wooley carried under his arm.

"Did you find that in her room?" she asked.

Wooley plopped sacks of grub, and an old German pistol onto a desk. He handed Eva several rolled canvases.

"Her room was mostly empty, but we found one bag, and a British passport in the name of Amanda Casper. We kept searching. Beneath the platform of the bed, we found these paintings and the gun."

"More paintings!" Eva marveled. "Why is our suspect so interested in art?"

Eva tore off a rubber band and unrolled one canvas. Her hand flew to her mouth.

"Oh no," she said.

Griff walked over. "What's wrong?"

Eva peered at pencil sketches of a German soldier. She lifted one sketch. Beneath it was another of a man's rugged face with a windmill in the background. She looked at the others, each of a Dutch scene.

"These are Grandpa Marty's drawings from the war. She stole them from his garage."

Griff picked one up.

"Maybe he's an undiscovered Master." He set it back down and turned toward the holding cell. "Let's find out why Amanda has his sketches."

Eva grabbed the hem of his jacket. "Forget it, Griff. She isn't talking. Besides, let's wait and see if Brewster can identify her."

"Okay. I'm diving into my burger." He swiped one from the bag.

Eva lifted Amanda's gun from the desk and asked Ryan, "Where did you find her weapon?"

He shrugged. "Like I said, it was under the bed with the paintings."

Eva leaned closer. It was a WWII German P38. She pulled Griff aside, burger in his hand.

"Griff, I won't say this to any other agent. When I first went to Michigan, I was so tired out. I fell asleep, hard. You may not believe this, but Amanda in there was in my dream. She tried to kill me with this gun. She had the same vivid eyes, same gun."

He arched his brows and began humming the tune from the *Twilight Zone* TV show. Eva punched his arm. He wasn't far off though. Dreaming of her future was downright eerie.

She forced down her burger. Many reports and hours later, Eva drove home. She crept into the house and found Scott asleep on the couch. She kissed his forehead, whispering she was home. He smiled in the dim light and went right back to sleep. After washing her face, Eva nestled an ice pack against her shoulder. She'd finally caught the sender of those slippers. Yet, she was no closer to the truth.

36

The following night, in her home office, Eva's intuition told her that Marty's last journal might reveal why Amanda had lifted his artwork. Perhaps Ralph already found out something that Eva didn't know. She set her take-out coffee by her elbow, eager for even the slimmest thread to Amanda Casper or Brittney Condover. Brewster had yet to confirm her identity. Eva dove into the pages with newfound gusto ...

In his Quonset hut in Thetford, England, Martin squinted in the weak light and picked up his pencil. He so wanted to tell Rebekah his thoughts. The Red Cross said she'd been sent to Auschwitz but couldn't trace her there. Anguish pierced his soul. Hot tears burned in his eyes. His heart was breaking.

Catching a glimpse of his open Bible on his cot, Martin was drawn to Psalm 3, written by King David when he fled from his son Absalom.

I cried unto the LORD with my voice, and he heard me out of his holy hill. I laid me down and slept; I awaked; for the LORD sustained me.

Martin dried his tears. The Lord had sustained him thus far. He took up his pencil and filled the empty pages in his journal. The lead became dull, so he sharpened the point and spent an hour pouring out his thoughts onto his journal pages.

Eli might be tending his tiny plant in the attic, the one by the window. Martin hoped he remained alive in Deane's attic. If only he knew how she was doing now that she'd married Simon. Years ago already, she'd purchased

Mr. Rosenbaum's truck and Martin painted it. Then he'd used that truck to carry grandfather clocks and Jews under the nose of Constable Kuipers.

At first, Martin transported clocks for Jews who sold their goods to raise money for escape. Then in 1941 he took clocks from vacant Jewish homes, storing them in Deane's shop for families if ever they returned to Holland. Kuipers was at the root of much grief. His stony heart had often led Martin to despair. He'd become Martin's worst enemy, dogging his movements, and harassing him unceasingly. After Deane's marriage, Martin saw a way out. On the last day before he was to take a merchant ship to enlist in the U. S. Army, Deane had come to his room.

"My boy," she'd said, tears filling her eyes. "I wanted to care for you in my brother's place. Your being here helped me fulfill my charge."

She'd lifted her hands onto his head and blessed him. "May the Lord our God bless all the days of your life. I may not live to see your children, but God showed me in a dream. You will survive the war and have a son."

Martin swiped teardrops off the journal page. He couldn't stop thinking about what happened to Rebekah. Had a secret informer led the Gestapo to find her? Martin may never know. He closed his eyes and asked God to protect Deane and Simon, Rebekah and Yaffa, and Eli. Yaffa was still milking at the dairy farm. At least Deane had said so in her last letter.

SOMETHING SHE READ STARTLED EVA. Someone had drawn a pencil line through Yaffa's name and written in Joanne. Why? That was her late grandmother's name. Why would Marty do that? Had he already met Grandmother Joanne in England? Or was she a different Joanne?

She checked her watch. It was nearly ten o'clock, the time Marty usually went to bed. But he might still be up. Eva hurried to the living room with her finger in the page of his journal. Marty slouched on the sofa watching a TV show about elephants. She picked up the remote and muted the sound.

"Grandpa, I need to ask you something important about your journal."

He smiled, fluffing the pillow beside him. "Come join me. I'm all ears."

Eva remained standing. She opened to the page and pointed.

"In here you mention Rebekah was taken from the tulip farm to a concentration camp. You worried about her safety."

Marty's shoulders drooped. "It was a terrible time for me. The Red Cross told me she perished at Auschwitz. I couldn't bring myself to believe it. Most everyone from that camp lost their lives."

"There is something else." Eva's eyelids started fluttering.

Her cheeks flamed, but she didn't dwell on Rebekeh. She was too anxious about her discovery.

"Grandpa, this note here."

She sat beside him. With a shaking finger, Eva pointed to Yaffa's name with the line through it. "You changed Yaffa's name to Joanne. Why?"

"I'm not sure. Let me see."

He took the journal with his hands trembling slightly. "Oh, I remember." But he just smoothed the page, saying nothing.

"Will you tell me, please?"

"Yaffa thought her name sounded too Jewish. She changed it to Joanne at the farm when she was in hiding."

"But didn't everybody there know she was Jewish?"

Marty pressed his lips together and then said, "Yes, but the invading Germans wouldn't. It looks like I forgot when I was writing, and so I went back and changed it."

"Did you know two Joannes, Grandpa?"

"No." He looked at Eva in a daze, then shook his head. "No, only one. Joanne Levi. I returned to Middleburg after the war and married her."

Eva's emotions surged. Goose bumps enveloped her arms.

"Grandpa," she said softly. "I'm Jewish? No one ever told me."

Marty lowered his head before gazing into her eyes.

"Joanne was so afraid by her wartime experiences, she never told anyone. Our marriage gave her new life. She used to tell me that she was twice saved. Once from the Germans, then later from her sins when she accepted Jesus' gift of salvation."

Eva was incredulous. "Does my dad know about his mother being Jewish?"

"No! Your grandmother was afraid even to tell Clifford. She believed she'd be taken to a concentration camp and killed as they did her best friend, Rebekah."

"This is all so mysterious. Did Grandma ever tell you about her family?"

Marty gripped her arm. "I have so wanted to tell you, but never found the words."

"Grandpa, I understand, but there are so many unanswered questions."

Eva was numb. She didn't even hear the tick-tock of the grandfather clock in the corner. Life had just thrown her an incredible curve. Marty got up and yawned.

He chirped, "Good night," oblivious that Eva's world had just been turned upside down. Scott found her on the sofa some minutes later.

She gazed at him with tears in her eyes. "You will not believe what I just found out from Grandpa."

A FEW DAYS PASSED WITH EVA still in shock over what she'd learned about Grandmother Joanne. The most difficult aspect was that Eva could never ask her anything. She had to shake off her troubles and bring her mind to what she and Griff had yet to solve about Amanda Casper.

This morning, she walked beside the FBI agent as they headed into the Smithsonian in downtown D.C. They encountered a twisted line of tourists waiting to pass through security.

Anxious to find out anything about the rolled-up drawings, Eva nudged Griff with her elbow. "Go over to the security guard."

He nodded, bypassing the long line. He approached a guard who supervised the screening of handbags and backpacks. Griff flipped open his credential case, his gold FBI badge glistening.

The uniformed guard stiffened. "So?"

"Sir, I am FBI Agent Griff Topping. My partner is Eva Montanna from ICE."

Eva didn't bother taking out her badge, assuming Griff would be believed. She simply added, "We are expected at the Preservation Center."

The supervisor peered at Griff's ID over the top of his half glasses and demanded, "Are you both armed?"

Griff straightened to his full height. "Of course."

The supervisor swung open a pedestrian gate and motioned at a desk. "Sign the guest form over there. Be on your way."

Griff tossed him a subtle salute and wrote their names on the clipboard. Eva spotted a small sign directing visitors to the Preservation Center. She started down the corridor, her heels clicking on the floor. Griff hustled to join her. The two special agents passed floor-to-ceiling glass walls, with Eva admiring various framed pictures displayed on easels.

"I never heard of the Center before," she told Griff. "Have you?"

"No." Griff scowled. "I have little interest in art."

Eva adjusted the canvases under her arm. "I discovered they are famous for restoring works of art."

Griff pointed to a technician bending over a painting on a table, and peering through a large magnifying glass. She used a tiny brush to repair a crack.

"Hey, Eva. That looks like back breaking work."

"And boring." Eva flashed a grin. "Do you think she'd rather be chasing art thieves through dark fields?"

"I sure would."

Moments later, Griff opened the glass door. "We each have our expertise. Right now, we need theirs."

Inside the high-ceilinged office, Eva stepped carefully on the shiny hardwood floors. Too bad she hadn't worn her flats.

She introduced herself and Griff to the receptionist, adding, "The chairman is expecting us."

The well-dressed woman consulted a log before picking up her phone.

"I heard you were coming. You may take a seat."

Eva was just about to do so, when a door behind the receptionist swished opened. A man in a gray business suit and green bow tie approached. He extended a hand to Griff.

"Agent Topping, I presume?"

Griff shook his hand and introduced Eva as a fellow agent.

The slight man faced Eva with a peculiar look on his face. "I am Cecil Prescott, Chairman of the Center. Frankly, your visit surprises me."

"Oh?"

Eva took a step back and glowered at him. She was in no mood to be harassed by an art expert.

Prescott gave an exaggerated frown. "I informed Agent Topping in no uncertain terms when he called that we are no appraisal service. Not even for government agencies."

"Sir, I understand your position, but—"

Griff plunged in front of Eva, interrupting her speech. "Excuse me, but my boss at the FBI phoned the Smithsonian's director. They reached an agreement. Our mission is most urgent."

"I see. You're pulling rank. I have no time for this, but follow me." Sarcasm lacing his tone, Prescott spun on his heel.

Eva nudged Griff. "Quick, before he changes his mind."

They scurried behind the chairman, passing through the metal door and down a hallway dotted with paintings and murals done in different mediums. He abruptly turned, and Eva sauntered behind him into the spacious conference room. Prescott jerked two chairs from the mahogany table, his irritation apparent.

He flipped his hand toward her canvases.

"Are those the pieces you asked me to review?"

Eva handed them over with a smile. "Please. We need to know their value."

"There you go again," he complained, rolling out the canvas. "I say again, we do not give appraisals like some TV show."

Griff pulled out his credentials and held them open. "And as I said, the FBI considers this a vital matter."

Prescott shot a glance at Griff's official ID.

"No need to throw your weight around, Agent Topping. I am civil service."

With a wave of his hand, Prescott unrolled the canvas along with the first sketch, a German soldier standing in front of building rubble.

He stepped back. "Oh my!"

Eva's spirits soared. She leaned forward, eager for him to explain how the sketch was worth millions.

But Prescott's touch to the canvas' edge held disdain. "Nothing like I expected. This is most unremarkable."

Griff snapped shut his credentials. "What do you mean?"

"Simply this." Prescott tossed aside the sketch and flipped to the next one.

"When you claimed someone traveled from Europe to steal these pieces, I relented and agreed to see them. My first instincts remain correct."

"And what is your opinion?" Eva folded her arms and glared.

As he adjusted his bow tie and confronted Eva with his deep scowl, she was tempted to add, "Mr. Pinhead," but clamped her lips shut. She waited.

"I say again, these are quite unremarkable. Compared to the master-pieces we see here, these look like they were done in a high school art class."

"That's absurd," Griff insisted. "Why would someone steal them?"

Prescott irreverently snatched out the last sketch. He gave an exaggerated shrug.

"I have no idea. Perhaps there is something about the paper, canvas, or technique that is not apparent at first glance."

"Where do we go from here?" Eva refused to accept defeat. "Are there tests you can perform on the paper?"

Prescott fiddled with his bow tie. "I suppose. Leave them here and I will assign one of our visiting scholars to examine them further. Give me a week."

He spun the pictures back into a roll.

Griff handed him a business card and said, "Keep these secured."

"Surely you jest." Prescott's vein pulsed above his cheekbone.

Griff lunged forward. "Mr. Chairman, I do not. We leave you with evidence in a terrorism case. If you lose these, you'll testify before a judge how that happened."

A visible shudder passed over Prescott's angular frame. He tapped Griff's card on the table, and then stowed it in his suit pocket. Next, he nestled the picture roll under his arm.

"A terrorist attack at the Center is my worst fear." His voice took on a serious edge. "We process some of the world's most valuable works. Let me escort you out, Agents Topping and Montanna. I promise, you will hear from me soon."

37

L ater that afternoon, Eva edited a report on her office computer when the JTTF receptionist sauntered up. Lana dropped a package on Eva's desk and walked off. Eva glanced at the familiar postal envelope from Chief Talsma in Zeeland.

Before taking out Marty's bills, she corrected her report and saved it into a file. Then she double-checked the status of her passport case. Next week, she'd appear before the Grand Jury. It would be a relief to have at least one case moving forward.

After inserting the date and time for the Grand Jury into her phone's calendar, she turned her attention to the envelope. Because it took time for Talsma to pick up Marty's mail from the postmaster and send it, some bills might be late. Eva cut open an end with scissors and slid out the contents.

On top was a Zeeland Charter Township newsletter.

Eva thumbed through it, noticing a colorful aerial map showing farmland in the township. The banner along the top boasted of the township's centennial farms. She smiled. On the list were several farms owned by local families for over one hundred years, including Martin Vander Goes' farm on 88th Avenue.

How nice for him to be recognized. She slid the glossy publication into her purse for him to enjoy later. Then she paused. Was this kind of publicity a good thing?

A handwritten envelope addressed to Martin Vander Goes at the farm unsettled Eva. It bore a return address of Jersey City, New Jersey. Perhaps someone had already seen that newsletter article. Could Trudi Kuipers Russo be writing to Marty?

Eva picked up the envelope by its edges and scrutinized the postmark. She was concerned about messing up fingerprints. Still, the mail handlers and Chief Talsma had already added theirs to the sender's. Eva's wouldn't make much difference. The inside was a different thing. She didn't want Marty's fingerprints anywhere near this letter. So to maintain the evidentiary benefit, she ran the blade of her pocketknife under the flap, slicing it open.

Then she used tweezers on her mini-Swiss Army knife to pull out the one-page note. Eva used a piece of paper to flatten it gently on her desk.

She quickly read:

Dear Mr. Vander Goes,

I am helping my grandmother locate a man who helped her in the Netherlands back in World War II. This young man was Martin Vander Goes. He was from Michigan and lived near a town called Holland. Her name then was Rebekah Abrams.

In my Internet research, I stumbled across an article about your centennial farm in Zeeland. From the map, I see you live near Holland, Michigan. Sir, if you are the same gentleman, please write me at the address below. If you prefer, call the number below my name. Thanks for your consideration and help.

The letter was signed by Cole Donner. It didn't appear to be from Kuipers' daughter. Eva's hackles rose all the same.

First, the weird "GPS slippers" arrived at Marty's. Then, the psycho Amanda Casper joined forces with Marty's neighbor Ralph using Family Finder. Amanda followed the GPS-laden slippers to Virginia, stole worthless art, and burned down the decoy house. Only by God's grace did Eva catch her. To top it all off, Eva discovered her grandmother, Joanne Vander Goes, was really Yaffa Levi.

She shuddered. To receive a letter pretending to be from Rebekah Abrams' grandson was too much. Eva doubted every word.

According to the Red Cross, Rebekah had died at Auschwitz before the war ended. Even the name, Cole Donner, sounded fake. Donner was one of Santa's reindeer. No. He wasn't real.

Eva resisted tearing the letter to pieces. She narrowed her eyes to slits. This was one more lure Amanda concocted to target Grandpa.

Then she realized something positive. She now had the address and handwriting of whoever was behind the letter. Eva vowed to bust wide open this ruse by Amanda Casper. The mention of Marty's years in the Netherlands seemed to link this letter, purportedly from Cole Donner, to the first threatening note Eva had found in Marty's truck. Her mind jumped from one question to another.

Was Ralph somehow involved in this fishing expedition? Was he still tinkering with their family data on the Internet? She yanked up the phone to call and blast him to the outer reaches of space.

Then she paused. Hadn't she purposely avoided contacting Ralph? She slammed down the receiver. Better to wait until she heard from Cecil Prescott at the Smithsonian. But there was something Eva could do.

She wheeled back to her computer and prepared a lead for the Terrorism Task Force in Newark. Griff had already opened a terrorism case on Amanda Casper, aka Brittney. The British deserter would face justice for torching government property. That meant every Joint Terrorism Task Force office would follow up on all leads, posthaste.

With a flick of her finger, Eva sent Cole Donner's name, along with his address and phone number, to Newark. A flashing icon at the top of the screen alerted her to another report in the same investigation. She clicked on a classified report from Griff Topping. In it, he detailed information from MI-5 agent Brewster Miles in London.

Eva rapidly read Brewster's intelligence. She let out a whistle. It was just what she thought. The mug shot photo confirmed Amanda Casper was Brittney Condover, the missing SRR officer. Brewster also revealed Brittney had highly secret training in disarming bombs and explosives. She'd also learned to assemble them. These revelations left Eva dumbfounded. Brittney was a bomb maker.

How could the one thing in the world that Eva fought the hardest against—terrorism—now involve her grandfather? It made no sense for the former SRR agent to target mediocre art pieces in Marty's garage. Perhaps Brittney had slithered to the dark side, as part of a complex scheme to blow up the Smithsonian National Art Museum. Eva forced herself to finish Brewster's report. He had already arranged with Griff to arrive in two days. Then he'd start interrogating Brittney at the British Embassy in D.C. He mentioned taking her to London for disciplinary action.

No way, Eva thought. That would happen only over her and Griff's dead bodies. If Brewster's interrogation failed, Eva had every intention of escorting the British terrorist to Gitmo. And she pledged to unveil the whole of

Brittney Condover's vicious schemes, *before* Brewster arrived. The "fake" letter from Cole Donner needed to be checked for prints. She and Marty needed to spend more time in his final journal and maybe even Grandma Joanne's diary.

Eva couldn't leave work for another two hours. But this was too urgent to delay. She scratched out a leave slip and dashed to her boss' office.

"Something urgent has come up. I need to leave early. Will you sign my slip for vacation time?"

"Nope." He waved her off.

"Sir, I must. My reports are finished for my Grand Jury appearance next week."

Her boss smiled. "Montanna, get out of here. Didn't you work the night through the other day? You've eclipsed your overtime requirement."

He tore up her leave slip and she thanked him profusely. Grabbing her purse, she stuffed in her Glock, hoping she'd have no reason to use her powerful gun.

Eva raced home determined to pull out any clues. She phoned Scott at his office just as she hit the remote button to open the garage door. Eva told him of her change in plans.

"No problem," he said. "I'm working late. You and Marty have fun."

"There's been a new wrinkle. Hold on a sec."

Eva nestled her G-car in the third stall of the garage before giving Scott the disturbing news.

"Some jerk sent Marty a letter, claiming to be Rebekah Abrams' grandson. The postmark is New Jersey, where Trudi Kuipers lives. How did he get her name?"

"Calm down. Rebekah Abrams knew his name, have you forgotten? I'll phone when I leave Capitol Hill."

"Sorry to be uptight, but this is strange." Eva turned off the car. "Stay safe."

They hung up. The first thing Eva did after going in the house was to lock the door behind her. She found Marty asleep in his room. She gently woke him from his nap.

"I came home early," she said. "How about coffee and an almond bear claw?"

He sat straight up. "My favorite. You know the way to a man's heart. I'll freshen up and meet you in the kitchen."

Eva washed her hands and brewed coffee. She set pastries on the kitchen table along with his last journal and her grandmother's diary. Marty entered, looking rested. He sat and bit into his treat. She settled in a chair next to him. Before telling him about the letter mentioning Rebekah, she asked him something less stressful.

"Grandpa, what's this about your being in a bomber squadron?"

His eyes drifted off. He ate his bear claw and drank his coffee before telling her, "I was fortunate not to be chosen as a gunner or bombardier. Many of those brave souls never returned."

"I can only imagine what it was like to lose your mates." Eva scanned the page. "This is the first I heard of your connection to airplanes. Maybe that's where our son Dutch gets his fascination with flight."

"Could be."

Eva sipped her coffee while Marty gathered his thoughts. When he set down his cup, he leaned toward her, his elbows on the table.

"They pushed us through training in a flash. You probably read how I was ordered to England to join a bomber group. It was sad to see those big planes roaring down the airstrip, some for the last time."

Marty stared out toward the tree line of Eva's backyard. His eyes closed and his chin dropped. Thinking he needed a short respite, Eva cracked open his journal, eager to get to the bottom of this today.

38

SEPTEMBER 1943 – THETFORD, ENGLAND

Martin Vander Goes hadn't fought against the Germans on their eastern front or in the Soviet Union's "Patriotic War." Rather, on this stormy autumn day in Thetford, he toiled behind a makeshift desk at Bentley Park. It was his job to stop anyone entering the large English mansion, by all accounts a palatial estate.

He fidgeted on the uncomfortable chair appreciating one benefit of this clerical assignment. Valuable artworks adorned every wall, which inspired him to do a little sketching of his own. The British government had commandeered Bentley Park with permission of some British aristocrat. Martin was grateful for his training in an engineering group, and proudly served as an aide in the U.S. Army Air Force, 388th Bombardment Group.

Yet during his orientation, his commander had cautioned Martin, "Even though our group is stationed at Bentley Park, the earl maintains an apartment here. Conduct yourself properly."

So really, Martin was a guest at headquarters. Because the earl allowed the Army to control access to his house, Martin took seriously his sworn duty to enforce the security agreement.

Above the roar of the wind, sounds of crashing trees made him jump. He looked to the vestibule beyond his station at the front door. He felt sorry for the men working outside felling trees behind the main house. The guys were also building a new air raid shelter.

Lightning crackled. Seconds later, thunder boomed. Martin rushed to gape out the large plate of glass. Rain fell in gray sheets. Darting back to his post, he prepared for something to happen, but what?

He picked up his pencil and worked on his reports. In truth, something besides Army requisitions plagued his mind. He needed to finish what he'd started days ago. Martin shoved aside a newspaper and took out a sketch from his folder. Deftly using the flattened side of his pencil, he shaded in the flight jacket collar of Staff Sergeant Vinnie Thomas.

Since Martin had first sketched a bomber pilot, he'd received orders from thirteen more crewmembers. He studied Vinnie's portrait. The way the staff sergeant peered out through the Plexiglas bubble in the bomber's nose seemed lifelike. Martin concentrated on highlighting the contrast of his wide-set eyes.

A shadow loomed across his sketch. Martin swiveled his head and gazed up at a tall figure. From the awkward angle, all he could see was a tailored tweed jacket.

"Nice work you do there," the interloper remarked.

Martin rose. He'd seen this face before, but where had he met this man?

"Thank you, sir," Martin managed in spite of his failing memory. "May I help you?"

The well-dressed man glanced at Martin's name on his Army blouse, and thrust out his hand. "Vander Goes, I am surprised to see you in my home."

Martin's brain fired on all cylinders. He searched the files of his past. Finally it hit him. He did know this man—Blake Attwood—and smiled graciously.

"Sir, I'm thrilled you made it back. Ever since placing you on Simon's boat in the canal, I wondered if you made it back safely. You encouraged me to help the Dutch Resistance and I did. After Pearl Harbor, I enlisted in the U.S. Army."

"So I see. As Bentley Park's owner and its present earl, the war we fight against fascism is of great concern to me."

Martin snapped his feet together. "Sir, I did not realize this is your home."

"Yes. A pleasant place before the war, but I hardly recall those days. My father was the earl until the Germans sunk his ship in the Channel."

"Oh, I'm so sorry for your loss," Martin said with compassion.

"Thank you. I remember your Aunt Deane, but old chap, remind me of your first name."

"Martin Vander Goes, sir. And you are Blake Attwood, correct?"

"Very good. Now I am the Earl of Condover."

Martin stood taller in the presence of the earl, who stepped around Martin to catch a better view of the sketch.

"I recall admiring your drawings in the Netherlands."

"Would you like me to do one of Bentley Park?" Martin asked.

"What a smashing idea. Deane has a keen eye for fine art." Blake gestured with his arm. "Do you notice the many works displayed in my home?"

Martin grinned. "I study your collection every spare moment. The pieces are exquisite."

"Tell me, how is Deane?"

"I've received a few letters. From her code, I believe she continues in the Resistance."

Blake nodded thoughtfully. "The network of brave souls resisting the Nazis continues to grow."

"She married Simon, her childhood sweetheart. He's the fisherman who shuttled you to your rendezvous with the sub. They have many people staying in her home. These guests, you understand, don't want to be found by the Germans. Many Jews are hiding in fear."

"Private Vander Goes, you showed courage in those days after Germany's invasion. It is fortunate you escaped the tentacles of the Abwehr, Germany's intelligence service. Others in the Dutch Resistance have not been as lucky."

"What do you mean?" he asked, afraid for his aunt.

"Dutch agents are being arrested at an alarming rate." A shadow crossed Attwood's youthful face. "I think someone has compromised the line."

"I suspect Constable Kuipers, who was promoted by the Germans, is really an Abweher agent."

"He very well could be from what you told me at the time. Have you heard from Deane lately?"

"Not recently enough. Your news makes me anxious for her safety."

Blake straightened a crooked painting on the wall, and then faced Martin, a serious glint in his eye.

"Let me find out what I can. It may take time."

Martin blew out his breath. "I would appreciate anything you can tell me."

"Does your commander know of your important activities? Your many talents?"

Not wanting to boast, Martin merely shrugged.

"Well, never mind. You are welcome in Bentley Park. I am beholden to you. I might not be here but for your help in finding me passage out of

Middleburg. And my country has given me the rank of lieutenant commander since I saw you last."

Martin tapped his heels together. "Yes, sir."

"At ease, private."

Martin relaxed his posture, and Blake tapped Martin's sketch.

"Are you an artist for *Stars and Stripes*? Your work is splendid."

"Sir, I am not. My assignment is to restrict access to your home."

Blake clasped his hands behind his back. "I am grateful to you and your aunt. When we first met, I was passing through Middleburg on my retreat from Holland ahead of the German advance. I hold a commission in His Majesty's Naval Intelligence and was collecting intelligence on Hitler's efforts to secure Dutch harbors."

"Will we beat them, in the end? I mean, General Patton is sidelined, and he's our finest general."

"Too bad he slapped that soldier. Patton is not out of it yet," Blake replied, eying Martin up and down. "With your country's aid, we have a fighting chance."

"General Eisenhower will give a broadcast later today. Do you know what it's all about?"

"I do. The Allies signed an armistice with Italy. Germany no longer has the Italians as a buffer." Blake rubbed his chin. "Hitler must be having a fit."

"Yes, sir."

Blake stepped closer, as if putting Martin in his confidence. "Vander Goes, when I met you and Deane, I failed to mention a possible family relationship."

"How so?"

Surely, the Earl of Condover was mistaken. Martin had no connection to English nobility.

"Family on my mother's side is from Goes, in the Netherlands. They descended from Peter Vander Goes. Do you know of him?"

"My parents mentioned him, and so did Deane. Peter had something to do with government and knew Johann Gutenberg, who invented the printing press."

"Brilliant! The very one."

Surprised, Martin straightened his back.

Meanwhile, Blake shifted his eyes toward Lt. Col. Francis Henggeler's office. "Have you heard about the new command of Monuments Men?"

"Not yet. You have me curious."

"Some people say it is rumor, but I am in a position to know." Blake lowered his voice to a bare whisper. "Your Army is organizing a unit to sweep through Europe protecting valuable art and historic buildings. They require soldiers like you, who know art when you see it."

Adrenaline pumped through Martin. A smile lit his face, but then he thought better of his chances.

"I'm a mere private. They'll find people better connected than me."

The next smile was Blake's. "I intend to offer an excellent word for you."

"It may require the recommendation of a high-level Army officer."

"I say, your commander uses my house as his billet and sleeps in my bedroom. He will be interested in my opinion."

Martin tried absorbing the earl's offer. He suppressed an urge to shake his hand. That wouldn't be proper. So he settled for, "Thank you, sir. I am most grateful."

"It is the least I can do for the lad who guards my door." Blake stuck out his hand. "And for the man who guided me safely from the clutches of the Gestapo."

The British commander shook hands with Martin, an American private. Martin felt as if he was actually family with the Earl of Bentley Park. He also realized that meeting him more than three years ago in the Netherlands was no accident. Surely God's hand was behind it all.

39

On a cool but sunny mid-morning a week later, Martin finished guarding the entry desk at Bentley Park. He snatched up his folder and hopped in an Army jeep. Then he sped away, veering around a bold peacock strutting down the middle of the road. Blake's dumb pet had kept Martin awake for the past two nights with its continual squawking.

Leaving the grounds, Martin considered Blake's promise. He'd heard nothing more about the Monuments Men. Fighting disappointment, he'd thrown himself into sketching. With his folder lying on the passenger seat, he drove straight to Knettishall airfield.

The B-17 Flying Fortresses had sortied early this morning to Germany. Martin gunned the engine, desperate to meet the *Screamin' Eagle* crew upon her return. He rounded a bend in the road just as a Fortress descended, passing close over his head. Jagged holes marred its tail.

"Must have run into Luftwaffe fighters," Martin muttered, pulling onto a taxiway.

He watched the Fortress land and taxi toward the ground crew. They frantically directed the plane to a parking spot. Martin rumbled past other bombers receiving post-flight services from separate crews.

From behind the wheel of his jeep, he spotted a small crudely-made wooden shack. Its hand-painted sign proudly stated it was the parking spot for the *Screamin' Eagle.* Crewmembers sat nearby on crates, some smoking cigarettes. Martin angled behind the shed and cut the engine. He swiped his folder and hurried to the waiting airmen.

"Hey, buddy," a tech sergeant said, nodding at the folder. "You got my transfer orders back to the States?"

A private with red hair sauntered over. "What he's carryin' is too big for orders. What ya got there?"

Martin proudly held up his sketch for them to see.

"Wow!" a couple guys chimed in unison.

The sergeant grabbed the drawing. "That's Vinnie. I'd recognize his nose anywhere."

"I like how 'ya show him in the turret, holding the trigger of his chin gun. He's an ace gunner," observed Red.

Martin took back his sketch and slid it in the folder. "Right you are. Vinnie asked me to meet him at the airfield. I just finished it, so here I am."

The sergeant looked skyward. "The *Screamin' Eagle* is due any time."

Another crewman walked up to Martin. Bandoliers of 50-caliber rounds draped around his neck and hung down to his waist. "What's up?"

"Vander Goes here drew Vinnie," Red said, jerking his thumb at Martin. "It's for real."

The crewman pocketed his hands. "I heard of you. Would you draw a picture of me, so I can send it to my mom?"

A misfiring engine caught Martin's attention. His head jerked up in time to see a bomber touch down on the runway. Only two engines were running. It skidded on one wheel, the wing tip scraping along the runway. The loud screeching sound hurt Martin's ears. The plane spun off the runway. Martin froze. Grass and dirt sprayed up in the air.

The crew jumped off their crates and ran full speed toward the airstrip, fire extinguishers in hand. Several airmen scurried from the plane. They carried a motionless buddy.

One of the ground crew hiked back with his unused extinguisher, saying, "He'll make it."

"Is that the *Screamin' Eagle*?" Martin asked.

"Nah. It's the *Sally-B*. Their tail gunner saw our *Eagle* goin' down in flames over France."

"How terrible!" Martin's pulse skyrocketed. So many brave men were getting killed.

"Our crew bailed out. Say a prayer for 'em and keep Vinnie's picture." He set down his fire extinguisher and ran back with a stretcher.

Martin kicked at the gravel. About a quarter of their planes didn't make it. This was the first time he personally knew one of the missing crew. It was even scarier for the bombardiers. They had to fly twenty-five missions before they could head back to the States.

He walked to the jeep with a shudder. Would any of the guys he'd talked to moments ago survive their future missions?

On the bumpy drive to Bentley Park, Martin silently prayed for the *Screamin' Eagle* crew. He'd heard stories of airmen parachuting in the English Channel and being picked up. Those downed in France were either hidden by the French underground or captured by Germans. He prayed the *Eagle* guys would be saved by the underground.

He parked the jeep and hurried to the Quonset hut, which served as his barracks on the acres behind the enormous mansion. He sat on his cot, looking at the sketch of Vinnie. If only one day he could give it to him in person.

Corporal Wagner stalked into the barracks. "Vander Goes, did you see Col. Henggeler since you got back? He's asking for you."

"Did I do something wrong?" Martin jumped to his feet.

"Dunno." Wagner flopped on his cot. "He ordered me to find you. You'd better get in there."

Martin rushed off in a tizzy. He ran up the steps and into the front vestibule of Bentley Park, nearly colliding with an officer. It was Lt. Colonel Henggeler, who was just leaving.

"Vander Goes, I've been looking for you. Follow me."

Martin snapped to attention and saluted the colonel. Henggeler returned the salute, and turned on his heel to his office. Then the base commander tugged at a squeaky desk drawer. He wasted no time fluttering a document. Martin held his breath. Was he in trouble for racing down to the airfield?

"Some people may guess you have influential friends in Washington."

Martin stood at attention. "I do not have friends in the Army, sir."

The colonel pointed to a seat. Martin complied, perching on the chair's edge. Henggeler snapped the drawer of his Army-issued desk shut.

"It has come to my attention you've been sketching the likeness of our soldiers. Quite good likenesses too."

"Yes, sir. Is there a problem?" Martin stiffened, waiting for the rebuke.

"None at all. President Roosevelt is being pressured by art lovers back home to ensure the Germans don't steal every masterpiece in Europe and that we don't bomb to smithereens such precious works."

Martin felt tongue-tied in the presence of his intimidating base commander.

Colonel Henggeler jabbed a finger at the document. "President Roosevelt has formed the Monuments, Fine Arts, and Archives program. They'll use the acronym MFAA, but already the press calls these military personnel and civilian advisers the Monuments Men."

Martin squirmed under the colonel's intense gaze. This must be it, the special program the Earl of Condover had mentioned. But Martin kept his trap shut. He didn't want to mess up his chance of ascending to the elite team.

"Private, how would you like to work for the Monuments Men?"

Martin's spirits soared. To avoid the impression he wanted to leave the 338th Bomber group, he simply nodded.

"Well, I hope you like it," Henggeler barked. "Because based on my recommendation, you are assigned to the Third Army. You report to Washington, D.C. for training."

Martin stood and saluted. His life was changing again, for the better he hoped. A question seared his mind as he walked down the steps of Bentley Park. Was he ready for the trust placed in him by the Earl of Condover and Colonel Henggeler?

40

MARCH 1944 – LONDON, ENGLAND

The war in Europe raged on. Martin was again stationed in England, but not at the palatial Bentley Park. This afternoon, his training in D.C. a faint memory, he ducked into a darkened basement near London, chilled to the bone. His eyes gradually adjusted to the dim light.

After scrambling for a seat next to Private Crane, he told Bobby, "I'm so ready to do something besides listen to lectures."

Bobby slouched on the wooden chair. "Yeah, what do these eggheads know about war?"

"They know art, and that's our mission."

Martin had no idea when he'd actually get to search for any missing art. He gazed around the room used by the Monuments Men. Snow swirled in white tufts around the windows that sat two feet from the ceiling. These high windows brought natural light into the otherwise dismal level below ground. At least during the past week, cold temperatures had moderated. Spring couldn't be that far away, could it?

"My brother is fightin' with the Fifth," Bobby said. "He's a truck driver."

Martin pumped his fist. "Rumor has it our guys along with the Brits dumped bucket-loads of bombs in Berlin. Was your brother in that raid?"

"Wish I knew. I like to think he's givin' it to the Germans right and left."

Shifting on the flimsy chair, Martin shared Bobby's sentiments. The battles seemed far off from this cramped lecture hall. For the past few weeks, museum and art types trained him, Bobby, and other soldiers about German forces marauding through Europe. Martin saw an imposing figure stride to the front who hadn't spoken before.

His eyes flew to his syllabus. The tall captain pacing by the lectern was Robert Posey. Before the start of another boring lecture, Martin stroked the sergeant chevron on his sleeve. A thrill shot through him. Just last night he'd torn corporal insignias from his uniforms, and proudly sewed on his new chevrons. He was rising in the ranks.

Just the other day, his lieutenant gave orders to Martin and six other fresh sergeants when they'd received their chevrons. "Listen up," the lieutenant had said crisply. "We're shipping to the front soon. You'll each command a team of four, and will investigate sites where we believe Hitler is hiding art treasures he's plundered. Art experts will accompany some teams, but you need to learn enough to recognize art when the experts aren't along."

Private Crane was on Martin's team. He'd spent time working for an architect in New Jersey. A shrill noise made Martin flinch. He snapped his head forward. Captain Posey tapped a pointer on a chart resting on the easel. He was an architect with the Army Corp of Engineers. Posey's stiff posture and Army uniform gave him a commanding presence.

Martin leaned forward expectantly.

Posey cleared his throat and began his lecture. "General Eisenhower, the Supreme Allied Commander, accepts our recommendations. Some of the world's most treasured buildings have been ruined by relentless bombings. Unfortunately, our artillery will continue invoking damage. General Eisenhower orders the safety of allied troops and civilians *must* take precedence over protecting these treasures. Those on building restoration teams will find much work to do."

Another new sergeant next to Martin shielded his mouth and said, "I studied mechanical drawing and worked for a construction company in Chicago."

Martin was more interested in Posey's briefing than small talk. He tried to listen as the captain explained, "We fully expect some of you will find and preserve artworks. Just this week, an intelligence memo came to my attention."

At the words "intelligence memo" Martin's mind flew to his work for the Dutch Resistance. Whatever Posey had to say, he didn't want to miss a word. He blocked out the sound of Bobby tapping his fingers on the desk. The colorful artwork flashing on a large screen had him riveted. That's because Martin instantly recognized the *Ghent Altarpiece* completed in 1432.

Posey raised his voice. "Notice Jan van Eyck's brilliant work. You may know he is from southern Netherlands and Belgium known as The Low Countries. This *Altarpiece* is priceless."

Martin's father and mother had greatly respected the Flemish painter. Martin watched in awe as Posey put up another larger photo of van Eyck's magnificent work. Robed angels flocked around a red altar and bowed before a white lamb, its head gleaming.

Posey again tapped the pointer. "Be on the lookout for this panel, *The Adoration of the Lamb*. See how the lamb bleeds from the throat and is being worshipped on four corners by angels, martyrs, prophets, and apostles. It represents Jesus' crucifixion."

Martin's pulse quickened. As part of the Monuments Men, might he actually find such a famous painting by a true Master?

"Hermann Goering, commander of Hitler's Luftwaffe, has ordered the SS to steal the *Altarpiece*," Posey gravely intoned. "Hitler wants it to decorate the new headquarters of the Third Reich."

Murmurs spread through the attendees like wildfire. Martin felt outrage at Goering's order, but then caught himself. Why be shocked at anything the Nazis did? He'd witnessed firsthand the terrors of the Gestapo. Posey rapped his pointer for quiet.

"See here, gentlemen. The *Ghent Altarpiece* was stolen from the Chateau de Pau in the south of France where it had been stored for safekeeping."

"Our guys better stop these Nazis," Bobby hissed. "There's no end to their evil."

Martin said through clenched teeth, "I know. I've seen their dirty deeds."

His old anger burned again. The ferocious Nazis were wreaking carnage across Europe, bullying Jewish families to turn over their artwork as well as their businesses. The families did so in a vain attempt to preserve their lives.

His aching heart longed for Rebekah. But she had perished from tuberculosis at an Auschwitz concentration camp. He turned his head to wipe his eyes. He didn't want to tear up in front of Bobby. After all, Martin was his superior officer and had to remain tough.

He forced his attention to Posey, who pointed at the screen. This new selection showed a beautiful rendition of a purple-robed man sitting on a white horse in front of other men on horses.

"Oh my," Martin murmured.

"What's that painting?" Bobby asked.

Martin simply shook his head as Posey raised his voice. "Whoever finds this painting will be famous throughout history. Van Eyck's *Just Judges* is another panel of his fabulous *Altarpiece*. Hitler's deputies are frantically searching to grab this panel for his birthday present. It would complete the *Ghent Altarpiece*."

Posey folded his arms and asked with a slight grin, "Does anyone know why Hitler may not have a happy birthday?"

Martin's hand shot up.

"Yes, sergeant."

Surprised to hear Captain Posey address him by his new rank, Martin swallowed.

"Sir, the *Just Judges* was stolen several years ago and has never been found."

"Correct." Posey's grin widened. "Sergeant Vander Goes, you are interested in van Eyck?"

Martin squared his shoulders. "Yes, sir. My family is from the Netherlands. They believe my ancestors knew Jan van Eyck and his relatives."

Several in the audience turned to stare at Martin. Bobby rolled his eyes. Martin couldn't figure if Bobby disapproved of his family connections or the others' caustic glares.

Posey was nodding his approval. "Well done, sergeant. Keep an eye open for the *Just Judges*. Unfortunately, both that panel and one of John the Baptist were stolen seven years ago. On April tenth, nineteen thirty-four, to be exact."

A picture of the John the Baptist painting flashed on the screen. Martin watched and listened with extreme interest.

"This panel was discovered in a baggage area of a Brussels train station. Unknown persons demanded a ransom for its return. A note left in place of the *Just Judges* mentioned Germany being forced by the Treaty of Versailles to return it. I fear Hitler may have his hands on both of these fine works."

The screen went dark. Posey returned to his lectern. "Tomorrow I will outline our plans to protect landmark buildings. You'll receive a binder with artworks and buildings to safeguard. You are dismissed."

Martin assembled his notes, his mind percolating with fresh ideas. An art expert from New York bumped into Martin's chair, causing his papers to slide to the floor.

"You're only on this team because you carry a gun. Don't be fooled you know anything about art. "

Bobby doubled his fists. "Hey, watch it!"

"At ease, private," Martin ordered, hoping to defuse the tense situation.

A tapping sound grabbed his attention. Captain Posey had returned to the lectern.

"Excuse me. Excuse me. May I have your attention?"

To a man, all talking stopped. No one, not even the New Yorker, resumed their seats.

Posey asked, "Sergeant Vander Goes, are you from the Netherlands?"

Martin stood erect. "Sir, I lived on the island of Zeeland, in the town of Middleburg, during the Nazi invasion."

"Do you speak and understand German?"

"I do, sir." Martin wondered where these questions would lead.

Posey looked about the room. "Is anyone else fluent in German?"

Bobby shook his head. So did everyone else.

"Sergeant, I will meet with you briefly," Posey said, pointing at Martin.

Bobby squared his shoulder and faced the New York art expert. "Too bad you don't know German. Maybe you'll get lucky and be assigned to Sergeant Vander Goes' team so he can talk for you."

Martin ignored Bobby's comments and collected his papers. Then he went forward with sinking spirits. Because he knew German, he was about to be kicked out of the Monuments Men.

41

MAY 1945 – MUNICH, GERMANY

Martin couldn't have been more wrong. He had served with distinction in the Monuments Men for the past fourteen months. On this wet morning in May, he stretched his legs beneath a table in the mess hall at Seventh Army headquarters in Munich. He opened the *Stars and Stripes* newspaper, eager for a war update.

His eyes snagged a terrific headline: *Germany surrenders in Holland.*

He quickly read the article. A week earlier, Canadian General Foulkes and German Commander-in-Chief Blaskowitz had reached an agreement. German forces in the Netherlands were capitulating. It was official. Germany had finally lost the war.

Martin wanted to jump up and holler hooray! But he thought of the millions of lives lost. He didn't stir. But then it occurred to him—with Netherlands in Allied control, he should write to Aunt Deane this very instant. He thrust down the newspaper and dashed to his quarters where he grabbed his writing case. If only this letter would reach her in Middleburg.

A dreadful thought loomed. What if she died or was languishing in a prison camp? He shook off such awful possibilities, and hoped he would see his brave aunt again soon.

He snatched up his pencil. Pouring his thoughts on paper, he told Deane how he was in Munich and praying for God to protect her.

I'm in the Monuments Men. We're tasked to find great works of art carried away by the Nazis. When my captain discovered I spoke German, he assigned me to his unit. My travel through France and Luxemburg has been quite successful, but also dangerous. In Lorraine, France, we carefully entered the Priory Church of Mont Saint Martin near the Luxembourg border. Its roof had been blown off. Rain washed away the plaster walls. Beneath the old plaster, Captain Posey found a wall painting of the Annunciation. It had had been painted sometime around 1350. I could hardly believe the extraordinary find!

Yesterday we stopped at King Ludwig's Neuschwanstein castle. It's filled with amazing art and jewelry stolen from the Rothschilds and other Jewish families. I ache all over. We carried tons of art, statues, and carvings down hundreds of steps. There were no lifts.

Aunt Deane, how are you and Simon? Do you hear from Yaffa? If so, please greet her for me and write back, letting me know how she is. I am heartbroken over Rebekah's death. So many are gone; I cannot comprehend the loss. That I don't have to liberate those stinking camps is best. My hatred for Kuipers and his random killings still haunts me. I never forget your blessing to me before I left. Your love and care sustain me through many dark hours.

Love, Martin

He sealed and addressed his letter, stowing it in his blouse pocket. Clatter from a nearby table drew Martin's interest. He walked over to where Bobby stood with his arms crossed. U.S. troops and Russian officers, who had assisted in the monument restorations, played dominos. Several small pieces bounced off a table.

"Take a look, Sarge." Bobby jerked his head.

Curiosity getting the better of him, Martin peered closer. Instead of dominoes, he observed tiny porcelain figurines. A uniformed American lieutenant drinking coffee with a Russian colonel grinned up at Martin sheepishly.

"Look here, Colonel Romanov got himself a hundred pieces from the eighteenth century."

Bobby shot Martin a questioning glare. It seemed obvious, but Martin had to ask. He strode up to the Russian colonel and picked up a figurine.

"Where did you get these?"

Romanov leapt to his feet, and puffing out his chest, he announced, "I find 'dis in de palace at Sans Souci."

Though intimidated by the colonel's mammoth size, Martin couldn't restrain himself.

"You mean you *stole* these from the Palace of Sans-Souci."

In a flash, the colonel's subordinates circled around Martin. Romanov took a swing at Martin. He ducked. Bobby lowered his head, ready to pounce.

The lieutenant quickly stepped between the men, sternly correcting Martin. "Sergeant, I don't think you mean the colonel came by these items by wrongful means."

"Doz Krauts killed my men." The massive Russian shoved the lieutenant aside. "But ve von da fight. To da victor, doz the spoils go."

Martin whirled, facing Bobby. "Private, go fetch Captain Posey."

Bobby hustled off. Romanov scooped his booty into a pile and with one enormous hand, swept them into his knapsack.

The lieutenant pulled Martin aside. "Look, buddy. Stop kickin' this bee's nest. You're gonna start an international incident."

Martin had another idea. He wanted to obey Captain Posey's instructions.

"These figurines look like they're part of Germany's national treasure. It's wrong to steal from Germans even if they do it to everyone else."

Romanov headed for the door, only to be intercepted by Posey.

"Colonel, excuse me. I am Captain Posey and commanding officer of this unit."

With a fierce glare at Posey, who he outranked, Romanov clutched his knapsack.

Posey didn't flinch. "Pursuant to agreement between our governments, I understand you have artifacts from the Palace of Sans-Souci."

Colonel Romanov drew his arm tightly around the knapsack. Posey held out his hand.

"I will take the figurines and provide you with a receipt. If these items aren't returned to the German people, they'll be given to the Russian government."

Martin steeled himself for a shouting match and serious reprimand. To his surprise, the loud-mouthed Russian simply handed his knapsack to Posey. Bobby flashed a crooked smile and Martin felt relieved. Any doubts that he'd done right rolled off his shoulders. He darted away to post his letter to Deane, a whistle flying from his lips.

THE NEXT MORNING, MAY 13, 1945, following Posey's orders, Martin completed an inventory form for the figurines taken from Colonel Romanov. Posey accepted Martin's inventory with a smile. Then he nudged him to a quieter area.

"Assemble your team," Posey said with enthusiasm. "We leave for Austria."

This was a sudden change of plans. Martin tensed.

"What is our mission in Austria?"

Posey's eyes sparkled and he clapped Martin's shoulder.

"Our troops discovered sealed-up salt mines near Altaussee, Austria. That's a hundred and forty miles southeast of here. We're taking the trucks. Meet outside in one hour."

"Yes, sir."

Martin saluted his superior officer. Adrenaline spiked through him as he gathered his team. Bobby helped corral everyone and pack up. The entire group left in a light drizzle. Martin was Posey's driver. The commander's zeal for the mission was contagious, and Martin drove the Army jeep with gusto. They set off at a good pace, but that soon ended on the slick roads.

For many tiresome hours, it became stop and go. Go and stop. Turn and go. They waited at Allied checkpoints, and carved out detours around roads that had been demolished or filled with rubble. Long after leading the mighty six-by-six trucks, Martin's left foot turned numb.

He stomped on the metal floor, which made his right foot press on the gas. He ended up gunning the jeep, and jerking Posey's head backwards.

"Sorry, sir." Martin eased off the gas. "My foot's asleep."

"We'll be there before long. But be prepared. Our work in Austria will take time."

Believing Austria to be beautiful, Martin hoped that would be true. He steadied his feet.

"Good, sir. Maybe we will stay there until our discharge."

"I think not. Our task is urgent. Russian troops continue to advance. General Patton wants us to be the ones emptying the mines and transferring their contents to safety."

"Does General Patton think the Russians will steal the art?"

Posey cleared his throat. "Based on your experience yesterday with Colonel Romanov, what do you think?"

"That General Patton's instincts are correct," Martin replied, grinning.

"Exactly. Looks like we are nearing the mine."

Martin spotted the handmade sign and turned, this time trying not to jolt his superior officer. In his rearview mirror he saw the five trucks of the Monuments Men following in the steady rain.

"Sir, how was this mine discovered?"

"Our troops found the mine shaft entrance, but unfortunately it had been blown up. Intentionally, I might add. While our soldiers were inspecting the entry, an archivist from a local museum told them the mine held treasures, put there by the Third Reich."

"Whoopee!" Martin's hands flew off the wheel. "I mean, do they know for sure what's inside?"

"We're guarding the mine and searching for explosives." Posey shifted his weight on the hard seat. "This archivist seems reliable. He refused to join the Nazis, and so they fired him. Mine workers that he knew discovered crates of explosives being hauled in and labeled as marble slabs."

"That's a clever ploy. Why explosives, sir?" Martin kept his eyes on the uneven road.

Posey thumbed through a stack of reports. "It says here a Nazi official living in the area insisted explosives be used if Allied forces closed in on the mine. He wanted to prevent the art from being returned to the Jews."

"I hope they never had a chance to set off the explosives."

"You'll be happy to know art lovers were actually working as caretakers. They convinced German guards to blow up the entrances and preserve the art. I understand the explosives are deep in the mine. The military guards fled. Our troops are receiving good intelligence from the civilian caretakers."

They reached a crossroad. Martin was unsure which way to turn. He asked Posey, who consulted his map.

"Turn left. The mine entrance is a mile down the road."

After Martin cranked a tight turn, Posey pointed ahead to a building swarming with U.S. soldiers.

"That's the HQ for mine operations. We'll billet there. Park in front."

Martin slowed to a stop, excitement filling him. Would he be the one to find the stolen van Eyck painting down in the mine? Or was that wishful thinking?

Trepidation slowed his steps. First, they had to deal with explosives lining the mine. That was not Martin's specialty. He hopped out of the jeep, and did the only thing he could do. He put his future in God's hands and hurried over to help his captain.

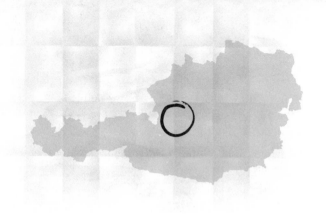

42

THE AUSTRIAN MINE

With great vigilance, Martin listened to the civilian caretakers explaining about the treasure being held in the mine. He had to interpret their animated instructions. A few times he faltered, searching for the correct English word. Sweat dripped from his brow. Finally, the hour-long meeting came to an end.

Martin wiped his face and left the HQ building eager to investigate the mine. He bypassed the jeep, and took the wheel of a three-axle cargo truck. Posey eased into the passenger side. Bobby drove another one of the big six-by-six trucks, as did three other privates. Then Posey, Martin, and the privates lumbered down a gutted road, bringing the caretakers along.

At Posey's direction, Martin led the way to the mine entrance. He jammed on the brakes. Another six-by-six truck blocked the entrance. Its tailgate hung down. An Army colonel in a rain-soaked uniform directed some privates boosting a large crate onto the canvas-covered truck.

"Okay, Martin," Posey said. "Sorry for the rain, but there's nothing to be done."

Martin killed the switch, stopping the engine. Posey plunged out, signaling his party forward. He walked to the rear of the truck being loaded, where he crisply saluted the waterlogged colonel. The superior officer returned the salute.

"Good afternoon, sir," Posey said. "My team and I arrived from Army headquarters in Munich. I understand everything in the mine is being guarded and I'm curious to know what's in there." Posey pointed at the crate.

The colonel stiffened. "I am on General Eisenhower's staff. This crate is headed for Allied headquarters in Paris."

"Yes sir," Posey replied, assuming the demeanor of a junior officer. "May I inquire as to its contents?"

"Certainly. It contains Michelangelo's *Madonna of Bruges*, which was once in the Church of our Lady of Bruges."

"You are correct about that, sir. However, the Madonna was stolen by the Third Reich from the Bruges church. Has General Eisenhower issued a requisition order?"

The shorter colonel stared up at Posey before thrusting out his bottom lip.

"Not necessary. I issued the order, transferring it to Ike's Allied headquarters."

As Bobby crept up alongside him, Martin lifted a hand. He watched the standoff between the captain and colonel with growing unease. From what he'd seen, Martin didn't think Posey would back down. And he was right.

Instead, Posey snapped at Martin, "My leather case."

Martin pulled out the stack of papers and handed them over. Posey waved his papers.

"With respect, colonel, I am here with the Monuments, Fine Arts, and Archives program. General Eisenhower commissioned us to ensure all stolen art is returned to the proper owners. I think 'Ike,' as you call him, will be highly embarrassed if the Madonna shows up at his headquarters."

The colonel's face beamed red. His hands flew to his hips.

"Captain, you have no authority to countermand my orders."

Posey reached back and tugged on Martin's jacket sleeve. Then he motioned for the colonel to step aside from Bobby and the other soldiers.

"Sir, may the three of us speak privately over there?"

The colonel acted as if ready to explode. He hesitated, but did follow Posey and Martin for ten yards or so.

His face grim, Posey kept his voice low. "I understand the temptation to ship the Madonna to the Supreme Allied Commander, and hope for a promotion. But I must report this effort to avoid the proper safeguarding of such a priceless piece. When I do, you might end up being a private loading trucks for Sergeant Vander Goes here."

Posey jerked his head toward Martin.

"I see." The colonel snorted as if wanting to rip Captain Posey to pieces.

At length, he stalked to the truck, ordering his aides, "Return that crate to the mine."

While Martin hid a grin, Posey's face was a portrait of seriousness.

"You see, sergeant, there's not much difference between certain American colonels and certain Russian colonels."

"It makes me wonder, sir, if other works have already been transported from the mine."

Posey raised his eyebrows. "An astute observation; however, we may never know."

He handed Martin the papers to stow in the leather valise. Finally, they approached the patiently waiting caretakers. Posey told Martin to bring his men.

"And you will interpret for our guide, Herr Freitag. After he takes us through the mine, we'll prepare our action plan."

Martin relayed to Bobby the captain's orders. Soon, the group huddled into a rickety elevator, boasting a single lightbulb. With the flick of a lever, the operator began their descent. After dropping to a depth greater than two football fields, the elevator shuddered to a stop. Martin filled his lungs with air. Never before had he been so deep below the earth.

Herr Freitag pushed up his thin glasses. He raised a rickety slatted wooden door and flipped a light switch. A sixty-foot-wide and forty-foot-high corridor stretched out before them. Martin exhaled, waiting for Posey to lead the way. He trailed behind the captain with a question eating at him. Where were the explosives?

Posey acted unconcerned. He gestured with his arm as they walked along the rugged corridor hewn from rock. "See these side rooms jutting off? The carved out rock has been smelted for its salt. It's left hiding places perfectly suited for storing art and treasures."

Freitag turned on another light in one of these storage rooms. Martin explained the guide's German comments. Then he lunged toward a bunch of canvas bags.

"They're filled with Nazi gold!" Martin shouted, his words echoing off the rock.

Bobby whistled and peered around his shoulder. Freitag urged them to explore another room. He switched on a light, explaining through Martin, "This room is filled with sculptures."

Posey strode to a covered object and lifted a canvas. Staring at him was a life-size unclothed woman. He dropped the canvas and hurried back to Martin.

"As you see, we'll be very busy. Pick up the pace before the Russians crash our party."

Bobby made a wisecrack about the fat Russian colonel.

Martin jabbed his side with his elbow. "Sshh."

Posey shot Private Crane a withering glance. Then he nodded at Freitag, who snapped off the light. The team headed down the corridor until they reached another lighted room. Martin was amazed by the tangle of wooden cases, each standing on end. They hadn't laid eyes on any masterpieces, let alone a van Eyck. His spirit began to wane.

Then in precise German, Freitag quickly got Martin enthused to complete the mission. He said excitedly, "Each case contains one or more paintings. The outside printing identifies the contents and the city where these pieces were stolen from."

Posey wrote on a small pad, as they viewed room after room stuffed with wooden crates. When they returned to the corridor, Martin whispered to Bobby, "Touring these endless rooms reminds me of a house of mirrors from the fair."

"Yeah, Sarge. Or some eerie, haunted house."

They laughed, lagging behind their guide. At long last, Freitag looped back around to the elevator. Posey leaned over, telling Martin to explain their future plans.

Martin fumbled for the German word for inventory before saying, "Herr Freitag, Army guards will remain here after we leave the mine. Each morning, we will enter the mine, examine the crates, and record an inventory. Hopefully, our inventory will match yours."

Freitag frowned and blinked his shrouded eyes behind frameless glasses. His odd response gave Martin pause. Posey nodded for him to continue.

Martin took a deep breath, wondering if he had offended Herr Frietag. "After we complete the inventory, the crates and contents will be loaded on trucks and taken to Munich. The art will be returned to the lawful owners, if possible."

Frietag's dour face erupted into a smile. He rattled off a few choice words to his caretakers. They all applauded. He said something to Martin, who told Posey, "Herr Frietag and his colleagues will be grateful to see the art, jewels, and gold returned to their rightful owners."

Posey and Freitag shook hands in agreement.

The guide turned off the last light, and Martin scooted into the elevator for their much-awaited ascent to the top. This intense day had sure opened his eyes. The leaders of the now demoralized Third Reich had pilfered massive amounts of the world's art, much from Jewish families. When they reached the top, he couldn't help breathing a sigh of relief.

He turned to Bobby. "At least we didn't stumble onto any explosives."

"Not yet anyway," Bobby replied, wiping his forehead.

Martin wet his lips, anxious over what tomorrow might bring.

THE LAST OF THE EXPLOSIVES were hauled from the mine over the next few days. Martin busied himself examining the paintings. He soon made a troubling discovery. The salt from the mine was damaging the priceless works of art. Posey too was alarmed.

"Sergeant, complete your inventory with all due speed. I want these paintings removed pronto."

Martin passed along Posey's orders. Thereafter, each day from dawn until dark Martin labored deep in the mine with his crew. He painstakingly examined and packaged ancient Greek and Roman decorative works, Byzantine mosaics, and paintings by Rubens, Goya, and Cranach. Also, he took time to inspect paintings of lesser value.

On the third day, as Martin and Bobby closed up a crated painting, voices yelling bounced off the rock walls. Nearly a dozen troops barreled past, going farther into the mine.

One of his team ran by shouting, "Sergeant, they found some ..."

His voice trailed off. Martin spun around. "Bobby, did he say they found someone? German soldiers are hiding in the mine. Come on!"

Even though they had no weapons, Martin and Bobby joined the chase. They ran through a darkened section of the mine toward flickering lights. Martin and his private stole into the lighted room. Captain Posey was surrounded by U.S. troops.

Martin dashed up, panting for air. "Sir, who did you find? German soldiers?"

Posey pivoted on his boots to face him.

"Did you learn anything from my lectures in London?"

Startled by the unexpected question, Martin searched his memory.

"Indeed, sir. I enjoyed your lectures and took good notes."

Posey began ripping away the crate's front panel.

"Let this be a test. What do I have here?"

He tore off the panel and shone his light on a framed piece. A chill exploded through Martin's body. Hairs on his arms and neck prickled. He stood in awe.

"Sir, you found the *Adoration of the Lamb*! The centerpiece for van Eyck's *Ghent Altarpiece*! To think, you have the honor of discovering such a valuable painting stuck in a salt mine."

Posey's eyes sparkled with delight.

"Martin, we've struck pure gold. Each of these cases is labeled. All the panels are here."

"All, sir?" Another chill shot through Martin. "I mean, even the stolen *Just Judges?*"

Posey grinned sheepishly. "Point taken. No case holds such a label, but we can hope."

The captain stopped a soldier moving another crate.

"Corporal, find a photographer."

The corporal rushed off to comply with orders. Meanwhile, Martin couldn't stop admiring the *Adoration of the Lamb.* The colors were rich and stunning. As he gazed upon the sacrificial lamb, love for Jesus overflowed in his heart. Tears stabbed his eyes. These he dashed away with his sleeve. To witness van Eyck's masterpiece was truly a highlight of his life.

Posey stepped forward with a generous proposal. "Martin, you and I will have our pictures taken with this beautiful painting. We will be the first of many people wanting such a picture."

Bobby dipped his head and stared. "My ma will want to see me next to this too."

Martin agreed to let him be photographed next. The photographer took pictures for close to an hour. Martin wished the others would leave. He wanted to fall to his knees in worship. Not to the painting, but to the real Lamb. Jesus Christ had saved him through these many difficult years of war and allowed him to witness the greatest testaments to Christ's sacrifice in the art world. Martin was overcome with wonder.

TWO WEEKS AFTER Posey found the famous panel, the masterpiece from the *Ghent Altarpiece* still sat in the "studio," as the troops called the room in the mine. Every few days, a VIP arrived to have his picture taken with the *Adoration of the Lamb* and Michelangelo's *Madonna of Bruges.* Even General Patton paid homage. Trucks waited to load these valued pieces; however, General Eisenhower had yet to arrive. Martin stayed on edge, not knowing when that would be.

Early this morning, he supervised troops loading the trucks with gold. Its value: a whopping five billion dollars. Martin couldn't comprehend such an enormous sum of money. After dispatching seventy-seven truckloads of gold and art, Martin checked off on his clipboard the last three trucks he'd inventoried. He watched them lumber away, sandwiched between an armored convoy. Aircraft flew overhead to give air cover all the way to Munich.

Martin stood back, feeling grateful for all he'd accomplished. Though his work was ending here at the mine, he regretted van Eyck's panel of the *Just Judges* wasn't found.

A letter he'd just received at mail call rustled in his pocket. Yaffa, or Joanne as she now called herself, had written. Martin was anxious to read how she was surviving with the fighting over at last.

"We're almost done here, Sarge," Bobby said with a grin. "I'm headed home next week. What about you?"

Martin gripped his clipboard. "I plan to ride the train to Middleburg. My Aunt Deane will want to see me."

"Who's your letter from? Your girl back in Michigan?"

"No, I haven't heard from Helen in ages. I guess she forgot about me."

Posey came up and asked Private Crane to see about a crate that had broken open. To Martin's surprise, his commanding officer shook his hand.

"I've seen some of your work, sergeant. When you get home, don't let life keep you from your creative side."

"Yes, sir," Martin said.

"No, no, private. That is the wrong crate." Captain Posey dashed off, leaving Martin standing alone to ponder his future. Perhaps Joanne would be able to visit him at Deane's. A searing thought passed through his mind. Should he go to Auschwitz instead?

Maybe if he saw where Rebekah died … Then Martin changed his mind. He longed to see Aunt Deane and Simon. He preferred being with the living than chasing ghosts.

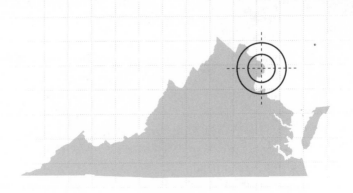

43

NORTHERN VIRGINIA

A thud startled Eva. She jerked up her head to look at Marty. His head had dropped to the table. Was he ill? She pushed aside his journal and sped over to him.

"Grandpa, are you all right?"

He moaned. "I'm sick to my stomach. Too much coffee."

"Let's put you in bed. You rest and I'll make tea and toast. Mom says that always does the trick."

He leaned on her arm as they slowly walked to his room. Eva eased him on the bed and draped a quilt over him. She felt his forehead. It was cool, thankfully. He was already sleeping. The poor man, she mused. He'd been through many changes in the past month. She laid aside her questions about Grandma Joanne. The main thing was for his health to revive.

She went to the kitchen, where she fixed tea and toast. Then Eva heated chicken broth in a pan. Before bringing in the bed tray, she first checked on Marty. He'd rolled onto his side.

She whispered, "Grandpa, it's Eva. Are you hungry?"

Silence met her. She tried again and this time he croaked, "Okay."

A fluff to his pillows and she sat him up, leaning him against the pillows. Then she collected his tray before he fell asleep again. Eva tucked a napkin in his shirt collar and fed him broth. After a few spoonfuls, he rallied. He ate his toast and Eva talked about happy times and what his grandkids were doing in Richmond.

"Today, they're touring Walton's Mountain," she said.

"Oh, I love that TV show. Can we phone the kiddos later? I miss them."

"Me too." Eva handed him a teacup. "Maybe they'll be home soon."

He finished his tea. Eva removed the tray and then patted his hand.

"You lie down. I'll be quiet."

Marty threw off the covers. "Nope. I'm better already. I want to call Ralph and check on my house."

He walked to the kitchen so erect that Eva wouldn't have guessed there was anything wrong. She set the empty dishes in the sink and stowed the tray in a cupboard. Was it wise for Marty to even talk with Ralph? Eva finally decided he should be able to find out about his own house.

Marty called Ralph, only he wasn't home. So Marty left a message on a recorder. Eva convinced him to sit with her in the den. For the next hour, they talked over his time with the Monuments Men.

"Eva, when I locked my eyes on van Eyck's painting, the *Adoration of the Lamb*, I felt like I was standing on holy ground."

"Your part in such a critical but little known part of history makes me want to write your memoirs. Your journals are pretty complete, but I'd like to add your current thoughts. I have my tape recorder and can get started if you're ready."

Marty smiled. Eva wasted no time delving into his time in the Austrian mines. He had such clear memories of events that they made tremendous progress recording his thoughts. Then she posed a question about his Dutch Resistance contacts.

Marty's hands flew to his cheeks. "There was a double agent who fled Holland before the war's end. Mr. Oostenburg was captured. So was his daughter Lucy. She survived Dachau, but I never saw her again. When I was stationed in Munich, I didn't realize how close she was to me in that awful camp."

He wiped his eyes. The clock struck four, and Eva turned off the tape recorder. She had a final question.

"Have you had any recent contact with Blake Attwood? You were billeted at his great estate, Bentley Park."

"The Earl of Condover, you mean." Marty's eyes shifted toward the hall. "Wait! You just reminded me of something."

He left the room, returning moments later carrying something white. "I've saved this all these years. It's my sketch of Bentley Park."

Eva gently took the 4 x 6 drawing. "You have captured a beautiful estate. Is this a peacock in full array?"

"Yes indeed. Blake kept one as a pet. I didn't like being kept awake by its lively chatter."

"Would you like me to find out if he's still alive?"

"The peacock?"

"You're funny." Eva folded her hands. "I meant Blake Attwood."

A serious look appeared in Marty's eyes. "Eva Marie, I'd like nothing more than to see his face and give him this sketch."

She wrapped him in a tender hug, her mind concocting a scheme to begin her search by reaching out to Brewster Miles.

THAT EVENING EVA BEGAN TYPING Marty's memoir, leaving it in novel form just as he'd written it. However, she didn't get far. Ralph called and Marty put him on the speakerphone.

"The farm's overhead garage door is open," Ralph complained. "Your garage floor is all broken up. How come?"

Marty tossed a questioning look at Eva. He dodged a direct answer by replying, "Ah, we're having new concrete poured later."

"It's a real mess. Anyways, I assume someone's shortwave radio signal or squeaky brakes made your door go up. But I punched the closer button in the garage, jumped over the safety beam, and closed your door. How about that!"

"Thanks for letting me know. Is everything else okay?"

"Sure thing. When you comin' home?"

Marty ran his hand through his thinning hair. "Ralph, I'm not sure, but are you looking into my family for your book or what?"

"What do you mean?"

"My granddaughter told me about some computer work you did looking for me and my family. Why?"

Eva had no idea Marty was going to quiz Ralph. She might as well use this chance to confront the neighbor. She leaned toward the speaker.

"Ralph, this is Eva. You went on Family Finder pretending to be Marty and using the name Dutch Dingo. Is that right?"

A loud noise blasted their ears. When it stopped, the connection was dead.

Marty shook his head. "Ralph talks so fast, he confuses me. Why was my garage door up? Is he in there snooping around my paintings?"

"I am sorry to say it is possible. Ralph has your key. Maybe we should have Chief Talsma retrieve it for us."

"Let me sleep on it. Ralph is an oddball, but until now I have trusted him."

She patted his arm. "Scott should be home soon. I'll dig up a snack."

Eva's sense was right on the money. Scott sauntered in ten minutes later and shared root beer floats with them. He yawned and led the way to bed. That night, Eva finally was able to sleep without waking once, which was a good thing because she slept little on the following nights.

She appeared at the Grand Jury for her passport case. She ran down leads for another task force office. After a long and productive talk with Brewster, Eva sat on surveillance in D.C. and Virginia's suburbs. By Saturday, she hadn't written one word in Marty's memoir. Instead, she did the laundry, while Scott washed the Explorer. Then he drove halfway to Richmond to pick up the kids from Eva's folks.

They arrived home at noon. Dutch raced in the house from the garage.

"Gramps, see my copter. Wanna watch it soar?"

"Sure do, buddy."

Marty rose from the sofa. Soon Eva and her kids, young and old, played in the backyard with the radio-controlled helicopter. Eva enjoyed watching Andy and Dutch playing video games with their great-grandfather. When Marty had enough laughs, he dropped to the sofa for a nap.

Joy filled Eva's heart for the first time in weeks. She loved Marty's presence in their home. Besides, she was hooked on learning more about the Netherlands and her ancestral home. She also was discovering things she never knew about WWII, such as the Monuments Men.

She fired up her laptop at the dining room table, with an idea to do some typing. Sounds of video playing from the family room broke her concentration. Chatter from the kids, laced with giggles, caused her to type the same sentence twice.

Eva hit the delete button to erase the duplicate sentence. Gazing into the living room, she saw Marty on the sofa, his white hair glistening in the sunlight from the window. His head drooped at an awkward angle, and his mouth hung open. He breathed evenly so she figured he'd be okay for a few minutes yet. Her eyes landed on the dining room painting. It was the one she'd taken from Marty's farmhouse.

Awash in his memories, she imagined his flight up the steps of the Dutch windmill to watch in horror as German troops stormed into Holland. Because of Grandpa Marty, two Jewish girls hid for a time in de Mulder's mill. Eva mentally retraced his risky journey from the mill back to Aunt Deane's. She mulled over Deane hiding valuables in her two-door safe. Kuipers' coercion for valuable jewels came at a price for her family.

Eva locked her eyes onto the eighteen-inch-wide by twenty-four-inch-high frame on her wall. She rushed to it, and took down the heavy painting. In the kitchen, she switched on the bright overhead light. Eva flipped the painting over.

On the top edge of the wooden frame a number "17" was penciled in. She was stunned. Hadn't she read in Marty's journal how the safe combination had been written on a painting in Deane's shop? Her eyes jumped to the frame's right side. There penciled in was the number "6." She saw along the bottom a number "38." Had this very painting hung in Deane's jewelry shop sixty-five years ago? If so, how long had it been in the family?

Eva carried the heavy painting back to the dining room and laid it on the table with a thump. She stepped into the living room and perched beside Marty on the sofa. He grunted once, straightening his head.

She smiled warmly. "Sorry, Grandpa. Were you having a nice dream?"

"Oh no." Marty blinked. "I wasn't sleeping. Just resting my eyes."

She slipped his hand into hers. They were thinner than in the past, but still calloused from years of working the farm.

"Can I ask you something?"

"Fire away." Marty rubbed his hands together. "As I said, I'm awake."

"Do you remember Deane's large safe?"

Marty nodded briskly. "She kept family treasures in it."

"Such as the necklace you buried in the garage."

"That's right."

Eva edged closer. "You wrote of a painting with the safe's combination. Do you know what happened to it?"

"Not for sure." Marty swiped at his chin. "She had several nice ones."

Then he pointed to the dining room. "That's one of Deane's in there."

"I took that painting from your wall at the farmhouse," Eva said.

"Okay," was all he said.

Eva took his hand. "Come see what I found."

Marty leaned on her hand and lifted himself up. In the dining room, she turned over the painting, showing him the number on the top slat of the frame.

"Does this look familiar?"

Marty looked at the right vertical edge of the picture frame, then to the bottom.

"This is the one!" His eyes sparkled. "This windmill was right next to the safe, alright. When I looked at it just now, I smelled Deane's shop and heard her clocks ticking."

"How did this painting come to be in your home?"

Marty twisted the frame from back to front. Eva gazed with him at the oil painting. Its dramatic hue of orange from the setting sun was the painting's focal point.

"The war ended, but I was still assigned to the Monuments Men. I had leave coming so visited Aunt Deane."

Eva realized that in all of her reading, she'd neglected to ask about how her great-aunt fared after the war. Eva corrected her oversight by asking, "Were she and Simon still living in her home?"

"Yes! But they survived a terrible famine. The Allies made food drops near the war's end, which sustained them. Simon had a bad cough, and Deane wasn't well."

Eva felt sorry for her brave ancestor. "Your journals bring Simon and Deane to life. I do wish I could have known them both."

"I found her feisty as ever. And forgiving. The locals shaved off Mrs. Kuipers' hair and made her parade around with other collaborators. Deane pitied her and brought her bread."

"Really?" Eva reared back in surprise. "Even though Constable Kuipers killed people and extorted Deane's jewelry?"

Martin nodded thoughtfully. "Deane never held that against his wife. I learned much about being a Christian from my faithful aunt. Kuipers was tried and convicted. When he left prison, he took his wife and daughter to Germany."

"I found his granddaughter teaches in Jersey City," Eva explained. "I called a few times, but Trudi is never in. Nor does she return my messages. She may be ignoring her past."

Marty sat at the table, and cupped his hands under his chin. "I was crushed to learn de Mulder became a Nazi sympathizer during the war. You probably read how the Germans captured his son. They blackmailed the miller into collaborating with them and turning in Dutch patriots."

"Did you ever think that's how the Gestapo found Rebekah at the tulip farm?"

"It did cross my mind."

Eva frowned. "But then why didn't he tell them about Deane hiding Eli and his family?"

"Hmm …" Marty's voice fell away. Then he suddenly asked, "Guess who else I found at Deane's?"

"Ah …Yaffa?" Eva took a seat beside him. "I mean to say, Grandma Joanne?"

"No, that came later. Eli Rosenbaum and his parents lived all those years in the attic. The Nazis never found them. They remained in Deane's house and were hoping to go to Israel."

"They eventually did, which is a wonderful result. May I ask about the painting? You must have brought it home from the Netherlands."

"Certainly. Deane also gave me the ruby necklace for my bride. Of course, she didn't know then I would marry Joanne. Because after I saw Deane, I took the train to see your grandmother. Memories of finding her and hiding her in the mill overwhelmed me. I asked her to marry me on the spot. She said yes, and the rest, well you know the rest."

No, Eva didn't know the rest. But his voice sounded tired and she wanted to focus on the painting and artifacts. Marty smoothed the painted windmill with his hands.

"The last thing Deane wanted me to do before leaving Middleburg was to take this picture. She also gave me all the family heirlooms from the safe, using the combination printed on this frame. I dug up the linen scrolls in the backyard near the shed. She must have had a sense she was nearing the end of her life."

"Was she? I mean, did you ever see Deane again?" Eva asked.

Marty shook his head sadly. "She died in her sleep two years after Joanne and I married. Simon wrote me all about it."

Gooseflesh covered Eva's arms. Life and death were in God's hands.

She was silent for some time, reflecting on Aunt Deane's legacy of love. This raised a new question.

"And the pouch," she said. "Did she ever say what was in it?"

"No. Now that I am thinking of them, what did I do with the scrolls?"

Eva tapped the wooden frame. "Let's concentrate on this painting. Do you know who painted it?"

She didn't tell Marty just yet how Brittney Condover had stolen his artwork from his garage.

"Nope. I told you everything I know."

"Any idea when it was painted?" Eva asked, trying to nail down what Brittney was really after.

Laughter rang from the family room down the hall and Marty turned, as if eager to join in the fun.

"So glad the kiddos are back. They make me feel alive. Anyway, the painting could be more than one hundred years old. Guess that makes it an antique, like me."

An idea formed in Eva's mind. Without telling Marty the details, she kissed his cheek.

"Writing your memoirs gives us a special time to bond. I love you, Grandpa."

He hugged her. Eva savored their special moment together. But her mind kept dragging her back to Brittney Condover. Could this be the painting she'd been after?

44

Eva's heels clattered on the hardwood floors the following morning. She approached the Smithsonian's Preservation Center for a second time. A different security officer guarded the entrance from when she and Griff had first visited. Would this guard give her trouble over the Glock she carried in her large shoulder purse?

Though Eva readied for a fight, her admission went smoothly. She simply signed in as having her weapon. Then she picked up the handles of a double-layered shopping bag. What would Cecil Prescott think of the item she was bringing him this time? His voicemail message resounded in her head as she reached for the Center's door.

"Agent Montanna, please remove the exhibits you left. It is as I thought. Nothing of value."

Eva had been disappointed by his message and curt tone. She'd so hoped the other pictures would have disclosed Brittney Condover's motive in stealing worthless art from and burning down the decoy house. Eva had held out hope Chairman Prescott would have found hidden treasure. That was not to be.

The paintings Brittney had stashed in her hotel room were stolen from Marty's garage attic. And Prescott had made it clear he wanted nothing more than to be free from Eva's blue-light specials.

She pulled open the door, annoyance rising. Didn't Chairman Prescott realize Marty's work had been good enough to get him appointed to the

Monuments Men? She had a mind to tell him about her grandpa preserving great works of art. Prescott would have to be impressed.

Then Eva caught herself. Why should she care what Prescott thought?

She checked in with the receptionist and sat anxiously in the reception area. Prescott appeared without his suit jacket, but still wearing a crisp shirt and bow tie that seemed to be his brand. He carried a roll of brown paper under his arm. When she stood, he thrust the rolled-up prints at her.

"Our visiting scholar examined these specimens. They are certainly nothing one would knowingly steal."

He cleared his throat and adjusted his bow tie. "Of course, no one should steal. You know what I mean."

Prescott's eyes shifted to Eva's shopping bag on the floor.

She smiled. "I brought another painting, which I suspect is the actual target of the terrorist we have in custody."

"No." He raised his hands, palms out. "We will not act as an 'Antique Road Show' for government agents trying to solve cases. I was humiliated to even ask a visiting scholar to evaluate those … whatever."

He gestured with disdain at the rolled-up prints Eva had stashed under her arm. Then he spun on his heel. Eva steeled herself for an uphill battle.

"Please hear me out, sir."

Prescott bobbed his head around. Eva quickly lifted the shopping bag.

"I don't like bothering you or the Center, but this could be evidence in a Federal crime. If you prefer, I'll ask the FBI Director to make another request of your boss."

Prescott bristled, but he leaned over and peered into the bag.

"What do you have this time?"

With her fingers, Eva deftly closed the opening. She must lay the groundwork before Prescott saw the contents. "Are you familiar with the Monuments Men, as they were called in World War II?"

"Of course." Prescott arched his neck, trying to see in the bag.

"My grandfather, Marty Vander Goes, was an Army sergeant assigned to help Captain Posey and the Monuments Men. Marty has great interest and knowledge in art history."

Prescott's jaw relaxed. "Go on, Agent Montanna. The Monuments Men saved the world's masterpieces from ruin. I respect their heroic efforts."

Eva had his interest; now she made her move. "Marty inherited this painting from his aunt in the Netherlands, which he believes is roughly one hundred years old. This makes me wonder, then, why a foreign terrorist steals worthless prints from a home she thinks is Grandpa Marty's and then sets it ablaze. She also takes his sketches from his garage attic."

Prescott's eyes widened. He took a step back.

Eva seized upon his growing curiosity by lifting her shopping bag. "Undiscovered by the thief was a painting on Grandpa's dining room wall. When we left Michigan for Virginia, I brought it along, thinking it would make his transition to our home easier."

"Most commendable. Perhaps in doing so, you saved a precious work of art as your grandfather did."

Eva's eyebrows arched. She never thought she might be preserving art too.

Pulling out the framed windmill painting, she asked, "Will you help me determine if this is the picture the thief was looking for?"

Prescott handled the painting with great care. But then his face fell. He furrowed his brow and shook his head.

"This is slightly better than those." He nodded at the rolled prints Eva had placed on a chair.

"Would you be willing to examine the painting further?" Eva pressed.

"Certainly not," he snapped. "It would be an insult to ask any expert."

Eva studied his tight lips. She wasn't ready to concede.

"You and I find ourselves in situations foreign to us. I'm accustomed to dealing with facts and evidence. Nothing abstract."

She nodded at the windmill painting and kept her voice level to conceal her rising ire. "Chairman Prescott, you are more familiar with the abstract. You and I speak two different languages. But here is what I need your help with. Why would someone go to such extremes to steal an abstract object of so little value?"

He glared at Eva a full minute before tucking the painting under his arm.

"I will not give you an excuse to have the FBI Director contact my boss. A visiting scholar will be assigned to give you an opinion about this piece. Good day, Ms. Montanna."

From his hurried steps away from her, Eva felt anything but victory. She sighed and picked up the roll of Marty's sketches. There was something she could do with these. As she left the Center, Eva's heart filled with love for her dear grandpa. She decided to frame his prints and hang them in his room.

It was eleven o'clock on Wednesday and Eva sat fuming in her office. She waited for the criminalist from Homeland Security's D.C. lab to arrive. But Alfred Swift was not true to his name—he was thirty minutes late. Fred, as he called himself, had phoned Eva a few days ago, demanding to meet in her Virginia task force office at this date and time.

His refusal to compromise forced Eva to cancel her meeting at the Department of Justice. A simple explanation flitted across her mind. Fred had some personal reason to come to her office at this hour before venturing to his lab. Eva shrugged off his tardiness and finished her own delinquent work hour reports. At five minutes after twelve, the receptionist finally buzzed Eva's desk.

"Fred Swift is here to see you."

"Let him know I'll be right out."

Eva stalled, taking her time clearing off her desk. She ambled to the reception area where Fred extended his hand. He was a very skinny man, as if he ate only raw vegetables. Round wire-rimmed glasses sat crooked on his elongated nose.

"Good morning, Special Agent Montanna." His grip was firm, much stronger than Eva expected.

She pointed to the open conference room door. "After you, Fred. Did you have much traffic coming out of D.C.?"

"Nope, I live Oakton. I haven't been to my lab yet."

Just as Eva thought. He had either a school or dental appointment. Since he wasn't drooling and his speech seemed normal, she guessed he'd just left his kid's teacher. Eva shrugged and settled into a comfortable chair around the conference table. Fred took a seat across from her.

Eva reached for a notepad. "I assume you're here to tell me what you discovered about the GPS device we submitted."

The criminalist opened a leather valise. The rigid plastic envelope he withdrew looked like a Christmas tree, tagged with red and green evidence tape and labels. He slid the small tracking device from its wrapping.

"This is an extremely interesting discovery for our lab."

"How so?"

Fred laid a typed report on the table.

"This GPS is highly sophisticated and not run-of-the-mill."

He glanced over his spectacles as if beginning a college lecture. "We see similar devices with commercial applications. However, this one caused us to connect with our counterparts at the Pentagon and at the CIA."

"Really!" Eva shot forward.

She wished Griff was here, and not in Georgia for training at FLETC. Fred picked up the small GPS between his forefinger and thumb with a sense of mystery.

"This is Russian," he whispered. "Or I should say, old Soviet because it dates to the Cold War. Since the Iron Curtain fell, these devices turn up in the intelligence services of former Soviet-bloc countries and even the Middle East."

Eva did some fast calculating. "Russia put this in my grandpa's slippers?"

"Unlikely. New Russian GPS devices are more advanced than this one."

"Okay, you have me guessing."

"Agent Montanna, we are not sure of the origin. The GPS transmits a signal just like your cell phone. In fact, it is a one-way cell phone."

Fred's news unsettled Eva. She didn't know what to make of it all. "Well then, whose number is it calling?"

"Hold on. It's not so simple. Just like the equipment our intelligence services create, this device is designed *not* to be tracked."

Eva was incredulous. "What else can you tell me?"

"Sorry. We know very little more," Fred admitted, taking off his glasses.

"Let's begin again. Tell me everything you have."

Fred pinched the bridge of his nose. "Okay. A similar one was previously found secreted in the handbag of a wealthy Colombian woman. Her husband was a drug lord who was assassinated by a rival."

"Oh great!" Eva's blood pressure rose and pounded against her ears. "You're saying Colombians are targeting my grandpa?"

"In another case, the GPS sent a signal to a number used by a Bulgarian intelligence service." Fred returned his glasses to his nose and picked up Eva's device.

"Yours is programmed with the same number. It can't be traced, but we suspect some freelancing Bulgarian intelligence officer is responsible."

Eva felt like screaming or slamming the wall. She shook her head to clear it.

"Fred, it makes no sense. Grandpa has no money. He's surely no competing drug lord. What else can we learn?"

The analyst shook his head. "Nothing, except we'd like to keep the device. I could compare it to any others we might stumble onto in the future."

He might stumble onto something in the future? This wasn't good enough.

But Eva decided Fred was a dead end. He was simply a bureaucrat with no curiosity or intellect. She picked up his report and slid her chair away from the table.

"Fine. Continue treating it as evidence and protect the chain of custody."

She showed him out and rushed back to her desk, calling Griff. Of course it went to his voicemail. She left an urgent message, her mind in high gear.

Bulgarian intelligence services pointed to Brittney, who was in league with one of their rogue agents. Something didn't sit right. All she had so far were insignificant paintings. Yet Brittney was using all of her skills and training to pursue something. Eva felt stumped at not knowing what that "something" was.

45

Two days later, Griff returned from his training and Eva accompanied him to the British Embassy on D.C.'s northwest side. Brewster Miles led them to the SCIF, where Griff started trading stories with the MI-5 agent.

Eva's emotions were ramped up and she wanted to get down to business. Brewster calmly poured himself tea from a decanter. "The bombing in London delayed my coming to interrogate Brittney Condover," he said with a scowl. "Fortunately, no one was killed. Many were seriously injured."

"Our fight against terrorism continues," Eva noted, waving off anything to drink. "Which brings us to your renegade SSR agent."

She was antsy to discuss what Brewster had learned from Brittney. The many loose ends involving the discredited British agent caused her increasing alarm. How big was the conspiracy?

Griff seemed content to drink his coffee. "Brewster, you and I have seen each other through dark days. Tel Aviv comes to mind."

"Indeed." Brewster sipped his tea. "Our survival on the Island of Socotra surrounded by terrorists dominated my thoughts on the flight over."

Eva drummed her fingertips on the table. "And I worry about the present. Brittney Condover isn't talking to us. What did the wayward Brit tell MI-5? Anything useful?"

Brewster wiped his mouth with a napkin.

"I appreciate the arrangements you made for me to question her. And you were correct, Eva. She spit on my shoe."

"A real corker, as they say in Britain," Griff said, topping off his coffee. "So was it a total bust?"

Brewster traded knowing looks with Eva. "Not entirely. I am visiting with my good friends that I don't see often enough. Other than that, I learned nothing."

"Not one useful clue?" Eva clenched her fists, stressed at the lack of progress.

Brewster put down his cup. "Brittney is in some kind of mess but refuses to disclose what it is. I suggested if she admitted to violating British law, she'd do her time in England near family and friends. She growled, 'I am no traitor.'"

"So her pride is ruffled, but she's crossed the line in multiple ways. Is she delusional?" Eva asked.

"I pressed her hard. She insisted she's done nothing to aid our enemies."

Eva jumped to her feet and began pacing the room. "I think Bulgaria could be classified as an enemy of yours and ours."

"Without a doubt." Brewster tapped his pen on his file. "It is not what she said, so much as what she did not say. I think she is involved in criminal acts for financial gain."

Eva sat down and fidgeted with her cell phone. Her mind pulsed with how to make Brittney talk. In the end it came down to prayer and asking God for His justice to be done. As soon as she silently asked God for help, calmness filled her spirit. It was like a load of bricks tumbled off her shoulders. Eva poured some coffee.

"So, we'll keep her and charge her criminally." Griff leaned back in his chair.

At his suggestion, Eva popped to her feet again. "Oh no. She's a terrorist. She blew up Federal property. I'm sending her to—"

A phone next to Brewster rang, interrupting Eva. He answered and then paused.

"Yes," he nodded, "she is here. Put the call through."

Brewster handed Eva the phone. "You have an emergency call from outside."

Eva put the phone to her ear and heard sobbing.

"Kaley, is that you? What's wrong?"

Griff whispered to Brewster, "Her daughter."

"Mom, we need help. I've tried calling you forever."

Eva's heart flip-flopped. She spoke in low tones. "Kaley, I'm sorry my cell doesn't work where I am. Please quit crying. I can't understand you. Slow down and tell me what happened."

"They took Grandpa Marty, Mom!" Kaley yelled.

"Who took Grandpa?"

"FBI agents!"

"Did they say where they were taking him?" Eva cast a defiant look at Griff.

Kaley snorted, "No! What should I do?"

"Call your dad. Tell him that I'll work on freeing Grandpa. You stay home, so you'll be there when Dutch comes home from camp. Everything will be okay. I'm glad you got through. I'll call you again soon, honey."

Eva hung up, glaring at Griff. "What do you know about this? Your agents came to my house and arrested my grandfather."

"What?" Griff shut his notepad. "Who? Where did they take him?"

"FBI agents came and got him. That's all Kaley knows. They could be Bulgarian agents or SRR agents from Britain. Maybe they intend to hold him to swap for Brittney Condover. What's going on here?"

Eva's pulse spiked. Her eyes darted from Griff to Brewster. She snagged her purse with the Glock inside.

Brewster bolted to his feet. "Eva, this is serious. You and Griff go. I'll do some checking on my end." He started for the SCIF door. "Outside you can use your cells."

EVA GRABBED HER GEAR and blasted from the secured room. She and Griff talked constantly on their cell phones. He unlocked his Bucar and Eva beat him inside. He turned on the ignition, and to Eva's demand for answers, Griff roared away.

"Eva, here's what I found out from my boss. Marty was picked up by agents from our art and cultural property theft unit. They're questioning him at the FBI's Washington Field Office. We're heading there."

She was seething. "I am relieved he's not some hostage for trade. Is he in protective custody? That's nuts. He's perfectly safe with me."

"They're questioning him about art. Something about World War II."

Eva's hand flew toward the windshield. "Watch out!" she yelled.

A pedestrian stepped from the curb. Griff swerved and kept on driving. Eva tugged on her seat belt, her mind whirling with the implications.

"They should've called me and arranged to come to the house. Marty was assigned to the art protection detail under General Patton."

Griff pulled in between two no parking signs on "G" Street and threw a FBI sign on the dashboard. He locked the car with his fob and took off running.

Eva hustled to keep up with his long strides. When they reached security, Griff spoke to the guard and signed the register admitting them to the building. They entered the reception next to the interrogation rooms, but Eva stopped in her tracks.

There relaxing in a waiting room chair, clad in his signature bow tie, was Cecil Prescott from the Smithsonian. Eva felt betrayed. Prescott saw her, but refused to make eye contact. So, he was responsible for Marty being hauled into custody. Before Eva could confront him, a receptionist ushered her and Griff into a miniscule conference room.

"Wait here," the woman intoned. "The case agent will be here soon."

She left. Eva whirled on Griff.

"Case agent. Did you hear that? There is a case, and Marty's their defendant."

Griff pointed to a chair. "Eva, sit. She's the receptionist and doesn't even know if there's a case number. She uses 'case agent' generically."

Eva dropped in a chair, her emotions cascading. The door opened and an older woman with short graying hair walked in. She pumped Griff's hand.

"Agent Topping, we had cyber-fraud training together five years ago. I'm Sylvia Kemp, the agent assigned to the Bureau's art and cultural property crime unit."

"I recall the training, but not you. I'm assigned to the JTTF in Northern Virginia with Special Agent Eva Montanna." Griff turned his head. "Eva's with ICE. She and I have worked together for years."

Eva shook Agent Kemp's hand. "My daughter said the FBI has my grandpa, Martin Vander Goes, in custody. Did you arrest him?"

"Please, take a seat," Kemp said. "Let me explain."

Griff stepped between the two women and sat down. Eva remained standing at the end of the table.

As did Agent Kemp, who said forcefully, "This matter was referred by the Smithsonian. They discovered an anomaly involving art Mr. Vander Goes had possessed."

"Oh no they didn't!" Eva objected. "They know nothing about Grandpa Marty."

Griff started to interrupt, but Eva cut him off, fire stoking in her gut.

"Griff and I referred this matter to the Smithsonian. I brought Chairman Prescott several pieces of art. He's out in your waiting area. You could have checked your computer and read our entire case. Maybe you did and chose to go behind my back."

"Eva, you exaggerate," Kemp replied, pointing to the chair.

Eva held her ground. "You're unlawfully detaining my grandfather. That's no rookie mistake. Why not call Griff or me? We would've brought him in for an interview."

Griff rose to his feet and addressed Agent Kemp. "Since he's not under arrest, and in view of Eva's objection, it would be wise for you to cease all questioning."

"He's not being questioned. He's in the lounge drinking coffee," Kemp replied.

Griff lunged for the door. "You'd best get your supervisor in here, or I'm calling the director's office. I will raise this matter to the top."

"No need." Agent Kemp scooped her papers from the table. "I'll bring in Mr. Vander Goes and Daryl Radeck, my supervisor."

She darted from the room in a huff. Griff shut the door.

"Eva, you're right. She probably did read our file on Brittney Condover. I'm surprised she didn't call us."

"Griff. I'm furious, but I didn't mean to embarrass you in front of one of your agents."

"I would have said the same thing. It was better she heard it from you."

There was a light knock on the door and Agent Kemp stepped in, followed by Marty. "I'll leave you here to talk, while I find my boss."

Eva rose to embrace Marty. "Are you okay?"

"I'm fine. The FBI has great coffee."

"Grandpa, you remember Griff. He's seen you at the house several times."

Marty grinned widely. "This is exciting. They found something special about our painting."

Eva was incredulous. He didn't seem at all traumatized by his arrest.

"Can you tell me what they found?" she asked.

"The experts want to know why I have the windmill painting."

"What did you say?" Eva finally took a seat.

"The truth. I've nothing to hide."

Another rap at the door and in walked Agent Kemp. She was followed by a man in a dark suit and paisley tie who pulled a chair behind him. He slid a chair to the head of the table, pointing at the extra chair for Kemp to sit in.

Then he extended a hand to Griff. "I'm Daryl Radeck, supervisor of the arts squad." He faced Eva. "Agent Montanna, I'm glad to meet you. Sorry for the clumsy circumstances. Let me explain."

Griff and Marty sat on opposite sides of Eva. Radeck inched his chair forward and took charge.

"We skimmed through Griff's terrorism file on Brittney Condover. Her actions confused us, but we were more confused by the latest painting Agent Montanna took to the Smithsonian."

Eva interrupted. "You say you *were* confused. Are you going to be forth-right about your findings?"

"Eva." Radeck stopped. "Forgive me. May I call you Eva, Agent Montanna?"

"Of course." She glanced at Marty, who seemed to be enjoying all the fuss.

Radeck dumped a thick folder on the table. "We have as many questions. We received an informant's tip, you see, about a painting by a Dutch Master being sold for millions. Then the Smithsonian determined the last painting you brought them is an authentic seventeenth century painting of the De Rieker windmill in Amsterdam."

Eva wondered if Radeck's "informant" was Delores Fontaine.

The supervisor took out two stapled reports. "Here is Chairman Prescott's report," he said, sliding one to Griff and one to Eva.

Marty wiped his face with both hands. "This takes my breath away,"

"If I can keep your attention …" Radeck raised both thumbs toward his chest. "I'll summarize what we know and why we wanted to speak with you, Mr. Vander Goes."

The De Rieker windmill meant nothing to Eva. She turned her eyes back to Radeck. He waved a copy of the report in the air.

"The experts realized they were looking at a never before catalogued piece. At the same time, rumors began seeping out of the Smithsonian and because we have informers throughout the arts community, we heard of it. When we contacted the Smithsonian, Chairman Prescott admitted how he had received the De Rieker."

Eva glared at Radeck. He glared right back. "Do you know your grand-father was assigned to the Monuments Men under General Patton during World War II?"

"Yes. I discovered his position while reading through his war journals."

Radeck spun in his seat to address Agent Kemp. "Did you know he had journals?"

Kemp's face paled. Before she answered, Griff interjected. "We should all agree this will be a joint investigation. If the journals have value, Eva will make them available."

Radeck lurched around and nodded brusquely at Marty.

"Our research revealed Mr. Vander Goes was present in the salt mine of Altaussee, Austria, where many artworks stolen by the Nazis were found. We are just trying to assure everyone his painting wasn't misappropriated from the mines."

Anger surged through Eva. She bolted to her feet.

"Who do you think you're talking to? I've been a special agent longer than you. I've also been a supervisory special agent, like you, but gave that up to make cases again and make a difference. I know the Nazis inventoried every piece of art they stole. Every piece Adolf Hitler didn't want in his offices was stored in the mines. You should have searched for the windmill painting in those records."

Griff's head pivoted to Radeck who was adjusting his position on the chair.

"The Smithsonian searched the captured records. So did we and no record could be found of that painting," Radeck said.

"Duh!" Eva snapped. "Grandpa Marty couldn't have stolen a painting from the mines if the painting was never there, could he?"

Griff rapped the table. "Agent Radeck, if you knew all that, why didn't you simply phone my supervisor and arrange a joint meeting?"

Radeck adjusted his tie. He seemed uncomfortable and Eva was fine with that. Where was all of this going? How could she expunge Grandpa's arrest record and his fingerprints? She might have to hire a lawyer.

Eva began calculating her next move when Radeck gushed, "I am so sorry. If only we had done so. Mr. Vander Goes explained the painting has been in his family for generations."

"Maybe you should bring in Chairman Prescott from the Smithsonian to brief us," Griff said, adding with a warm smile, "Since we're all working together."

Radeck nodded at Agent Kemp and she rose.

"Wait." Eva raised a hand to stop her. "Before you do so, let me make an observation Prescott has no need to know."

Agent Kemp sat down with a grimace.

Eva patted Marty's hand. "In reading my grandpa's journals, I learned at the beginning of the war a British earl named Blake Attwood visited Marty and his Aunt Deane Vander Goes in Middleburg. The windmill painting was displayed on the wall of her jewelry shop. Attwood admired it. His granddaughter, Brittney Condover, is in our custody after stealing cheap paintings from a decoy house she thought was Marty's and from his farm's garage in Michigan. End of story. Case closed."

"Wow! That's it," Agent Kemp exclaimed, her dour face brightening.

"You may be correct," Radeck said. "But how did Attwood know its value and how did his granddaughter track down Mr. Vander Goes?"

Griff stood. "Brittney had access to special means and tactics as a British agent. That will all become known, but I'm interested in what the Smithsonian has to say about the painting. Can we hear from the gentleman?"

Eva bristled. Imagine, Griff calling Cecil Prescott a gentleman. Griff was a better judge of character than that. She continued fuming inwardly, not trusting what Prescott would say or do. Perhaps he was getting his revenge on Marty because Eva made trouble for him.

46

Eva pocketed her hands, trying to calm down in front of Grandpa Marty. Agent Kemp returned to the conference room with Cecil Prescott, who carried a laptop computer. Everyone stood.

Radeck pointed to the chair Eva had vacated at the table's far end. "Mr. Prescott, I think you know everyone, except Martin Vander Goes. He possessed the windmill painting."

Prescott pumped Marty's hand. Yet he offered Eva a weak handshake and sat in her seat. Radeck hadn't referred to Marty as the painting's owner. Would that be Eva's next battle? She steeled herself for war against the surly chairman.

Prescott opened his laptop and looked at Radeck, who sat at the other end of the table. "Am I free to disclose what we've learned about the windmill painting?"

Radeck tented his fingers and nodded. Narrowing her eyes at him, Eva prepared herself to protect Marty no matter what. She would not let him be jailed on some bogus charge.

Prescott's eyes swept the room. Then he folded his arms.

"Agents Topping and Montanna were disappointed to learn our reluctant analysis found their first pieces were worthless. In fact, when Ms. Montanna picked them up, I was crestfallen because she brought me another."

His sudden smile to Eva seemed genuine. "But the moment you handed me the windmill, I knew you had presented us with a mystery."

"Why?" Eva interrupted.

Prescott's face beamed, as if he and Eva were dear friends. "Did you notice how much heavier that painting was than the others?"

Eva hadn't given that any thought. "Now that you mention it, yes."

"The extra weight roused my curiosity and that of our visiting curator. Soon, even though we value secrecy, murmuring began about our find. It's not often we see something new, you understand."

He brought a hand to his face. "Well, I do not mean new. Of course it is old, but to us and the whole art world, it is new."

Prescott's computer sprang to life with a clear photograph of the windmill painting, which sat on an easel with a purple drape behind it.

"I call this the *De Rieker Windmill*, because that's what it is. This is an unsigned painting of the De Rieker windmill in Amsterdam, Netherlands. The mill was built in the seventeenth century, in 1636, to be precise. We suspect the painting was created soon thereafter."

"Wow!" Agent Kemp cried.

No one paid any attention to her, but Eva wasn't impressed with the agent's supposed expertise. Talk about a sham. She meant to expose Kemp if need be.

Griff's mouth hung open. "No wonder someone wanted to steal it. How did you determine its age?"

Another photo flashed on the screen. This time Eva looked at the back of the frame. Prescott used a small pointer to tap at the corners of the painting's frame.

"The frame is crafted from oak, which partially adds to its weight. Oak was used until the mid-seventeenth century. Notice the corners are not mitered but are lap joints instead. Thus, the sides overlap at the corners."

"What does that tell you?" Eva asked, peering at Marty, who sat beside her. He was nodding with enthusiasm.

Prescott spun the computer around so he could see it. "Lap joints were used by Flemish Masters until the middle sixteen hundreds. So these joints confirm the frame is as old as the De Rieker windmill in the painting and perhaps even older."

"Maybe someone used an older frame on the painting," Griff opined, looking at Eva.

Her mind reeled. "Is it valuable enough for Brittney to try such extremes to steal it?"

"It is." Prescott again tapped his pointer. "Though we do not know who painted it, the canvas was made from a ship's sail. Flemish artists took pains coating the canvas with glues, making it so smooth the texture of the canvas doesn't show through the paint. This artist used the same method. It requires more study by our experts."

Marty was punching Eva's leg, but she was so engrossed in Prescott's account that she didn't acknowledge him. Finally Marty leaned over.

"I must speak with you privately," he whispered.

"Okay," she mouthed. To the others, she asked, "May we take a brief break?"

Supervisor Radeck stood. "We can get sodas and meet here in ten minutes."

The room emptied, leaving Marty and Eva alone.

Marty rubbed his hands. "Did you see the number seventeen at the top of the frame? Number six is on the right and thirty-eight on the bottom. It's Deane's safe combination and proves it was in her shop in 1940."

"I forgot! Grandpa, you're marvelous. The safe numbers are in your journal."

He stood, giving a mock bow. "Eva Marie, that's a nice compliment."

"I hope this solves everything." But Eva couldn't shake the feeling some other shoe would drop when the agents returned.

47

After their short break, Eva reassembled with the group in the conference room. Radeck shut the door. "Now that everyone is comfortable, may we proceed?"

Eva leaned toward Chairman Prescott, and asked if he would show photos of the frame's back section again. He turned his laptop computer around.

Meanwhile Eva bestowed another smile on Marty. "My grandpa just reminded me of something he recorded in his war journal back in 1940."

The image of the frame reappeared on the screen and she pointed to the number seventeen at the top. "Deane kept her valuables in a large safe in her jewelry shop. The safe's combination was written on the top, right, and bottom edges of the frame. You will see the number six on the vertical right edge."

Prescott toggled to other photos, which confirmed Eva's numbers were indeed on the frame's side and bottom. He aimed his pointer at the screen.

"This tends to prove the painting was in the Vander Goes family back in the forties, before Martin even worked in the salt mines."

Radeck pushed back. "I don't know. Those numbers could be anything."

"I'll let you examine Marty's journal where he wrote the numbers." Eva leapt from her seat. "You may photocopy relevant pages, to authenticate dates and ownership."

Eva straightened her back and thrust in her final arrow. "As a special agent with a top secret security clearance, I assure you, I am not lying."

"We'll see." Radeck tilted his head as if deep in thought. "What did Brittney Condover know that we don't?"

Prescott turned his computer around and manipulated the keys. He kept his eyes on the screen. "I may answer that, but first let me follow up on something I just learned."

"What's that?" both Griff and Sylvia Kemp chimed.

Prescott looked over at Eva, who remained standing. "Agent Kemp informed me Brittney Condover's grandfather saw the De Rieker in Deane's shop and admired it. Did he ever hold it when it was removed from the wall?"

All eyes flew to Martin. Eva figured she knew where Prescott was going. Was it possible the Condovers had the safe and needed the combination to open it? Come to think of it, Eva had never heard what happened to the safe. Of course, she'd neglected to ask.

She gave Marty a penetrating look. "Grandpa, did Blake Attwood admire the windmill painting?"

Before answering, Marty stared up at the ceiling. Then his eyes twinkled.

"Yes, he did. I recall he removed it from the wall. I watched him to make sure he didn't look at the combination."

"Do you think he did see it?" Eva shot back.

Marty rubbed his chin. "I don't think so. Deane told me later she too was concerned about him seeing the combination."

"Nice try," Eva said, turning to Prescott. "I hadn't thought of that."

"Neither had I," Radeck admitted.

Prescott smiled too broadly for a man just proven wrong. "That is good news, because it confirms something I have not yet told Mr. Radeck or Agent Kemp."

He spun the computer around once more. Eva recognized this new painting because she'd looked it up online after reading Marty's journal. She leaned forward, trying to anticipate what Prescott might reveal.

"Does anyone recognize this?" Prescott asked.

Hands around the table flew into the air, but not Griff's. He looked annoyed. "I feel inept. What am I looking at?"

Prescott faced Marty with a grand smile. "Since you saw the actual piece, tell Agent Topping what it is."

"Gladly." Marty chuckled. "That is Jan van Eyck's fifteenth century painting of the *Adoration of the Lamb of God*. Our detachment of Monuments Men found it, along with all the gold and art hidden by the Nazis in the Altaussee salt mine."

"That's right," Prescott interrupted.

Supervisor Radeck beamed as if he'd won the lottery. "Mr. Vander Goes, you are indeed someone to admire."

He purred this, as if in the presence of a celebrity. Amazed by Radeck's newfound approval, Eva hid her smirk.

For the next few minutes, Prescott explained how the *Adoration of the Lamb* was the centerpiece of van Eyck's *Ghent Altarpiece* from the Cathedral in Ghent, Belgium. Eva was interested to learn that Jan van Eyck founded the Flemish Primitives between 1425 and 1432. However, as Marty's granddaughter, she grew ashamed how little she knew about art. Maybe that would change. She envisioned Marty taking her to all the great art museums and teaching her.

Bringing her mind back to the stuffy conference room, she heard Prescott say, "All the *Ghent Altarpieces*, minus one, were stored in the salt mine by German General Hermann Goering. He had intended to give the entire set to Hitler as a birthday gift for display in the Third Reich headquarters."

Radeck leaned back in his chair. "What is the relevance of all this to our meeting?"

"Good question." Prescott raised a finger in the air, like a teacher. "Recall I was curious when Agent Montanna brought me the De Rieker windmill. The Flemish Primitives painted on panels of wood. Canvas was not yet used. Van Eyck painted the *Adoration of the Lamb* on wood."

He motioned toward the computer screen. "Back when Blake Condover lifted up the windmill in the jewelry shop, he too would have realized it was as heavy as oak. He probably knew art."

"Yes!" Marty cried. "He has many masterpieces in his home at Bentley Park."

"You've been in his home? When?" Radeck quizzed.

Eva faced the supervisor and said, "Grandpa was stationed at Bentley Park during the war. Chairman Prescott, are you suggesting the Condover family has been searching for the *De Rieker Windmill* all these years? I thought you said it's painted on canvas."

"Let me show you a most startling discovery."

Prescott produced a new screen showing Smithsonian technicians removing a piece of canvas from the oak frame. "We discovered the seventeenth century oil painting is mounted over an oak panel, dating to the fourteen hundreds."

He flipped to another screen. "See these small square nails? Similar nails were used on the *Ghent Altarpiece*. That's how we know the oak panel you see here was framed in the fourteen hundreds."

When he next showed a tall vertical painting, Eva didn't know what to think. A man clothed in a royal blue robe sat upon a white horse. Behind the man were ten other men on horses.

"You found it!" Marty clapped his hands. "The *Just Judges* was stolen from the *Altarpiece*."

Agent Kemp's hands flew to her mouth. "Wow!"

Eva tossed Kemp a frustrated look. She needed to defend Grandpa Marty all over again.

"I'm also astonished," Eva said. "But let me assure you, Marty did not steal that painting from the salt mine." There was fire in her looks.

Marty leaned forward. "Eva Marie couldn't be more right. All of us Monuments Men searched for the *Just Judges*. For those of you who do not know," here he smiled at Griff, "the missing *Just Judges* stands five feet tall and two feet wide. The De Rieker windmill painting is much smaller."

"Most definitely," Prescott chimed, jabbing his pointer in midair. He went on to explain, "The missing *Just Judges* was once hinged to the *Ghent Altarpiece* and complemented the *Adoration of the Lamb*. On the tenth of April, in thirty-four, a thief unhinged the *Judges*, stealing it from the *Altarpiece* in Ghent's gothic Saint Bavo Cathedral. It hasn't been seen since. All sorts of intrigues were reported, with some claiming Germany schemed to get its hands back on that particular painting. You must understand that is credible."

Marty nodded briskly. "Yes. Germany was forced to return the *Judges* to Belgium under the Treaty of Versailles. The Nazis stopped at nothing to gain what they wanted."

Silence descended on the room. All this art intrigue made Eva's mind spin. She thought of her meeting with Delores Fontaine, who had insisted a Dutch masterpiece was for sale. Was Brittney Condover already pitching a masterpiece for sale, resulting in those calls to Delores?

Eva dropped in her seat. She had to ask. "So Chairman Prescott, what is the wooden painting beneath the De Rieker?"

"I am displaying only a picture of the *Just Judges*," he replied, tapping the screen lightly with his pointer. "A copy has been painted from its likeness. The original has never been found. Even those wanting to give the complete set to Adolf Hitler never found it."

Prescott then paused to look across the table. "You are all wondering why I even mention this. What I'm about to show you is a tightly held secret. I have threatened to fire anyone from my staff who risks disclosing this."

Adrenaline pumped through Eva and she watched Prescott stroke his keypad. A new image graced the computer screen. It was a black and white likeness to the earlier colorful image. There stood the same man on the white horse.

Prescott's wide grin looked strange on his normally stern face.

"This is a pen and ink drawing of the *Just Judges*. It is smaller than the painted panel. We carbon dated the wood panel and are positive this is the only existing version of the *Judges*. It is signed by Jan van Eyck."

"Incredible!" Marty cried. "I can't believe I never knew."

Radeck whirled on him. "That pen and ink drawing was actually behind the windmill?"

"Yes," Prescott answered for Marty. "I believe van Eyck drew the pen and ink piece as his prototype. Later, someone, possibly van Eyck's descendent, mounted the De Reiker over it."

He flipped back to the photograph of the finished painting, becoming almost giddy. He tapped his pen on two riders just behind the prominent judge.

"Look closely at these two men." His pointer remained on one face in the image. "This is a likeness to Jan van Eyck." Then he thrust the pointer at the other man's face. "This is most likely his brother before his death. Hubert van Eyck painted with Jan."

Griff laughed. "Alfred Hitchcock used the same trick when making his movies. He put himself in short cameo appearances. My favorite is *North by Northwest*, a classic thriller."

"Ahem," Prescott cleared this throat. "Back to the *Just Judges,* if we might."

He returned the pen and ink version to the screen. "Note the two men do not look like brothers in the prototype. We can only guess when Jan got around to painting the *Just Judges* he decided to pull an Alfred Hitchcock."

Eva raised her finger as though reluctant to interrupt Prescott.

"Yes, Ms. Montanna?"

"What is the value of the pen and ink? Is it possible the Condover family knows of its existence?"

"This is priceless." Prescott's eyes shone. "We have no way to estimate the true worth. Because the actual *Just Judges* painting is lost, then this is the only likeness in van Eyck's hand and signed by him. The legacy of past thefts makes the prototype even more valuable."

Eva and Griff traded keen looks. Meanwhile, Prescott wasn't finished. He rapped his pointer on the table.

"It is believed Belgian Arsene Goedertier stole the original. He sent several ransom notes offering to return the *Just Judges*. Months later, he suffered a stroke. On his deathbed, Goedertier admitted evidence was hidden in his office. Later, copies of extortion letters and a proposed extortion letter were found. No one really knows if he was the thief or if he knew where the painting went. He died without saying. It's been nearly eight decades and still no one has found the painting. I'm convinced this is the only original work."

"What about the Condover family?" Eva reminded Prescott.

He shrugged. "I suppose it is possible. It is certainly worth stealing."

"Amazing," Daryl Radeck barked from the end of the table. "There's enough evidence in the terrorism case to charge Brittney for attempted theft of a priceless work of art, but I'll leave that up to Agents Topping and Montanna."

Prescott turned off and closed his computer. "We at the Smithsonian would love to keep working on both pieces. And Mr. Vander Goes, with your permission, we'd like to ascertain who painted the De Rieker. Eventually, if you agree, we will disclose to the world the prototype of the *Just Judges* has been found. The world deserves to know."

Filled with wonder, Eva asked the obvious. "You brought in photos to show us on your computer. I assume both pieces are safe at the Smithsonian. Are they well protected?"

"More so than in your home, as you discovered."

Eva lifted her chin, making a decision. "All right, we'll leave them with you for now. Later, we'll determine their value and make future plans."

"I see." Prescott toyed with his bow tie. "Is it too much to hope you might donate them to the Smithsonian Institute?"

Eva thought back to the episode of Prescott's begrudging acceptance of the rolled-up dollar store paintings Eva brought him. A smile touched the corner of her lips.

"You are gracious to suggest it," was all she was willing to say.

Another idea rambled around in her mind and she wondered if this was the time to pursue it.

48

Although Radeck held the door for those leaving the conference room, Eva held back, telling him, "I'd like to speak with Chairman Prescott alone."

Prescott gaped at Eva and lingered by the table. Radeck agreed to her suggestion. "Sure. I'll walk the others to the elevator and wait there for you both."

After Eva shut the door, she turned to Prescott. A question furrowed his brow.

"Chairman, I appreciate your work and delight in your good news. I have another possibility."

His eyes glittered like diamonds. He rubbed his hands together.

"You have another ancient painting?"

"No." Eva smiled. "But I have a necklace with rubies that came to my family about the same time as the paintings. I've never known whom I could trust with such information."

"Could it have belonged to the van Eycks?"

"We don't know any more than what I just told you."

"Our experts could help you to learn more. You know it is safe with us."

"When things slow down a bit, I will contact you."

She turned to open the door and Prescott whispered in her ear, "Be sure to keep your jewels very secure."

It had been a week since Eva and Griff had the good fortune of meeting their newly devoted friend, Cecil Prescott, at the FBI. On this morning, as she and Griff stopped at the bank, Eva couldn't help chuckling.

"Griff, you should have heard the chairman when I called him yesterday and said I wanted to show him the ruby necklace. He insisted, 'My dear Eva, call me Cecil.'"

Griff erupted in laughter. "You have made a friend of him for life. I'll wait here while you enter your safety deposit box."

He folded his arms like a watchful sentry, which made Eva grateful he'd agreed to come along. She walked into the vault, inserted her key, and pulled out the box. She reached around her house deed and other papers to remove a smaller box that held the necklace. She nestled it into her leather valise and locked the deposit box.

"We're all set," she told Griff. "I don't like carrying something so valuable around with me."

"I have a remedy," he replied with a mock bow. "Your chariot awaits."

She slugged his arm and they scurried to his Bucar. Eva buckled her seat belt. As Griff sped away, she clutched the side of the door. He drove through traffic like a madman to meet Prescott at the Smithsonian.

"Okay, you've convinced me," she yelled. "You're a speed demon."

Griff laughed and wheeled into a reserved parking place. "Your good buddy Prescott told me to take the spot he reserves for dignitaries."

"To think we once were on his 'get lost' list."

Eva quickly gathered her belongings. She and Griff hustled around to the front door and breezed through security. Their seats in the reception room had barely gotten warm when Cecil retrieved them. His lean face was ringed with smiles.

"Good morning, you two. My staff and visiting scholars are waiting to examine in our laboratory."

He looked at the valise Eva carried. "Is that it?"

"Yes, and I am anxious to learn more about this necklace."

Griff and Eva followed Cecil down a narrow hall, its hardwood floors highly polished. He looked back at her.

"My most trusted technicians hope your piece might have been van Eyck's."

Griff nodded. "We do as well."

Eva gripped the valise tighter, unsure what they would find. Prescott punched a combination and held open a door for them to pass through.

Inside the spacious lab LED spotlights hung from the ceiling and shone brightly on a waist-high table covered in purple velvet.

Her reception was much friendlier than on her first visit. Eva glanced at several technicians standing behind the counter, their faces tense. In starched white coats, they resembled medical doctors, only they wore no stethoscopes. Prescott was all smiles introducing Eva and Griff to his staff.

"My experts know every manner of antiquities. And these agents from Homeland Security have brought us rare jewelry. At least we hope so."

Eva took out the box, then handed the oil cloth to Prescott. He unrolled the cloth and removed the necklace with care. Gently, and with great respect, he laid the piece on the purple velvet. White lab coats gathered around, the taller ones gazing over the shoulders of the shorter techs.

Griff leaned over whispering into Eva's ear, "Vultures after roadkill."

She smirked, keeping her eyes focused on her family's necklace. A technician lifted the jewels up toward the lights.

"It looks real to me," she said, gingerly sliding the chain and medallions through her gloved fingers.

She studied the back of each medallion. She pulled a jeweler's loop from her pocket, put it to her eye, and examined each diamond, and each ruby. Finally, she tenderly returned the necklace to the velvet.

"Not only is this real, the necklace is extremely old. Its rubies are some of the finest I have ever seen."

A thrill shot through Eva. Oh, how she wished Marty could be here. The technician conferred with Cecil. Three other heads strained to glimpse at the unique find.

Cecil huddled with Eva and Griff. "I am told your necklace is rarer than many in the collection of the British royal family, and much older. This is determined by the method used by the silversmith to fashion the necklace."

"What do you suggest I do with this piece?" Eva wondered aloud. She was mystified by the necklace's connection to the Vander Goes family.

Cecil fiddled with his bowtie. "May I suggest you leave it in our possession to further examine and evaluate? We are all curious to know its history. I think you should insure it for four million dollars until we can arrive at a better idea of its worth."

Eva rocked back on her heels, totally stunned. She was speechless.

"Sweet." Griff clapped Eva's back. "I always knew you were one in a million."

The chairman bubbled over, smiling at his technicians. "One never knows the true value until auction. The highest bidder sets its value. If you decide to sell, there will be quite a stir. That will also be true when the public first learns of its existence. We at the Smithsonian stand ready to announce it for you. As you can imagine, it won't be quite as large a fuss as the other discovery we are anxious to announce to the world."

Eva debated as to the best course of action. Cecil wasn't letting her off easily. "Will you entrust us with the necklace? Our experts are eager to analyze this prize."

Griff flashed a goofy grin. "Do you want me to fly you back to the bank?"

"Okay. I won't be running that gauntlet with you anytime soon." Eva closed her valise. "Cecil, the jewels stay with you until I obtain insurance."

He held the door open. "Oh my dear, we will supply you with whatever documentation an insurer needs."

"Thank you," Eva replied with a nod.

Griff walked her to the elevator. He stayed strangely quiet. Then he pushed the button joking, "Your family amazes me. All this wealth, yet you hang out with a common guy like me."

"Let me ask you this," Eva said, facing him. "Can you handle the doldrums of chasing fanatical terrorists around the world?"

Griff's eyes flickered. "Guess who surfaced? Our Romanian escape artist. Interpol caught him on video boarding a plane to Bulgaria."

"You're kidding, right? Or are you saying Brittney is in league with Andrei Enescu?"

"The British traitor still isn't talking and Andrei is on the run." Griff hopped onto the elevator. "Who knows? Stranger things have happened to us."

Eva rode the elevator in silence, digesting the news. If only there was some way to make Brittney tell what she knew. Yet Eva was smart enough to realize her latest arrestee would never divulge a thing. No, she and Griff would have to step up their efforts to find Andrei. Her future path becoming clearer, Eva left the elevator with renewed purpose.

49

A few days later, Eva straightened Marty's covers on his bed. He was in the family room, watching television. After fluffing a pillow, Eva reached for another. A book tumbled to the floor, its pages spilling open. Eva leaned over to pick it up. Her eyes caught a snippet of familiar writing. This must be Grandma Joanne's diary.

What was it doing under Marty's pillow? Perhaps he didn't want her to read it. She'd just closed the diary when he walked in.

"Mind if I take a little nap?" he asked. "With everything going on, I'm tired out."

Eva stepped away from the bed. "I was rearranging your bedding and this fell out. Is it Grandma's diary?"

Marty reached for the aged book and held it in his hands as if it were a beloved heirloom. "You had told me you wanted to read her diary. I stored it under my pillow so it wouldn't be lost."

"So you don't mind if I leaf through it while you're taking your nap?"

"Not at all, sweetie."

"Have you ever read it?"

Marty dropped to the bed. After helping him remove his shoes, she slipped the diary from his fingers. He'd already fallen asleep. Eva tiptoed from the room.

She made fresh coffee, thankful Scott had taken the kids to see a baby panda bear at the zoo. Eva opened the diary from the back, with no idea of what she was looking for. An old letter was stuck between two pages. She opened it, and the light-yellow letter crackled with age.

Her eyes squinted at the tiny letters.

Yaffa:

When I was released from Ravensbruck, the Red Cross took months to find you. My health improves from the tuberculosis. I am in a sanatorium in Stockholm, Sweden. Do you know how I can reach Martin Vander Goes? But for him, we would never have survived the ravages of the Nazis.

At Ravensbruck, I met a wonderful woman. We called her Aunt Corrie. She also survived the horrors of this place. She and her sister Betsie taught me how to forgive. She also taught me about Jesus' great love. He covered me every day through the cold, the hunger, and the beatings. I am now a Christian.

You are my dearest friend. I think of you as my sister, so the Red Cross will help with your travel expenses. Please come, Yaffa. I want to lay eyes on you and tell you of my wonderful Savior. I send this letter to the de Mulders at the mill in Middleburg. Perhaps they know how I can get in touch with Martin.

Your friend and sister for life,
Rebekah

A chill tore through Eva. Rebekah had survived the Holocaust at Ravenbruck, not Auschwitz. The letter from Cole Donner in New Jersey may be legitimate after all.

She paged through her grandma's diary to see if she ever wrote about Rebekah's letter. Finding no mention, Eva reread the yellowing letter. Rebekah had sent her letter a month before Marty and Yaffa, who became Joanne, married in the Netherlands.

Eva's heart flipped. She realized Grandma Joanne had never told Grandpa Marty that Rebekah lived. So why had she saved the letter?

Eva had no answers. But there was something she could do to make up for lost time. She picked up her cell and punched in the number for Cole Donner, Rebekah's grandson. Their lives intertwined in an astonishing way, and history was coming full circle. As the phone rang, she recalled her suspicions Cole had been an imposter.

A woman answered. Eva had expected a man and blanked on what to say.

"Ah … hello," Eva said. "I'm calling for Cole Donner."

There was a moment of silence before the woman demanded, "Who is this?"

"Eva Montanna. I'm responding to a letter Cole sent my grandpa. His name is Martin Vander Goes."

The woman said nothing else. Then Eva heard muffled sounds of the woman talking with her hand covering the phone. More muffled sounds, and then a man said, "Cole Donner here. To whom am I speaking?"

Eva quickly identified herself, adding, "My grandfather is Martin Vander Goes and we received your letter. I'm trying to help him sort things out."

"Oh, yes. Thanks for phoning. I was never sure if I'd contacted the correct person. I am trying to help my grandmother contact Martin, whom she knew in the Netherlands."

Eva held Rebekah's old letter in her hand. "My grandfather knew a young woman named Rebekah Abrams in Middleburg at the beginning of the Second World War. He is from Zeeland, Michigan. He thought Rebekah died in the custody of the Nazis. Are you telling me that she is alive and living in New Jersey?"

"Oh, no." Cole stammered. "I mean yes, she is alive, but she lives in Goes. That's a village in the Netherlands."

"Did she ever live in New Jersey?" Eva asked.

"No, but she visits here. My father, Rebekah's son, left the Netherlands when he was a young man and married my mom here in the U.S. I'm anxious to help Grams. She and her friend Yaffa were hidden by some nice people, including Martin."

Warmth spread through Eva's entire being. "I believe Rebekah and my grandpa knew each other. I'm reading his journals. He actually married Yaffa."

"Oh." Cole heaved a long sigh.

Eva could sense his disappointment. "She was my grandmother who passed away some years ago. She changed her name to Joanne. In fact, I never knew her name was Yaffa until I read his journal."

"Eva, I hate to interrupt this effort to reunite old friends, but my wife and I were just leaving to watch our daughter play water polo. I noticed your call came in with a blocked number. May I call you back?"

Eva rattled off her phone number. "I think our grandparents would be delighted to see each other again."

After Cole hung up, Eva sat in silence for a long while. She closed her eyes, finally coming face to face with being Jewish. Having put her faith in Christ years ago, she counted herself one of His own.

A sudden desire to know more about her heritage flooded her heart. She wanted to talk things over with her dad. His mother, Eva's grandmother Joanne, had been Yaffa Levi. And to this day he still didn't know. At least she didn't think so.

Her call to Dad in Richmond went unanswered. Even his voicemail didn't click on. She made another call, this time to Pastor Dekker from Marty's church in Zeeland. More than anything, she wanted to talk with someone who had known Joanne.

The receptionist put her through to his pastor. She told him of her recent findings.

Pastor Dekker was kind in his reply. "Joanne was always quiet, but she rolled up her sleeves. Whenever we needed soup delivered to the sick, she was right there to help. Eva, she was a caring woman."

"I appreciate you sharing that. Her death surprised us all, and I didn't have a chance to tell her of my love. What does it mean that her name was Levi?"

"A minister friend in Virginia is a Christian, but was raised Jewish. Have you heard of Sal Feldman?"

"Oh, yes," Eva answered. "He pastors a huge mega church, even larger than the one I attend. I know something of his testimony. He found the Messiah in college."

"I'll be happy to connect you two. He can shed much light for you."

"God's ways are a mystery," Eva said. "He has allowed me to discover my heritage for a reason."

She thanked Pastor Dekker and then waited to hear back from Sal Feldman. Her world had been turned upside down, but in a wonderful way. The Lord had certainly protected Marty through much peril.

If he had perished in the WWII, Eva wouldn't be here. She opened her Bible and began reading about Moses and Aaron. The ancient tribe of Levi captured her interest. Could it be possible that Eva's grandmother traced her roots to that priestly tribe?

50

A MONTH LATER IN THE NETHERLANDS

Eva and her family, including Grandpa Marty, all squeezed into a rental van. They drove from Schiphol Airport southwest of Amsterdam, heading for Goes, which was less than an hour from Middleburg. The beauty of the Netherlands rang in Eva's heart. Small farms dotting the flat land felt like home.

"Look," she said, pointing out the window. "The trees are tinged with orange, as if touched by a master painter."

Marty laughed heartily. "Finally, someone besides me is interested in art."

As Scott drove past a group of bicyclists, Eva replayed in her mind events leading them to Goes. They would go there first and then travel to Aunt Deane's old house in Middleburg. The suspicious letter from Cole Donner in New Jersey turned out to be exactly what it claimed to be. Rebekah Abrams survived the dreaded Ravensbruck. Her American grandson Cole had arranged for Marty to visit with Rebekah. Eva and Scott had pulled the kids from school to make this historic journey. Their ancestor, Peter Vander Goes, had originated in Goes.

Eva had dug up much about Nazi death camps since her conversations with Cole. She spread the map of Holland on her lap, thinking how some Jewish women were kept alive because they were strong workers. Others survived if they were pretty. However it happened, Rebekah had lived. When

Eva had told Marty, tears flowed from his eyes in a great flood. He'd dropped to his knees to pray for his first love. Eva had joined him at his bedside. What a profound moment that was in her life.

On the narrow road to Goes, Eva turned in her seat. "Grandpa, are you excited to see Rebekah?"

"Worried too." Marty moistened his lips. "Will she know me?"

"What the two of you had together can never be forgotten."

Marty's lips parted in a fragile smile. "I remember her eyes, dark and lovely."

"Your painting of her suggests she was pretty."

"She was a beautiful woman to me!"

Kaley giggled from the back seat and Eva turned, fixing her eyes on the road ahead. By Marty's account, Rebekah had been lovely and one of the few to still be alive when camp guards turned over the 500 women to the Swedish and Danish Red Cross.

Her heart ached at what Rebekah must have endured. Prisoners at Ravensbruck performed hard slave labor. Many were forced to undergo medical experiments such as bone transplants and bone amputations. Eva shuddered. But she was about to witness a happy reunion, she hoped.

Aside from the British woman calling turns from the GPS, everyone in the van remained quiet. The kids played with their handheld electronic devices, and Eva thought about how Middleburg had been rebuilt since the war. The GPS interrupted her mental travels by announcing, "Turn right. Then you have reached your destination."

Eva gazed over her shoulder. "We're here. Grandpa, are you ready?"

"Is this where she lives?" He peered out the van's window.

Eva checked the address again, then surveyed a plain two-story brick building. Two sets of windows on the first floor were separated by an unpainted door. Two more sets of bare windows completed the second story. The entire street held similar basic dwellings. Eva saw not a speck of litter anywhere.

She guessed Rebekah lived a simple life. Their van rolled to a stop where the front door of the house opened to the sidewalk. Eva and her family piled from the van, and out stepped an erect white-haired lady. She walked toward Eva, extending her hands. Eva grabbed both.

"You must be Rebekah. I am Marty's granddaughter."

Rebekah's dark eyes danced in merriment. "I never thought I would meet Martin's family. Or ever see him again."

Marty was climbing from the middle seat. As he straightened, he stared at Rebekah. For some moments, he didn't take one step.

Not until Rebekah cried, "Martin!"

She covered her mouth with her hands. He rushed toward her, his face shining. He seized her hands into his and stood there transfixed. He smiled broadly and she smiled in return. Eva turned away and rounded up her kiddos.

"Andy has my game," Dutch complained.

Eva ruffled his hair. "We're meeting new friends, so I want you to be happy. You don't need your game right now."

"Eva," Rebekah called. "Did Martin tell you that he and his aunt helped me and my friend Yaffa to hide?"

Before Eva could reply, Rebekah came over and touched both her hands to Eva's cheeks. Rebekah blushed. "Of course you know. Yaffa was your grandmother."

Marty waltzed over as if years younger. He tenderly caught up Rebekah's hands again. His blue eyes crinkled. "I was told you didn't survive. Oh, Rebekah, I am so grateful you did."

She tugged on Marty's hands and swayed on her heels. In English laced with a Dutch accent, she said, "And I thank the Lord my American grandson found you."

Eva gathered her family and introduced everyone. Dutch handed her a tin of cookies Eva bought at the airport. Rebekah invited them all into her modest home.

"My daughter lives here with me," she said. "Joyce is working today. I hope you meet her."

A square table in the dining area was set for seven places. Bread and cheese were heaped on large platters. Rebekah went into the kitchen and brought out two steaming serving bowls.

"I hope you like the hachee. The tender meat tastes best with the mashed potatoes. Please save room for apple tart."

With everyone sitting around the table, Rebekah passed the rye bread. Marty held onto the plate.

"Rebekah, this looks delicious. May I thank God for this food?"

She dropped her eyes and smiled shyly. "I would be honored, Martin."

Marty and the family bowed their heads.

"Our God and our Father," he said. "We thank You for delivering us here safely. Most of all, we thank You for preserving Rebekah's life during the war and mine too. We praise You for answered prayers and for the lives of our children and grandchildren. You have been most faithful. We ask You to bless this food. Thank You in Jesus' name. Amen."

The passing hours were filled with laughter, tears, and reminiscing. Eva helped Rebekah wash dishes and became better acquainted with her. Kaley and Andy took Dutch to a nearby park. As late afternoon approached, Eva wanted to be on the way to their lodging and to a restaurant for dinner. Rebekah had already done enough entertaining.

As they lingered in the living room, Eva sought everyone's attention.

"I have an announcement," she said. "It involves our plans for tomorrow and Rebekah too, if she's interested."

Dutch interrupted, "Are we gonna change hotels again?"

"No, we won't," Eva promised.

"Good." Andy shoved his hands in his pockets. "I like watching people golf."

"Me too. Will you teach me, Dad?" Dutch asked.

Eva faced her grandpa. "I have a secret I can now share. Rebekah's grandson Cole and I have researched online. Through Family Finder, we've learned Aunt Deane's house and jewelry shop have changed hands several times."

"How do you know this?" Marty interrupted.

Eva patted his hand. "From the power of Internet technology. Anyway, I've seen pictures of her house and shop. Alan Rosenbaum, Eli's grandson, has recently bought both properties. He left the attic just as it was during the war."

"Oh, Martin." Rebekah clung to his arm. "Eva shared this while we washed dishes. She asked if I could visit Middleburg with you."

"Please do."

Eva couldn't help beaming at Marty's quick reply. "Alan invited us to tour the shop, which is his home. He's converted Deane's house into a museum. If we leave our suitcases at the hotel, we'll have enough room. And if we head here to Goes early enough, we can easily pick you up and make it to Middleburg in time. How does that sound, Rebekah?"

Their hostess looked tired. Still she said with enthusiasm, "I can think of nothing more fitting."

Marty gazed at her intently, and she dropped her eyes. With Eva's kids getting antsy, she expressed thanks and loaded the family back in the van. Marty held onto Rebekah's hand until the last second.

They reached the Middleburg hotel an hour later and ate a light supper. After settling Marty and kids in their "Golf Suite," Eva wandered with Scott along the golf course. They stood by the green's edge, under the bright full moon.

Her heart surged with emotion. "Everything that happened is a miracle of life."

"I need to tell you," Scott said, sweeping her hand into his. "You are a wonderful woman."

Joy flooded her. Eva looked up, searching his eyes. He bent down and kissed her. When he lifted his head, she leaned against his chest, drawing from his strength.

"Sweetheart, I am so thankful for you every day," Eva said tenderly. "We are blessed not to have suffered what Marty and Rebekah did, being torn apart like that."

"Do you think they'll stay in touch with each other?"

"I wonder. Grandpa seems subdued. But I'm sure he's overwhelmed. He thought she had died. He probably regrets not finding her."

Scott smoothed her hair. "Eva, you haven't told me. How do you feel learning your grandmother was raised Jewish? Do you long to search for her family?"

"Amazed describes it best." Eva let her breath out slowly. "Pastor Feldman has arranged for me to take classes about Jewish heritage, learning of the feasts and traditions. My dad is coming too. Our Lord Jesus was Jewish. I belong to Him no matter my bloodline, but it's fascinating to look upon history with new eyes."

Scott whistled. "That's a turn of events."

"Dad was as shocked as I was at first. Then hurt."

Scott drew her into a warm embrace and she relished his love like never before. The future beckoned with the unknown. For tonight, Eva felt content to savor her life just the way it was.

51

The next morning, Grandpa Marty and Rebekah huddled next to each other in the van's middle seat. The Montanna crew was heading from Goes back to Middleburg. Eva delighted in Marty and Rebekah talking in English and sometimes in Dutch.

Her grandpa rarely spoke in Dutch. To Eva, it was like music to her soul. The couple kept busy laughing and gawking at the sights, as though the long intervening years had been erased. A sparkling waterway came into view. Eva figured Deane's house was close as the GPS intoned the distance remaining.

"My old neighborhood!" Marty cried. "Turn left at the canal."

As if on cue, the British GPS lady chimed, "Turn left at the water. You have reached your destination."

After Scott cranked a left turn, Marty pointed right. "Simon moored his boat there."

"I haven't been to Middleburg since I left." Rebekah tapped Eva's shoulder. "Martin took me in Simon's boat when I hid at Veenstra's Tulip Farm."

"Stop!" Marty pointed to a tall flat building along the canal.

Scott wheeled to the curb.

"Nope, that's not it." Marty sounded dejected. "The windows are wrong."

He gazed further down the street that ran parallel to the canal.

"Go on ahead, to the next block."

Scott pulled forward and then slowed.

Marty clapped his hands. "Hoorah! We found it."

Scott parked the van in front of a tidy building. The sign read in giant letters, *Deane Vander Goes Holocaust Museum.*

Marty pushed his face to the window. "That next building used to be her shop."

With the family unloaded, Eva peered at the sign on the house. Her Dutch was sufficient to know it was open only on weekends. But she'd e-mailed Alan and he agreed to meet them this morning. Eva knocked, but there was no response.

Martin walked over and looked in the windows of Deane's old house. He cupped his hands around his eyes. "The front hallway looks just like it did back in 1940."

"We're ahead of schedule," Eva said, turning away. "Let's come back."

Marty looked down the street. "Can we drive to the mill? I know the way."

He opened the van doors and the family piled back in. Marty sat up front with Scott, directing him to follow the road adjacent to the canal. As they drove the narrow street, Marty gave a guided tour of the route he'd ridden on his bicycle.

"I delivered articles to Mr. Oostenburg, the undertaker, by peddling down this street. And I ran down the alley, taking food to Rebekah and Yaffa, two scared Jewish girls hiding in the mill."

Scott edged the van close to the windmill. Its gate was closed. A hand-painted sign proclaimed tours were available only on weekends.

"Too bad, Grandpa," Eva said. "Let's look around. I want to take your picture."

They unloaded again. The kids ran up the ridge while Marty and Rebekah sped to the fence, chattering in Dutch. When they fell silent, Eva walked up with her camera. At the sight of tears trickling down Rebekah's cheeks, Eva lowered her camera.

Scott walked up with his keys, and Marty gestured with his arm.

"Across these fields, I spotted French paratroopers falling out of the sky. And there," he whirled around, pointing behind him, "German patrols marched down this road and past the mill, while Rebekah and Eva's grandmother hid inside."

Eva sensed the tremendous strain he'd lived through so many years ago. And yet his faith in God stood firm. And he had passed that faith to his son Clifford, Eva's dad. She used her hand to shield her eyes from the bright sun.

"It's no wonder Grandma Joanne never talked about any of this," Eva remarked.

Rebekah drew near to her side, and Eva confided, "She feared mentioning her Jewish heritage, even in America. It takes my breath away, such terror you all lived through."

"Do not blame Yaffa." Rebekah wiped her eyes with a tissue. "Your grandmother knew the results of pure evil. I saw acts of hate at Ravensbruck, but Aunt Corrie showed me the way of true light. The Nazis meant it for harm, but God used the awful things to bring me to my wonderful Shepherd."

Eva grabbed her gnarled hand. "You are a brave woman. As a federal agent, I hunt the guilty, but I've never faced what you did. I understand what you mean about God using trouble for our good. Sometime, perhaps I can share with you all He has done for me since the terrorists killed my twin sister on September 11th."

Rebekah's gaze was tinged with sadness. Marty slipped her arm into his and walked with her back up to the ridge. The children giggled, taking pictures of the mill with their phones.

Scott scurried toward Eva. "I don't want to throw water on your party, but Alan is probably at Deane's house waiting to show us around."

Her hand flew to her mouth, and she called, "Come on, everyone."

Marty and Rebekah turned slowly. Their faces radiated happiness. Eva quickly snapped their picture in front of the mill before herding her clan into their car.

BACK IN FRONT OF DEANE'S row house, a wiry dark-haired man about ten years Eva's junior waved and greeted them on the street.

He met Scott first and shook hands. "Eva," he added, turning to her. "It's good to meet you. Papaw Eli told me about your time with him in Israel. I was in China then."

Alan's English was nearly flawless, except for a slight accent. His job as an international sales rep explained his comfort with Americans and the English language.

Marty pumped Alan's hand. "I wish Eli and I stayed in better touch. He likes to use the texting and I haven't mastered that, I am afraid."

"Papaw often speaks of your bravery."

"This is my friend, Rebekah." Marty reached for her hand. "She was Rebekah Abrams during the war."

Alan nodded graciously. "Back then, Papaw and Deane prayed many hours for you because the Nazis had taken you."

At Rebekah's quiet smile, Alan gestured around Deane's old home, which had been converted into the Holocaust museum.

"Eva, based on your e-mails of what you found in Martin's journals, I included new displays for Deane's museum. First, let me take you over to the old Vander Goes jewelry shop. It is now my home."

Scott helped Eva round up the kids who had started roaming toward the canal. They stepped into a modern house, with hanging lights and a leather sofa. Marty turned in a circle, staring at a corner.

Eva lightly touched his arm. "Does anything look familiar?"

"The windows are the same. The large safe sat over there. The jewelry cases were set up where Alan has built his kitchen. Your home is nice."

"So you approve?" Alan asked, his voice tense.

"My boy, I find it remarkable that you are living here."

Just then the phone rang on a side table. Alan dashed to answer it. He spoke in Hebrew and then handed Marty the receiver. "Papaw regrets not being here. He wants to talk with you."

"Oh good."

Marty grabbed the phone. For several minutes he and Eli chatted, with Marty saying Rebekah's name again and again. Eva wandered to a window, imagining Constable Kuipers striding in and basically stealing Deane's jewelry. Kaley came over and pointed to her necklace. "Mom, did this gold Dutch shoe come from Aunt Deane?"

"I wonder," Eva replied. "My grandmother gave it to me when I was younger than you."

Marty said good-bye and put down the phone. Alan grabbed a key ring. "Allow me to show off the Deane Vander Goes Museum. Follow me."

"You first," Eva said to Marty and Rebekah.

The two of them walked beside Alan in the alley, and the tour group hurried behind. Scott snapped photos along the way. Marty suddenly stopped.

"Eva, the shed stood here. You know, where I buried our family's valuables."

Scott took pictures of Eva and Marty in the backyard, and then everyone filed through the rear door of Deane's house. Marty drifted around the kitchen as if in awe.

"It's exactly like it was back then. Alan, you are a marvel."

"Some items aren't from Deane's house, but they are from the same period," Alan explained. "The kettle is not hers, but the teacups are."

"May I?" Marty asked, reaching for a blue and white cup.

His finger lightly touched the curved handle, his eyes wet with tears.

"Alan, you have preserved her life in this place. Thank you, dear boy."

Marty wiped his eyes and Rebekah grabbed his hand.

"I can picture you at this table, Martin, eating the same bread you brought Yaffa and me at the mill."

Alan ducked into the living room. They all followed.

"The radio is a replica. Imagine Martin and Deane listening to war news being broadcast on the BBC. They endangered their lives even having a radio. Papaw Eli came here after we bought Deane's house and shop. He drew sketches for me."

Eva whirled. "Grandpa, some of your sketches should be on display here."

"Maybe so," Marty replied, rubbing his chin. He sauntered into the front hall. "I feel like I'm seventeen again and just arrived off the boat. Look, the same blue delft tile is on the wall. I sat here tired out and anxious, waiting for Deane."

"And you worried you were in the wrong place, because Mrs. Rosenbaum let you in and you didn't know her yet." Eva grinned at Alan.

Marty seemed restless. He paced back to the living room window. "I sat here, reading my Bible and watching for the Gestapo."

Danger lurked in the shadows and Eva shivered. Both her grandmother and grandfather could have lost their lives to such radicals. It made her think. She spent her career enforcing the laws to prevent such mayhem from happening again. But Brittney Condover had been right there to snatch what she wanted, ready to smash everything Eva's family held dear. The British SRR agent was a lost soul. How in the world could she come from the same family line as Eva and Marty?

Alan burst Eva's reverie by beckoning her upstairs. He waved and the troops followed. He turned at the top step and said, "Deane and Martin had their rooms on the second floor. Wait until you see the attic. As many as four families crowded together."

The Montanna family climbed into the cramped attic. Eva dipped her head below the rafters and whispered to her son, Dutch, "Grandpa Martin helped to hide Jewish people up here to keep soldiers from finding them."

His innocent blue eyes rounded. "Why did soldiers wanna kill them?"

Marty laid a hand on the boy's shoulder. "Because they hated people they did not know. Though the attic is empty, I can see Eli playing his violin by this tiny window. I can hear his mother weeping and even smell the stale air."

"I wish I could have hidden up here," Rebekah whispered to Eva.

Eva put an arm around her shoulder. The two women clung to each other.

"The suffering you endured is beyond my understanding," Eva said, straightening her back. "That's why I'm helping Grandpa with his memoirs, to be a light to the future."

"Yes, we must shine for Jesus."

As Rebekah wiped her eyes, Eva gave her a moment alone and stepped over to the high window. Sunlight poured in. She thought of Brittney spending the rest of her life in a cell because she chose the wrong path. On the other hand, the Rosenbaums took refuge behind these walls because they were Jewish. Yet Deane had made them her family in the face of brutality. She had loved them as her own.

Marty joined her by the window. "Deane told me something I've just remembered. Sometime after the First World War, her father, who would be my grandfather, read from the family Bible how Elijah saw dry bones being restored. Grandfather Vander Goes told Deane, 'My descendants will see Jews returning to the land of Israel.' Can you imagine that? He was right, all those years ago."

Gooseflesh prickled Eva's arms.

"I don't pretend to understand, Eva Marie. Come see my old room."

The family trailed behind him as he slowly took the steps that wound to the second floor. He led Rebekah into the room that had been his.

"Every day on my knees in this room I prayed God would send His angels to preserve you. I thought He failed me, but I was wrong. He did save you."

It was a tender moment.

At length, Alan ushered everyone downstairs, where Eva asked if he had many visitors to the museum.

He shrugged. "Yes and no. I'm open on weekends, and accept donations to help with repairs. The city threatens to increase taxes because they say we're a tourist attraction. That is not what I mean it to be. I created this museum to honor the memory of our family and the goodness of Deane and Martin."

Eva drew back and whispered something to Marty. At his nod, she told Alan, "My grandpa mentioned burying family heirlooms in the alley. We recently found Deane's jewelry. While not yet appraised, we think it will fetch a high price. Marty would like to donate a portion to an endowment. Perhaps on that basis, the city will agree to make it an admission and tax-free Holocaust museum."

Alan clapped Marty's shoulder. "You are most generous."

"I want Deane's legacy of love to survive, Alan." Marty replied. "There's enough cruelty in this world. Jesus teaches us to love our enemies, which Deane taught me amidst great odds."

Eva and Alan discussed the details, pledging to remain in touch. Scott took dozens of photos, with Eva snapping a few so Scott could be in them too. Their drive back to Goes was filled with joking, but also tears. Marty walked Rebekah to her door, and spent thirty minutes talking to her alone.

She lifted up her hand and waved. Then she disappeared into her home, closing the door.

Marty eased back into the van with a sigh. The kids seemed clueless and kept chattering away. Andy vowed to "jump out of an airplane with a parachute." Eva sensed Marty's anguish. Had this trip been wise at his age? But when they reached the hotel he rallied.

He drew her aside. "I have something to show you."

"About Rebekah?"

Sorrow flickered over his face. "No. Joanne and I had a daughter who was born here in Middleburg. Hilda became sick when she was three months old."

He reached into his pocket and blew his nose on his hankie. "My little girl is buried in the cemetery. That's why we left the Netherlands and moved to Michigan. Will you drive me there?"

"I am so sorry."

She threaded her arm through his. Marty had experienced more tragedy than she ever knew.

"Let's go right away. You hop in the van and I'll tell Scott we're taking a drive."

"Eva Marie, because I lost Hilda, you have always been my special girl."

A lump formed in Eva's throat and she blinked back tears. What else was Marty burying deep in his heart? She so wanted to help him find happiness.

They took an impromptu trip to see Rebekah. Martin watched her fix a simple meal of vegetable soup and fresh bread. She urged them all to sit around the table.

"In the excitement, I forgot to serve my apple tart the other day," she said.

After everyone assembled, she prayed a blessing for the food and Martin's family. He ate his soup, but couldn't take his eyes off the older version of the young woman who'd attracted his attention. His feelings for her hadn't changed.

As she served the dessert, he observed her long fingers, now ravaged with arthritis. He wanted to protect her from life's pain all over again. He knew he loved her more. He helped her carry dirty dishes into the kitchen.

Eva brought in empty glasses. She smiled at Rebekah. "Your soup was so flavorful. I would help wash dishes, but I see Grandpa is doing that."

"Thank you, Eva." Rebekah's brown eyes sparkled. "Martin is a good helper. Just make yourselves comfortable. I brought out picture puzzles. There is one of a windmill you and the children might enjoy putting together."

"We spotted a boat basin a short distance away," Eva replied. "Will you miss us if we take a walk?"

Marty didn't wait for Rebekah's opinion. "That's a fine idea. Do that."

The family was barely out the door when he threw a dishtowel over his shoulder and took up his position next to his long lost friend at the sink.

"Rebekah, I'm happy to be with you."

She rinsed out a bowl. "Martin, your family is precious."

"The Red Cross told me you perished at Auschwitz," he said, his voice cracking. "All these years, I thought you were dead. So did Joanne, I mean Yaffa. She quit using her Jewish name."

"I never knew you married Yaffa until my grandson told me. I wrote a letter to Yaffa and the Red Cross sent it to her. Perhaps she never received it."

Rebekah wiped her hands on a towel and stood staring into Marty's eyes.

"I have never stopped thinking of you." He held her hand.

"Martin, during my whole time in prison I thought about your kindness to me. I knew you to be a Christian. When I met Aunt Corrie in the camp, she shared with me about Jesus being a Jew, and how Jesus changes people. To me, you were like Christ."

"My dear." His head swam.

Rebekah stiffened. "But I always wondered. Did you help me because you cared for me or because of your Christian obligation?"

"Oh!" he cried.

Tears clouded in his eyes. Joy and doubt filled his heart at once. Marty gazed out the window to compose himself. Then he faced her with resolve.

"Rebekah, after I took you in Simon's boat to the resistance contact, I escaped back to America and enlisted in the Army. I spent years in Europe hoping to be with you again soon. When I tried finding you, I heard you died of tuberculosis. Only after my efforts to locate you with the Red Cross failed did I turn my attention to Yaffa."

Tears streamed down her face and she sobbed, "If only I had gone to the dairy farm like she did."

Marty pulled her to him, folding her in his arms.

"Sshh. We found each other and do not ever have to be apart."

"We are separated by a large ocean."

"Rebekah, are you willing to be together?"

"Oh, Martin." She leaned against him and trembled. "Can this be happening?"

"I refuse to let an ocean stop me. You know, I sailed to the Netherlands alone when I wasn't yet eighteen."

She looked up into his eyes. "I am willing. How can we do this?"

Marty's mind whirled. But he found words to reassure her.

"You are my forever love. Your grandson lives in New Jersey. If you move to America, we can live at my farm. If not, I will move here. Never will I leave you again."

Eva had a hard time convincing Marty to leave Rebekah even for a few days. But in the end, Rebekah insisted that he go with Eva and his family to England.

"You owe it to them, Martin, to see where you served in the Army," Rebekah said, folding her arms. Her dark eyes held a plea. "But call me every night!"

"I will help him do so," Eva promised.

Marty wavered and debated, but finally he agreed. He grabbed Rebekah's hand.

"Eva can vouch for me," he said with a smile. "I painted your portrait by the windmill and that painting is now in my house."

Scott drove aggressively to Amsterdam to make their flight for England with five minutes to spare.

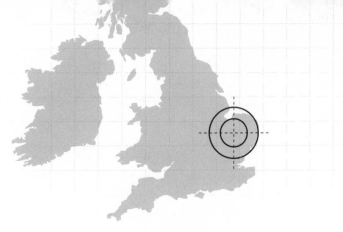

52

A FEW DAYS LATER IN THETFORD, ENGLAND

It was after midnight when Eva and her family reached the historic Fox and Hound Inn near Thetford in Suffolk, England. She slept hard until a rooster crowed, waking her at dawn the next morning.

The proprietors, Tom and Annie Fox, fed them all a hearty breakfast of coddled eggs, sausages, potatoes, and fresh melon. Tom mesmerized the kids with his colorful tales of mysterious happenings in the area.

"I'm told this whole house shook when American bombers took off for Germany from Knettishall. Stop when you pass by the old airfield. You can still see the main runway."

"Mom!" Dutch dropped his spoon on the floor. "Can we stop and look for bombers?"

"Another time, buddy," Scott said, bending down to recover the spoon.

Eva downed the last of her delicious coffee. "Grab your gear. We've an outing."

"Beat 'ya," Andy challenged his brother.

The kids ran up to the room to fetch their caps and jackets. Eva waited on the sunny porch drawing in the final precious moments of her vacation. Soon enough she'd be chasing after terrorists. But first she wanted to see Marty enjoy their next stop.

Dutch raced down the steps, carrying the model airplane Scott bought him at Heathrow. It was an exact replica of the plane they'd flown from Dulles. He took it everywhere. Scott opened the right front door of the British van and jabbed a finger at the steering wheel.

"Kaley, you're always whining about not getting to drive. Here's your chance."

She quickly dove into the third seat. "No way, Dad. Brits drive on the wrong side of the road."

Scott laughed and edged behind the wheel. Andy climbed in next to Kaley and tapped Scott's headrest. "When I'm old enough, I'll drive on the other side, Dad."

"Okay." Eva lifted Dutch into the back seat. "You sit next to your name-sake, Grandpa Marty."

Dutch showed his model airplane to Marty. "Wanna hold it, Gramps?"

"Sure thing, kiddo."

Eva scooted into the left front seat, and Scott pulled from the parking area, with the trusty British GPS voice telling him, "Turn right at the next intersection."

"Where we going, Mom?" Kaley clicked on her seat belt.

Eva looked over her right shoulder and peered at her children.

"Bentley Park. We are meeting an important man. You all be on your best behavior. No touching, pushing, or shoving. Be quiet too, unless you're asked a question. Do you understand?"

Moans from back.

"Sounds pretty boring," Andy said, shoving out his lip.

Marty interjected, "Is the Attwood family still in residence?"

"You'll see," was Eva's reply. She grinned at Scott. Marty craned his neck to see out the window.

"Does any of this look familiar?" Eva asked him.

Marty ran fingers through his hair. "No, but I remember being here, long ago."

"We're going to see where Grandpa was stationed during World War II," Eva explained. "Grandpa, why don't you tell the kids about it?"

"Okey dokey. Can you believe I was a year older than Kaley? I sailed the Atlantic by myself to live with Aunt Deane, where we just visited. To my horror, Germany invaded the next day. It took a while to leave the Netherlands, because of the war. Eventually I enlisted. The Army sent me here to Knettishall Army air base."

"We're near an Army base?" Andy asked from the far back seat. "Cool."

Eva swiveled her head again. "We watched the movie *Winds of War*. Do you remember when Pug drove up to a big house to meet British generals?"

"I guess so," Andy said.

Kaley leaned forward. "He can't remember a thing, Mom. My brother needs help."

"Gramps," Dutch said, pretending to fly his plane. "Did you fly one of these?"

Marty gestured out the window. "I wasn't too far from here. I lived at Bentley Park, which was being used by Allied forces. We slept in huts out back."

"Like when we go camping in tents," Scott added.

They passed a high stone fence on the country road. Scott turned into a drive, aiming the van between two piers.

Andy whistled. "Look at those giant stone lions. You really lived here, Gramps?"

A tall gate barred their way. The van came to a stop, and Scott punched some buttons on a keypad.

A male British voice inquired over a speaker, "May I help you?"

"We're Scott and Eva Montanna and family. We are expected, I believe."

"Indeed. Let me check." The voice paused. "Oh yes, when the gates open, drive to the front entrance. An aide will meet you."

Seconds later, the gold and black gates swung open. Scott pulled through and followed the asphalt drive stretching out like a tunnel beneath giant trees. The drive curved to reveal sheep grazing on vast lush meadows spanning before them. Eva's pulse quickened. Around another bend, the view was breathtaking. The stately brick mansion with long wings on both sides was larger than her old high school.

"It's right out of a Jane Austen novel," Eva quipped. "Like fairyland."

What she didn't say was how greatly the magnificent estate, with its formal gardens and private lake, contrasted with Rebekah's humble circumstances in Holland. On each end, brick chimneys pointed skyward. Four stories of windows faced the meadow. The entry door was built on the second level. Two sets of winding steps led from the parking area up to the entrance.

A unified gasp came from the rear of the van.

"This is incredible, Mom!" Kaley exclaimed. "I can't wait to tell Glenna Rider I went to a castle."

Dutch asked loudly, "Does the king live here?"

"England is ruled by a queen, silly," Kaley corrected.

"All right," Scott said. "Let's be nice."

He ascended the rolling drive, giving them all a better view.

Eva filled in some details of what she knew. "This home belongs to Grandpa Marty's long lost cousin. His name is Blake Attwood. The former King of England gave Blake's grandfather the right to own this home and also gave him a title, the Earl of Condover. His home is called Bentley Park."

"So, Dutch," she said, looking back at him, "the king doesn't live here, but a friend of the king does and he is our distant cousin."

"Eva, this is so special," Marty called from the back. "Thank you for coming here."

A man wearing a suit and tie pointed them over to a parking spot. Scott had barely turned off the van when the man opened his door.

"Welcome to Bentley Park. I trust you had no trouble finding your way?"

Eva untangled her long legs, ready to see inside this splendid home. Dutch already had burst out of the sliding door. The aide waited for Eva's two teens to climb out of the rear and then took Marty's arm.

"You must be Martin Vander Goes. The earl is most anxious to see you again." He led Marty to the steps. "Are these too much? If so, we can enter through the lower door and use the lift."

Marty straightened his back. "Years ago I took these steps two at a time."

"All right. Follow me, please," the aide intoned.

"Wait," Marty said. "Is Blake Attwood really still here?"

"The earl has not been feeling well of late."

Marty walked up the steps, holding onto the railing. When they reached the top, Eva whispered in his ear, "Is this anything like you remembered?"

"Oh, far grander today. Back then, Army jeeps parked all over the grass. No flowers bloomed. There was a peacock, though."

"Yes," Eva said with a laugh. "The bird kept you awake."

They entered through a massive wooden door into a gigantic three-story-high room. A wide staircase led to the upper stories. The highly polished floors made Eva glad she'd worn her running shoes. On heels, she might take a tumble. Various paintings decorated the carved wooden walls. No doubt the earl owned a few masterpieces, Eva concluded.

A glittering chandelier displayed in the center of the foyer had smaller ones on each side. Eva stood beneath the gleaming lights in awe. A well-dressed woman walked in with a handheld computer. She shook Marty's hand, and he introduced his family.

"I am Victoria Rich, Blake Atwood's personal assistant," she explained. "It's been too many years since we've had children at Bentley Park. Please make yourselves feel at home."

Eva motioned for Dutch to back away from a marble sculpture.

"This home is beautiful," she said. "I can only imagine walking along these stunning grounds every day."

Ms. Rich checked something on her computer. "The earl will tell you that it is quite an undertaking to keep the place in order. He is ready to see you, Mr. Vander Goes."

She beckoned Marty with a wave. Her heels clicked on the shiny floors as she took them through a corridor off the large foyer. After passing a library lined with books, Ms. Rich entered a cozy sitting room, its wooden walls giving a warm feeling. An elderly gentleman sat next to a fireplace in a leather upholstered chair. He looked in terrible shape. His hair was thick and white, but his coloring was gray. Red splotches covered his face.

Ms. Rich approached him quietly. "Your Lordship, Mr. Vander Goes and his family, the Montannas, are here to see you."

She turned to Marty. "Mr. Vander Goes, do you recall meeting Mr. Attwood when you were stationed here in the war?"

"I certainly do. Blake, it's me, Martin." He leaned over and patted the earl's hand.

"Forgive me," Blake sputtered. "My legs are not strong enough for me to stand."

He started wheezing and coughing. Ms. Rich handed him a glass of water. He sipped some and handed back the glass.

Marty seized his frail hand. "It's wonderful being here, sir. Thanks for inviting us."

Blake nodded weakly at the leather chair beside him.

"Take a pew and dispense with the 'sir.' You are no longer in the Army Air Corp, private. We are equals today."

Eva stepped forward and pressed her hand in Blake's. So did Scott.

"Grandpa Marty actually became a sergeant," Eva said. "He's told us about your love of art and encouraging him to join the Dutch Resistance."

Blake folded his trembling hands. "If the children want a diversion, I can have my staff saddle up the horses. They could ride for a while and never leave the grounds."

"You are kind to offer, but the children aren't dressed for riding," Eva replied. "However, they would enjoy exploring the grounds."

She motioned for the kids to come closer. "Meet Kaley, our oldest, then Andy, and Martin, who is named after my grandfather. To avoid confusion, we call him Dutch."

"Of course he would be Dutch." Blake cracked a smile. "In honor of our Dutch heritage."

Blake pressed a button on the table next to his chair. "We'll see to it that they at least see the stables. I have a foal that descended from the great Secretariat."

"Sweet," Andy piped. "We just saw that DVD. He's the best horse ever."

A woman wearing a black uniform and white apron walked in silently on rubber shoes. Blake told her in a hoarse voice, "Please arrange a tour of the grounds and stable for these nice young people."

Eva wanted Marty and Blake to reminisce, so she and Scott followed their children to the door. On her way, she passed a framed sketch on the wall and recognized the initials on the bottom. She stopped before the likeness of a U.S. airman manning the machine gun in the nose of a bomber. The distinctive initials "MVG" were just like those she'd seen Marty sign on his other works.

Eva nudged Scott with her elbow. "Look, it's one of Marty's drawings."

From behind her, she heard Blake say in a hoarse voice, "Eva, I see you found a familiar artist. If you will join us here, I will tell you about it."

So she and Scott turned around and sat across from him and Marty.

Blake gazed with watery eyes toward the sketch. "Martin, do you recognize it? You drew Staff Sergeant Vinnie Thomas at Knettishall airfield."

Marty lowered his eyes. "I never gave him the sketch. His bomber ditched over France."

Eva wondered how he was dealing with so many powerful memories from the last few days.

"Your grandfather was popular when stationed at Bentley Park," Blake said. "We did not have good cameras then, and Martin sketched the air crews. As he just said, nose gunner Thomas' plane was shot down over France."

"When I transferred out, I left the drawing with the commanding officer in hopes Vinnie survived."

Blake shifted in his chair. "After the war, I found your sketch in the house. We checked and discovered the Germans held Thomas and his crew as POWs until the war ended."

"He lived?" Marty raised his chin. "I always wondered about him and that picture."

"That is not the original. I duplicated and mounted it here. It took years, but Ms. Rich found Thomas living in St. Louis and sent him your sketch. I received a thank you letter from his children saying his health was poor. Your drawing arrived in time to lift his spirits."

Eva smiled at Marty. "That is terrific news."

"Well, it solves one puzzle in my life." Marty clasped his hands. "There are a few more that need attending."

Before Eva could explore what he meant, Blake broke in, "If you and Scott enjoy art, stroll through the grand hall where you entered. There are some nice pieces. Your grandfather and I have much to talk about."

TAKING THE EARL'S HINT, Eva and Scott withdrew to the great hall. They meandered through the densely wooded grounds for close to an hour. Scott photographed the kids near a beautiful peacock and hen. Eva brought her children to a swing hanging from a large elm tree, and they had fun pumping with their legs, high in the air. She turned to Scott.

"We can let them play here a while. I want to go in and check on Marty."

"I am enjoying being out here with you, but I suppose it's time. Lead the way."

The two of them found Marty drinking tea with the earl in the same sitting room.

"Perfect timing." Blake gestured to their former seats. "Martin has given me the sketch he made of my estate when he was stationed here. And we have had a riveting conversation. I feel like you are family. Let me explain the agreement he and I just reached."

Eva's eyes darted to Marty and he smiled broadly.

Blake adjusted his lap blanket. "My granddaughter Brittney is my only heir. She survived her father but is a total disgrace. I can only imagine greed led her to America to steal Martin's necklace and a van Eyck drawing Martin didn't even know he had. I once suspected it when I handled Deane's windmill painting in her jewelry shop."

"What made you think that?" Eva probed, eager to find out what he knew.

"You ask a legitimate question. Family legend is the easiest way to explain it."

Scott leaned closer. Eva inched her chair forward. Blake was providing answers to her many questions.

He lifted a wobbly hand. "Brittney was our pride and joy. She changed her name from Attwood to Condover because of our family's peerage. When she entered our military, I was thrilled. I am at a loss to explain her sordid behavior. She may serve time in an American prison, and should. Once released, she will be tried by our government for treason. The final straw was when she stole artworks and my gun collection from Bentley Park."

"She was arrested with a P38," Eva noted.

Blake shook his head. "From my collection, no doubt."

He wiped his eyes and Eva felt compassion for the elderly gentleman.

"She had the cheek to sell my paintings to a Bulgarian spy," he said with a sigh.

Blake stopped talking. He slowly faced Marty as if it hurt to move his neck. "I am beyond humiliated. Please accept my sincere apologies."

Marty grabbed his friend's hand. "I already have. There's no need to apologize."

With pain edging his voice, Blake asked Eva, "Will you forgive my granddaughter? And me for failing her as I did?"

Eva came over and crouched by his chair. She looked him in the eye. "Blake, may I call you that?"

He smiled, so she continued. "You aren't responsible for Brittney's behavior. There is nothing to forgive you for. And I pray God will grant you peace in your life."

"My dear, thank you. Now let me tell you what I just told your grandfather."

Marty looked at Eva and in that moment she pictured him stationed here as a young private in the Army. With his sparkling eyes, he looked youthful.

Blake sipped his tea. "Bah, it's cold. Anyway, I am too old to manage the estate. I am not long for this world. Because my granddaughter endangered Martin and you," he made a sweeping motion with his arm, "I am deeding Bentley Park to you, Eva."

Stunned, Eva felt for her chair. She sat, but couldn't overcome the shock. Scott wore a silly grin. Eva had an absurd urge to laugh and never stop. Inherit this splendid estate? How ridiculous!

"Before you object, Eva," Blake said, bending forward. "You don't want to move to England and you probably can't afford to operate Bentley Park. I can't either. Martin and I have just talked about this. There is enough value in the Jan van Eyck sketch of the *Just Judges* to endow this estate forever."

Eva shook her head wildly. "Such a majestic estate should be preserved. But I do not own the van Eyck sketch. If Grandpa wants to sell it to fund a national trust to preserve the estate, he can do so."

"See here, Eva. Bentley Park is part of the Vander Goes heritage. I hope it will never be sold and that you will see reason."

"My one objection, aside from making an enemy of Brittney, is that the buildings housing Deane's jewelry shop and museum need funding."

Blake tilted so close to the edge of his chair, she was concerned he might fall out any second.

He cleared his throat. "Martin mentioned that. You should know I already talked with my attorney and financial advisors. They assure me that between the van Eyck and ruby necklace handed down from Peter Vander Goes, there is enough value to fund both, leaving your family plenty to live on."

Marty was nodding in perfect agreement. Unfortunately, Marty hadn't heard Brewster's report of the research he and MI-5 had done. The Earl of Condover was desperate to save Bentley Park.

"Blake, you are generous to me and my family. However, this is far too much to digest in one day. If you draw up a proposal, we will share it with our attorney and financial advisers in the States. First and foremost, I want to bring the matter to God and seek His wisdom. "

"Great." Blake rubbed his aging hands together. "That is all I ask. Set a time to meet here tomorrow. You listen to my advisors, and take the proposal home for consideration."

Eva and Scott traded penetrating glances. After more back and forth with Blake, she agreed to meet him in the morning. Scott went to round up the kids. Eva ignored their noisy banter on the ride back to the Fox and Hound.

The idea of being an heiress baffled Eva. How could she make such a weighty decision? After cajoling the rest of her family to play checkers on the porch, she and Scott took another walk.

"My lady, you are quiet," he said, reaching for her hand.

"I've never heard you call me that before. Aren't you sweet?"

"I don't think you understand what Blake is saying. Along with the estate, the peerage passes to you. You will have a British title. He said you'll become the Countess of Condover. Were you even listening?"

"No." Eva groaned. "And I can hear Griff's ribbing now."

"I like the sound. Countess Eva Marie Condover."

"Well, I'm not sure. I want to help the earl, but do I really want his daughter coming after me because she thinks I've stolen her legacy?"

"You're doing nothing of the sort. Blake has the right to name his heir. You are of the same family tree. Perhaps God arranged this for you to bring glory to His name."

She stopped at the fence line. "You are a wise man, Scott Montanna. Tomorrow after our meeting, I intend to ask Blake about the eternal consequences."

"Good. And Eva, you would look smashing in a diamond tiara meeting the queen."

She lunged for Scott's ribs, tickling him until he cried, "Uncle!"

Her evening passed in relative calm. However, once her head hit the pillow, she couldn't sleep a wink. Her mind refused to relax, so she took her concerns to the throne of Grace.

"Father God," she prayed softly, "will you help me do what is right in Your eyes? I am Your servant in everything."

She finished her prayer and drew the silky sheet to her chin as Scott breathed deeply next to her. Life's events rarely kept him awake. Eva struggled with her conscience for hours. When morning broke, she had at last reached a decision.

THEIR HIGH-LEVEL STRATEGY MEETING DRONED ON FOR HOURS. When Blake's attorney gave Eva a thick packet to take home, she slid a hand atop the envelope.

"Thank you. If you don't mind, I would like to meet with the earl alone."

The room emptied and Blake rang for more tea to be brought in. Eva poured out the steaming brew and nestled both hands around her cup.

"Blake, you are making detailed preparations for Bentley Park. I have an important question." She cleared her throat. "Where are you going from here?"

"We've just agreed. I'm not leaving Bentley Park."

She gazed at him tenderly. "Do you believe in the hereafter?"

"Oh, I see what you mean, Eva Marie."

He said her name as if she belonged to him. In a way, she did.

"I am listening," she said softly.

Blake brought the cup to his lips and drank. "Your coming here with Marty has restored my spirit, and my faith. Back in 1989 I heard Reverend Billy Graham preach the most amazing sermon. He taught me things I never heard in church."

"What kind of things? I am curious."

She set down her cup and sat beside him. He patted her hand.

"Much better. It was like Reverend Graham spoke to me. I had traveled the world and come up empty. Graham said, 'Christ became the lamb of God for you.' His finger pointed right at me, and I was changed from the inside out. All my strivings ceased. That makes it so hard for me about Brittney."

"There is hope for anyone in Jesus, if they seek Him."

Blake caught Eva's hand. "That's her problem. She blames God for taking her parents in the auto smash-up. She spews such vitriol toward God."

"You give me a better understanding of her troubles. I will pray for her."

"Before I leave this earth for my heavenly shore, to know you are praying for her soul will make my last days more bearable."

Tears ran down Blake's face. Eva hugged him warmly, wanting him to feel her love. Her heart filled with affectionate emotions, unlike when she'd first laid eyes on Blake Attwood. She clung to him, not wanting to ever leave Bentley Park.

53

I t was a month later, and Eva had trouble accepting she was the Countess of Condover. The title sounded silly, even if Scott got a hoot out of constantly whispering the newly-acquired title into her ear. As Bentley Park's new owner, Eva wondered what to do with the estate. Vague ideas wandered in and out of her mind, never taking shape.

She slipped next to Scott in bed, eager for his opinion. He was on the sea somewhere with Winkin', Blinkin', and Nod. She pulled the blanket to her chin, feeling chilled. How could Eva forget Brittney's quest to ruin Marty?

Her mind turned to her ancestors. Her great-grandfather had once told Deane his descendants would witness Jewish people living in Israel. They did. Before Marty left Holland to enlist, Deane blessed him, saying he would survive the war and have a son. He did. While Hitler's brutal regime had tried to blot from Joanne's life her Jewish heritage, Eva's grandmother came to love Jesus as her Messiah and so was in heaven with Him. Didn't their love of Jesus live on, in her?

It was then Eva understood Blake's granddaughter could never steal her family's legacy. She must relinquish her anger at Brittney. Only then would she be free to shepherd the great estate of Bentley Park. She flipped to her side, an idea sparking in her mind. Her excitement grew.

Blake still lived there, but his health was failing. Could her plans succeed in time? Longing to tell Scott, she touched his cheek.

"Hmm," he groaned, flopping over on his back.

"Are you awake?"

"I am now. Why?"

"Do you still love me, after all the changes?"

Scott reached for her hand. "Sweetheart, I will always love you."

"Me too." Eva squeezed his hand. "I had an epiphany about Bentley Park."

"Oh, I hope we didn't make a mistake ..." His voice drifted away.

He would offer no answers for her tonight. Eva lay still, struggling for peace. She had court in the morning. Griff had begged off, claiming he had a stop to make. True to form, he refused to tell Eva what it was. She wrestled with the future until she finally decided not to decide. Then she slept.

Peals of thunder startled her awake. She ran to the window. A violent wind roared. Rain fell in great torrents. The sun struggled to pierce dark, heavy clouds. Eva gasped. A double rainbow arced across the entire sky. Pink and purple merged with bright yellow and green. Awestruck, she dropped to the window seat. Surely this stunning display was God's reminder her future was in His hands.

She also took it as a sign to move forward with what she had to do. After quietly dressing in her walk-in closet, she drove the wet roads to the court-house where she snuck in the back row. The defendant faced the judge. Eva held her breath.

The judge sentenced Brittney Attwood Condover to prison for ten years for torching the decoy house. He reduced her time due to the house being unoccupied, but gave no consideration for her guilty plea. The instant he banged his gavel to adjourn, Eva seized her purse and left. She didn't want Brittney spotting her.

On the way to her car, Eva phoned Griff and told him the news.

"You better race back to the office," he replied. "I've something to tell you."

Eva went on explaining, "The Brits filed a detainer. They can grab Brittney when she's expelled from the States after her ten years."

Griff grunted in her ear. "Don't break any speeding laws, but you might want to hightail it back here."

He ended the call with a click. Eva pushed the accelerator, grinning. Delores Fontaine's original info had been spot-on. Apparently, Brittney had counted her chickens in anticipation of stealing Marty's van Eyck sketch. Though Delores had contacted Eva after hearing rumors, it was Eva who found the sketch. Or, rather Cecil Prescott from the Smithsonian did.

Eva owed Delores thanks in another way. The art curator had facili-tated the sale of the ruby necklace and van Eyck's drawing to a private collection. Proceeds were funding the Deane Vander Goes Holocaust

Museum in Middleburg, Eva's new estate in England, and college for her three children.

She sped to the office with nagging doubts. Though she'd forgiven Brittney, she would never be free of her treachery. Eva controlled the fallen British agent's ancestral home.

She stepped to her cubicle and glimpsed Griff studying his computer monitor. As she approached him from behind, he reduced his screen to black and faced her.

Eva nodded at his blank screen. "What are you up to?"

"Just waiting to hear how it went at court."

She rolled her chair into his cubical and crossed her arms. "What can't I see? Don't pretend you're buying Dawn a surprise gift."

"Okay, you caught me." Griff smiled sheepishly. "I was waiting to tell you until I had more facts."

"I knew it. What did you find?"

Griff maximized his screen. Eva stared at the image of passengers lined up at a Customs and Immigration entry point.

"Three days ago," Griff began, "these passengers deplaned in Detroit from a KLM Amsterdam flight."

He tapped his keyboard, and passengers moved forward in line presenting their passports.

"What's so special about that flight?" Eva demanded.

"Watch and see. The next guy approaching the desk is an American named Robert Shields from Chicago."

Eva squinted at the screen, then titled her head to reduce the glare.

"That's Andrei Enescu!" she squealed. "How did you get this?"

Griff leaned back in his chair. "Lydia Neff brought the video to my attention earlier. A CIA analyst claims he found this while randomly viewing entry videos."

"Random my eye. Some source tipped off the Agency. Why didn't they tell us so we could grab Andrei?"

He shrugged. "Maybe they'll follow him, and hope he leads them to a sleeper cell or something."

"The CIA isn't authorized to operate inside our borders. What are they up to?"

"I'll mark this spot on the video so you can work on it later. I'm taking the day off to go flying."

"What? You can't go flying around for fun." She pointed to his now darkened screen. "Don't forget the threats Andrei shouted at us."

Griff locked his desk. "And don't forget you tackled Brittney. I'm leaving our Romanian escapee in your capable hands."

"Are you sure you're not hiding something else?" Eva asked, rising from the chair.

A peculiar look flashed over Griff's face. "Uh oh, I guess I am."

He flew to unlock his desk and yanked out a piece of paper.

"Eva, you can't close Brittney's file."

She tossed her keys in her purse. "Why not? She's been sentenced, so the evidence will be destroyed or disposed of."

"I don't mean that evidence."

"Oh, the vacant land. The Marshals will try auctioning it off. If there are no takers, they're donating the property to the city of Bull Run."

Griff fluttered the paper. "No, there's another piece of evidence."

"What are you talking about?"

She tried grabbing the sheet. Griff hid it behind his back.

"Lydia gave me these lab results. It's about your leather pouch."

"Whew, I nearly forgot." Eva leaned on his desk. "Is it silver dust as I predicted?"

"Negative. It's ashes."

Eva's heart raced. She could hardly utter the words.

"You mean as in human ashes?"

"Correct."

Eva again tried snatching the sheet. Griff finally handed it over, and she scanned the report. At the bottom were the incredible words just as Griff had said: *Human Ashes.*

"This is insane. Was Brittney after these? Is there no end to her schemes?"

"Why would human ashes be kept for centuries?" Griff blurted.

"I wonder … could these belong to Jan van Eyck?"

Griff shrugged. "I know zip about art. Who died first—Jan or his brother, what's his name?"

"Hubert died years before Jan."

"There you go." Griff tapped the paper. "Jan saved his brother's ashes."

"Wow!"

Eva swallowed. She sounded as ridiculous saying "Wow" as Agent Kemp had.

"If it were my case, I'd dump the powder down the toilet and give the pouch to my kids for their Legos." Griff laughed.

"No, we need to identify these remains."

"We?" Griff raised his brows.

"Yes, we. We're partners, remember?"

Griff shook his head. "Nope. I've already reserved the plane."

He relocked his desk. With a wave, he left Eva to stew over the lab results. She wheeled the chair to her desk, and it didn't take long for her to call Lydia and grill her about the CIA's lame story of how they "caught" Andrei on film. Next, she called CIA agent Bo Rider, which went to his voicemail.

Eva scanned the lab report, ill at ease with ashes being kept in her safety deposit box. They deserved a burial. But until she knew whose they were, she refused to act. There was something else she could do.

She would read Marty's other journals, the ones tracing her family's history. And when he returned from his honeymoon with Rebekah at Bentley Park, Eva would corner him about the ashes. She suspected he was like Griff, hiding other secrets.

Before she decided her next step, her cell phone rang. It was Kaley, who hollered in her ear, "Mom, my gold Dutch necklace is gone!"

"When did you last see it?" Eva quizzed.

Kaley made little sense, so Eva convinced her that she'd have to investigate later. She hung up the phone. This was unbelievable. Here she was in the crosshairs of another possible theft. Eva vowed to protect her family at all costs, and she wouldn't quit until she knew everything.

NOTE FROM THE AUTHORS

We wrote this work of fiction to entertain. We also wove in historical facts to enlighten the story. In *Stolen Legacy*, we tell Martin Vander Goes' life story in the Netherlands during WWII. The accounts of Germany's invasion and aid given to the Netherlands by the British and French are true.

The Knettishall airfield in Thetford, England, was the base from where B-17 bombers of the U.S. Army Air Force, 388th Bombardment Group attacked Germany. A historic person, Capt. Robert Kelley Posey, was a commander in the U.S. Army Monuments Men. The account of his group discovering gold and art in the mines at Altaussee, Austria, is based on fact. The quantity of gold and masterpieces described were found in the mine. The German and American military officials' attempts to decorate their military headquarters with stolen masterpieces did happen.

After the war, Capt. Posey served as an architect instrumental in designing Sears Tower in Chicago, which was the tallest building in the world when it was built in the 1960s. Jan van Eyck created the Ghent Altarpiece, and the theft of his Just Judges is real. However, the pen and ink prototype and Deane's painting of the sixteenth century De Rieker windmill were created by the authors for your enjoyment.

De Zwaan, the giant windmill toured by Eva and Marty in Holland, Michigan, is the only authentic working windmill in America. Built in 1761 in Krommenie, near Amsterdam, it was moved to Holland, Michigan, in 1964. De Zwaan is a fun place to tour with your family.

Lastly, as many of you have read or heard us say, we really enjoyed Bo Rider's kids who we wrote about in *The Joshua Covenant*. That led us to feature the teens, Gregg and Glenna Rider, in *Night Flight*. Well, it's happened again. After the manuscript for this novel was completed and in the editing process, we wondered what we'd do if we had been blessed with an inheritance such as Eva Montanna's. In fact, we wondered how it impacted Eva's life. So we are creating an epilogue, which we want to share as a special treat for you, our "die-hard" fans after you finish *Stolen Legacy*.

Send us an email at SLepilogue@DianeAndDavidMunson.com, and we will send you the digital epilogue. Many of you already tell others about the family friendly and wholesome novels we write. Will you, our friends, also consider writing a review on Goodreads.com, ChristianBook.com, Amazon.com, or Barnes & Noble.com? You can also 'like' us on our FaceBook page at Diane and David Munson, or other social media. You can also donate our book to your church library and tell your friends about us. If you do, send us a link or a note, when you request the epilogue. If you don't, we'll happily send you the epilogue anyway. Thanks for encouraging our continued writing. We couldn't do it without y'all!

—Diane and David Munson

THE MUNSONS' THRILLERS MAY BE READ IN ANY ORDER.

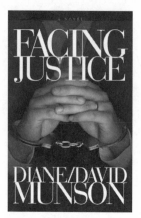

ISBN-13: 978-0982535509
352 pages, trade paper
Fiction / Mystery and Suspense
14.99

Facing Justice

Diane and David Munson draw on their true-life experiences in this suspense novel about Special Agent Eva Montanna, whose twin sister died at the Pentagon on 9/11. Eva dedicates her career to avenge her death while investigating Emile Jubayl, a member of Eva's church and CEO of Helpers International, who is accused of using his aid organization to funnel money to El Samoud, head of the Armed Revolutionary Cause, and successor to Al Qaeda. Family relationships are tested in this fast-paced, true-to-life legal thriller about the men and women who are racing to defuse the ticking time bomb of international terrorism.

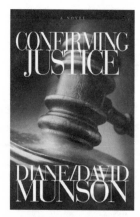

ISBN-13: 978-0982535516
352 pages, trade paper
Fiction / Mystery and Suspense
14.99

Confirming Justice

In *Confirming Justice*, all eyes are on Federal Judge Dwight Pendergast, secretly in line for nomination to the Supreme Court, who is presiding over a bribery case involving a cabinet secretary's son. When the key prosecution witness disappears, FBI agent Griff Topping risks everything to save the case while Pendergast's enemies seek to embroil the judge in a web of corruption and deceit. The whole world watches as events threaten the powerful position and those who covet it. Diane and David Munson masterfully create plot twists, legal intrigue and fast-paced suspense, in their realistic portrayal of what transpires behind the scenes at the center of power.

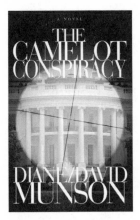

ISBN-13: 978-0982535523
352 pages, trade paper
Fiction / Mystery and Suspense
14.99

The Camelot Conspiracy

The *Camelot Conspiracy* rocks with a sinister plot even more menacing than the headlines. Former D.C. insiders Diane and David Munson feature a brash TV reporter, Kat Kowicki, who receives an ominous email that throws her into the high stakes conspiracy of John F. Kennedy's assassination. When Kat uncovers evidence Lee Harvey Oswald did not act alone, she turns for help to Federal Special Agents Eva Montanna and Griff Topping who uncover the chilling truth: A shadow government threatens to tear down the very foundations of the American justice system.

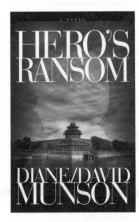

ISBN-13: 978-0982535530
320 pages, trade paper
Fiction / Mystery and Suspense
14.99

Hero's Ransom

CIA Agent Bo Rider (*The Camelot Conspiracy*) and Federal Agents Eva Montanna and Griff Topping (*Facing Justice, Confirming Justice, The Camelot Conspiracy*) return in Hero's Ransom, the Munsons' fourth family-friendly adventure. When archeologist Amber Worthing uncovers a two-thousand-year-old mummy and witnesses a secret rocket launch at a Chinese missile base, she is arrested for espionage. Her imprisonment sparks a custody battle between grandparents over her young son, Lucas. Caught between sinister world powers, Amber's faith is tested in ways she never dreamed possible. Danger escalates as Bo races to stop China's killer satellite from destroying America and, with Eva and Griff's help, to rescue Amber using an unexpected ransom.

ISBN-13: 978-0982535547
320 Pages, trade paper
Fiction / Mystery and Suspense
14.99

Redeeming Liberty

In this timely thriller by ExFeds Diane and David Munson (former Federal Prosecutor and Federal Agent), parole officer Dawn Ahern is shocked to witness her friend Liberty, the chosen bride of Wally (former "lost boy" from Sudan) being kidnapped by modern-day African slave traders. Dawn tackles overwhelming danger head-on in her quest to redeem Liberty. When she reaches out to FBI agent Griff Topping and CIA agent Bo Rider, her life is changed forever. Suspense soars as Bo launches a clandestine rescue effort for Liberty only to discover a deadly Iranian secret threatening the lives of millions of Americans and Israelis. Glimpse tomorrow's startling headlines in this captivating story of faith and freedom under fire.

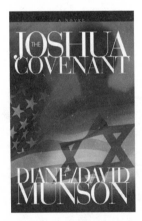

ISBN-13: 978-0-983559009
336 Pages, trade paper
Fiction / Mystery and Suspense
14.99

The Joshua Covenant

CIA agent Bo Rider moves to Israel after years of clandestine spying around the world. He takes his family—wife Julia, and teens, Glenna and Gregg—and serves in America's Embassy using his real name. Glenna and Gregg face danger while exploring Israel's treasures, and their father is shocked to uncover a menacing plot jeopardizing them all. A Bible scholar helps Bo in amazing ways. He discovers the truth about the Joshua Covenant and battles evil forces that challenge his true identity. Will Bo survive the greatest threat ever to his career, his family, and his life? Bo risks it all to stop an enemy spy.

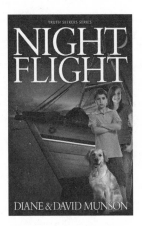

ISBN-13: 978-0983559023
224 Pages, trade paper
Fiction / Mystery and Suspense
14.99

Night Flight

In *Night Flight* the Munsons crank out a high ve-
locity thriller for the young and young at heart.
When CIA agent Bo Rider's kids ask for a dog,
Bo adopts Blaze a mature dog for Glenna and
Gregg. The teens are shocked when Blaze con-
fronts shady criminals making counterfeit money.
They discover what their parents never told them:
Blaze is a retired law enforcement dog. When the
crooks are arrested, Glenna and Gregg become
witnesses and take refuge with their grandparents in Treasure Island, Florida. When Grandpa
Buck learns what Blaze can do, he permits the
kids to put Blaze to work solving crimes. Glenna
and Gregg use the reward money to help a friend
with an urgent need. Danger follows them from
Skeleton Key in the dark of night as Blaze reveals
a surprising twist.